# The Ice Palace Waltz

Dear Beth,
Do ask your
mother everything you
want to know -
never too late.
Best
Barbara

Barbara L. Baer

Published by Open Books

Copyright © 2020 by Barbara L. Baer

Interior design by Siva Ram Maganti

Cover images "Ice building at sunset in cold winter" © by aphotostory and "Bride and groom at the window" © by Sotnikov Misha

Learn more about the artists at shutterstock.com/g/aphotostory and shutterstock.com/g/SotnikovMikhail

ISBN-13: 978-1948598286

"Always when markets are in trouble, the phrases are the same. 'The economic situation is fundamentally sound.' Or simply, 'The fundamentals are good.' All who hear these words should know that something is wrong."

– John Kenneth Galbraith, *The Great Crash 1929*

An apocryphal story attributed to Franklin Delano Roosevelt: "It wasn't I who got us out of the Depression, it was 'The Goldbergs.'" "The best I can do is start at the beginning and hope. But starting at the beginning isn't always that easy. People don't just appear, they come from someplace. Everybody has ancestors and everybody is descended."

– Gertrude Berg, *Molly and Me*

# Family Trees

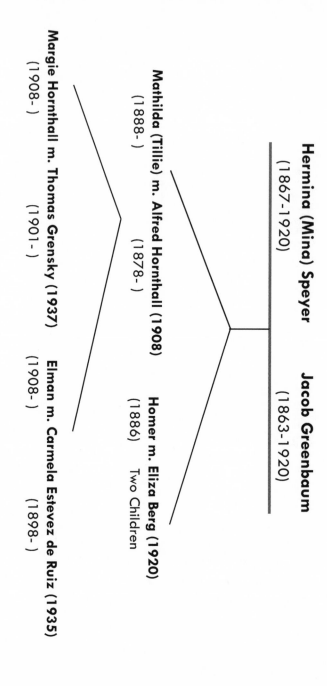

Hermina (Mina) Speyer
(1867-1920)

Jacob Greenbaum
(1863-1920)

Mathilda (Tillie) m. Alfred Hornthall (1908)
(1888- )          (1878- )

Homer m. Eliza Berg (1920)
(1886)     Two Children

Margie Hornthall m. Thomas Grensky (1937)
(1908- )          (1901- )

Elman m. Carmela Estevez de Ruiz (1935)
(1908- )          (1898- )

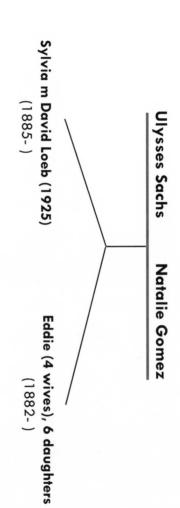

**Ulysses Sachs    Natalie Gomez**

Sylvia m David Loeb (1925)
(1885- )

Eddie (4 wives), 6 daughters
(1882- )

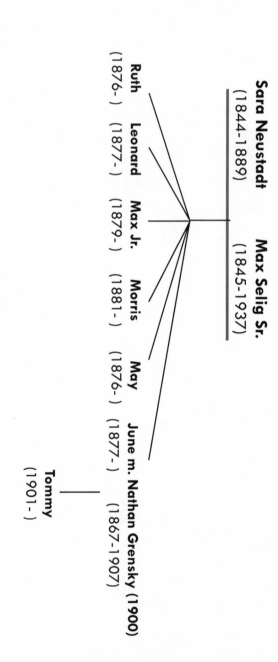

Sara Neustadt
(1844-1889)

Max Selig Sr.
(1845-1937)

Ruth
(1876- )

Leonard
(1877- )

Max Jr.
(1879- )

Morris
(1881- )

May
(1876- )

June m. Nathan Grensky (1900)
(1877- )        (1867-1907)

Tommy
(1901- )

# Part One

# ONE

## LEADVILLE, COLORADO
## 1889

IN THE LEADVILLE BARS during long and frigid winter nights, the main topics of conversation went from universal disasters, earthquakes and fires, to local particulars, mine collapses, fires and the falling price for silver. Any gloomy mood was lifted by stories of miraculous wealth from metals, first from gold along the Arkansas River, then silver from the Little Pittsburg and the Bonanza, the Matchless, Fairview and Climax mines. Each story of Leadville's boom days increased the drinkers' thirsts and revived memories of that time a decade and more earlier when the snowbound mining camp in the Rocky Mountains had been the richest square mile on earth, a time when veins of silver washed like rain from the Mosquito Range into the Arkansas River Valley.

Maximillian Selig was equally at home at the Elk's Club Bar, the Texas House or Hyman's Lodge where Leadville's leading citizens gathered to play cards and be served drinks by ladies too scantily dressed to be declared decent. Max Selig, his companions might say, was an all right kind of Jew. He told a good story, held his poker hand steady, his blue eyes on his cards. When he won the night's purse, he stood all his companions, from the mayor to fire and police chiefs, to drinks.

Max justified his evenings out to his wife Sara as necessary to their survival.

"My dear, do you remember that the fire wagons didn't come fast enough to keep poor Chaim Levy's shop from going up in flames when his stove exploded? With my connections, the fire trucks won't wait to come to us."

Sara visualized fire consuming Selig Bros Groceries and Dry Goods, not an idle fear in a town built of wood where entire streets had burned like match sticks in the past.

"And Sara, beloved wife, I pick up the business news and the politics from men who are making it before it comes out in the *Herald Democrat*." Drinking together, Max explained, made Leadville more democratic.

"You're right, husband," Sara answered as she returned to her mending. In the morning, she knew her husband's nose would be redder than usual and he'd wipe it often with his handkerchief, telling customers, "Morning chill in the air, early this year." But soon he'd be hauling the bags of grain and flour from wagons into the store as briskly as a young man.

When Max had a big win at Faro, or if miners repaid his grubstake, he came home with arms full of flowers, a bottle of champagne for Sara, and a silver dollar for his "Leadville babies," June and May, the two youngest of the family's six children, born in the mining town. "Not the cheap stuff," he said, pouring the girls a bubbly sip, "that's no more than sugar and water with some yeast, but real champagne all the way from Paris, France. To our own Champs de Élysées!"

Max pretended the champagne bubbles were going to run off the glass before he sucked it all up. "We didn't know the hard times here, girls. No Harrison Avenue as you see it today. No raised sidewalks with timber supports as we have now. If you can imagine, there weren't lodgings enough for all the men arriving in carriages or on horseback. They kept coming faster than the camp could put up shelters for them. I've heard tales that the poor men slung themselves over ropes to sleep, one on top of the other, like wet clothing your mother hangs on the line. After a few hours rest, back they went into the cold where avalanches and cave-ins threatened. That was the kind of silver fever they had."

"The miners are still poor, Papa," said June, the youngest, only twelve, but more outspoken than May, a year older but quieter, who let her sister take the lead.

4

"Yes, they are, and you both have good hearts to care about them," Sara said.

Sara never stopped May or June from adding a few more beans and a little extra flour for a miner or his wife. The girls saw how the men never stood up straight and how the women covered their sunken mouths with their hands to conceal their missing teeth. Every Saturday, Sara and her daughters delivered food baskets to *shul* to be distributed to the Orphan and Widows Home because that was *tsedakah*, charity that Jews performed to help those less fortunate than themselves.

Max and Sara also liked telling stories about the Jews who'd made fortunes in Leadville. "Meyer Guggenheim, our co-religionist," Max recounted, "no sooner bought up another man's hole in the ground than a silver vein gushed up. His sons inherited his Midas touch and got even richer in the smelting business."

"And don't forget Mr. Charles Boettcher and Mr. David May." Sara looked up and smiled. "They arrived with hardly more than supplies in their carriages and now they're rich men with department stores across the country."

"Two ladies showed us pistols today, Papa. They said that if we asked them to, they'd fire them out the window for us." June looked at her father to know if he'd be angry they'd spoken to the parlor girls at Miss Lil's.

"The poor soiled doves still have to defend themselves, human nature being what it is." Max turned to share a look with Sara who sighed. "Dears, though our family does not enjoy the luxuries of the rich, there are many less fortunate than ourselves. We have not made the fortunes our co-religionists managed, but we are a happy family."

---

Brothers Max and Isaac Selig had been bachelors, twenty-two and twenty-three, when they left Mannheim on the Rhine in 1868, crossed the Atlantic in second class to New York City, took a train to Chicago where their eldest brother, Joseph, waited on the platform. After settling them in above his store, Selig Fine Grocers, Joseph showed his brothers around the business, two rooms on the ground floor with a storeroom in back. "We can use you strong young fellows. Business is always best kept in the family."

From her spot at the cash register, Joseph's wife Cecile encouraged conversation between her brothers-in-law and two sisters, Sara and Harriet Neustadt, also from southern Germany, who shopped at Selig's. Cecile soon hand delivered invitations for Friday night supper to the Neustadt sisters: getting the brothers married would ensure their staying in Chicago, she believed. The Sabbath meal was a success. Max favored the elder sister, Sara, who was robust and laughed at his jokes, while Isaac was drawn to Harriet, a slender young woman who blushed easily and had grey eyes fringed with black lashes. Their next meeting, Isaac asked for one of Harriet's pastel scenes she said she had painted from childhood memories of walking along the Rhine.

The Selig brothers and the Neustadt sisters married in a double wedding the following December in the Sinai Reform Congregation on Indiana Avenue. Max and Sara's oldest son was born within the year, and the next came a girl, then two more boys, all strong and healthy. Isaac and Harriet's first born, Jed, came prematurely in the middle of a heat wave. Baby Jed barely survived. "Unhealthy conditions, crowded conditions of the city," Max repeated every time the baby was ill. Despite family loyalty, the younger brothers chafed under Joseph and Cecile's commands and were resolved to move their families west to start a business on their own.

"In the mountains of Colorado, such silver is being brought up from the earth that men come from everywhere to make great fortunes," Max told Sara. "A green grocery and dry goods store will make us independent and assure our children's future."

Sara didn't worry about herself but questioned her sister's strength to withstand hardship. "Harriet and baby Jed may not thrive without the benefits of civilization."

"Our strength lies in family," Max continued to insist. Finally, the wives agreed.

---

In Leadville, everything that could go wrong for Harriet and Isaac went wrong. Jed was four when a runaway horse leaped from the street to the sidewalk and struck mother and son with its hooves. The boy died of head injuries and Harriet, whose leg was broken, never forgave herself for having lived while Jed died. She limped and used a cane, but seemed to recover her spirits when she became pregnant with a second child. Her pretty eyes sparkled and she laughed at her husband's comments about the town ruffians. At six months, Baby Samuel died of a fever.

"It is not your fault," Sara told her sister over and over. "You shall have more."

"I cannot endure it." Harriet turned away. She stopped going out except to sit in the graveyard in the new Jewish section of Evergreen Cemetery to mourn her sons.

Most days Sara cooked two meals, one for her family and one for Harriet and Isaac. In good weather, she walked down Harrison Avenue to her sister's where she often found Harriet in bed with nothing warming on the stove. On Fridays before sundown, Sara brought Harriet starched sheets and *challah*, along with egg noodles prepared the way her mother had taught her in Germany, stirring extra cream and butter into the white sauce to put weight on her sister. If Isaac happened to be at home, Sara listened without comment to his complaints about his brother Max's drinking, gambling, under-the-counter grubstakes to miners that seldom paid off.

Sara never refuted Isaac's accusations. Max was not a temperate man but Selig Brothers thrived because of his lively interest in customers and his connections, whereas dour Isaac, who never lifted his head from order forms or the cash register to greet people, would have driven customers to the competing stores.

Max and Sara's two eldest, Leonard and Ruth, had hated everything about the mining town. On the rare occasions the family took the train to Denver, they begged to be left behind with distant cousins who lived in the city where they could run on paved sidewalks and in green parks. "Everything here is so clean, Mama. Let us stay for school. I'm afraid when we pass those houses with the bad women.

And the drunkards make me so frightened," Ruth said. She once made her little sisters, May and June, wash out their mouths with soap for answering female voices who called down to them from upstairs windows where undergarments were hanging in full view of the street. From then on, the younger girls kept a secret: Miss Lil sometimes invited them into her warm parlor for hot chocolate to hear the Negro, Mr. Moseby, dressed in a green satin coat, play ragtime on the piano. Ruth would have punished them with worse than mouth washings if she knew.

At seventeen, Ruth married a bank employee twice her age and moved to Denver. At the wedding, May and June wished their oldest sister *mazel tov* and danced in wild circles at the reception, not least because they were happy to see Ruth go. Leonard followed his sister to study engineering and married a Denver girl related to Ruth's husband.

The middle Selig boys, Max Jr. and Morris, were fearless explorers who snuck off after school to descend into mine shafts and uncovered open pits with smoking depths, so dark and fearsome they seemed to go right down to the underworld. They scrambled to the top of Carbonate Hill where slag dunes could have collapsed on them. They went hiking the mountain trails without fear of being caught in a blizzard, though they had once been rescued. "We would have been fine," Morris said. Their curiosity and daring might have been fatal if Leadville's Jewish veterinarian, Dr. Ballin, hadn't caught them trying to steal a ride on a black horse he'd been treating. Ballin offered the boys an apprenticeship as an alternative to a visit from the sheriff. With Dr. Ballin, Max Jr and Morris learned to poultice infections, splint broken bones and clean gunshot wounds when men came to the veterinary's back door rather than risk the law.

Dr. Ballin told Sara, "If you can keep them out of trouble a few more years, your boys will grow up to be doctors." From that time, Sara hid money from her husband to send both boys to medical school in the east.

---

Max and Sara Selig's good fortune came to an end one February night in

1889 during a blizzard so heavy that Sara begged her husband to stay in.

She followed him down the stairs to the store. "Must you really go out in the storm? You can't see your hand before your face."

"I won't be long, only an hour or so. I'd not like to disappoint friends," he replied as he disappeared in clouds of wind-blown snow. Sara bolted the door, crossed the storeroom floor and climbed the stairs. In the sitting room, May and June sat bent over a book. Sara opened the *American Israelite* which she never seemed to have time for, and listened to her girls reading aloud from *The Blue Fairy Book* by Andrew Lang. The stories reminded her of how she and Harriet had gathered wildflowers blooming in the spring along the Rhine. Where had Harriet's lovely water colors gone to? They were so skillful. Poor Harriet. Even the alpine flowers that would soon rise through snowmelt in the meadows had not inspired her sister to paint again.

Sara turned toward the door and cupped her ear. "Did you hear anything, girls? It must only be the strong wind rattling that old door."

"I think it's the wind, Mama," June said, but in the next moment, they all jumped from their seats at the sound of a crash.

Sara opened their inside door and peered down the stairs. "It could be a drunkard blinded by snow who has fallen against the door."

Then they heard a louder crash. June stood alongside her mother to peer down. There was no light in the store, only the sound of cans being thrown from the shelves.

"Someone has broken in down there, Mama." June clung to her mother's arm.

Sara wrapped her shawl more tightly around her shoulders, took a candle in one hand, her walking stick in the other. "You girls stay here. Out-of-towners don't know we keep no whiskey or spirits here. I'll show the intruder my cane and that will be enough."

"No, Mama, don't go." The girls hung on her skirts to keep her with them. "Sit down again. Papa will be home soon, please, Mama."

"And when will that be? After this devil has run off with our goods!"

Sara pulled free and started down the stairs. The girls stood at the top watching her candle's halo flicker on the wall. Her cane went *tap, tap, tap* until it stopped. Then they heard their mother cry out, "Who are you? What do you want here? Put that down. Don't you dare strike me!"

June ran halfway down the stairs, close enough to see a cloaked figure with a hatchet in his hand. The blade shone wet and black. When she screamed, the intruder flung himself past the broken door.

June bent over her mother to shield her from the freezing wind coming from outside. She heard the clopping of hooves on the hard snow, a horse whinny, and felt sick from the smell of blood that rose from a wound on her mother's head.

"Get your brothers!" Sara said in a hoarse voice. "Go, girls."

"We can't leave you, Mama," June knelt beside her mother.

"We have to do what Mama says. Our brothers will save her." May knelt beside her mother. "Maxie and Morrie will know what to do. I'll get them and you find Father."

"The Elks Club is closest. I'll start there." June wrapped her mother's shawl around her, turned back for one look back. Sara was not moving.

"We're closing the door as best we can, Mama, and going for Papa and the boys," May said as June pushed aside the broken door and they faced the fierce wind.

June ran with the storm at her back until she reached the immense wooden door of the Elks Club. She rubbed snow from the window with her jacket until she could see inside. Her father was facing her, his head thrown back, wiping foam from his whiskers, grooming himself like a lion. She knocked hard. No one came. She hammered with her fists until a man opened up and peered out. "Get out of here, girlie. No place for you."

"I need my father, Max Selig, there. Tell him…" She couldn't say more.

After what seemed a long time, her father lay down his cards, said something to his companions, and emerged in the icy air, his whiskers immediately taking on frost.

"Someone…a man with a hatchet hit Mama in the head. She's calling for you." June began shaking so hard she couldn't get more words out.

"My God, girl, what are you telling me…speak up? Did you say

Sara?" Steam was rising from his breath as if from a boiling kettle as he spoke.

"Mother is lying on the floor. Someone hit her and she can't get up."

"Was she speaking? Did she call for me?" Max cleared snow from his brows and his beard. "Damn this storm."

June nodded, and began crying.

"Damn it all to hell, I'm coming, Sara," he shouted.

When they pushed aside the broken door, they saw Sara. Max threw himself over his wife, pleading for her to open her eyes, to say a word to him, but she did not stir. He looked up at the girls. "There's been a gunslinger from Jesse James' gang sighted in Fairplay. A posse's out looking for him."

By the time Max Jr. and Morris arrived with May in Dr. Ballin's horse-drawn carriage, Sara's wound had stopped bleeding but where the bandit's hatchet had gone in, a slice of blackness looked deep against her greying blond hair.

"The worst danger is pressure building in the skull," Morris said to his father. "The only brain surgeon we know is in Denver. There's no one here who can operate."

"We'll start by carriage and meet the night train in Fairplay," Max Jr. said.

Together the brothers lifted their mother and carried her out the door and into the carriage where they covered her unconscious form with a blanket. Morris added his coat. Max Sr. tried to climb in but his sons held him back.

"You and the girls catch the first train tomorrow morning," Max Jr. said to his father. "I'll sit in back with Mother and you drive, Morrie. We've got to get to Fairplay."

At that moment, Sara turned her head but didn't open her eyes. She groaned once and was still. No color spotted her usually ruddy cheeks.

"Damn it all, I'll be with her!" yelled their father.

"There's no room, Papa. I'll be with her every moment, talking with her," Max Jr. said. "You'll catch the Rio Grande at six tomorrow morning. June, take Papa upstairs."

June managed to pull her father back indoors and up the stairs to their rooms where she began moistening his lips with whiskey until he reached for the bottle. All the snow seemed to fall from him at once, making a dark puddle on the rug that for an instant made June think she was seeing her mother's blood.

"It's all my fault, my dearest Sara. I'm not worthy to be a Jew, a husband, a father to you, my angels. Sara, my dearest, my beloved Sara." Max threw himself face down on the sofa and sobbed.

———————

Sara Neustadt Selig died two days later in the Denver General Hospital with her husband and weeping children at her side. The sheriff declared her death a heinous crime and put a five-hundred-dollar bounty on the head of an unnamed outlaw of the Jesse James gang.

The community of Leadville and the Selig family stood close to the grave in the Jewish section of Evergreen Cemetery. A young nephew, Hermann Selig, came from Chicago. Hermann's father, the eldest brother Joseph, sent his brothers shipments of dried beef, fresh fruit and vegetables from Chicago.

"I apologize for father. Health won't permit him to travel," Hermann said to June.

"It's good of you to come so far." June held his hand for support.

Max Sr. kept his composure until the mayor of Leadville said, "Sara Selig would have been out shoveling on a day like this, to make a path for customers. From upstairs, there would have been a fragrance of her brisket, making us all hungry." At that moment, Max wailed, "My Sara, my beloved," and fell back into the arms of his sons who led him to a bench.

Harriet stayed in the carriage, her black veil pulled over her face. The recent snow had warmed the earth enough so that with great effort, the men dug a grave to bury Sara. Days later, Harriet came to visit her sons' small headstones, and lay small bouquets of white smilax on her sister's fresh grave.

# Two

## August, 1895

June Selig was waiting for her older sister May to finish dressing for Saturday services. May held up a moss green dress with black piping and a lace collar. "Should I wear this green? You say green suits me but I don't know."

"Green is such a good color for you, and today you'll look especially pretty with pink in your cheeks," replied June. "Now get into that dress or we'll be late. I'll take the flowers out of water and carry them."

Once out of the house, the young women walked briskly in the cool September morning down Harrison Avenue to Pine Street. On the corner of Pine and Fourth, they stopped across from the two-story matching towers that rose above the entrance of Temple Israel. Though the *shul* was only a single large room with a rustic wooden outside siding, golden stars painted on the arched, dark blue ceiling always made June feel as if the heavens had been brought beneath this roof.

"It still makes me so proud of Papa and our brothers, and happy that Mama saw the results of their work," said June.

"And sad," May continued her sister's sentence, "that she had so little time here because she loved the Temple and the Sisterhood."

In the vestibule, the page from the *Herald Democrat* describing Temple Israel's opening in 1884 hung in a bronze frame. *In 33 days, the Jewish men of Leadville, men who spoke English, Yiddish, German, Russian, or Hungarian, stripped down to their shirt sleeves to hoist beams and hammer and lift the walls in time for sunset on Rosh Hashana.*

*Rabbi Sachs came from Cincinnati to blow the* shofur *for the first service.*

As June was placing the tall white lilies in buckets before the choir risers, she saw that May was only half paying attention to getting their arrangements in place. Every time the door opened and closed, a stem dropped from May's hands. Who was her sister expecting to come through the door? June wondered. Of course May was awaiting the same person she had dressed so carefully to please. Who could that be? May hadn't spoken of anyone special. Was there a newcomer to Leadville? June was curious and a little envious of her sister's excitement, but if May found a love interest, it would make staying at home in Leadville with their father less of a burden.

Following a year of mourning Sara's death, after the *yahrzeit* recitation of the *kaddish* and lighting the memorial candle in *shul,* Max had resumed his evenings out with the town's notables, though there was less money for poker because everyone had become poorer. The silver market showed no signs of recovery; young men and women, whole families, were selling their businesses and leaving for Denver, Salt Lake City, even San Francisco. The Jewish population dwindled with the rest, but Max Selig, always the gambler, believed they'd come back to mine a new vein of silver or even gold. And because Sara was buried in Evergreen Cemetery, Leadville would be his home. On colorless winter days, the bright green cabbages and oranges from California, the red apples from Washington State, made shoppers come into Selig's grocery to spend a few pennies on fresh fruit and vegetables. Even in pinched circumstances, May and June still gave the poorest miners' children extra beans and flour, a free carrot or turnip.

"Practice your *tsedakah* elsewhere," Uncle Isaac still said if he caught them.

"We think of Mama," June and May answered together. "Mama helped others."

Max Jr. and Morris' practice as the town's youngest physicians barely met expenses because the brothers let poor patients pay less, or traded services in exchange for treating them. June knew her brothers were ambitious to join hospitals beyond the Rockies where they could continue to learn from superior physicians, but for now they stayed in Leadville out of loyalty to their father.

As June stepped back to survey her floral arrangement, May confessed her secret.

"He's the most educated and refined man I've ever met, June."

"I guessed there was a special person. Is he new to town?"

"Yes, he's just arrived, all the way from Europe. His name is Nathan Grensky. Two days back, he came into the store to see Morris. It seems they'd met at the library where Mr. Grensky told our brother that he'd been feeling lightheaded ever since coming to Leadville. Imagine the shock of leaving a city like London which is at sea level and arriving here in Leadville in the high mountains!"

"And that's not all he left. Think of the culture in London, and then coming here."

"I did think of all that."

"London!" June said. "Does he have fancy ways and look down on us?"

"No, Mr. Grensky does not appear high and mighty despite his fine starched cuffs and good tailoring. To my regret, I'd not powdered my nose and I knew it was shining."

"You have a darling nose—let me powder it now." June knew that her sister worried that her nose was too long; in fact, the tip of May's nose did droop a little and reddened from cold or excitement, but a man of character would overlook this, June thought as she applied a thin layer of powder.

"He asked about the book I'd been reading and when I showed him the cover, he said that the poet Heinrich Heine had been his favorite since childhood but since he'd begun reading in English, Mr. Emerson's poems and his philosophy of life greatly pleased him. Imagine my surprise that the very book I was reading was so dear to him!"

"He appears to be a man suited to your heart."

May blushed. "I would have given him my copy of Emerson if it hadn't seemed too forward. I brought it today to present to him." May lifted *Poems* from her bag. "He's tall and attractive, Sister. If only he doesn't mind that I'm rather small compared to you."

"If your minds are harmonious, that is what matters."

"Oh, June, I think that's so and I know you'll find Mr. Grensky as fine as I do. Without boasting about himself, he admitted that he transacted business in French, German, and English when he worked for the Rothschild Bank in London."

"Rothschild Bank! My goodness. What brought him to Leadville?"

"His uncles are the Grensky brothers. They required an accountant, and would only have someone in the family and so he has traveled all this way."

"Grenskys. They're so unpleasant, both the men and their wives, and they make it clear they look down on Father."

"But *this* Mr. Grensky is not displeasing at all!" May answered vehemently. "The Grensky wives are hard little women but we should pity them for they've lost their babes and are childless, like poor Aunt Harriet. Nathan does not have their characteristics."

"Nathan! My goodness, May. How quickly Mr. Grensky has become Nathan."

"At his request." May lowered her eyes but June saw a becoming blush.

"I'm sure to be pleased if you like him so much."

"I admit that I do, June. As I said, my heart went out to him before we met because of Morris' description of the uncles' meanness toward him. Since, my admiration has only increased. His uncles are so stingy they've improvised an apartment above their business rather than have him at their home, and he says it is cold."

"I feel your friendship for him already. Perhaps you can be of some help improving his situation, May."

"I wish I knew a way but I believe he's a private man."

As the sisters finished arranging the lilies and sat awaiting the arrival of congregants, June formed an image of Mr. Nathan Grensky, tall, somewhat stooped, and probably near-sighted from so much reading figures, middle-aged but not too old for May. Her sister had never had a suitor and yet she composed deeply romantic verses from her imagination and her reading. June would be sure to tell Mr. Grensky that recently Prang's Greeting Card Company of Boston had bought several of May's seasonal short poems and would be publishing them.

The moment June saw the tall stranger who lowered his head to enter the *shul*, she realized how wrong she'd been imagining Nathan Grensky as bent and middle-aged. She would have picked him out of any crowd as the most attractive of all men present.

June caught Mr. Grensky's look of recognition as May waved her hand, but in the next moment, his gaze turned in her direction and their eyes met. For an instant, a spark seemed to flash over the heads of everyone else, a current arcing between them that heated her face and traveled down her neck until she felt herself too hot under the light blouse she wore. She dabbed her forehead to wipe away the perspiration.

Nathan sat three rows ahead and on the other side of the aisle beside the Grensky uncles and their wives who dressed, no matter the climate, in stiff black gowns and bonnets. From her seat on the aisle, June had a perfect angle to observe his fine profile, clean-shaven firm chin, straight nose, dark brown hair trimmed above his white collar. She was sorry she'd already packed her new cambric blouse and navy-blue skirt in her suitcase because May said how it flattered her tall figure. But what am I thinking? June asked herself. This is about May's happiness. What I wear is no matter. Mr. Nathan Grensky is May's heart interest.

The choir was taking their places and the room quieted. The illuminated Torah that Meyer Guggenheim had ordered from Switzerland was brought from the holy Ark.

June only realized the service was over when the congregation stood, shook hands and wished each other *shabat shalom,* which she murmured without knowing how she found her voice. Then she was hearing May apologize to Nathan for the simplicity of their service. June found herself looking into his grey-blue eyes.

"I haven't introduced our youngest sister. June, this is Nathan Grensky."

June felt her forehead hot and supposed it turned fiery as May continued to talk.

"I imagine that my sister would like to hear your first impressions of our town. We've lived here all our lives and cannot see it as a stranger might," said May.

"Let me think for a moment." Nathan paused. His eyes stayed on June. "I marvel that one can buy anything, from fine Oriental carpets to pistols and a large selection of gravestones, all within a block. The game rooms and saloons on Harrison Avenue never close the entire night. From my room, I've heard what sound like gun shots."

"Oh dear," May laughed, "I'm afraid you've seen far too much."

"I am also surprised at the number of perfectly good items that people abandon on the street. In Germany, everything was repaired and reused. Apparently, here in America there is such bounty one can throw so much away."

"Oh, no, we're really quite poor now," said May. "But you're right about things being discarded. If you've never been in a mining town, you don't know the speed that wealth got made and just as quickly was lost, rich one day, nothing the next. Men bought what they wanted, or gambled it away. Much of what you see abandoned probably comes from those who are leaving Leadville and can't afford to carry away their possessions."

June marveled at her sister's fluency before this handsome man. Usually May was the shy one but now June felt so choked with feeling that she couldn't speak a word.

"Children are at constant risk from deep and dangerous mine shafts that often lie amidst homes," continued May. "All manners of pits and holes are dug everywhere and then left uncovered when they are no longer being mined. Our brothers—you know Morris and Max Jr.—survived childhood adventures only by good luck and strong constitutions."

"I've seen these holes and am reminded of little burrowing animals I remember in Germany," said Nathan.

"You mean gophers!" May laughed.

"Gophers!" Nathan laughed with May but looked at June. "My first impression, I will be truthful, was of a town I could find no comfort in."

"No comfort!" May reached out to touch his arm. June winced. How forward her sister was all of a sudden. No, this was a good thing, June told herself, to feel so at ease.

"I'm sorry it's been so difficult, and such a shock." June finally joined in.

"But not lacking in friendliness. Your *lustige* family, May, and your brothers, have been kind."

"Do you mean *happy* family?" June asked. *Lustige* had several meanings in English; the word could mean happiness and also desire.

"Yes, happy is the word." Nathan answered. "So you speak German?"

"Our mother read to us in German. The poetry sounded like pure music. I always hoped to learn more," May said.

At that moment, their brothers approached.

"Glad to see you here, Nathan. Your color is improved," said Morris.

"It is the company. Your sisters are most kind."

Max reached out and tapped Nathan's gold watch that hung across his vest. "Never show your watch outside your vest in this town. Someone will relieve you of it. And do let me take your pulse."

"Brother, must you always be the doctor! Even here!" protested May.

Max pulled back Nathan's cuff and placed fingers on his wrist.

"How are you feeling overall?" asked Max.

"Sometimes I'm chilled to my bones, but then again, it's cold in my apartment."

"Not good," said Morris. "You must insist on a better stove in your rooms. You told me you'd contracted rheumatic fever as a child."

"That's true, but I recovered. I was a great walker in London, but now to go from my room to my uncle's home, only several blocks away, puts me out of breath."

"The high mountains are no place for you. I say so frankly." Max shook his head. "But since you are here, you must come see us for a thorough examination. Hopefully, your heart will adjust to the altitude. The lungs can also become compromised so avoid catching cold that can become pneumonia. My sisters will have invited you home for cake, I imagine. Father enjoys new faces. Unfortunately we must work this afternoon."

"The Sabbath…oh, Morrie," said May, then turning to Nathan, "But you'll come for coffee and a cake, won't you, Nathan?"

"I'm afraid I must regretfully decline for the same reason."

"Work on the Sabbath? Your uncles should give you this day off," said May.

"Business comes first for them. Otherwise, they are observant."

June noted that Nathan said *observant*, not *religious*—a nice distinction for a man whose native language wasn't English.

"About the watch, my brother was only warning you to be careful," said Morris. "We live among desperate people in hard times. My brother and I treat knife and gunshot wounds every day. If fights don't kill them, the poor devils do themselves in with every manner of liquor. If we had a dollar for every man poisoned by drink, we'd be rich. Not that the miners' lives concern your uncles."

"Maxie!" exclaimed June. "What a lack of politeness. Mr. Grensky is not responsible for his uncles' business."

"I apologize, though spirits merchants sell addicting alcohol to the most vulnerable of men," said Max.

Morris pulled at his brother's sleeve. "We must be going. Tell Papa we'll be in time for supper," he said to May.

"You mustn't take our brothers too seriously." May said. "They have recently returned as doctors and can't control their penchant for giving diagnoses. They are kind and treat the destitute without pay."

"I am sorry I cannot accept your *lustige* invitation." Nathan glanced at June as if he knew how the word affected her, as if it was already a sign of trust between them.

"We'll walk with you to Harrison Avenue, Nathan," May suggested.

"Thank you, ladies, if it's not out of your way."

"I should go directly home, I've much to do." June knew that getting away from the strange and insistent feelings aroused by Nathan was the only right thing to do, and yet she could not move away from the attraction she felt to him.

"June is going to miss our poetry reading," said May. "She is leaving us here, but we are proud for her. June has been awarded a scholarship to Women's Educational Preparatory College in Baltimore. The first woman in our family to attend college."

"I am sorry to hear that you are going so far but I congratulate you on your merit." Nathan looked into her eyes and she looked back. Then he began to cough.

"June, we've kept Nathan too long." May spoke vehemently, raising her arms and accidentally striking June's shoulder with her elbow.

"I'm sorry. Forgive me, Sister."

"No, forgive *me*." June hugged her sister around the waist. May deserves her happiness, June thought. If I can help her by leaving her alone with Nathan, I must do so.

Yet she didn't make her excuses and move away from Nathan.

"If we walk only a little farther, we'll see the snow-covered peaks," May said.

They walked until May pointed to the crests of Mount Elbert and Mount Massive shrouded in clouds.

June didn't plan her next words.

"It's already snowing but in the meadows below the peaks there are still Alpine flowers in bloom. May, what would you say to an excursion with Mr. Grensky to Twin Lakes tomorrow? It will be the last time I will be able to do so."

"Tomorrow being Sunday, I am free from my uncles," Nathan answered quickly.

"But how will we go?" asked May. "It's quite far. I'm not sure of the way."

"We'll arrange for a carriage," June answered. "I know the way perfectly."

# THREE

"IF WE HAVE TO make emergency calls, we'll be without transportation," Max Jr. said to June when she asked to borrow their carriage for the trip to Twin Lakes.

"Think of the good it will do Mr. Grensky to be in the really fresh air," June addressed her younger brother, Morris.

"We'll be all day at St Luke's and we won't need the carriage, Brother," Morris said. "I'll ask Horace to get our pair ready for you, but don't press Mr. Grensky to walk more than he should. If his breathing sounds labored, you must stop."

"We'll be careful, won't we, May? We'll show Mr. Grensky the late wildflowers in the meadows and the views across the lakes."

May nodded but didn't look up to share June's assurances. June was aware that her sister had been peculiarly quiet during supper; ordinarily, she would have asked if May was feeling unwell, but instead of inquiring, she rose first from the table and cleared the dishes before anyone else got up. She turned her back to hide the color that rose to her cheeks as she thought of seeing Nathan Grensky in the morning.

June woke up before dawn but didn't want to disturb May who was sleeping. She could barely wait until light came through the window of their room, quietly got up and began to pack their picnic lunch into a large basket. "It will be a good day. No clouds," she said when May came to the table for coffee. Neither of them looked in the others' eyes. Finally, May said, "I'm concerned about Nathan's health. You heard our brothers say that he must avoid getting a chill. Perhaps we should cancel this journey, for Nathan's sake."

"Oh no, that will only disappoint him. He won't catch a chill this early in September. Think of the memories he will have through the winter, how it will buoy his spirits during the dark days to have seen Twin Lakes and the wildflowers. We'll show him the ruins of the Interlaken Hotel and tell him how it rivaled any in Switzerland when people came to Leadville for vacations and summer sports. May, the carriage is on its way, so don't be such a worrier. It's my last time this year seeing the lakes."

June caught a glance of herself in the mirror, saw her cheeks glowing against the red and white cambric blouse she'd unpacked and tucked into her dark blue skirt and made tighter with her wide belt. When May came into the kitchen again, dressed in a brown cardigan over a beige skirt that Ruth had passed down, June knew she should suggest a change to brighter colors. Yesterday morning, she would have encouraged her sister to look her best; any other morning she'd have fussed with May's hair, pressed tendrils around her face to bring out her wistful brown eyes. They'd always been each other's best friend and confidante, hardly a secret between them. But today, all June said was, "You need a little rouge to pinken your cheeks. You don't want to look peaked."

"I am tired from sleeping badly but since you insist we go, I cannot refuse."

———

Over the twenty miles to Twin Lakes, the bumpy roads threw them against each other, June and Nathan Grensky on one side of the carriage, May facing across and facing in the direction they were traveling. Each contact with Nathan caused June's heart to pound so hard she thought that everyone had to hear it. Midway, when they got out to stretch, June asked May if she preferred to take the seat beside Nathan.

"I'll remain facing forward, otherwise I get a headache," May replied.

They re-entered the carriage and rode silently until Mount Elbert came into view.

"Is our mountain as grand as the Alps?" June turned to Nathan.

"The Alps have nothing more splendid to offer," Nathan replied.

"But you'll be disappointed in our little lakes, I'm afraid. Just ponds compared to what you've seen," June continued.

"I've never been more enchanted." Nathan caught and held June's eyes. *Enchanted.* The word made her tremble almost as much as *lustige.*

At that moment, the coach tilted to one side again and June fell into Nathan's lap. "Excuse me," she said, pulling herself up again. He looked at her with grey eyes that seemed to tell her, do not apologize, the touch of you is as welcome to me as it is to you. *No,* June thought, do not imagine such intimate feelings. *No.*

Twin Lakes, small, roundish bodies of water were divided by a marshy rise that separated them. The three started out along a path beside the closest lake where piney slopes of Mount Elbert reflected in the glassy waters, an ice-blue under the blue sky. Higher up, dense clouds hung on the mountain peaks.

"It will be snowing there already." May shivered as if she could feel the cold.

"But it's still summer here." June pointed out violet and coral wildflowers with creamy tongues down their center. "These are Columbines. They're my favorite flower."

Nathan knelt to look more closely at the delicate petals. "Yes, I recognize them, we also have Kolumbines, sometimes they are blue and called Akelei, I believe."

"Blue! Imagine!" exclaimed June. "These taller ones are Bright yarrow and Glacier lilies. And there's Purple prairie smoke. The blooms have stayed late this year."

"Just for you," said Nathan.

June trembled all of a sudden, from her knees down, as if she no longer had her habitual strength to hike for miles. She leaned against a small pine.

"You're certainly our botanist this morning, Sister. Usually you're running off and showing your mountain hiking skills while I linger over a flower."

May's words felt like blows.

"I only thought our guest would like to know." June studied the toe of her boot. "May writes about our flowers in her poems. She knows their Latin names as well."

"When I was small, I kept a notebook with flowers I knew by name," Nathan said. "I was enchanted by the woods as a boy."

*Enchanted.* The word released butterflies in her stomach.

May coughed. "As I feared, the carriage ride has given me a small headache. I'll sit here in the sunshine with a book while June takes you further. She is a great walker."

Nathan asked politely if May preferred they stay with her. May shook her head.

"You go on. Remember, June, our brothers advised against anything strenuous."

"We'll only look around the lake and be back." June knew she should now offer to stay with her sister as she'd done many times when they'd come for hikes with their brothers; those times, May's decision to stay back had never mattered because her sister daydreamed along the paths, lagged behind and usually turned back.

May picked up her book. "You two go off now."

"I feel returned to health in this beautiful place." Nathan seemed to have no difficulty maintaining June's pace as they continued toward the scattered homes of summer visitors, shacks and shelters for fisherman, and in the distance, the abandoned Interlaken Hotel.

June stopped to point out the hotel's peaked roof through the trees.

"It's fallen to ruin, unfortunately. Before we go that far, let us sit on this nice rock and rest," she said.

But Nathan stayed standing. Was he alright? Had she taxed his strength?

"We're at a higher altitude now. Perhaps it's too much exercise for today."

He shook his head. His gaze on her again felt like electricity, a thrilling pain.

"Miss Selig, I know we have only met yesterday."

A mix of fiery hot and icy cold went through her.

"Nathan, we're less formal in the west. Call me June, please."

"Yesterday, June, you said you would not be here much longer."

"But I'll be back, perhaps as soon as winter holidays." June didn't drop her eyes as she said words that she knew she should not say but could not hold back. "Until yesterday, I wished nothing more than

25

to travel and see everything beyond Leadville, but now I'm regretting my departure. I wish I weren't going so soon."

"You mustn't regret getting an education," he said. "But to be truthful, and risking your displeasure, I fear that I shall never see you again."

June choked out, "Never see me again? Do you fear that may happen?"

"Yes, and it pains me because I greatly wish to see you again."

"Will you be returning to Germany before I am back in Leadville? I know it is hard for you here."

The lake that had shimmered before her turned dark under a cloud.

"My uncles have made it clear they need me to stay but your brothers advise me to leave because the altitude is not good for my health."

"Then of course you must follow their advice." June stood up as she protested against sacrifice of health. She felt close to tears and unsteady on her feet.

He waited a moment and said, "I shall be here when you return."

The words made her feel as if he'd caught her from falling. She blushed and blurted out, "I'm a great letter writer. Writing is a passion with me. I consider composing a letter almost a sacred duty. We'll write to each other."

She must bring May's name into the conversation now, must say something about their shared love of poetry, how writing letters mustn't exclude her sister. "May will be here. She admires you very much."

Nathan seemed to ignore her meaning. "I should not, I have no right, but I cannot help myself. I declare admiration for you, June. More than admiration. I have another feeling that I have never known and that I dare not speak."

Nathan was so close that June could feel the warmth of the sun on his jacket, and through his jacket. She stood as tall as she could on tiptoes, her eyes level with his. Nathan's dusky eyelids, the pink edges of his earlobes, the deep dimple in his chin, and his mouth all so close that she began to lose her balance and tilted toward him.

He gently caught her shoulders with both hands and drew her against his body. He touched her hair and she loosened the coil at the back of her neck, dropping the ribbon that had secured it. Their faces were unbearably close. He raised her chin and brought her nearer until their lips came together in a softness and warmth she had never known.

Finally, breathless, they gasped and pulled away. "This is my first kiss," she said.

"It is mine as well." He took her by the hand and now they sat on the rock.

For moments, they remained silent and still, only the beating of their hearts and a light sound of ripples on the lake. Then he pulled away to look into her eyes.

"Yesterday, sometime before ten in the morning, I disliked Leadville and thought I would leave soon, but then the world stopped moving, as if it had been spinning in one direction and suddenly reversed course. That change happened when I saw you, June. And only an hour later, we spoke and I heard your voice for the first time. You must believe me when I say that nothing like this has ever happened in my life. I can't believe it's happening now, and that I'm so unmannerly as to force my confession on you."

She looked at his grey eyes, as deep as the sky and water. "I felt at that very moment a spark of electricity passing between us. Do you believe that could happen?"

"I know it happened. All night I continued to feel that current. I didn't mind sleeplessness because I saw your lovely face before me."

"Nathan, I must tell you...I must confess..."

"You must believe me when I say I've never taken advantage of a young woman before this moment."

"No, no, no! You're not taking advantage. It's my selfishness I'm speaking of. I must confess the most serious selfishness in the world. My beloved sister May met you first and she has confided in me that she has a special feeling toward you."

"I am grateful for that, and for your brothers' friendship."

"May has hopes of greater friendship. She introduced me so I might approve of you. Now I have spoiled her hopes. It's unfair that I've been the favored one once again. Our father never offered her a chance of applying for college. He chose me over her as he always has. Today I have taken advantage again and committed the very worst betrayal."

"I appreciate your sister. I'll be her friend as I would have been if you and I hadn't met, but I'd not feel more. Only for you, June, do I feel overwhelming love."

"Not met, that's impossible!" June clasped his hands, laughing and crying at once.

"It was five minutes before ten. You arrived just before services began," she said. "May saw you and you saw her, and then we saw each other."

"And then that moment happened and cannot be denied." Nathan drew her close again and they kissed until both were breathless.

June finally pulled apart. "I must go to May, but I don't know how to tell her."

"She will understand when I explain," he said.

"No, you mustn't. Her feelings will be so hurt if you confront her. She felt so hopeful that you and she might become closer, that affection might grow between you."

Nathan kneeled to pick up the ribbon that had fallen to the ground. He held her ankles, her knees close to his face.

She looked down. "Thank you. I'm so happy, Nathan, and only a little unhappy."

"Don't worry about May. I promise we shall be fine friends," he said.

When they arrived back around the lake, May seemed not to have moved from the bench she'd made of a fallen tree trunk.

"Did you walk as far as the Interlakken?"

"No, we only reached midway between the lakes and rested. May, my dearest sister." June approached her. "I'm sorry we were so long. We…"

"But you don't appear sorry, or tired." May stood and moved into the shade of a thick pine. "Your color is as pink as I've ever seen it and your eyes tell me you're happy, not sad. Your lips are swollen. You've been kissed and your hair has been loosened."

"Oh, May, how can you say that!"

"Because it's so obviously true. I am not surprised by anything you do, June. You have always done just as you wished."

"That's unfair, Sister." June's voice felt thick with tears as May turned her back. "Oh May, I had no intention for this to happen. Look at me, please."

"Miss Selig, May," Nathan's eyes expressed concern and he stepped closer but May moved out of reach and put her hands out in front of her.

"May!" June's voice pleaded.

"Say no more. You two need not further trouble me with your pity. I have a talent for imagining happiness for others. As June said, I write poetry inspired by imaginary love and loss. My portion is loss, June's is love." She turned to June. "I told you Nathan was too attractive for me but I hoped you would give me a chance to get to know him."

"May, if he had been anyone else but Nathan."

"I'm doing my best to not run away and hide." May raised her hands again as if to ward off any more words. She bit her lips. "I'm feeling cold. Look, clouds are coming. We might be rained on and we haven't had a bite of food."

"Let me get the blanket from the carriage to warm you," said Nathan.

"Nathan must need it more than I do, only he feels nothing of the chill now. Take care, June. We are not all as well-favored by health as you. Don't be selfish in all things. We must take Nathan away now before he catches a chill to make you regret this day."

# Four

## The Ice Palace
## 1895

JUNE CARRIED HER BAGS up two flights to her college room on the eve of Rosh Hoshana. Her roommate had already unpacked and left a note saying she'd return later. She signed her name Miriam. Was Miriam Jewish? June wondered. Was she away attending services somewhere in Baltimore?

As June imagined the *shofar* resounding to the beams of Temple Israel, she sat alone looking out her window on the green campus of the teacher's preparatory college. The absence of services mattered less than feeling constant pain remembering May's hurt, her sorrow, and the cool goodbyes between sisters. She had no one to confess her selfishness to on the High Holidays, so she made a vow that in this New Year, she would ask forgiveness from her heart and win back May's trust.

Instead of writing to her sister, she expressed her feelings to Nathan.

*My dearest Nathan, Far away from my family and from you, I offer prayers for your happiness on Rosh Hoshana, a Year of great meaning for us. I also ask for forgiveness in the heart of my sister who I wronged without wishing ever to do so.*

Nathan wrote on the same day but they only read each others' letters two weeks later. June learned that the Selig's supper after services had included him. He reported that May cooked an excellent supper of brisket, with her own *tsimmes* and honey cakes for dessert. Reading this didn't make June as happy as it should have; despite her resolves to devote only good thoughts to May, she felt waves of jealousy and regret at not being able to cook Nathan's first dinner. But he would not want to read her small-minded thoughts. She complimented his penmanship, his neat sloping letters with big S's and elegant swirls. In his reply, he told her about his education.

*In our German schools, our pages had to be perfect. There were no corrections allowed. If you made so much as one mistake, you wrote the entire page over. After I lost my parents and was sent to live with relatives, the discipline enforced in gymnasium served me well. Your brother, Morris, has entrusted his* Roget's Thesaurus *to me, a well-thumbed copy that I shall consult chapter and verse for future letters.*

Postal delivery depended on the weather and, it seemed to June, on magic; sometimes bringing several letters in one week, followed by a month's drought. Over the long autumn of their first separation, June wrote more words to Nathan than she did for class assignments. She wanted to know all about his childhood, his studies in Paris and work in London, and his hopes. In turn, she wrote what she remembered about her early years in Leadville and the awful night of her mother's murder.

In letters to May and her father, June told of her studies and observing Sabbath with her roommate, Miriam, at their home in Baltimore. May answered with news that Prang's Greeting Cards had purchased two poems for Mother's Day. "I composed what I imagined must be that blessing to have one's dear Mother close as we used to have ours in happier days."

June believed that May was sharing loss. She hoped the letter offered forgiveness.

───────────

Nathan also watched the Leadville Ice Palace rise from the ground, "as if Grimm Brothers side by side with Israelites laboring in Egypt came alive before my eyes."

*November 22, 1895. The men unloose great blocks of ice from frozen ponds and lakes. These blocks are then carried by all means of transportation to be laid together and mortared with water to freeze at night. Then these free men, not enslaved except to their dream, stagger to a saloon to drink and play cards until all hours, rising to go again to the ice fields the next day. There is a fanciful, optimistic element in the Western American character. Residents believe this Palace of Ice will lift spirits and bring back prosperity. It appears to me that the imagination of Leadville itself may be recovered if not its financial well-being. My uncles of course see only the possible benefit to business—they will sell more*

In the next letter, Nathan worried that a sudden warm spell in mid-December would melt the Palace. He reported how day and night, crews sprayed the blocks with water until at last the cold returned to freeze hard the walls and towers.

When Max Jr. and Morris took Nathan to Twin Lakes to watch them skating in preparation for races at the Ice Palace, he found their rock covered in snow.

*I rested my cheek against its coldness, certain that stone had recorded the first moments I dared declare my feelings. I confessed to your brother that an adventurous doppleganger took me over that day, removing all fear and giving me courage to declare myself to you, and with your approval, let Morris know my intentions.*

Morris, Nathan then revealed, along with his brother, had romantic intentions of their own. They'd not yet met two sisters named Suzannah and Fanny Guthmann, recently arrived from Mannheim, but they had received photographs of the young women who were staying with relatives in Cincinnati.

*They intend to travel east to meet the sisters, and, if the matches seem desirable, to set an early wedding date and bring them back to Leadville. Your oldest brother favors the elder sister, Suzannah, while Morrie likes the looks of Fanny. Though both girls appear very fine, no one can compare to your beauty. There is no one to compare to you, my darling.*

In mid-December, when June thought she couldn't stand another day in Baltimore, her father wired funds for her ticket home. "Ice Palace complete. Must come." She spent all her pocket money in Hutzler's Department Store buying a dark green cashmere scarf for Nathan, a lacy white blouse for May, and a volume of Louis

Stevenson bound in red leather for her father who loved the South Sea adventures.

Often Nathan concluded a letter with Heinrich Heine's words, "When two who love are parted, they talk as friend to friend."

––––––––––

For weeks, as Nathan had reported, every Leadvillian worked around the clock for the grand opening of the Ice Palace on New Year's Eve. Children left school early to kneel beside their mothers and fathers replacing paving in sidewalks, filling potholes, painting and scrubbing and polishing storefronts. Max Sr. was stocking grocery shelves. Max Jr. and Morris purchased a new examining table for the inevitable falls on the ice. Even the Grensky brothers, loathe to spend money, had agreed to pay Nathan's fare to Denver to bring back two extra cases of Dewar's whiskey in time for the opening of the Ice Palace on New Year's Eve. Nathan did not tell his uncles that June's train would be arriving the same morning from Baltimore via Chicago.

June was still tidying her hair and pinching her cheeks when the train pulled into Denver's Union Station. Out her window, she saw a tall, slender man in a long grey coat and fur hat who looked so distinguished among the bushy-haired, bearded crowd that she felt a moment's panic. Letters written, unguarded words of yearning and hope, intimacy of poems and promises to 'my dearest, darling love'— she'd been so young, bold and foolish, unworthy of a sophisticated European who would now find her girlish and dull.

But when Nathan rushed forward toward her and she was in his arms, she forgot her doubts. She trembled beneath his cool hands that caressed her cheeks and knew that he felt as she did. She snuggled under his coat until the world and all the passengers milling around them disappeared.

The Denver, South Park and Gunnison railway carriage offered no privacy though passengers heading to the Ice Palace were imbibing at such a rate that they hardly noticed the couple huddled together in the corner. The men passed bottles of whiskey from hand to hand, and after a few hours, were lurching forward and sideways as the train climbed over passes and through tunnels. "I'm glad I didn't bring my uncles cases of Dewar's from the baggage car," Nathan whispered. "Not a drop would be left."

By the time Mount Massive and Mount Elbert came into view ten hours later, June had a headache and thought Nathan looked pale. The train blew its whistle and slowed into the Leadville station where Max Sr., whiskers bristling and a nose as red as Saint Nicholas, greeted his daughter by throwing his arms in the air in wonder at how grown up she looked, and then turning her around and around.

"My dear, dearest, my young scholar, you've returned home to me at last. Mr. Grensky, thank you for conveying our June safely."

"You've already missed the most splendid parade, Sister." Morris and May walked toward them, talking over each other about the marching bands and dancing dogs in the parade that morning.

"The parlor women rode ponies and showed their white knickers and red stockings," said May.

"They most surely did!" Morris whistled. "I'm sorry you missed it, Nathan."

"I had to secure this very valuable person. I must bring the much less valuable cargo to my uncles." Nathan pointed to the baggage car that was being unloaded.

"You're joining us to dance the night away," Morris called after Nathan.

"Thank you, Nathan, for your good care," June said. "You'll come to dance?"

"Yes, of course I shall," he called back. "Goodbye until tonight, June."

"And we're taking you to the Palace, Sister," Morris said over June's protest that all she wanted was to sleep.

He bundled June and May side by side under a blanket and pushed off, steering from behind. Everything seemed in motion around June, toboggans sliding in all directions, some overturning in snow banks alongside the tracks, the riders apparently having such a good time or too inebriated to feel any pain.

Max ran alongside until they'd picked up enough speed to coast up Eighth Street in view of the Palace that suddenly rose up before them: walls, towers, red and blue flags flew from turrets "Look at this," May pointed to the ice-statue of Lady Leadville holding a banner that read $200,000,000. "That's what Leadville made in silver in one year."

"Leadville is showing herself recovered, for all to see," said Morris. "You had to be here to watch the Palace grow. The towers are ninety feet high, and the walls five feet thick. Look—isn't it like a magic castle?"

"It's all I've heard about and more!" June said.

"June must be tired and she'll want to change her clothes for the dancing. She'll dance all night with someone we know." May looked away when she said this and June lowered her eyes. Was May hinting that no one else had any idea of their romance? Had Nathan not written that he'd opened his heart to Morris?

———

June had less than an hour to re-acquaint herself with the familiar corners of the small room she'd shared with May for so long as her sister hummed to herself as she pinned her hat. They didn't speak as they gathered coats, fur caps and muffs to meet their brothers and father in the carriage below. Every coachman and pair, all of Leadville with bells and ribbons streaming from their carriages, seemed to be rushing to the Palace together.

"We'd get there faster on foot," Max Jr. grumbled.

"Patience, Brother," replied Morris. "Father is comfortable and our sisters' good boots are for dancing, not snow. We'll get there soon enough."

Darkness all around made the Palace shine like a star leading them forward. Gas lamps illuminated ramparts and archways glowed with such blue lights that June thought for a moment that the ice vision was floating off the earth into air.

When they finally reached the hitching posts in front, Morris helped his father and sisters out of the carriage. He tied their horses and gave them feed bags. Around them on the smoothed ice, children skated in circles while their parents hurried forward.

May and June entered a passageway where many people jostled to see the beer bottles, stuffed game animals and fish frozen into the ice walls.

"The Coors beer bottles you see here," Morris pointed, "they're colored water. As soon as they arrived for display, they got drunk up. We refilled the bottles with brown water and resealed them."

Once they emerged from the passageway into the main hall, the sisters heard the nosy crowd become silent, all eyes fixed overhead on frosted icicles hanging from trusses, lamps embedded in ice pillars, colored lights glistening above.

"Doesn't it feel as if galaxies are floating above the ice?" Morris asked.

June nodded. "I can't believe our citizens did all of this in a few months."

On a balcony over a wood dance floor, an orchestra played, "The Vienna Waltz."

"May I have the first dance?" Nathan appeared at June's side. He was wearing a dark suit and looked so remarkably handsome that June barely restrained herself from throwing her arms around him.

"Before all the others who admire you have a chance to ask," he bowed.

"You shall have all the dances." June fit herself into his arms.

Women in fur and jewels, men in top hats and long black coats, whirled around the tall couple, came close and then moved away. June and Nathan seemed to be separated from others not only by dancers giving them space, but because they saw no one else. Even familiar people stopped to look at June, seeing the independent girl who had helped manage a household without her mother, a girl they'd watched win the school prizes, suddenly grown up, her thick chestnut curls looped into a womanly chignon.

The dancers requested three "Vienna Waltz" encores. During the final one, June noticed that May danced with Jerry Murphy, the Irish clerk at the Emporium. June always liked Jerry, who played the fiddle so fast he made you laugh and stamp your feet keeping time. June also remembered that May had been Jerry's favorite. When they shopped at the Emporium, he asked to see her poetry because he penned verses as well, though he said he never used the learned words as May did. Still, June never expected Jerry Murphy to be dancing with May. Irish and Jews lived in separate worlds. Perhaps at this carnival of ice, everything could be more democratic, as she'd read happened in Venice, Italy, when nobles and commoners mixed together during that famous Carnival time.

The two couples left the dance floor to drink a seltzer. May's cheeks shone and Jerry's lithe body moved in anticipation of dancing the polka the orchestra began playing. June saw they were close to the same height, some inches shorter than she and Nathan, and that they seemed to share each other's merriment in the evening.

"Do you mind if we watch?" Nathan wiped perspiration from his brow. "I'll catch my breath and we'll begin again."

"Of course I don't mind." June squeezed his hand as Jerry took May back on the floor, whirling and turning her sister twice as fast as the rest.

"June," Nathan said.

"Yes, Nathan." She waited a moment. Even with the music and crowd around her, the great ice hall seemed to have become quiet.

"June, I'm nearly ten years older than you are. I'll be twenty-eight this summer."

"When? I don't know your birthday. How could I not have asked?"

"August 27."

"Thank heavens I'll be home. Life is ahead of us, Nathan. Ten years is nothing when we have each other." June brought his hand to her lips, which soon became a kiss.

"I'm not a wealthy man but I will save every penny." As he said this, Nathan began to cough. He took a long while to stop and catch his breath.

"It's the dampness." June felt a chill down her spine, and longed again for his hand on her back, the warmth of dancing with him, to rid her of the sound of that deep cough. She could climb high mountains and swim in the cold lakes, while a few waltzes took all Nathan's strength. It's his first winter in the altitude, she thought, and the long train rides to and from Denver that morning had tired him. When warm weather came, they'd walk together and the exercise and good mountain air would make him stronger.

After supper in the Palace restaurant, they danced one more "Vienna Waltz" and went to collect their coats as the crowd's voice rose as one for "Auld Lang Syne." Before they entered the tunnel to leave the great hall, Nathan and June kissed under the ice arches and lunar lights.

As June turned the key and opened the store door, she heard, "June! June!"

"Coming, Papa."

Nathan kicked snow off his boots and helped her remove her coat and her outer shoes. "Shall I come up with you?"

"I don't know. Papa may have drunk too many whiskeys." June took Nathan's hands from his gloves and warmed them between her own.

"We'll talk to him together," Nathan said. "We don't want to wait until others tell him about us."

"He doesn't like surprises. If he's seen us at the Palace, I shall be candid."

"June! What's keeping you! Don't let the cold in."

"We're coming up, Papa."

They walked softly upstairs, opened the door a crack to the sitting room where Max sat in his wing chair warming his hands before the stove. Frost still clung to his beard and whiskers. Evidently he'd not been home long enough to build up the fire.

"I'll get more logs," she said.

"June, you don't need to do that now. I want to speak to you."

Before Max said more, Nathan stepped forward. "I come to ask your blessing to ensure your daughter's happiness. I apologize for not giving you warning of my intentions."

June could hear no quaver in his voice and marveled at his sureness.

"Intentions! What can those be? You're a bookkeeper, Grensky. I shall take care of my daughter as I've always done." Max's black eyes narrowed as he squinted at Nathan. "You—a stranger. A nephew to the Grenskys."

"Papa, please don't be insulting to Nathan. He's not at all like his uncles. That remark is not worthy of you."

"You are a child! How dare you say what's worthy of your father!"

Nathan coughed into his kerchief.

"Will you tell this sick man he needs to go home and get a good night's sleep!" Max wagged his finger at June. "He doesn't belong in the altitude."

"Papa, he's tired. He's been to Denver and back to bring me safely home."

"Ah, now I understand why he was so eager to make that trip."

"We both are tired, Papa. I sat up on the train for three nights. I mean no complaint. I'm grateful for the opportunity to see the Palace and to be home with you."

"You cannot be grateful and speaking to me as you're doing." Max pounded the floor with his stick.

June could count the times her father had been angry with her, or that she'd spoken oppositional words to him. Her mother had been the disciplinarian, her father the whiskered, crinkly-eyed parent with stories and sticks of gum that mysteriously appeared from behind her ears. After her mother's death, June had been her father's companion. Never before had she given him cause for anxiety.

"Perhaps you'd fix us all a hot whiskey, June. It would take the chill off. Since Grensky will be staying to hear what I have to tell him, he'll need some revivifying spirits before he goes out in the cold."

"Yes, of course I will, Papa. Nathan, will you take a hot toddy as well?"

"Thank you, June."

They remained silent waiting for water to boil. Outside the snow fell steadily. June poured a finger full of whiskey for herself and Nathan, two for her father, before stirring in sugar and lemon.

She delivered the cups and sat down beside Nathan on the couch across from her father. They blew on their hot drinks before sipping.

"Daughter, you're too young to know better but Grensky has been out in the world and should be ashamed, taking advantage of a young, inexperienced girl. I'll be glad to hear that he has no intentions beyond dancing with you for all to see."

June took a deep breath. "Papa, I'll be nineteen this summer. I've always had a mind of my own. I'm not a child being taken advantage of."

"I didn't ask you to speak. I'm addressing myself to him." Max pointed his thick and reddened finger at Nathan. "Exactly how long have you been taking advantage of my daughter behind my back? You've not been in our city long. She's been at her studies."

"Papa, Nathan is the most honorable man in the world. What words to use!"

"June, hold your tongue. Grensky, answer my question."

"We met at Temple in September just before June left, Sir. We've not seen each other again but we have been writing letters."

"Letters! Between the two of you, with no one else reading them!"

"Of course not, Papa. I'm free to write to whom I please."

"I esteem your daughter. She has a fine character. You must be proud."

"For how long have you *esteemed* this youngest child of mine who has been deceiving me with letters behind my back.?"

"As he said, Papa, since September. Our correspondence has brought us close. We know each other as well as any two people who've had years together. I may be young but I also know that my mind is made up. I wish only to pass my life with Nathan."

"Balderdash! The first well fitted-out young man you meet has turned your head, that's all. There's nothing more to it. You'll meet other young fellows, June, and I'll like their families as I do not like… what I know about Grenskys is no recommendation."

Max paused. It was his nature to be pleasant and accommodating but the shock, June realized, was too much. He'd worked hard for his sons' educations, two doctors and an engineer, survived his wife's murder, and, crowning his efforts, been able to send his youngest daughter to college, though scholarship funds covered most of the expenses.

"As Sara's daughter, blessed be she in memory, such ungratefulness and betrayal should go against your nature. You've become a Cordelia, the daughter her father loved best who renounced him."

"Papa! What literary references you can summon. I didn't know you'd read *King Lear*. But you're not quite right. Cordelia insisted on honesty in declaring her love for her father. I love you wholeheartedly and always will."

"I saw the shortened version dramatized at Loeb's Theater. And dammit all!" Max pounded the table so hard he hurt his knuckles. "My youngest daughter will be a teacher, perhaps principal here in Leadville where she will look after me in my old age." He turned his reddened eyes on Nathan. "You wish to take her from me! I won't have it."

"Oh Papa! Please don't strike the table again. You've skinned your knuckles."

"My flesh wounds do not matter. Only, here, where I hurt." Max struck his heart and then let his hands fall in his lap. "Don't take all my words personally, young man. My son Morris reports that you have the character your Grensky kin lack."

Nathan deeply blushed. "I cannot answer for my uncles."

"He's not at all like them. He wishes to be free of them," said June. "But to earn and save for the future, he must continue in their employ."

"So you will leave me all alone?" Max gripped his walking stick.

"I won't leave you, Papa. You sent me away to college, far from home. You have May here, and your sons are only a few streets away."

"We'll abide by your decision in everything, Sir," said Nathan.

"Will you then!" Max shouted, his voice already hoarse.

"Except to give each other up." June took Nathan's hand. "We will love each other forever and against all obstacles."

"You've always been a bold, prideful girl, June, prone to stubbornness that your dear mother, blessed be she, would have curbed. I don't believe you know your own mind, no matter how much you believe you do. Passing fancy, I'm sure of it." Hot tears came to his eyes, tears of frustration and exhaustion. "Mr. Grensky has turned your sister's head as well with his poetry."

Only now, when her father brought up May, did June let her guard down.

"Oh please, Papa, we never meant to hurt her. It's breaking my heart."

"What is this about? Are you both in love with the same man then?" asked Max, a smile creeping onto his face. "May will be quite happy with Nathan. They share interests in poetry. June, you will return to your studies and come to your senses to realize your duty lies here, with your father. Moreover, Nathan Grensky, I don't believe you will last a year in Leadville, You haven't the constitution for it."

Nathan stood up. "Mr. Selig, with due respect, your daughter May and I are friends but not more."

"You shall become more, as you have with June. What is wrong with May you cannot love her?"

"May is a fine young woman but it is June I love."

"June will return East. Time will change her mind."

"No." June stood and took Nathan's hand. "I shall not change my

41

mind. I'll wait as long as you wish for your permission to marry Nathan."

"Marry! Marry? Who said marriage! Are you trying to kill me tonight, June?"

Nathan answered. "We love each other and we wish to marry with your blessing."

The ice on Max's whiskers had melted and was puddling onto his waistcoat. His wrinkles seemed to deepen and lines appeared around his eyes, making his bushy white brows stand in points. June resisted her natural impulse to kneel beside him and dry his shirt or bandage his raw hand. Instead, she added logs to the fire and refilled his toddy.

"If it were your sister May before me, my words would be enough to make her obey. I know you're a determined, headstrong girl, June. Your strengths are also your weaknesses—you'll discover this one day. But I see from your expression that by denying you, I am playing the Capulets and Montagues, stoking your will to rebel."

"Papa, you amaze me with so much Shakespeare."

"I learn from mistakes of others. I shall not forbid you continuing to see Nathan while you're home this time, but no more about an engagement. And only so many letters between you, perhaps one per month will be enough for your foolishness."

"I'll finish my course of study," said June.

"And you will take a teaching position," Max said.

"I will do everything to receive your blessing, you know that, my dearest Papa."

"That's settled." Max sighed. "Say good night to Nathan and go to bed."

"So you do not deny us our affections, Papa?"

"That I did not say. For the present, you may meet in the company of others."

"Thank you, Mr. Selig. I will obey your wishes in everything," said Nathan.

June led Nathan down the stairs and through the store, which was cold and damp. With the door open, the biting wind blasted them. For an instant, June saw before her the wound, the blood, the black slice into her mother's head. She clung to Nathan. He held her against

42

him as revelers came weaving toward them.

"My father will come around to understand we are not to be parted." June leaned toward Nathan and they kissed. "Papa will bless us, my darling."

June was about to put the inside chain across the door when she realized May wasn't yet back. For a moment, June hoped her father had seen May dancing with Jerry Murphy. He'd not tolerate that. But then, she didn't wish any wrath to fall on May.

# FIVE

## NEW YEAR'S DAY
## 1896

NEW YEAR'S DAY, MAY made June's favorite oatmeal porridge with raisins, poured cream over the top and brought the steaming bowl to the table beside her sister's bed.

"I know you want to sleep but we must be at the Palace for our brothers' race. I'll bring your coffee right now. Cream and sugar still?"

"Oh yes, lots of both. Where's Papa?" June yawned and stretched.

"He's gone on ahead to watch our brothers warm up for the speed skating competition. We'll meet him there," May said.

"Did he say anything about last night?"

"He was out before we had a chance to talk."

June smelled the fragrant porridge and tasted the sweetness on top. "Thank you. It's delicious. In the dormitory, I'm always hungry. They don't serve us much because the girls are always worried about their figures."

"I've hardly asked about your studies and I want to hear everything," said May.

"I wish they were more interesting. I know I sound ungrateful, but I'd give it all up to be home and not so far."

"From Nathan?"

June looked at May. "Yes, of course, and from you and Papa."

"You mustn't think of leaving your studies, June. You'll have a way to make a living if times ahead are more difficult. You finish breakfast and we'll get going. We can talk on the way."

When they came downstairs, Uncle Isaac was adding receipts at the register.

"It's New Year's Day, Uncle. Everyone is at the Palace, so come with us," May said. "You won't want to miss our brothers in the competition."

"No time," he answered, rearranging jars of molasses. "Too much to do."

"Poor thing," said June once they were outside and signaled a toboggan driver.

"It's probably better here than at home with Aunt Harriet," said May.

They caught a toboggan and arranged themselves under blankets. Their driver, bundled up in scarves, told them to hang on as he pushed downhill before he jumped on in back to steer their sliding rush. All around, a carnival atmosphere of toboggans, home-made sleds, and riders on horseback waving flags, sped past them.

The wind in their faces kept the sisters from talking until they reached the end of the descent where their driver ran behind the toboggan to give them more speed for the uphill slope to the Palace.

"I don't know if we can talk about Nathan, or if you prefer we do not," June said.

"Of course we can talk. He's already your fiancé if I'm not mistaken."

"May, do you mean that your heart is free from pain when you think of Nathan?"

"Mostly, I suppose I do. Shall I tell you an amusing story Morris related to me about Nathan?"

June nodded and May began describing the night their brothers and father took Nathan to Madame Lil's Parlor House on West Fifth Street.

"Madame Lil's? I don't understand, May."

"Neither did Nathan, according to Morrie. Initially, he expressed surprise at the sumptuous decor, the Oriental carpets, and the number of women sitting and chatting with men in the parlor but didn't understand where they were until Madame Lil suggested the men accompany young ladies upstairs."

June stared at her sister. "I don't think this is an amusing story. Why did my brothers...and Father?" June felt herself rigid with anger.

"I don't know except they wanted to show Nathan a good time. Perhaps to show him how some of our most dignified citizens spend their evenings."

"A good time! They don't know him at all. It was a terrible mistake!"

"June, don't worry. Like yourself, Nathan was not happy. He remained in the parlor listening to the piano while Papa and Morrie went upstairs, then he left."

"They took Nathan where he did not ask to go, under false pretenses." June's face burned. She wasn't in any position to bring this up with her father but she'd remember when he was being so high and mighty about how a good daughter should behave.

"Where was Maxie? I can't imagine he would like this," June said.

"You're right, our older brother was not there. I should have made that clear. Morrie confessed all this to me because I think he felt they'd done a foolish thing and he'd better tell me before I heard gossip, or worse, that it got back to you the wrong way. Nathan remained the perfect gentleman. It all ended quite unremarkably."

"How can you be so unmoved? I can barely endure hearing this."

"Sister, we girls in the west aren't easily shocked, remember? We knew a long time ago how Stillborn Alley got its name." May was looking down at her hands. "I hoped the story wouldn't upset you, but I see that it has."

June wiped her eyes to dry the tears clinging like snowdrops on her cheeks.

"One day I'm sure that Nathan and I will have a good laugh over it but for now I'm very angry at our brothers and Papa, and he's angry at me because we told him last night we wished to marry. I will try to retain my good humor toward our father and enjoy this time at home even though he's opposing my happiness. He believes Nathan and I won't be able to wait until he gives his blessing. We'll wait."

"June, you have always done as you wished. It won't hurt to wait for happiness."

"I saw you dancing with Jerry Murphy. You looked happy yourself."

"Happy that I'm asked to dance?"

"Yes, of course, and that you danced so well together. You weren't home when I saw Nathan out last night. It was late. How long did you stay to dance?"

"I have my own key, and I have a secret that you must keep." May waited until June nodded. "Papa might be angry with you now, but he'll accept Nathan because he's our faith and a good man. He'll never agree to me seeing Jerry Murphy."

"Papa surely saw you dancing last night."

"Papa was watching you and Nathan, king and queen of the ball. He didn't see me, I mean, he couldn't have imagined that Jerry Murphy and I are more than friends."

"Do you mean Jerry is more than a friend?"

"Jerry and I were on the musical committee for the Palace. I always liked him and he confessed that he had feelings for me."

"That's true, Jerry paid you special attention, and appreciated your poetry."

"You can imagine how grateful I was that someone preferred me," May said.

"May, you're not telling me that Jerry really is your sweetheart?"

"Why not? Should I have no one? Jerry admires me as I am and I reciprocate."

"Jerry can admire you, but he's not a Jew."

"I know, he's a simple clerk and he's Irish, but he's got a wonderful sense of humor and makes me laugh. I'm a clerk, too, for Father. Jerry says I have an Irish poetic soul, so you see we are not that different. He has high ideals about many things."

"Papa will never allow you to marry Jerry."

"I'm not thinking of asking Papa. When I go to meet him, Papa thinks I'm at the Hebrew Benevolent Society."

"Concealing your feelings, having a double life, how difficult for you, May. Should I be worried about your health?"

May laughed. "I've never felt better. Don't you think I am improved from when you last saw me, at Twin Lakes if you remember, when I had the ground knocked out from under me by my own sister?"

At that moment, the Palace ramparts with American and Colorado State flags flapping in a brisk wind came into view.

47

"Almost there, ladies. One last push." The driver trotted behind the toboggan to keep it in the iced grooves.

May leaned over and whispered, "Although thwarted love is the most popular theme with Prang cards, after condolences, I'm no longer looking on. I don't think you should begrudge me my share of happiness, Sister."

"Oh, May, of course I don't." June took May's hand and kissed her cheek. "I wish you happiness, though I don't know how this can be without Father's approval."

"Father will not determine my life and that's all I have to say."

The toboggan slid to a stop where an attendant reached down to help them out.

"Aren't you June Selig?" the driver asked as they paid him. "You were always good to my father who has passed on. You think we're gonna make money here?"

"We hope so," said June. "I'm sorry about your father. Was it an accident?"

"No, his lungs. Mother has moved back to Indiana but I thought things might change for the better with the Palace, so I'm staying here. Have fun, ladies."

As they entered the smaller ballroom set up for the speed skating competition, they saw their brothers already poised on the starting blocks. Max wore a red sweater and white bloomers and Morris had on blue and white. The sisters climbed into bleachers set up for spectators. It seemed everyone's breath was rising with a single exhale and hanging in the air like puffs of steam, and then came the gunshot, two dozen men bent over, heads almost touching their skates, tasseled caps bobbing, racing around in a circle. Once, twice, a third time around. The Selig doctors stayed close until the final fourth lap when a new dentist in town streaked ahead to the finish line. Morris came in second, Max Jr. third. All the racers hugged each other and headed for the bar.

# SIX

## LEADVILLE
### SPRING, 1896

ON A BLUSTERY, BITING April morning during a cold spell that had returned too late to refreeze the melting Ice Palace, Nathan Grensky bundled up, walked quickly up Harrison Avenue against sleet and driving wind toward the shelter of the County Court House. A month earlier, an unseasonable warm spell in March had melted the walls of the Ice Palace, and with it, Leadville's hopes for a long season of profits. As the Palace ice bricks weakened, its walls sank like a tired stalwart, limb by limb, melting into the muddy snow.

Nathan reached the Court House door and pushed it open. Far in the back, one man sat alone in the dimly lit office with a pile of papers on his desk.

At least it's warmer here than in my office, Nathan thought.

"I intend to become a citizen of the United States." Nathan removed his Homburg and handed the man a sheaf of papers.

"You come to the right place. Head accountant for Grensky Brothers Liquors and Tobacco, eh?" The clerk read Nathan's employment record. "Raking in the dollars? Bad luck about the thaw, wasn't it now?" When Nathan affirmed, the clerk asked his arrival date in America but demanded no proof. He wrote, "January 1, 1895," cutting by six months the four-year residency required for complete naturalization.

"What must I do now?" Nathan signed the papers of intent.

"You wait two years and then you take a test. Then wait two more.

49

You'll have no problems with your application, Mr. Grensky. We need educated men like you. Them ignorant eastern and dark people, send them back to Russia and Italy, is what I say if anyone asks me."

Nathan wanted to tell the clerk that he hadn't asked and that "these" people deserved a chance as much as he did, but said only, "One day I will marry here."

"With a real western lady, I suppose," the clerk winked. "We've got more beauties here than they got in Paris. And let me tell you, if you wasn't to become a citizen, and you got married to one of our girls, your good American wife, now she might be forced to lose her U.S. citizenship marrying a foreigner, so then where would you be? You're doing the smart thing becoming a citizen."

"My future wife intends to exercise her right to vote that your state allows."

"Female radicals don't have no place here," the clerk closed his record book.

Nathan again held his tongue. He felt satisfied to have begun the process of naturalization but disliked the exchange between himself and the clerk. Back in his room that night, dark except for a gas lantern beside his bedside table, he wrote to June to tell her about his application. "I regret not responding to the clerk for his prejudice. I still have vivid memories of those souls less fortunate than myself who made the crossing to America in steerage. They were not treated as humans should be."

Once Nathan started writing, the memories flooded back and he couldn't stop his pen moving across the paper. He and June had talked about her mother Sara's death, and she knew he'd been orphaned very young, but he hadn't wanted to burden her with the saddest days of his life, not the survived Rheumatic Fever, how his mother bathed his forehead to bring down the fever, but what had happened to her and his father soon after his recovery. Now he wrote it out.

*Two years after my illness, Father, who worked in a broker's offices that shipped wines and spirits along the Rhine, caught typhoid fever, probably carried by bargemen coming from the south. The disease was common then and there was no cure. Mother fell ill also. The doctor could do more than administer ether to relieve their suffering until they died. I was kept in another room inside the house that the doctor boarded up when he left. Only wardens were allowed in to remove their bodies and leave me food because they all feared contagion. I weep for the first time in my adult life now as I remember this.*

Nathan paused, unable to stop his tears, not wanting to feel this sadness.

He blew out the lamp and tried to sleep. In the morning, he'd finish with a more cheerful tone. But as soon as he was lying on his bed and watching the shadows on the ceiling, he got up again to pace the room, heart thudding in his chest as he remembered, how, after the quarantine period when his father's family had come to fetch him from the house of death, Aunt Theodora held her kerchief over her nose and refused to touch him. Once home, they scrubbed him until his skin was raw, and for two weeks after his arrival, his aunt kept him sleeping in the barn, just to be certain he no longer carried the infection. Theodora and Mendel were childless and knew little of kindness. Over the years, they counted every *pfenning* that his upkeep cost the family, reminding him he had a debt to repay when he began earning.

There was no love in that cold house but there were books that saved him from despair. He lived for reading adventures in faraway lands. Later, in the gymnasium, he excelled in ancient history and languages, won medals for excellence every year, dreamed of becoming an archeologist like the great German explorer Heinrich Schliemann who had discovered the city of Troy. But when he turned sixteen and passed his gymnasium examinations with highest marks two years ahead of most classmates, neither his aunt nor his father's middle brothers, Adler and Adolph, also wine brokers in Mannheim, permitted talk of going to the university to continue study. He must begin to work to repay their expenses. Within weeks, a cousin found him a position at the Warburg Bank in Hamburg and he left his aunt and uncle's home without barely an embrace between them.

At the Warburg Bank, he always dressed neatly, accomplished his work without complaint, and kept to himself. If he'd have joined one of the Hebrew cultural societies in the city, or attended parties he was invited to, he might have made friends, but he was used to solitude and preferred to read or attend concerts and theatrical evenings alone. Simply being out of Uncle and Aunt's house was such a pleasure, he wasn't aware of suffering from melancholia, only that sadness rather than happiness lived inside him.

*Melancholia?* The word he said aloud surprised him. He looked up in the dark, wondering if he'd ever felt happiness until now. Certainly he'd not suffered ill treatment from employers and fellow bank tellers and had been treated with respect. In 1893, when he was twenty-six, the Warburg Bank sent him to France to study the language, and then to London to perfect his English. The Hamburg bank apprenticed him to Rothchild.

The kindly older men at Rothchilds praised his gift for languages and repeated what the Warburg's had predicted, a fine career in international finance. Again, he could have accepted the social invitations that would have advanced him, but instead he found excuses to stay in his room reading English novels, then venturing out to the Covent Garden Opera House and the theaters along the Strand. He had fallen in love with the city and had no plans to return to Hamburg when a letter arrived from Leadville, Colorado, in America. Adolph and Adler, his father's two older brothers, had emigrated there and they needed an accountant. "You owe it to your family who brought you up and cared for you at their expense," they wrote. Enclosed with the letter were vouchers for ship's fare on the Hanseatic Line, Second Class. He felt he had not been given a choice.

Nathan boarded the ship in Bremen where he shared a cabin with three German Jews who had jobs waiting for them in the Chicago Exchange. On the deck above them the First Class passengers strolled and listened to orchestras playing for their entertainment; below, on the bottom decks beneath the water line, the steerage passengers, crammed together, came up for air once it was dark. The wealthy did not bother his sleep but Nathan would never forget the poor souls, many sick, beneath his cabin and the roiled Atlantic Ocean.

Nathan wrote this until he felt he'd come full circle in his account to June. He was exhausted and blew out the lantern whose fumes were irritating his throat.

In the morning, he walked up and down the room, again dark except for the candle at his bedside, and very cold. Since the first night he'd climbed the dusty cold stairway and opened the door onto the small, cramped space with a bed, table, wash basin, he'd felt cold. From the first, his uncles had reviewed the previous accountant's faults, how the young man had warmed himself too much and cost them in coal.

"You can only trust your own," Adler said, "to conserve expenditures in the interests of the family business. We don't mix much here. We keep to ourselves and attend to our business. We're much relieved you've answered our call, Nephew."

When they brought him later to meet their wives in their home on Banker's Row, Flora and Hildegarde each repeated the phrase, "We keep to ourselves."

--------

During his luncheon break, Nathan returned to the letter he hadn't sealed. June knew that he and Morris had become friends, and he wanted to repeat her brother's words the first time they'd met. "'Fate has a way of throwing people together,' your brother said. Little did we know, my dearest, our good fortune. All that I have written of misfortunate is redeemed by the miracle of your love!"

# SEVEN

## THE MINERS' STRIKE
## 1896

"CITIZENS ARMING THEMSELVES AGAINST citizens, is that what you want in our town? The miners want only enough to feed their families and you begrudge that?" Max Selig Sr. was red in the face as he waved a cane in the face of Adler Grensky who'd just reproached him for 'foolish charity' toward the miners.

"No one of you benefits if poor men and their families become more desperate," Max concluded without ceding the floor as if he dared Adler to answer to the audience of Leadville's Jewish community packing the Temple Israel on a Thursday evening.

Nathan was sitting at the back taking notes for his new friend, Jacob Heimberger, the editor of Leadville's weekly *Herald Democrat*. "If you can cover the meeting for me while I locate the gun mounts encircling the mines, I'll get photographs with my new Kodak and have proof of the mine owners' intentions," Heimberger instructed Nathan.

Nathan worried that he couldn't take notes quickly enough in English, and that he had no experience for the job of reporter, but as the men and women stood to speak, he got down the key quotes and knew he could write up the discussion.

A night earlier, Jacob had taken Nathan into the tangled lanes where the miners and their families were putting up barricades.

"So many children will not live to their fifth year, and you'll see why. It's highly unsanitary. I'm no doctor like your future brothers-in-laws, but it doesn't take medical training to see that in this climate and altitude, a malnourished child breathing coal and mining dust from morning to night can hardly survive," Jacob said. "Are you getting cold, Nathan? Let's stop for a cup of tea at my home and you'll meet Lily, the joy of my life as June will be of yours. The secret's out, my friend. I congratulate you."

"Did Morris tell you?" Nathan asked. "I suppose everyone knows."

Jacob nodded. "You made a fine couple at the Ice Palace."

"I proposed that night, which made June's father none too happy but I felt I'd been dancing in heaven with her in my arms."

"Max Sr. will come around. He's lost his wife so he's trying to keep June close," Jacob answered.

"I understand that. This fine house is your home?" Nathan was looking up at carved eaves on a small home with a porch. "I could almost be in my *heimat*."

"It's my dear Lily who has undertaken so much, even down to hammering nails and painting this porch, though now I've told her to rest. In a moment you'll understand."

When they were seated around the Heimberger's dining room table, Lily brought steaming cups of fragrant dark tea and spooned sugar into their cups.

"Lemon?" she asked Nathan. "I believe Europeans still favor lemon over milk, except the British of course."

He smiled and thanked Lily who was clearly pregnant, her apron hiked above taut belly, her round face and blue eyes warm and welcoming. Such a pretty woman's face made him miss June all the more.

"Nathan, since you can look at our troubled town with a fresh eye, I'm interested in your observations of our western man," Jacob said.

Nathan blew on his tea. "I'm no expert but in my hours of solitude I reflect on my travels and what I have observed." His eyes went to a shelf above the buffet where Jacob had at least a dozen cameras of different sizes and shapes. "If I had your abilities to record moments, I could remember more."

"Yes, the camera is for a newsman almost as valuable as the pen," Jacob said, his own black pen poised above a notebook.

"I don't believe you should quote me. I wouldn't want my ignorance in print."

"Let me decide. I keep notes on every topic imaginary. I'm not Charles Dickens but I have that great writer's compulsion to note it all down. Do go on, dear Nathan."

Nathan sipped his tea and turned his face toward Jacob, then Lily. "It appears to me that in youth, the American man in the west is rapacious and out for himself. Perhaps there is a change as a man ages. Of course, that's a generalization. June's father, Max Selig, has most likely been a generous person from early on, whereas my uncles are still directed at making money at the expense of others, so no two are alike, but I believe the world over, youth takes chances and here in the west, many risks."

"True. Some men are never satisfied, no matter how wealthy they become. Your uncles seem indifferent to their reputations, if I'm not offending you by saying this."

Nathan shook his head. "I confess, they underpay me based on their promise of a share in the business. I don't know how long I'll stay with them. I am only looking as far ahead as the summer when June will return to Leadville."

———

As June was reading Nathan's letter describing his first time as a reporter covering the miners' conflict in Leadville, the quadrangle of the college darkened for the night. She visualized Jacob Heimberger walking beside Nathan as a cold evening fell over Leadville. She knew the Heimberger couple only slightly from *shul* and remembered once when she'd been perhaps sixteen, Jacob had asked her about her favorite authors. She'd been reading *Great Expectations* and answered Charles Dickens. His face lighted up and he told her that when he worked for the Philadelphia *Inquirer* and the paper published letters of Charles Dickens, their circulation had swelled. Dickens was his favorite author, too.

June circled back to a sentence at the beginning of Nathan's letter. "Jacob's Lily looks strong and healthy in her pregnancy, though, as

Jacob confided earlier, there were always risks giving birth in this altitude. Your brothers will make sure Lily and her baby are safe." June felt both warmed that Nathan was making intimate friends but also left out of this circle. If Nathan made his own life in Leadville, perhaps he wouldn't need her. At such a distance, with so little time together, she often felt overcome by doubts, as if the night at the Ice Palace and his declaration were a dream.

---

June repaid her father for the train fare to return to Leadville over the summer vacation by working in the store during the day and tutoring high school students late afternoons three times a week. The nights she kept free to be with Nathan. She and May left home together, then separated at the Tabor Opera House when Jerry Murphy appeared, his face so cleanly shaven that his rosy cheeks looked like polished apples. He tipped his hat to June, exchanged greetings and a sentence about the weather, and then he was off with May on his arm. June liked Jerry and wouldn't betray May, but when her sister arrived home at night with liquor on her breath and her hair clearly hastily pinned up, June closed her eyes tightly to prevent images of embraces, perhaps in a room somewhere, from coming too vividly to mind. If Nathan had not spurned her sister, if over time he'd developed a warm friendship for a young woman as compatible as May was, would this dearest person be endangering her reputation to spend most of the night out with Jerry? How could she judge May's yearnings, when she herself clung to Nathan from the moment he walked toward her? If no one was in sight, she kissed him fervently, taking away his breath.

Now as she walked beside him toward the Heimberger's, they came to streets where miners' barricades blocked their passage. The men were armed and suspicious of strangers until Nathan expressed their sympathy with the strike. "We're on our way to Jacob Heimberger. He is telling your side." The men let them pass with warnings to be careful. Nathan knew that Jacob thought conflict was inevitable, that any incident could spark open warfare.

The evening before June was to return to Baltimore, she and Nathan reached her door but June did not turn the key to go in. She pulled him close. "I want to stay here with you at your side, to help in any way possible in the struggle. Why should we wait to marry? Every moment away, I feel I'm losing forever. I miss you so."

Nathan tilted June's chin toward him and held it gently.

"My darling, I feel I share every feeling with you, wishing only for your return to Leadville, but if we disobey your father and he doesn't give his blessing, we'll regret it. The day I leave my uncles, I'll have no remorse, but I'd regret disappointing Max Selig."

For that instant, June envied Jerry and May's abandon, more in accord with her heart's desire than being obedient to her father.

Only a week after June returned to her studies in September, Nathan's first letter enclosed the front page from the *Herald Democrat*.

"We were awakened by a blast. More explosions followed. By the time I arrived with Jacob, there was fighting on Seventh and Eighth streets," he wrote.

June read the press cuttings from the *Democrat* and gazed at the stark pictures Jacob had taken of barbed wire barriers, mounted guns, wounded men lying amid debris.

Soon, the events happening in her mountain town began to be reported across the country. The governor of Colorado ordered the state militia to leave their barracks and march to Leadville to put down the strike. When the troopers arrived, a Denver paper reported that they met a warm welcome from better-off citizens guarding property as volleys of gunfire came from the miners. The only official who supported the miners seemed to be the sheriff of Lake County, and he was thrown into jail.

All that week, June couldn't pay attention to her teachers whose courses on classroom decorum seemed to be only about manners young ladies must follow. At Leadville High, June's teachers hadn't been able to afford to worry about seeming 'feminine'; they had ruffians to keep in their desks and dealt blows to the tops of students' hands, and sometimes, to their backsides. They could be inventive as well. June remembered Mrs. Langford making rowdy tenth-grade boys calculate the latitudes and longitudes to locate a treasure chest where she'd hidden some gold-wrapped chocolates. Now some of these same young people, her classmates, were in the midst of a battle where Nathan himself might be in danger. Twice she wrote to him, "My darling, take care and do not put yourself at risk."

———————

Through the winter and into spring of 1897, the citizens of Leadville lived under martial law. In March, Eugene Debs came to town. He told the striking miners that the owners had all the money and power. He didn't tell them what they should do, but Nathan reported that Debs' somber words ended the strike.

*The militia is leaving. The miners gained nothing, nothing. How much it must have cost Mr. Debs to deliver this message. In the audience, we felt his pain. What many fail to understand is that Leadville is losing more than the miners' rights. People are leaving for opportunity elsewhere, not only because the price of silver is falling but the good will of the Ice Palace days has been erased. My heart is sore for this strange town with its rough edges and such great efforts to make a better life.*

It was finally May who wrote the most touching letter in which she listed the Jewish families who were leaving Leadville, friends, neighbors, the Temple Sisterhood.

*We'll be a ghost town, with scarcely a minyan. Jerry and his friends make food parcels for the miners. He's in touch with men in the unions in California and may move there to avoid arrest here. Papa now thinks the world of Nathan who has taken the miners' side against his uncles. He admires Jerry without knowing anything about our relations.*

# EIGHT

JUNE FELT IT WASN'T fair that her brothers were getting married so soon after traveling to meet the Guthman girls in Cincinnati, while she and Nathan were forced into waiting on her father's whim. Still, the December wedding meant she would soon be home to see Nathan.

Two weeks before she was to leave Baltimore for home, she was questioning how she might use her education beyond teaching affluent girls to become proper young ladies before they found husbands. In a letter to Nathan, she praised the dedication of women who worked with the poor. "My heroine is Lillian Wald. She had every privilege and chose to live in the Henry Street Settlement House to help the poorest Jews," June wrote.

When a letter arrived from Nathan, June always sat a moment at her desk before opening the envelope. She gazed at his photograph taken at the end of the summer. He had worn a new shirt with a soft white collar that came up under his wonderful firm chin. The indentation in his chin seemed more decisive every year. His face spoke of character and firmness, but no picture existed that could show his lean physique, the warmth of his skin. She had only to close her eyes to remember the feelings that gave her such painful pleasure. She brought the photograph close and kissed his lips.

"My beloved June." Nathan's neat hand usually filled pages but this letter was hardly one paragraph. He hoped she was well and then wrote that he wished never to compromise her dedication to a larger purpose.

*I shall not stand between you and your ideals by confining you to a married life and its restrictions on your freedom. You're still very young.*

*If you reconsider our promise, you will hear no reproaches.*

June stared at the letter and cried. "How foolish I've been! But how can he believe I'm not constant and true! Has he no faith in our love?"

Miriam, her roommate since their freshman year, asked what was wrong.

"Forgive me. I'm sorry to disturb your reading, Miriam."

"I hope there's no bad news from home. You're so far away from family."

"I'm wondering if Nathan is entirely committed to me." June burst into tears.

"Of course he is." Miriam held June's shoulders until her sobbing quieted down, and then gave her a tissue. "What has passed between you?"

"Nathan seems to have taken my wish to be a dedicated teacher as a way of telling him that I don't want to marry, which is the opposite of what I meant."

"He's a complete gentleman, June. You need to assure him you don't mean having to choose between him and your sense of honorable work."

"I want to marry more than anything. Nothing else matters to the way I feel about him. Our lives will be happy only if we're together, I'm sure of it. Perhaps he thinks that I have doubts about his health. Or that he wishes to return to London rather than wait on my father's permission. The altitude and our climate is not good for him."

"You'll write to him how much you love him, and that will make him happy."

"The mail is so slow, I'll not sleep at all until I know he's received my letter."

"Then get it in the mail today. There's still time if you hurry, June."

"Thank you, Miriam." June squeezed her friend's hand and sat at her desk.

*My darling Nathan, My wish to be your wife is unchanged. I've promised myself to become your wife because that is what I want above all else in the world. If you have changed your mind and chosen otherwise, you are free. But I see myself fulfilling every ambition and duty only if I am at your side. Otherwise I shall be a shadow of myself.*

---

"Long distance! Miss Selig, long distance on the telephone." A girl called up.

"I hope it's her sweetheart!" Miriam hushed the girls. "June's been waiting and it's almost made her sick with worry. She has barely eaten a thing."

The sound of Nathan's slightly hoarse voice raised her fear that he was ill.

"All I want is to marry you and make you happy. I have no second thoughts."

"Nor do I, not a single one. I miss you so, my dearest. Are you feeling well?"

"I'm quite well now. I love you heart and soul."

June heard giggles behind her and tried to speak more softly. "I hope you haven't caught a bad chill."

"Do not worry, I'll be in perfect health the moment I see you."

"It's so painful to be apart. I'm counting the minutes until I'm with you."

---

Nathan met June at the Denver station early in the morning, and this time they had an empty compartment to reunite and sit with their arms around the other.

May was alone waiting for them on the platform in Leadville. "The Guthman girls are in a suite at the Hotel Vendome and are expecting us to visit."

"But I'm tired and so is Nathan. Can't we go tomorrow?"

"Our brothers' brides are not to be contradicted. You'll see. Come on."

Nathan picked up June's case. "Your brothers are happy, which is what matters. I'll leave you to meet them."

"Goodbye, Nathan." June restrained herself from kissing him—the little prick of guilt before May was still there. "Until tomorrow," she whispered. "Tomorrow."

---

The future sisters-in-law were finishing coffee and had eaten most of the cakes on a plate when June and May knocked on their suite in the Vendome. After greetings, the elder and more talkative sister, Susie Guthman, commented on the bitter coffee.

"It tastes wonderful to me. I haven't had any since the morning," June said.

May reached for the last cake and handed it to June. "My sister has been traveling for three days to be here in time for the wedding. The train just arrived from Denver. It's a long and tiring ride."

"You don't have to tell to us!" said Susie who sat on a couch with her small feet up as she described the wonderful family home in Mannheim, all the comforts they were used to in Germany, and the indignities of traveling west. "Leadville is as poor and shabby as they said to us in Cincinnati, but they did not warn us enough."

"This hotel is proper, isn't it?" May asked.

"Ve've seen better. It's the street out there, and surroundings," Susie grimaced.

Fanny Guthman nodded agreement with her sister while casting a shy smile at June and May. June decided that Morrie had made the better choice and hoped that Fanny was stronger than she looked; at least Fanny would have a doctor for a husband. June hoped that opinionated Susie had a generous heart and would make her Max Jr. happy.

May and June had no warning for Susie's next outburst. "We vill never see Mama and Papa no more. Now ve take husbands in America," said Susie.

May and June looked at each other. Perhaps Susie didn't mean to blame their sadness on Leadville or the brothers, but it seemed America and all in it offended her.

"We understand you're both musical. Our brothers sing in the Temple chorus. *Sie singen gut,*" June attempted in German.

Susie answered in English, shaking her head, "Ve must lose much culture here."

Susie continued to spit out her guttural English in a way that June found unpleasant, especially when she complained about the plainness of Temple Israel where they'd be married. "Small and narrow, without height, like a cottage," she said.

At the moment when June was about to lose her patience with Susie, Nathan called from the hotel lobby inviting them all for an early supper. "He knew I was hungry, and he's rescuing us," June whispered to May.

At the first sight of Nathan's handsome face and well-made clothes, the Guthman sisters became fluttery, and there were no more complaints about Leadville. Nathan had the further inspiration to order wine with dinner, an expensive Riesling that turned the sisters into cooing doves. They parted so amicably that June had no choice but to accept Susie's invitation to view the bridal boxes that had arrived from Germany.

———

The next day, when the brides unwrapped their lace gowns, June gazed upon the tissue-thin organdy, the infinite number of small pearls and roses embroidered over bodices and veils in their boxes. She felt no envy over the elaborate dresses and the satin slippers. She'd have been happy to be married in her plainest outfit if it could bring the date closer, and she felt angry all over again at her father's demands that she and Nathan wait. You are being selfish, she told herself. It's your brothers' time. Be happy for them.

———

Leonard and Ruth, June's eldest brother and sister, arrived the day before the wedding. Leonard was an engineer in Denver and came to visit his father once a month but Ruth so disliked Leadville that she never came. Ruth, thick and flushed with her own importance as President of the Sisterhood and the Hebrew Home Society, let it be known that in Denver, Ruth Selig Fleishman was a personage. Her three little girls appeared with their mother the night before the wedding dressed in ruffles, bows and puffy sleeves that cut into their plump white wrists.

"I don't understand why Maxie and Morrie aren't marrying at our

Temple Emmanuel in Denver, which is superior in all regards. Temple Israel is more like a log cabin than a true *shul*," said Ruth to the Guthmans during their supper on the eve of the wedding. Immediate agreement was reached and the women spent the rest of the evening finding everything wrong with Leadville while May and June sat apart.

"I'm tempted to tell them about the Selig adventures," whispered May. "Madam Lil is probably laughing with our brothers as we sit here. Shall I tell the brides anything? Just a hint?"

"You're wicked, May. They might pack up and leave."

"Well?" May raised her eyebrows.

"That is exactly vhat I say! The *shul* is no more than cottage!" Susie's loud voice interrupted all other conversation, but when she'd stopped, June spoke.

"I've been to Temple Emmanu El in New York City. It is as grand as anything in the world but I wouldn't trade our little *shul* for Denver and New York put together. We've always worshipped here and here's where I'll marry," June said.

"Dear June, you are restricted in your experience." Ruth sipped her coffee.

"I only say it's a pity that our dear Susie and Fanny won't be dancing at the Windsor Hotel in Denver. Harold Tabor built The Windsor when he was still in his chips and spared no expenses," said Ruth.

"Harold Tabor built our opera house and this hotel where you're staying," May said to Fanny with a wink in June's direction. "Our famous Senator took his pleasures here with his paramour, under this roof, perhaps in your very suite."

"You might watch your words!" exclaimed Ruth.

"Oh, tell us more." Fanny leaned forward.

"It's common knowledge and tragically romantic. A beautiful dance hall girl named Baby Doe stole Senator Tabor from his admired wife and caused his downfall."

Susie and Fanny listened attentively as May told of Harold Tabor, Leadville's first silver millionaire, a United States Senator, who left his wife to marry Baby Doe, lost his reputation in Washington as well as his mining wealth.

"In the end, they were penniless. She died starving, lost in the snow," May said.

"More a story of a man's foolishness than a tragedy," Ruth said. "One day, I'll tell you what we had to endure in this town and you'll understand why I praise Denver. We survived our youth, which is better than the fate that befell our poor uncle's children, and our own dear Mother whose head was hacked into two by bandits."

Leonard's wife, a timid woman named Lillian who lived in her sister-in-law's shadow, stood up to follow Ruth to the door. As she pushed in her chair, she said, "In Denver, we have true theater that is the envy of the country. There is a drop curtain with ancient Greek ruins pictured on it, quite unmatched outside of Greece. Here, you're lucky if you get dog shows and trapeze acts passing for culture."

"Thank heavens Lillian agrees with me, even if my own sisters do not." Ruth wrapped a protective arm around Lillian who bowed her head.

"Ruth is my guide in everything. You cannot make a wrong turn if you are following Ruth."

"We have Shakespeare performances at the Tabor Opera House here," May said.

"I'm sure it was exciting, if you like real shooting." Ruth turned to Susie. "Someone usually fires off a gun during a performance. More importantly, Sisters, one cannot keep a kosher home here. Morris and Max have been living together too long to keep kosher, but we will do our best to supply you from Denver, for however long you are obliged to live in these conditions. I get headaches merely remembering."

At the mention of food, Lillian swore that Ruth's *kugel* could not be matched.

"We shall see." Susie drew in her breath. "I am known for the *kugel*, to the last sultana. But it is my brisket that I vill make for you first ven ve are bei home."

Ruth, despite her headache, had the last word. "The duties of marriage I shall endeavor to describe when our two younger unmarried sisters are not present."

Duties? June wondered. Duty in no way described her feelings for Nathan nor what their marriage would be. There was nothing dutiful about their love. They would give themselves freely, eagerly.

———————

As the organist's first bars of Mendelssohn filled Temple Israel, the congregation and guests turned to admire Susannah and Fanny Guthman as they came down the aisle in frothy wedding gowns so wide they scraped the wooden pews as they passed.

"Our temple gives them too brief an entrance," Nathan whispered. "They'd have liked to turn around and come back again for a second walk down the aisle."

"It will be plenty long for me." June clasped his hand, knowing he could feel the small diamond ring he'd given her the evening before.

The two Selig brothers joined their brides before the Ark. They looked as tall and handsome in their white shirts and black suits, June thought, as any Biblical illustration of Jacob or Joseph. At the sound of the Cantor's rich tenor chanting *Baruch Atah Adonoi Eloheynu,* June's eyes filled with tears. When the Cantor told her brothers to remove the veils from the faces of their brides and kiss them, everyone called out *Mazel Tov! Mazel Tov!*

As June wished her brothers happiness, she was certain that no other couple was as perfectly matched, nor had such feelings and understanding, nor, she felt, looking over at Nathan's fine profile and squeezing his hand, such a physical appreciation of each other as they had. It was only a matter of time before she held his body close every night.

The Hotel Vendome closed its doors to all but the wedding guests, over a hundred for the dinner and reception, Jews and Gentiles together making toasts and remarking on the excellence of the five-course supper Susie had commandeered the kitchen to prepare.

The Grensky wives, Hildegard and Flora, rushed to welcome the Guthman sisters as if they'd brought an essence of southern Germany with them. Compliments on dresses, coiffures, the flowers and particularly the wedding supper flowed from their pursed lips, though they hardly acknowledged June, May or Max Sr. They made dates to play cards, and extended invitations to musical evenings. "Dear girls," June heard Flora Grensky say to Susie, "if only we'd known you before this blessed time, you'd have had your party in our home, so much nicer than a hotel. We will try to make life bearable here."

"I told them they should have transferred the ceremonies to Denver, to our Temple Emmanuel. It would have been ever so much nicer," said Ruth. "The ballroom at The Windsor has crystal chandeliers from France and parquet floor for dancing."

"There's nothing wrong with these floors, not for Leadville," said Flora Grensky, tapping her feet and surprising June with her defense of the town she usually scorned.

June, Nathan and May separated themselves from the discussion. Max Sr. had enjoyed many drinks, but asked for one more glass of champagne before the music began. "It's real Paris champagne. You girls remember you tasted it with your dear mother, blessed be her name."

"We do," answered May and June, and kissed their father's cheeks.

"If only Sara were here now, she would have gathered everyone in the family for this happy event. We would have Harriett and Isaac here. How can my brother miss the marriage of his nephews?" Tears welled in Max's eyes.

"Papa, don't cry." May wiped a tear from her father's cheek.

"I know he's truly sad that Uncle and Aunt could not forget their own sorrows to celebrate their nephews' happiness," May whispered to June. "Does Fanny make you think of anyone?"

"Aunt Harriett, and I hope life will be easier for her. Papa still doesn't suspect anything about you and Jerry?"

"No, I don't think so. It's not easy to lie, don't think it is," May looked down.

"I'm sure it isn't, and it seems that your life is making you tired. Are you eating enough nourishing food, Sister?"

"Tonight, I gobbled up everything. We don't want to hear from Susie."

They laughed, and soon newly-married Fanny sat at the piano. She played a Chopin Nocturne delicately, so that once again both June and May thought of their Aunt Harriett, not the music but the delicacy of her watercolors that still hung on their wall.

"She plays well but Papa is snoozing," May whispered. "It would take Sousa and his marching band to wake him. I'll bring him home. You stay and dance with Nathan."

"Thank you, dearest," June said. "I only hope that happiness comes to you, too."

May's lower lip trembled. "I wrote that Jerry moved to San Francisco, didn't I?"

"You didn't. You only wrote about our co-religionists who left. Did he have to move such a distance from you?"

May nodded. "After the end of the strike, the mine owners have kept Pinkerton men here. Jerry had become a wanted man and it wasn't safe for him to stay. No, don't frown, June, he did nothing but stand up for others' rights. There was such rancor here, such hatred on both sides. San Francisco is a staunch labor town. I'd join him there if you were home to look after Papa."

"Oh, May, you wouldn't!"

"Oh yes I would. We meet in a hotel in Denver, both of us incognito," she smiled.

"What do you mean?"

"We get ourselves up so even you wouldn't recognize us. I've been collecting odds and ends from the theater where Jerry was much admired." Before June could express her shock, May held her elbow. "You see, my life is not as dull and ordinary as you might imagine. Now go, June, you waltz for both of us tonight." May kissed her lightly and reached up and patted Nathan on the cheek.

# NINE

## 1898-89

From November until April, blizzards kept Rocky Mountain towns isolated by fierce storms and record snowfall. During a lull between storms, telephone service to Leadville resumed long enough for Nathan to call June.

"I should be sharing the difficulties with you," June cried. "I will come."

"June, stay where you are. It's like the siege when the militia put down the strike. A dozen feet of snow has fallen this week, no one on the street, few customers though your father and sister are raiding their shelves to help others. We're fine. Summer and your graduation will come soon enough."

"Soon enough? No, it's forever," she cried, feeling she'd die of longing for him.

---

When Nathan's next letter, written in January and delivered to June the middle of March, she read with amazement his account of circumstances that had kept young Coloradans, ready to go fight the Spanish in Cuba, from leaving the Rockies.

*You most likely know many of these young fellows from school who had signed for the war. There was a parade and flags and marches but our weather continued to keep anyone from traveling, and in the end, our mountain contingent missed the boats for Cuba. In my view, they can only count themselves lucky not to have died of wounds or the Yellow*

*Fever. At present they are consoled by free drinks which our patriots are offering in the local establishments. Apparently all feel like heroes and will continue to speak of their intended valor.*

———————

On a chilly April morning, Nathan walked to Jacob Heimberger's offices at the *Herald Democrat* where the editor was writing a story about the winter's damage.

"When you're done, will you come with me? I'll explain on our way."

"Why so mysterious?" Jacob put down his pencil.

"Anything I do gets back to my uncles. They reproach me for choosing June, the daughter of a shopkeeper, over a woman of their choice with money. They might even try to prevent me from completing citizenship."

"So that's your secret?" Jacob laid his glasses on his desk and took his coat. "Why would they object to your becoming a citizen?"

"They fear my independence. Uncle Adolph refuses to raise my salary with the reason that I've chosen to remain penniless by marrying June Selig."

"Your June is a treasure." Jacob took Nathan's arm. "She's the finest kind of new American women, educated, a mind of her own. She's also grown more beautiful as I've known her, Nathan. You can be proud and happy. Tell those uncles to go to hell."

"If only I could. I simply can't break away because they withhold what I deserve. The more time I put myself under them, the more they must recognize my due."

"I doubt they have that kind of honesty, but let us hope so," Jacob said.

The two men reached the Lake County Courthouse where the same clerk who'd taken Nathan's application still presided over the deserted office.

Nathan swore allegiance to his new country and renounced all foreign sovereigns. The exact words he was required to say, "Revoking allegiance to Emperor William the Second," made Jacob turn his back and cover his mouth to suppress a laugh.

After the oath, Nathan signed papers, and they walked back outside into the grey day. More snow was on the way.

They entered the Vendome for champagne to celebrate. Jacob lifted his glass.

"I'd have liked saying the reason I'm becoming a citizen is to vote against William McKinley in the 1900 election," Nathan said

"That would have caused trouble. Most men don't have the brains to be citizens. They vote what they believe is self-interest even when it clearly is not. I'm not optimistic we'll ever be a country that votes for the people's good. I doubt Bryan has a chance."

"Do you think not? His idea of generalized reciprocity makes good sense."

"Yes, if people voted with their reason. As a scribbler, I'm bound to be realistic. Here's to ideals, my dear friend. When you renounced William Two, I decided to swear an allegiance myself." Jacob brought his glass to eye level. "I swear that our *Herald Democrat* will uphold the American Constitution on good and bad days in Leadville. I'll face my subscribers' objections and continue to question McKinley's promises for his 'full dinner pail' as an outright campaign lie. Here's to what's assured. Your future happiness with June."

"And to your wife and the children. May we enjoy health and happiness."

---

On a warm July day, the Baltimore Women's Teachers Preparatory College held their graduation ceremony. After introductory remarks, June Selig, the class valedictorian, lifted the skirts of her black gown and walked to the podium. She looked down upon her classmates' black mortar boards decorated with bright ribbons.

June usually felt confident as a speaker, but now her throat was so dry and her pages looked so far away on the podium that she didn't know how she'd deliver her speech entitled, "What Lies Ahead for a Woman in the New Century?" She hesitated a moment, made herself draw a deep breath and began.

"With so many of you, I share the honor of becoming the first female in my family to have been given a college education. I am grateful for this opportunity." June thanked her father, her teachers, and her classmates, "who shared their homes with me when my family was so far away."

She smiled at Miriam who winked back, helping June overcome nervousness.

"You might not know that our mountain state of Colorado was among the first and is still one of very few in our nation where women vote in a popular election. In 1893, the men of Colorado passed a State Amendment that meant my mother, my older sisters and all other females in Colorado could vote. We recently elected the first female senators to our state legislature. I wish to see universal suffrage for our sisters and daughters in every state."

A small number applauded while many fanned themselves with their programs. June knew from experience that most of her class-mates and teachers held the cautious political opinions of their upper middle class families. She saw that Miss McClellan had lowered her eyes. June loved this older English teacher all the more because Miss McClellan disagreed with her politics but encouraged her indepen-dence. In heated discussions about books, Miss McClellan had always listened to June's arguments.

When June stepped down, the Head Mistress offered a farewell prayer, asking all to lower their heads and give thanks to God. Before she was done praying, the girls jumped up and threw their colorful streamers into the air. June joined everyone for punch and congratula-tions but she could barely wait to take her bags and start for the station.

---

The next morning, June stepped from the train carriage onto the platform of Union Station in Chicago where Nathan waited with a bouquet of pink peonies. She flung herself into his arms, almost crushing the flowers.

"We'll frame your diploma and my citizenship papers side by side as evidence that we waited as long as any knight and maiden kept in a castle," he said.

"Oh, Nathan, I'm so proud of you! A citizen! Was the exam difficult?"

"Not at all. The most amusing part was renouncing my allegiance to the German emperor. Jacob nearly burst out laughing."

In the muggy warm air, Nathan took off his coat and June shed her long-sleeved jacket. They held each other closely, skin against skin. June forgot her modesty. She clung to him. No one knew them here. What if Nathan, like Jerry Murphy, simply swept her off her feet and took her to a hotel? She wouldn't mind lying that they were married but she knew deep down Nathan would never do that. She wondered sometimes if her feelings, the almost unbearable rush of blood to all parts of her body when she dreamed of sharing a bed with Nathan, meant that she was over-sexed. She couldn't ask May, which would imply judgment of her sister's behavior.

———————

June's cousin, Hermann Selig, placed the betrothed couple on separate floors of the three-storied home in the Hyde Park section of Chicago that he shared with his widowed mother, Cecile. June hadn't seen her first cousin since he'd traveled to Leadville nine years earlier for her mother's funeral. Since then, Hermann had earned a law degree from the University of Chicago, become junior partner in a prestigious firm and grown a round belly across which he wore a large gold watch on a gold chain. Still, his twinkling dark eyes put June instantly at ease. He gently teased her, reminding how her brothers had taken him to a parlor house to hear the Negro piano player and see the ladies.

"You as well! Papa and Morris took Nathan there once. He wasn't pleased."

"Well, I enjoyed myself. A pretty girl gave me cherry cordial. At fifteen, very protected by Mother, I felt wonderful. I swear this beautiful young woman flirted with me. I hold fond memories of Leadville."

"You'll come west to our wedding, won't you?"

"Of course I shall. Your Nathan seems a fine fellow. Almost as handsome as you are attractive. Don't blush. I'm a bachelor who speaks from experience."

Hermann opened the curtains that revealed the lake, stirred up under a sudden summer rain. "My mother urges me to marry while saying there's not a girl in Chicago fine enough for me. Mother was a Loeb, which explains a lot. They're a particular family, difficult to please. Papa wasn't quite good enough for her, even though he became the mayor of Morrisonville for a few years. That's a good story I'll save for supper. How is your father? Such a merry fellow. Has he remarried after his loss?"

"No, Papa hasn't remarried, though he's still vain about his full head of hair. We have to insist he go to the barber or it would hang to his shoulders like Buffalo Bill."

"Buffalo Bill! I remember how I hoped to see him burst through saloon doors and start firing a pistol. Scared Mother to death. She's the one who insisted you and Nathan sleep on separate floors. I'm afraid she thinks it a bit scandalous to host an unmarried couple in the house. As well as a graduate, you've grown into a true beauty, Cousin."

When Hermann left, June stood at the window. The rain made everything from sky to earth seem emotionally stirring. She and Nathan had never spent a night under the same roof and the intimacy of sleeping in this close proximity would have to content her while at the same time keeping her awake wishing for more.

---

After supper, Hermann saw his nearly deaf mother Cecile to bed, dimmed lights, lit candles and brought out brandy snifters.

"You'll join me?" June and Nathan nodded. "You know that Father wasn't the least inclined to go far west like his brothers—breaking ground, establishing new territory, living in duress as he called it. Not for him. Father liked his creature comforts."

"Uncle Joseph was much praised for his success, as I remember, and he always supplied father in dried meat and other goods hard to come by. We wouldn't have survived without family support," June sighed. "I'm afraid nothing will help now."

"Leadville has grown poorer since you visited," said Nathan.

"We won't be there forever." June said. "The altitude isn't good for Nathan. My brother Morris is planning to move to Los Angeles and open his medical practice there. He tells us there are palm trees and sunshine all year long. His new wife has fragile health. My older brother Max—you remember Max—has been honored recently by the State Medical Society for his work with childhood infections and offered a position in Salt Lake City General Hospital. Both of them want to leave to expand their careers but they hesitate because of our father."

"I'm sure there's great opportunities in Los Angeles and Salt Lake but I'm a Chicagoan, bully on my own city, second to none, New York included. My firm represents Armour and Swift." Hermann drank his brandy and lit a cigar, but hearing Nathan's cough, he snuffed it out.

"When my brothers leave Leadville, we will lose its best and most civic-minded doctors. I don't know who will be there for Father, or Nathan."

"I'm quite well, my dear," said Nathan. "I'm obligated to stay in my uncle's business for the present. I'm also close by to help June's father with his accounts though business falls off every month."

"I don't know particulars of your miners' strike but fortunately McKinley will again defeat that demagogue Bryan and bring us around to good times." Hermann mouthed his unlit cigar.

June and Nathan shared a glance. "I'm a new citizen who won't be voting for McKinley," said Nathan.

Hermann laughed and shook his head.

"We may not agree on politics, dear cousins, but I'm very glad that you're here. I miss my father and I envy you, June, having Uncle Max hale and hearty. Did you know my father was the first mayor of our faith west of the Mississippi? Not as far west as you ventured, but a certain amount of adventure all the same."

"You sent the newspaper clippings about Uncle Joseph," June said.

"But I don't think you know how he won his election."

"No, I don't think I do," said June.

"Like your dear Papa, my father was no teetotaler. It was a year that Prohibition was being voted into city charters around the Midwest. Papa campaigned on the wet platform. I believe this must have been before your father arrived, June, when my father was only in his early twenties and had not yet settled in Chicago. After he won the election, there was a torchlight parade. The saloon keepers marched through the streets carrying him on their shoulders to celebrate his victory."

"He sounds a lot like Papa. I'll tell him this story as soon as I'm home. I'm sorry about the passing of Uncle Joseph."

"He died too young but exactly as he wished, following a large Chicago steak and a brandy. Let's drink to stalwart generations of Seligs, and to you two young lovebirds."

---

The next days, Hermann quizzed Nathan about metals and metallurgy in the west. Every time Nathan talked about silver, lead or molybdenum, Hermann said copper.

"Not silver. Not lead. I can't pronounce that third one and won't try. Copper. Piping and plumbing, water supplies, refrigeration, wires of all sorts for conducting heat and electricity. Armaments. Cousin, investment in copper shares will assure your future."

For a moment, the wild twinkle in her cousin's eyes gave June pause. She saw her father's recklessness, his gambling in the commodities market, the grubstaking he'd committed to men whose promises of silver veins seldom came through.

"I'd like to have family here, Nathan. I can find you a good position in the bank that my firm represents."

"Nathan speaks four languages," said June. "He worked for the Warburgs in Germany and Rothschild in London. He's experienced."

"It's been years since that time, my dearest, and I never rose above teller."

"But you could have if you'd wanted to."

"Perhaps. Thank you for your confidence in me, Cousin, but it's been very long since I've had contacts at a metropolitan bank or used my languages."

"It will all come back the minute you get your hands on contracts. We're the leading law firm for trusts. The international department is growing. A man with languages will go far here but only if you keep some of your radical ideas to yourself. Jews have to be doubly prudent and give no hint of impropriety."

"I suspect the trusts employ their size to control salaries and prices," said Nathan.

"Exactly right, that's the beauty of trusts. Efficiency, dear Nathan. In America, we simply have to be the biggest and the best to conquer the world."

"What about the workers?" June asked.

"Cousin, the workers will all be in much better hands when business is run efficiently. I know you feel affection for Bryan but as I see it—as most sound business people see it—he'd take us back to the Stone Age, long before silver. I hope you'll join our Chicago office in finance one day."

# TEN

## 1900

SOON AFTER THEY RETURNED from Chicago, Nathan began investing small amounts from his salary in shares of United Copper. "Backed by Standard Oil," he quoted Hermann to Morris and Max who also put money into the metal. Hermann advised placing their savings accounts in Butte Montana Bank that offered the best interest rates. Soon the Seligs were all customers of the Denver branch of Butte Savings, including June who banked her dollars from substitute teaching. The principal of Leadville High School promised a regular position the following school year when a teacher would retire.

"Papa," June told her father one night in late October, "next September, I'll have my own classroom, so you see, I'll have done all you asked. We waited until I finished my degree and now will you give Nathan and me your blessing to marry?"

Max waved his hands back and forth in front of him. "Don't rush me, daughter. Always in such a hurry. You've only just come home to help out your family and you want to leave us."

"I'll be here in Leadville, I'll visit every day. Nathan and I will be your family."

"The time will come," answered her father. "Now shuffle those cards."

June knew better than to sulk in front of her father but she hit the pillows with her fists once she was alone. Her father was so stubborn. He didn't understand the needs of a twenty-three-year old woman in love, a woman whose heart and body yearned from the moment she opened her eyes until she closed them at night to give itself to this love. More than four years she and Nathan had waited, and now that they were so close to that moment, father was still indulging himself, keeping her living at home even though he had May to take care of him as well.

Her recompense was seeing Nathan every day for at least an hour, and on Sundays, they had the entire day before them. She cooked lunch and sent him home in the evening with packets for the week. When they visited the Heimbergers, they held hands and didn't feel embarrassed if Lily teased them about children. The conversation was always lively and political because Jacob refused to give up on Americans becoming more enlightened, though he didn't think it would happen before another decade passed in the new twentieth century. One evening over glasses of beer, he held up a copy of the penny press that featured pictures of wealthy Americans on their yachts. "As if warming by a rich man's fire could make you warm," Jacob said. "Only accounts of wild west shootouts and climbers rescued from peaks on mountains get such attention. People love to read about a death they've avoided, scandal they feel superior to, and the rich, best if the rich are the scandal."

"I don't see how McKinley wins in places like Leadville and around the country where people are so poor and the man has no interest in their lives," June said.

"It's disheartening." Jacob shrugged. "It's ignorance on top of something in our natures that willfully fails to see where our interests are being lied about. I always have hope or I wouldn't get my fingers ink-stained. But now we need sustenance. Don't leave any of Lily's sweet poppy cakes, and let's play out our cards. Lily dear, would you put on the recording 'Keep on the Sunny Side' to lift our spirits."

---

Another evening out, Nathan and June attended a production of Shakespeare at the Weston Theater. In the middle of Prince Hamlet's "to be or not to be" speech, a young man in the row ahead of them fired a shot in the air. Nathan protectively flung himself across June as the man bounded to the stage where he brandished his gun. "Go on man, do it, get on with it or I will if you can't pull the trigger!"

The actor leaned over and whispered something to the young man who returned to the audience where everyone was laughing.

"I wonder if we should attend wearing armor," Nathan whispered.

---

On a chilly Friday evening in late November, Nathan invited June out for a walk. She expected they'd see the Heimbergers and commiserate on McKinley and Roosevelt's landslide victory for a second term, but Nathan turned down West Seventh onto a quiet block where he stopped, pressed her arm and turned her to face a two-story wooden-shingled home with a broken fence and debris in the yard.

"You see the house needs painting and repairs but can you imagine living here?"

June didn't hesitate before answering, "I'm capable of working with my hands to make it our very best little home."

"We can rent out the ground floor and occupy the second story, that is, until there comes a time when we have our own larger family."

"Oh, Nathan." June gripped Nathan's hand. "I'll make this house entirely *gemutlich* but we won't become too attached because we'll leave Leadville before long. Every winter is harder for you and you know how my brothers warn about the altitude."

"There's a window on the north side where you can see the mountains," he said. "The air will be fresh there, free from soot and dust."

---

After Saturday lunch, June poured her father a glass of whisky and sat beside him.

"Yesterday Nathan took me to see a house on Seventh Street."

Max raised a bushy eyebrow and took another sip of his whiskey.

"What is your answer, Papa?" June looked into his face.

"I give you my blessings. Should I raise my hand like a King Lear who has changed his mind?" June laughed and flung herself onto her father's chest.

"Now, now, my dear, I was going to be the one to initiate this conversation. Nathan wished my opinion on the house so I went with him to see it. Though not in a fine neighborhood, I agreed the walls seemed solid. I've grown to respect Nathan's prudence, and all his helpful ways. He's been loyal to our May who unfortunately has found no beau and must content herself with her father for company."

"But we'll never leave May out of our new family, nor you, dearest Papa." June held his hand and kissed his cheek. "Thank you, Papa. Nathan is all I've ever wanted."

"And your teaching? What would your blessed mother say if you dismissed the years of study we afforded you?"

"I can always teach, wherever we go," she answered.

"And who is speaking of going anywhere? For that I do not give my permission. Let me say m*azel tov* and that will be enough for today. When shall you be married?"

"We'll marry soon, in January."

"Such a rush. Just like you, June, so headstrong. Won't you wait until summer?"

"No, we've waited long enough. We have savings enough for a small wedding."

"No, June, I shall provide a wedding to be remembered for my dearest girl."

# Eleven

SUNDAY AND MONDAY BEFORE the wedding, June and May decorated Temple Israel with palms and ferns. Above the altar they banked white southern smilax, while Nathan helped Max Sr. hang a wedding bell made with a clapper of white roses. Fresh flowers in January were June's extravagance and when she unpacked the pink and yellow roses from their wrappers and opened out the bunches, the fragrances transformed the cold and dark days of Leadville winter and seemed to whisper the secret that she and Nathan shared with no one but the Heimbergers. They'd purchased tickets on the Union Pacific to take the train to Southern California for their honeymoon.

At home, late into the night on Wednesday, the evening before the wedding, the sisters wrote place cards and wrapped chocolates in silver foil for guests to take home from supper at the Hotel Vendome.

———————

The morning of her greatest happiness, June wrote in the white taffeta wedding book that May had given her: "*My sweetheart came to see me in my wedding gown before I stepped into the carriage.*"

The moment June saw Nathan's carriage arrive to pick up her father, she started downstairs to greet him. May tried to stop her. "It's too cold, and you mustn't let him see you."

"Why shouldn't I take every minute of joy from this day?" she replied and ran out into the street. Nathan, in his grey morning coat, his top hat and gloves, seemed surprised for a moment then held her close in the extreme January chill that June hardly felt. She had no superstitious foreboding; she was marrying the handsomest and best man in the world who had traveled thousands of miles to arrive at the exact moment for her to catch sight of him and fall in love. The old superstition about beloveds keeping apart until the marriage ceremony was powerless, intended for the faint-hearted uncertain of their love.

As they held hands and gazed in each other's eyes, passengers in carriages and men on horseback coming and going on Harrison Street lifted their Stetsons and hollered, "A fine lady you got there!"

When Nathan coughed deeply in his chest with that worrisome rattle, she urged him to return to his carriage. "My winter catarrh. You will restore me to perfect health, my love."

---

May came down the aisle on Dr. Max's arm wearing cream lace over a pale pink taffeta skirt. Dr. Morris followed with his sister Ruth, in a long dark skirt and pleated jacket that May whispered to June looked like a turkey with its feathers out. "To go with the wattle under her chin," May giggled. Ruth's plump daughters flanked her, carrying pink and white bouquets. Then came the joy of Leonard's and Harriet's efforts, a pale daughter scattering petals alongside Ruth's youngest girl.

The organist began Mendelssohn's Wedding March. Guests turned their heads to see Max Sr., resplendent in a snowy white stock collar over a long black coat, mustaches waxed to polished pewter. On his arm, the bride in her simple cream gown made a classic figure, her chestnut hair coiled in a sleek chignon held in place with a white rose at the nape of her neck. Her only bridal jewelry was Nathan's wedding gift, a gold tulip pin fastened at her throat. His grey tie was held in place by the pearl stud she'd given him.

The Lake County judge performed the brief civil marriage before Rabbi Sachs began the service conducted in English and Hebrew. Rabbi Sachs from Cincinnati—the same rabbi who as a young man had blown the *shofar* for the first Rosh Hoshana at Temple Israel so many years earlier—had come west at Max and June's invitation. Now grey and bent, Rabbi Sachs still had a voice strong enough to reach the back rows.

At the conclusion of the ceremony, the rabbi gave the groom permission to kiss the bride. June lifted her veil and Nathan swept her into his arms, kissing her so vigorously—"*With such a smack,*" June recorded in her diary—that they heard giggles throughout the congregation. When they walked down the aisle, their eyes, even their breath, seemed to come together. No one could doubt their future happiness.

Carriages transferred the company to the Hotel Vendome for the reception. Before the meal was served, Max Sr. stood to read from *Songs of Solomon.* "Many waters cannot quench love, neither can the floods drown it," he began. Glasses were filled and refilled with champagne. June drank the sparkling wine with pleasure but had little appetite for several courses of rich food her brothers' wives had ordered. She felt almost feverish while Nathan's hands remained cold.

A trio played during supper and more musicians arrived for dancing, including the surprise performer, Jerry Murphy with his fiddle. When May offered Jerry a glass of beer, the small man with his cap at an angle accepted and bowed, as if he were no more than a special guest come all the way from San Francisco to play for the evening.

June danced the first waltz with her father and then turned to her husband. They held each other differently, more modestly than during their courtship when being in each other's arms to dance was the closest they could come to further embraces. Now she savored every formal step, every restrained touch, knowing in only a few more hours she would close the door to their compartment and pull back covers on their honeymoon bed as their speeding train headed for California.

When June and Nathan revealed their destination to be La Jolla, California, everyone but the Grenskys applauded.

"Extravagances upon extravagances," June heard the Grensky wives say. "Two weeks! What a scandal. Where will the money come from? From our business!"

June heard her cousin Hermann reply, "Madams, they can drink champagne and spend the night in the Waldorf Astoria. They are invested in copper."

May emerged from the Vendome's kitchen with a bag of rice she handed to guests. The grains tossed into the air came down mixed with the falling snow. June realized too late that the bouquet she'd intended to throw to May was still in her hands.

Jacob Heimberger didn't usually write the *Herald Democrat's* social column but for Nathan and June he made an exception. "The Selig-Grensky nuptials were pronounced by all as one of the prettiest and swellest in years. The bride was the cynosure of all eyes, the groom as tall and distinguished as any man might wish to be."

---

June and Nathan could hardly believe the sights before their eyes, the fragrances and the sun's glow that engulfed them when they descended from the train at the tiny La Jolla station. Palm and avocado and orange trees lined the road to the Pacific Ocean as their open carriage rolled along the sea. They both knew the Atlantic as a hard and grey ocean with hammering surf. Here the Pacific stretched a wide untroubled blue-green to the horizon. The caresses of light, the colors, the perfumes of gardenias and lemons enveloped them. Whether the richness of oxygen at sea level or the infusion of the ocean's salt and moisture, Nathan's complexion seemed instantly to change. He filled his lungs and said in amazement to June, "I feel as if my life has come back to me."

---

*"We were absolutely happy. A perfect union of heart and soul."* June wrote in her white wedding book. She didn't write that most nights she never parted from Nathan until dawn because modesty prevented putting into words such intimacies even in her private book, and there were no words for the physical delight they gave each other, passion, tenderness, understanding, and yet mystery, mystery and wonder, at the force in his naked body as her slender husband embraced her. What words could describe how it felt being touched and touching where fingers and lips had never gone before? Love overwhelmed June in its intensity, its variety, moments of burning impatience and hours of sleep in silky repose.

When June dipped her toes in the lapping waves at the La Jolla cove, the water felt warmer in mid-winter than mountain lakes in August. Her bathing costume was a cumbersome arrangement of black skirts that reached below her knees where stockings began. At first the skirt inhibited strong kicks, but once she slipped into the gentle swells and began to swim, she became part of the whole ocean, the sweet air, the clouds. She waved to Nathan, who called from the shore. "Don't go too far." She blew him a kiss.

As strong as she could be in the water, stroking arm over arm without tiring, she felt as if she'd melt in his arms when he kissed her wet body on the shore. *We loved enough for a lifetime*, June wrote when they returned from the sea before a midday meal to the La Jolla Shores. *Yet I am greedy and I hope for more.*

As the first week came to an end and the next seemed to stretch forever, they began receiving wires from the uncles Adler and Adolf, with only one word. "Return."

"There's no reason for troubling you this way, is there?" June sighed.

"I know that, my darling. They are worried men."

"They are envious of our happiness. We won't let them spoil it."

---

Two month's after the newlywed's return, Max Jr., in Leadville on a visit, confirmed what June suspected. He assured her she would be the healthiest of mothers and could teach until the summer vacation. He worried more about Nathan's health.

"His voice was stronger in California. He had…he had strength." She blushed.

"He was at sea level where he belongs. Leave Leadville, Sister, before the altitude causes permanent harm. You mustn't wait for a serious stage of heart congestion."

"He won't risk leaving his uncles yet."

"He's risking everything by staying," answered Max.

---

Dr. Max arrived to deliver Thomas Maximillian Grensky in Leadville

General Hospital in November, 1901. "A child of the new century!" Max declared, holding up screaming, red-faced, black-haired Tommy for June and Nathan to see. "A big boy. Congratulations, Sister. You gave your doctor little to do. You're going to make a full and perfect recovery and have many more. Let me hope Susie and I will give this boy a cousin. I envy you."

"Such a dimple in his chin," said May, leaning over the baby. "My godson is going to be a devil with women, I can see that."

"Have you made plans to move from here?" Max asked Nathan. "Don't delay."

# TWELVE

BY THE TIME TOMMY GRENSKY was three, he had memorized lines from *A Christmas Carol* which he loved delivering to his father who rested every evening after work. At meals, Tommy also recited Tiny Tim's words, "A Merry Christmas to us all and God bless us, every-one," whatever day or month it was. He could hardly be stopped from calling his great uncles Grensky *Scrooge*, which June supposed her own father had put in Tommy's mind.

June was always happy when Tommy lightened their worries over Nathan's health; she tended to be overprotective of Nathan and less so of Tommy who seemed as strong as she was.

When their close friend Jacob called to ask for help at the *Herald Democrat* offices one night, June questioned going out on a cold evening when he was so tired.

"Jacob's never asked for my help," Nathan said.

"I'll go," she offered.

"You stay with Tommy. Jacob called because he needs me."

At the *Democrat* offices, he found Jacob pale and drenched in perspiration.

"Would you take dictation?" Jacob asked. "The shellfish dish I ate earlier at the Vendome is making my head swim. I'm sure it will pass." After Nathan wrote down Jacob's words, the editor still couldn't get up to type. "If you can do it, we'll get this damn story about the botched robbery into Friday's paper and I'll go home to bed."

Nathan called Lily to send their carriage for Jacob. When the two men arrived at the door, Lily met them before the horses had even stopped.

"Jacob seems truly ill. Call the young doctor who has taken over the Selig brothers' practice," Nathan said.

Dr. Whelan arrived in fifteen minutes. Together with Nathan and Lily's help, they got Jacob into bed. When the doctor read the high fever on the thermometer, he said to Lily. "Keep him quiet. If his fever doesn't go down, use cold compresses and even bathe him in ice water. I'll be back early tomorrow morning."

Nothing Lily nor Nathan could do kept Jacob's fever from rising nor keep him awake. He fell into a coma. Two days later, Jacob Heimberger died with his family, Nathan and June, at his side. The doctor made a provisional diagnosis of death by cholera or typhoid contracted from eating the shellfish.

———————

Nathan had stayed up two nights with Jacob and then another to write a eulogy, but when it came time to deliver his speech in the cold air at the gravesite, his voice failed. June took the paper from his hands and read as loudly as she could to the large crowd huddled together in the Jewish section of Evergreen Cemetery. People stood ten deep, weeping in stunned disbelief over Jacob Heimberger's death. June led Nathan away quickly but he stopped, turned and stumbled. As June pulled him to his feet, they heard a miner praising Jacob for fairness, for speaking for them when they'd had no voice, and Nathan fell onto his knees.

———————

The effect the altitude had on Nathan's heart began to manifest more than ever after Jacob's death. To June, Nathan seemed to lack the will to fight a cold. He gave in and went to bed for days, too exhausted to dress. He told June it was as if he was plunged into the darkest river of his life. Not even Tommy's hopeful voice could lift him. Financial rises and falls in national markets added to his bleak outlook.

"Even if we have enough to leave," he told June when she urged their departure two months after Jacob's death, "what will Lily do without us?"

"I know it will be hard but we must. She has family elsewhere.

Nathan, we have copper shares we can sell. If you made up your mind to leave your uncles, we could still go to Chicago, you could work for Hermann until you find a job in California. Or I can teach. I don't want to be in Lily's position, blessed be Jacob's memory."

"My uncles owe me a settlement and they won't give a penny if I leave," he said.

"But does it matter as much as our lives? What matters most, Nathan?"

"Just give me a few more months." He closed his eyes.

June watched her husband fall into a troubled sleep, heard his breath rasping in his lungs. She still loved Nathan as entirely as she had from their earliest courtship but the love was different now, less passion and more care because of his weakened constitution. Gone were the nights that thrilled her until she felt her body a part of his, one shimmering and vibrating whole. She didn't dare do more than caress his forehead, kiss his cheeks because the stress on his heart would be too great. But this wouldn't be forever, she was sure. When they left Leadville for California, for that tropical paradise at sea level, their nights would be their greatest pleasure again, making all the hardships of the day seem as nothing.

---

When summer came, Nathan rallied but fell ill again in the winter, and by the spring of Tommy's sixth birthday, June kept wiping tears from her eyes as she lit candles on her son's chocolate cake and realized her beloved husband couldn't have blown out a single small flame. This was the seventh year since their marriage and Nathan's twelfth in Leadville and still she could not get him to leave his uncles' employ. All she could do was wait for the moment when he would realize that the Grenskys were never going to give him what he deserved. From a pot of water on the stove, she kept a steam vapor rising in the air to help Nathan breathe more easily.

---

A cold October morning, with snow already in the air, Nathan stopped by the telegraph office on Harrison Avenue to check the morning ticker that came in from the New York Stock Exchange. He recognized the date on the narrow serrated paper coming out in long curls—October 14, 1907—but had to look again and then again at the numbers spitting from the ticker: United Copper, listed first, had doubled from the twenty-five dollars Hermann had bought the stock for, to fifty dollars a share. The numbers kept rising. As he stood watching, he saw his shares were trading at sixty dollars.

"If only it were silver that the bankers wanted," said a man in a torn topcoat and rumpled hair who greeted Nathan. "When I think of what we've gone through for silver."

"Silver may never go back up, Mr. Duncan. Copper is the new gold." Nathan recognized the foreman of a mine that had closed rather than pay the miners what they'd asked for. Now he was one more ruined businessman, and Nathan pitied the man.

"Take care, Grensky." Another former man of wealth, Harold Best, tipped his hat as Nathan walked to the door. Best stopped him. "Grensky, you got copper information? I heard it's moving up. You have shares? Maybe you'll lend a little."

"I own only a few shares," Nathan replied.

"Lucky dog, at this rate a few has got to set you up for life," said Best.

Nathan tied down the flaps of his fleece-trimmed cap under his chin, and resisting the desire to walk quickly, he took his steps slowly and steadily against the wind's blast back toward Grensky Brothers, Dealers in Liquors and Tobacco. Alone at the front door, he couldn't help shaking his head at the image of a copper-winged fairy, a dragonfly or a bright small angel dancing before him. Copper at sixty dollars a share! He turned his key in the heavy lock. His heart was pounding hard as it always did with exertion or excitement. He had to be careful. He was glad to be alone but alarmed at the cold in the unheated office. When cold got into his lungs, making June insist he stay indoors to wait for the day to warm a little, his uncles Adolf or Adler sent a messenger to his home. "Important business awaits. Do not tarry." Now he paused at the foot of the steep stairs to his office to swallow a nitroglycerin tablet.

---

Still alone on the second floor of his uncles' building, with only the clerk downstairs, Nathan quickly ate the sandwich June sent with him, drank a cup of hot tea, and bundled up. When he stepped outside, snow was blowing in gusts and the temperatures had further dropped. At the telegraph office, he didn't have to ask the clerk to read the ticker tape because there was a group of men already crowded to see the machine. He stood in the back and waited until someone called out, "United Copper, up over sixty dollars a share."

Nathan returned to the office and called Hermann in Chicago.

"Sell the copper?" Hermann laughed heartily. Nathan saw in his mind's eye his wife's barrel-chested young cousin, waist coast strained over his belly. "We haven't hit the ceiling yet, Nathan. Don't talk of selling, not a word, bad luck."

"With my profits, I won't need luck. I want only retirement from my uncles."

"Hold tight, Cousin. I'm watching like a hawk over our copper chickens. We're staying in until at least tomorrow. We're going to make a killing, Nathan, trust me."

———————

That evening, Nathan left work while it was still light, walked to the florist, a miner who had taken over an empty storefront on Harrison Avenue. Nathan bought two dozen golden and russet mums and had the shivering boy wrap ferns with them before he tipped a dollar and walked out into more cold air.

When June saw the flowers, she hugged Nathan.

"I can tell something good has happened. Did you make the decision today and tell your uncles that we're leaving?" June clutched Nathan's cold hands and rubbed them.

"I have bigger news, my dearest. I can hardly believe it myself." He coughed.

"Come and sit by the stove. Let me heat you warm milk with honey. Your eyes look almost feverish with excitement. I don't like that look, my love."

"Don't you want to know what happened this morning?"

June drew him to the couch. "Of course I do, but first, warm milk. You need to breathe calmly and that helps with a few spoons of whiskey. Come sit here by the stove."

June could hear the rattle in his chest when he spoke. "June, the good fortune we've been waiting for has come. Copper is flying high, for reasons I don't understand. When Hermann sells our shares tomorrow morning, we'll be free to leave Leadville with a nest egg, enough to settle in California. I can hardly believe my own words."

"I hear the good news and also the hoarseness in your voice," said June.

"Don't worry, dearest, soon we'll be far away from the cold and I'll regain my health, I'm certain of it."

"Nathan, I'm so happy. We always believed good would come from the copper. I'll call in Tommy so he can hear your news, too. He's got so many ideas about California we won't be able to keep him quiet on the train ride west."

"Our share value has more than doubled."

"That sounds almost too good to be true," June said.

"I felt the same way which is probably why I didn't return to check the ticker tape at the end of the day. At noon, shares were trading above sixty dollars."

"But you decided to wait until tomorrow to sell them?" June asked.

Nathan nodded. "Your cousin is sure they'll go higher."

June took a deep breath. "We must rely on Hermann. Now, let's call Tommy and have our supper. Perhaps we'll wait until you've sold the copper to tell him. You look very pale despite the good news."

---

Nathan woke in the middle of the night drenched in sweat and began shivering, his heart pounding. June wasn't sleeping. She felt his forehead, brought a glass of water for his nitroglycerin.

"It's the excitement. It will be all over tomorrow when you sell the shares. Then you are not going to linger any longer. We'll leave with Tommy. May can come to help Papa follow us to California."

---

Tuesday morning at 9 am Rocky Mountain time, Nathan learned that United Copper had fallen back to thirty dollars a share. As he stood among other men reading the ticker from New York, the pressure in his chest built up so terribly it was as if the losses crushed his very bones and ligaments as well as his hopes to leave for California.

When he called Chicago, Hermann remained adamant that they should wait to sell. "United Copper will bounce up again."

Nathan hadn't the strength to argue. The rest of the day, his bookkeeping figures swam in their columns before his eyes. By that afternoon, he learned from a weeping Hermann that United Copper was now selling for ten dollars or less, and they couldn't sell them for what they'd cost. "I'm heartbroken for you, Nathan. There are no longer buyers, only sellers of United Copper. If only I'd listened to you yesterday. Unless I find a way to cover our margins, we'll lose everything."

Nathan's chest pains were so strong he could take only shallow breaths to speak. "We haven't lost everything. We have savings in Butte Montana."

Nathan didn't finish his sentence. He fell forward onto his desk where Adolph found him an hour later, unconscious and breathing with difficulty. When smelling salts beneath his nose didn't bring Nathan back to consciousness, he called a carriage to take his nephew home. June met them at the gate.

"I don't believe I can help you carry him," Adolph said.

At that moment, Nathan lifted his head. "I can walk," he said.

"You're not walking. Thank you Uncle Adolph. We can manage now." June lifted Nathan until he was standing and they managed to get him up the path and inside.

"Did you take your glycerin?" June stroked his forehead, clammy and cold.

Nathan nodded, letting her lead him to the couch. "I need more."

June kissed her finger to his lips, then brought the bottle of nitroglycerin. He swallowed four tablets. "A night's sleep and I'll be recovered. Don't alarm Tommy."

"I'll heat the beef broth with farfel; that will warm you up," she said.

As she waited for the broth to simmer and watched the ribbons of farfel rise to the surface, June was thinking which brother to call. Max was closest in Salt Lake City. Morris was in Los Angeles. Max first, she decided.

From the living room, June heard Nathan's hoarse voice as he tried to read to Tommy. Even from the next room, the deep, watery rumble in his chest sounded ominous. Every few sentences, he stopped for breath and coughed. "I'm sorry, son, I need to rest my voice," he said.

"It's time for bed," June said. For once, Tommy didn't protest. He pressed his face to his father's and felt the tear slide down.

"I can hear Papa's heart beat," Tommy said as June tucked him in.

"I'm calling your Uncle Max. It's a good thing we installed this telephone."

She dialed the numbers for Salt Lake City and waited for the operator.

Max took no time with courtesies. "Get him to Denver as soon as possible. I fear he's reached a crisis. Now, Sister, don't despair. He's a young man and we'll pull him through. I'll wire Morris immediately. Be quick, you cannot wait."

---

A frigid dawn was breaking Thursday morning when they caught the Rio Grande for Denver where they shared a carriage with two men from Fairplay. Nathan's eyes were closed the minute they sat down so he didn't see the headline on a passenger's paper, *Copper Breaks Heinze: Waterloo Comes to Young Napoleon and Banks Totter*. The second traveler's paper also had big print on its front page: *Black Thursday*.

The locomotive engine stalled and started again as it climbed the high passes and chugged through the mountain tunnels. June followed every breath Nathan took. "It is his heart. He's never adapted to the altitude," she told the two men. "It's not tuberculosis."

"You got to be born here to survive the Rockies," one man said.

"Good luck to you, Missus," replied the other.

In Denver, a stretcher waited with two nurses on the platform. Nathan seemed only half aware of the activity as they transferred him into the carriage where the horses jerked them all forward. June held

Nathan's hand. He squeezed in return.

———————

Orderlies and nurses wheeled Nathan down a long ward on a gurney, lifted him onto a bed, and drew curtains around him. One young man asked June to remain outside. In minutes, an attending physician arrived and closed himself in behind the curtain. When he emerged, he told June. "Your brothers have wired they will arrive shortly. There's a storm between here and Salt Lake City."

"What about my husband, what about Nathan?"

In answer the doctor patted June's hand. "We're doing our best," he said and pulled her outside into the corridor. "We'll know more soon."

In the dimly-lit waiting room, June sat alone. Beside her a Denver paper lay on the table. In bold letters, she read: *Utter Collapse of United Copper has Disastrous Effect on Stock Exchange. Banks close, Butte Montana among them.*

How could a bank constructed of solid brick and glass like Butte Montana become insolvent? June wondered. Cousin Hermann had transferred their savings account to the Montana bank because it paid high interest.

"We have our savings in Butte Montana." The night nurse came to light lamps.

June whispered, "We do also, but my husband mustn't know what happened."

"You poor thing, with him so desperate."

Finally the physician called her to sit beside Nathan. He squeezed her hand.

"I've lost everything." Tears rolled from his eyes.

"My dearest love," she said. "We will be all right if only you regain your health. Nothing but our love and Tommy matter." She kissed his feverish cheeks. "Just rest."

When Max arrived the next morning and Morris the following afternoon, they had Nathan moved to a private room. The hospital staff seemed impressed, June thought, with her brothers' credentials.

In shadowy light, June gazed at her beloved's pale and handsome face. His coughing had been quieted by a sedative but in his half-sleep, he wasn't peaceful; every few minutes she held him still to wipe hot perspiration from his forehead.

Nathan's fever seemed to rage like the storm outside the window as his heart struggled to pump blood. Max gave some hope that if the fever accompanying the congestion passed, if Nathan did not develop pneumonia, he'd survive this attack. He must never set foot in Leadville again. The very place where she'd been born and grown up was the antagonist in the life and death struggle her beloved Nathan was waging.

————————

The night June returned from Denver, still dressed in the black woolen dress she'd worn accompanying Nathan's body back to Leadville, she wrote for the last time in her wedding book.

*My sweetheart and I are separated for life. I am crushed and broken-hearted. How can I bear this separation and how can I endure the years without his blessed and loving companionship? And Tommy, my cherub, you have lost the dearest father in the world. Your heritage, my treasured child, will be the remembrance of Nathan's noble character. He was high minded, true hearted, innately refined, well and broadly educated and ever seeking to improve himself.*

June opened her wedding chest with her trousseau linen and Nathan's letters and placed the book where she would not see it soon. When she closed the chest, the intense fragrances of lavender, cedar, and linen starch lingered.

————————

At Evergreen Cemetery, the newly dug grave lay opened with her beloved's casket. Rabbi Rosen, who had arrived from Denver to conduct the service, stood too close to June. His breath smelled like cigars. Ruth whispered at her side that the rabbi's wife had recently died, leaving him with two young girls who were orphans. "As is Tommy."

"Tommy is not an orphan," June answered. "He has a mother to raise him."

At the conclusion of the service, Adolph Grensky spoke loudly. "Butte Montana Savings will recover but we'll have hard times and have to tighten our belts. There'll be no easy credit for chasing fool's gold which I always called copper." Adolph's brother Adler said, "It was fear of failure rather than failure itself that brought us to this pass."

June kept her eyes on that awful opening where Nathan was lowered.

---

That night, as she stood listening to Tommy whimpering in his sleep, June had no idea how a boy barely six years old would understand that he was fatherless anymore than she herself could accept losing her husband. She wiped her eyes with her apron as the candlelight patterned the dark wall. Tommy's stuffed bears lined up on his dresser, their variously bent ears casting shadows on the wall. Every birthday, May sent her nephew a new Teddy from San Francisco where she now lived.

The day's snow clouds had cleared, leaving a hard freeze upon the Arkansas Valley. Through the window, a full moon shone light from the snowy faces of Mount Massive and Mount Elmore upon June's patch-work rug. She shivered as she stood by her son's bed. The cold of the hospital where Nathan lay would always be within her, a suffocating cold. She'd never feel sure or secure about anything again.

In the moonlight, June stood looking at her son. Tommy had Nathan's chin with the dimple she loved so much. His smile, like Nathan's, turned up the corners of his mouth as he dreamed. Tommy's physical likeness was, June thought, more to Nathan, but his nature, his character, seemed inherited from her father. Tommy was a fun-loving, easy-going child, lacking Nathan's serious turn of mind. In another way, he had his Aunt May's adventurousness and begged to visit her in San Francisco where he could see tall-masted sailing ships on the waterfront.

# THIRTEEN

THE GRENSKY'S TWO-STORY home at #202 Banker's Row loomed forbiddingly as June and Tommy walked toward it. Like other stately residences on the best street in Leadville, #202 boasted gables, pillars, and a wide front porch leading to a massive front door, but only this house had a window in the left gable with a huge eye leering out at anyone passing beneath.

"Kids call it the Eye of the Haunted House." Tommy pointed up at the window framing a white glass cornea and black pupil. The lintel itself looked like an eyelid.

"They called it that when I was your age," said June. "It's always been strange."

Tommy gripped her hand tightly. "Are you scared that the aunts are spying on us from the eye?"

"I think it's painted over so you can't see through it to the outside. Don't be scared. They are your father's uncles' wives, part of family."

"Mama, I know they're watching us." Tommy stood next to his mother as June unlatched the gate. "I don't like these aunties. I don't like the uncles, either. I wish we didn't have to go inside. Can't we just go home?"

"No, we're here for a reason. They knew Nathan when he was your age, just a little boy. They will help us now." As June said these words, anger rose in her throat. She wished she didn't have to lie to Tommy. The uncles and aunts weren't kind, had never been generous nor loving to Nathan, quite the opposite, cruel in his childhood and mean until the day he died. She wouldn't say this; she wanted Tommy on his best behavior.

"Did they play pinochle with Papa like Grandpa plays with me?"

"I don't know. What matters, Tommy, is that you say please and thank you to everything. It's important that you do this because I'm asking them to help us."

Tommy twitched his lips to conceal a small smile. "Do you think they will?"

"I think they *must* help us. Your father worked faithfully for them."

Nathan's years of service had to make his uncles settle something on Tommy, June thought. Her brother Dr. Max had called urging her to move with Tommy and Max Sr. to Salt Lake City. "We have a large home and no children. There's nothing to keep you there." June replied that she was committed to teach. Dr. Max dropped his voice so Susie wouldn't hear. "I will raise Tommy as if he were my own son."

June knew her sister-in-law would grudgingly take them in because she couldn't refuse her husband, but Tommy had a stubborn, willful streak and he'd be sure to get into trouble with Susie who wouldn't let anything pass uncorrected. June and Nathan believed in kindness and trust rather than strict discipline with their son, and Grandfather Max was all treats, play and mischief, like a boy himself with Tommy. June didn't want to be a poor relation in Salt Lake City, nor in Los Angeles, where Morris also had a successful medical practice and no children. Morris' wife Fanny had survived several miscarriages and never regained her strength. Fanny was June's preferred sister-in-law but a rambunctious boy would be too much for her, as well as reminding her of childlessness.

June had considered joining her sister in San Francisco but feared May's life was too bohemian. What kind of example would it be for Tommy to know his unmarried aunt carried on with a man who led labor strikes and had been in and out of prison for his politics? She wasn't ready for San Francisco. If she received one thousand dollars from the Grensky uncles, she would repay loans for the funeral and put their house up for sale. She and Tommy would move in with her father above the store. Tommy needed the comfort of his grandfather more than ever, and with an infusion of cash from the uncles and her salary, they could all live together and keep open the store a bit longer.

When the tall door of #202 opened a crack, a cane and toes of small black boots emerged. The door pulled back a few more inches. June and Tommy saw two pair of boots and then, looking up, the small figures of Hildegard and Flora Grensky standing shoulder to narrow shoulder in the doorway. A wave of warm air mixed with a fragrance of camphor seeped out into the cold.

"You must come inside immediately or you'll let in the air," Flora said.

"Don't stand out there freezing and give us all a chill," Hildegard said.

Flora and Hildegard were hard to tell apart with the light behind them, thin, with greying hair coiled in buns at their collars. They wore identical raven-black dresses that emitted the peculiar odor of creosote or moth balls.

Flora pinched Tommy's cheek. "He looks peaked. You must feed him more, despite your loss."

*I do not starve my son the way you starve yourselves*, June wanted to say but kept her lips pressed together.

The door clicked locked behind them. She and Tommy followed the rustling cone-shaped skirts into a dark vestibule where they left their coats and shook off snow from boots. How could Flora imagine she'd not feed her son! She never heard a kind word from either woman. The Grensky uncles were by no stretch of the imagination joyful men but their wives were worse. June had hoped to see Adolph and Adler alone.

"Nephew couldn't save two pennies to buy her fur," Hildegard said to Flora.

June caught the whispered words she was meant to overhear. Fortunately, Tommy hadn't, or he would have piped up to say that his father had given his mother a fur coat, and he had a jacket with a real fox collar.

In the light, June saw Hildegard was slightly taller than Flora. The real likeness came from their posture, crimped shoulders that declared both had suffered cold and disappointments. Flora took Tommy by the hand. "We have chocolate that I suppose you don't get at home."

"My mama gives me chocolate!" Tommy said emphatically.

"Oh dear, he has a tongue. Your father never spoke out of turn," said Flora.

The sisters' stiff skirts swayed around their corseted bodies, making scratching sounds like insects rubbing their wings.

"We are familiar with death, my sister and I. We visit our own little cherubs in every weather. But we can never replace them as you can," Hildegard said.

"Replace?" June asked, truly not understanding.

"Why…we mean that you're young still and will find a protector and have more children, I suppose, with a second husband." Flora sniffed.

"I've never, never, never thought…" June bit her lip. How dare they say *replace* and Nathan in the same breath?

"Biscuits and chocolate for Tommy? You like biscuits?" Flora asked.

"Yes, please, I like the biscuits with chocolate horses on them."

"No, no. Biscuits *and* hot chocolate to drink, not both," said Flora.

"Thank you." Tommy tucked his hands under him on the couch.

All the time she and Nathan were married, the aunts had invited them once a year to supper where they ate dry-tasting food and endured criticism. Their invitations to the Grenskys to come to their home were always refused with one excuse or another.

"I made our appointment with your husbands," June began. "If this isn't the right time, we can return, or go to the offices."

She did not want to ever set foot in the Grensky building and especially dreaded seeing Nathan's office, but she and Tommy needed the uncles' help.

"I'm terribly sorry." Hildegard turned in the door frame. "It must have been the excitement of your arrival that made me forget to say that our dear husbands are unable to join us this morning. They're never free from the obligations of the business."

"But it's Sunday," said June. "I can wait until tomorrow."

"Work is never done for them," sighed Flora.

"Ever since the copper incident, they've been in danger of exhaustion." Hildegard looked back to Flora for confirmation. "They requested that we meet you in their stead."

"Exhaustion!" June raised her voice. "Nathan worked to his dying day. I don't mind returning when Nathan's uncles are at home. They are Tommy's blood relations."

Hot tears filled her eyes and her head pounded. So the uncles weren't coming. They had always broken promises they made to Nathan over his settlement, so why had she thought they'd be honest with her?

"Let's sit quietly and not upset the child more than necessary. We'll have our tea and chocolate, shall we?" said Flora.

The tea service had elaborately worked silver embossed with grapevines, but the cups were thick, certainly not the best Grensky china. June felt the insult when a chipped plate was served with the biscuits.

"Will you take milk and sugar?" Hildegard asked June. "My sister is preparing young Tommy's chocolate herself."

"Mama likes both cream *and* sugar." Tommy squeezed June's hand.

"Cream! I suppose with all the rich provisions at hand from your father's shop you're most likely used to cream rather than milk." Hildegard clicked her teeth.

Flora brought a cup of watery-looking brown liquid and placed it before Tommy.

"Just for you, young man. I made it myself. Now drink it all up."

Tommy took a taste. "It's not sweet enough, Aunts. More sugar, please."

"Isn't that the little prince!" Flora spooned two sugar cubes into the cup. "Now wait until they thoroughly dissolve so we have no more complaints."

June was about to nudge Tommy to drink, when Hildegard's cup clattered in its saucer like an announcement.

"Who'd have thought that copper would have had such an influence on us all? Just when we believed Leadville had recovered from the dreadful strikes and all that trouble with the miners, now we must suffer more difficulties. Banks are making credit scarce, but surely your brothers, June, with their fine medical careers outside this poor town of ours, have been spared our woes."

"They have established their practices elsewhere, it is true, but I don't expect them to support us. Tommy is your great nephew, and carries the family name." June drew a deep breath. "Nathan's uncles promised to settle a sum on him."

"We can speak for our husbands, June. Consider us their emissaries," said Flora.

June swallowed. "We hope you will find generosity in your hearts to help your nephew's only child as your husbands promised their father."

June didn't say that she had borrowed to pay for the funeral while the Grenskys offered nothing. Nor that at Selig Brothers the shelves were hardly stocked and the living quarters where her father slept looked more rundown every month. She wouldn't give the aunts the satisfaction of hearing that Max Selig's shakiness made it hard for him to work the register. Nor that Uncle Isaac was losing his eyesight. There had been too much enmity over the years for Grenskys to have sympathy for Seligs.

She started again. "Nathan was promised a settlement equivalent to partnership in the business. Your husbands stated this in letters. We are your only family in America."

In the next moment, as if they'd received a cue, both sisters brought kerchiefs to their faces and began to weep into them. Hildegard blew her nose hard.

"You must remind us that we are childless in the world. We had two girls."

"We prefer girls," sniffled Flora. "Which is why it is *ever so hard*."

The sisters just as quickly lowered their voices to the driest level.

"I never meant to remind you of your losses. I'm terribly sorry."

"I won't say that you and our poor nephew brought this on yourselves," Hildegard looked at the pattern in her tea cup. "But we do know the value of frugality."

"Even if we wished to help, at the present, bank credit is impossible to get," said Flora. "We can make no loans."

"I don't ask for credit or loans. I ask for only what is owed Nathan."

Hildegard continued as if she hadn't heard June. "Ever since you took Nathan to California against our advice, we felt the tropics affected him. That copper madness started there. We were informed of it."

"You mean you were spying on us?" June shook her head.

"From the start, Nephew's behavior had to be watched," said Flora. "Even before your marriage he paraded around with the scribbler Heimberger who stirred up trouble."

"Nathan abetted the ruffian miners. We know certain things," said Hildegard.

"Our wedding trip was seven years ago and we paid for it. If you hadn't called him back to work here, he'd be alive now. But you would not let us be, not even on our honeymoon. You threatened to give him nothing, just as you're doing now."

"I'm sure there were no threats," said Flora.

"As there is no threat now. What dreadful language, June," said Hildegard.

"There were promises, and threats. I dreaded the telegrams. Nathan returned out of loyalty and under pressure though I urged him not to. He believed that ultimately your husbands would do the right thing and he worked faithfully every day of his life for the business. Nathan sacrificed his health…"

"Let us not speak of sacrifices. What have we not given up in happiness, in family we are forever parted from, to remain at our husbands' sides! You needn't remind us of family obligation," said Hildegard.

"Your husbands didn't give him raises in salary. Only last Christmas…"

"Scrooge. Ebeneezer Scrooge." Tommy's high voice hung in the air.

Hildegard stood up, stepped toward Tommy as if she were going to slap him.

June rose up between them. She stood nearly a foot taller. Flora backed away.

"Don't threaten me, June Selig. As for your child, he has not earned favor here that might have won some indulgence from us."

"You take pleasure in reminding us that our cherubs departed at Christmas. Christmas is when we bid the angels goodbye." Hildegard dabbed at her eyes.

"Please, Aunts, let's not quarrel. Nathan and I always had the greatest sympathy for you and Tommy simply knows Dickens by heart. I've come because we need help."

"Aren't you the modern woman with a college degree? Nathan used to remind us, 'She's been to college,' as if no one on earth was as good as June Selig," said Flora.

Flora stood shoulder to shoulder with her sister like angry black wasps. "Mama, don't beg them, please. They're mean aunts."

"You're a nasty child. You'll become a criminal." Flora shook her finger at him.

"Flora, don't say another word against my child. Tommy will grow up to be a fine man because he holds his father's example in his heart." June took one deep breath.

"I only ask for what is due Nathan. I won't beg for charity. I shall consult an attorney."

"Just you try! We know what's in writing and what isn't," said Flora.

Hildegard laughed. "There's nothing, nothing, in writing. We know that."

June grabbed their coats and tried to open the door. Locked. Her chest heaving, her head pounding, she waited until Flora arrived with a key and slowly inserted it in the hole, then flung open the door to the chill air.

Outside under the flat grey sky, the failure of her purpose mattered less than breaking free of that house. Tommy held her hand tightly and led her down the snow-covered walk to the street. "I'd like to throw a stone and put out that eye!" he said. "Like David did when he killed the Philistine Goliath and set the Jews free."

# Part Two

# ONE

## NEW YORK CITY
## 1907

JACOB GREENBAUM WAS EXPECTED home to light the Sabbath candles but neither he nor his cousin Yuli Sachs moved toward the passing carriages that would take them uptown. An hour earlier, they'd been standing across from the Stock Exchange on Broad and Wall Street alongside men who seemed as much in shock as they were. It was now Friday afternoon, October 17, a mere five days after the madness of Monday, the uncertainty of Tuesday, the catastrophe of Wednesday, and Thursday, the confirmation of their disasters. If the Roman goddess above the pillars of the Exchange had seemed once to bless them with gifts of prosperity, she now crushed them with her stone gaze.

Without saying anything to each other, they'd begun walking uptown, ignoring the calls from carriage drivers.

Jacob kept clasping and unclasping his hands.

"There, there." Yuli placed a slender hand on Jacob's thick arm. "I'm also thinking of our loved ones."

Jacob shook his head. "I'm trying to find one bright word for the Sabbath tonight but I've not come up with any. We can't start over again as our grandfathers did, Yuli. Our children can't provide for themselves. They're helpless as kittens." He thought how his darling daughter Tillie had never heard the words, *No, that's not possible. No, we can't afford it.* Tillie's embroidered silk petticoats came from Paris, her hand-benched slippers from London. Yuli's son, Eddie, was no more equipped to survive penniless than was Tillie. Jacob refrained from mentioning Yuli himself, as impractical as the children. Then there was Homer, his only son, a thorn in his side.

"I find the news of the Chicago Cubs winning the World Championship most encouraging," Yuli said calmly. "Athletics take my mind off troubling matters."

"Did you wager on Chicago to win?" Jacob wondered if Yuli might have a pocketful of cash to buy back United Copper selling for five dollars a share. Copper had to go up again. The world depended on the metal. How could it have fallen like a lead weight?

"No, I didn't wager. Damn it all, I intended to. The Cubs were a long shot."

---

Jacob was stocky, short and bustled with energy, while Ulysses, called Yuli, was tall, slender and laconic. Jacob had inherited his father's sober style in dress, three-piece suits of dark gabardine. He carried a cane for style because he liked tapping on the pavement ahead of him. Yuli walked with long strides and the grace of an athlete. He favored soft linen shirts and loose fitting jackets, a Paris Bohemian style. Jacob and Ulysses were double cousins whose grandfathers, brothers, had married sisters, all of them part of the first wave of Jewish immigrants arrived in New Haven from villages in Bavaria in the mid 1850s. Both men and women had worked in factories sewing whalebone into corset stays. A generation later, Jacob and Yuli's fathers had their own shop, Greenbaum & Sachs, makers of girdles and brassieres. There they invented and manufactured the Smoother, a one-piece pink slimming corset that made their fortunes. The families moved to Bronxville, then to Manhattan's Upper East Side where Jacob and Ulysses still lived with their wives and children in townhouses on 75th off Madison.

In 1905, Jacob sold the New Haven factory to his Russian foreman just as rubber began to replace whalebone stays. Jacob was forty-seven and Yuli forty-four, young enough to enjoy gentlemanly retirement though Jacob looked to increase their capital. He took an extended trip by train through Montana, Utah and Colorado to see for himself how the minerals in which he planned to invest were extracted from the rugged mountains. In Denver, Colorado, he met cultured German Jews who invited him to Friday night services in their impressive temple. These adventurous westerners, he learned, enjoyed considerable social status as benefactors of local charitable institutions. In Montana, he heard stories of how the Heinze brothers had bested John D. Rockefeller and formed United Copper. After this trip, Jacob placed the bulk of both families' capital in copper, the miracle metal.

In the spring of 1907, a year after the San Francisco earthquake, the New York stock market had seemed perilously close to falling but corrected itself before the end of summer. Jacob bought more United Copper and a two-cylinder, black Studebaker-Garford to drive both families to a rented summer home on the water in Bayville. Jacob himself was too restless to stay at the beach. Back in the city, he joined true New Yorkers who relished August as a time with fewer restraints, when Jews and Gentiles rubbed elbows at Sherry's or the Waldorf Astoria bars, all the men summer bachelors with roving eyes and quick palaver.

The family had barely returned from their holidays the first week of October when the financial crash caught them as unawares as if a tidal wave had arisen from a flat sea. On the day that United Copper rose to its greatest heights, Jacob's broker, Alfred Hornthall, warned him that the sudden jump in share prices looked suspect. Even now, Jacob remembered his trip downtown with Yuli at Hornthall's request, and the broker's unpleasant voice saying, "Mr. Greenbaum, I smell danger in the metals. You should be more diversified." At that moment, the two partners, Singer and Lasley, had burst in on them. Mocking Hornthall's timidity, they shooed him out of the brokerage office, after which Jacob placed the family homes as collateral to buy more United Copper.

---

The cousins continued walking uptown. Blocks and blocks went by without either saying a word. When they reached 34th and Fifth

Avenue, a line of people surrounding the four-story edifice of the Knickerbocker Trust Company blocked their way.

"Look here, Yuli, we've arrived at our second temple of reckoning," said Jacob.

The imposing marble columns and bronze doors of Knickerbocker should have assured stability against the fiercest financial storm, but the bank, whose main collateral had been the Heinze brothers' United Copper, didn't seem to be doing any better at providing protection than had the goddess who overlooked the Exchange.

Police on horseback were keeping people in the long lines that wound around the block. When Jacob had seen a bank run after the Silver Panic of 1893, he'd pitied the subscribers who'd jostled and fought to withdraw their savings before the tellers ran out of money and closed their doors. He'd never imagined himself among the unfortunates.

A mounted policeman's horse reared in front of them, forcing Jacob and Yuli to step back. Across Fifth Avenue, an even longer line of women stretched around the corner and out of sight. Jacob didn't know why they separated the sexes. Thus far, his wife Mina seemed not to know the extent of their losses, but with the speed that gossip moved in their crowd, she would learn soon enough the disaster they faced.

For a moment, Jacob visualized the crowd parting as he and Yuli walked through the doors of Knickerbocker Trust and felt the cool green marbled banking room surrounding them. Mr. Granger, who managed their account, would invite them to sit in the library or wait comfortably with coffee and cigars while he checked their balances and latest dividend payments. Jacob banked at Knickerbocker because the establishment had a dashing young president with the reputation of a prince of commerce, a magic touch, and because of high interest rates paid quarterly. As Jacob's account had tripled, quadrupled, over the last year—*through this very summer,* Jacob said to himself—Mr. Granger made it apparent they were special clients who had only to sign for a loan or any type of financing.

"Let's leave here. I'm feeling ill," Yuli said to Jacob. But before they could move, a frantic-looking man in a Derby grabbed Jacob's arm and shouted, "Pierpont Morgan must come to our rescue or we're all finished. Where is the Big Chief?"

"It's President Roosevelt's fault. He crippled the railroads, kept oil and the trusts from natural expansion—shackled the very strengths of the country," Jacob said.

"You're right of course," said another man, wearing a raincoat. "But now those very men our president called *the malefactors of great wealth* must rescue the country. Unusually hot for October! I dressed too heavily." He removed his hat to mop his brow.

"Unseasonable," Yuli replied cordially. "We'll weather it, if you excuse the pun."

There was a sound of weak laughter from those nearest by and the phrase, "Weather the storm!" moved backwards with the crowd.

"When Morgan arrives, we can put this all behind us like a bad dream," said the man in the Derby. "I can almost see J.P.'s black brougham drawn by white horses coming down Fifth Avenue."

"Unfortunately, that vehicle is nowhere in sight," said the man in the raincoat. "I've been at the 66th Street Broadway branch. I couldn't get a cent from my account."

"How ungentlemanly and unsportsmanlike," said Yuli. "Shopkeepers are causing this situation, I suppose. Not investors like ourselves."

"Not only shopkeepers. Look at the carriages and the chauffeurs in their fine autos." The man in the raincoat pointed to vehicles on both sides of Fifth. "I tell you, it's all up to Morgan, but he won't lift a finger unless he likes Knickerbocker's balance sheet. I heard his accountants are in the vault right now going over the books."

"It's all the fault of socialists and damn Roosevelt," said the man in the Derby.

"Should we contact Mr. Granger personally?" asked Yuli. "He won't refuse us."

"I don't think we'd get in." Jacob felt irritated by Yuli's foolish words.

"If I'm unable to scull with the Club, what is the meaning of life?" Yuli sighed.

"Don't talk foolishness, Yuli. I have confidence in the bankers' consortium to save what we have. Not what we had on Monday or Tuesday, of course. Let's talk no more about it and get home before the first star appears in the sky."

Yuli lengthened his stride, making Jacob take twice as many steps to keep up, tap tapping beside him with his gold-tipped cane. Though neither of them were particularly religious Jews, the Sabbath and High Holidays were times they observed their faith.

"You know that our little broker Hornthall is smitten with your Tillie," said Yuli.

Jacob stopped. "Are you mad? Hornthall knows, or he should know, that Tillie loves your Eddie and plans to marry him." Jacob pounded his cane on the pavement. They were in front of Sherry's on 44th Street. Jacob loved Sherry's like a second home. If only he could drown his cares with bourbon and soda in comforting darkness.

"How dare Hornthall presume? He cannot have made advances."

"I could be assuming more than was meant but if you remember this past Monday, the last time we saw Hornthall and he advised selling, he warned you to protect your family. I don't know if you heard him mention Tillie by name, but I did."

"Curse it all, Yuli, you're putting ideas into my head that have little basis in fact. All I heard was his damnable coughing. What I remember of Monday is how confusing it all was with copper going up and up, the partners advising me to buy, Hornthall sputtering like a consumptive telling us to sell. What exactly did he say about Mathilda?"

"He mentioned that he hoped your daughter would not have to face hardship due to the risks you were taking. I heard it as a warning but I deferred to you, Jacob, as I do, when it's a question of finances for the family."

"Are you blaming me for losing our shares! Why didn't *you* take Hornthall's side and insist we sell!"

"I didn't understand the situation and I thought that you did."

"It was sheer madness that day. And Hornthall is such a carper, Yuli. His doubting always gave me heartburn. Such a meager little man."

The cousins had reached the Plaza Hotel and the opening of the Park, also one of Jacob's favorite spots in Manhattan where he loved being among the bustle of evening traffic, the horse-drawn cabs letting out elegant ladies lifting their skirts to reveal a bit of ankle as they climbed into carriages.

"I never said Hornthall was stupid, but he's out of the question socially. I tell you something else, Cousin, if my son throws the Russian rabble in my face at the table tonight, I'll strangle him, I swear I will."

The only pleasurable thought Jacob had had so far this awful week was that if he lost everything, there would be nothing for his vexing son Homer to inherit.

"There's one more bit of news to impart, Jacob."

"It cannot be as unpleasant as your suppositions about Hornthall."

"Oh, no. It's about Eddie. It's rather interesting in fact."

"What about him? Does he have any good ideas to help us out of our dilemma?"

Yuli smiled broadly and nodded. "My Eddie is traveling to Hollywood, California, next week. Natalie's cousins have invited him to tour the picture-making business out there. You know how Eddie adores the flickers and it's a darn good time to go, I'd say. He hates unpleasantness, as I do."

Jacob restrained himself from saying *like father like son*, incapable of a sensible word or decision. "As long as Eddie's back to take Tillie to the winter parties, let him see Hollywood, California. Perhaps he'll earn something for his troubles."

# Two

Mina Greenbaum massaged the brisket with both hands, salt and peppering, smearing the meat with garlic before turning it over to work the other side. Mina purchased Chicago kosher beef, neither too fat nor too lean, from her butcher Krauss. After the beef was seared to a deep brown, Mina would smother it with onions, tomatoes, carrots, red wine, stalks of celery, bay leaf, thyme and rosemary. She and Delia Delatte, her cook, shared respect for their raw materials, not too much seasoning, nothing to make Jacob reach for Bicarb of Soda after supper. If a dish lacked a certain something, Mina added another bay leaf.

Mina left Delia to paint the braided *challah* with egg white and place it in the oven while she went upstairs for a quick wash and a change before Jacob came home.

She heaved a sigh of momentary pleasure unbuttoning her dress. Over the years, being such a good cook and having a hearty appetite, husband and wife had put on weight. Many women seemed happy to spend their days away from home, hardly setting foot in their kitchens, boasting how well their cooks prepared their meals. Mina couldn't understand why liberation from cooking gave them more pleasure than planning menus, making shopping lists and traveling with Delia to where fish was freshest, pickled tongue the most tender, vegetables and fruit from the country the brightest. Coming home, her carriage loaded down with pungent packages and setting out to prepare the day's food with Delia at her side, was Mina's true source of delight.

Though the Greenbaum and Sachs families lived in adjoining brownstones, Mina shared little in common with Natalie, cousin

118

Yuli's wife. Natalie was a high-strung, unreliable woman, in Mina's opinion. You never knew what she might say or do. She was a vegetarian and never let pass an opportunity to speak out on the evils of killing and consuming animals as the rest of the family was about to enjoy the brisket. But Mina loved Natalie and Yuli's children, Eddie and Sylvia, as if they were her own. On the many nights their mother hardly gave them enough nourishment to survive on, she fed them until they protested they couldn't eat another piece of strudel.

If Natalie was one kind of trial to Mina's patience, her son Homer was another. Who else but his mother could have loved the red-faced, hairless baby who seemed to have been angry from the moment he was born, as if the pains of childbirth had been his and not hers? Through his childhood, Mina lost a half dozen governesses to Homer's tantrums. When a stubborn German *Fraulein* refused to quit, Homer had chased the poor woman around the dining room table with a carving knife until she ran screaming from the house. At thirteen, Homer was reading Russian novels instead of preparing for his bar mitzvah, which he refused, accusing his family and their German Jewish crowd of being soulless moneygrubbers. The Russians, who mostly resided downtown, had souls, he argued, while the uptown Germans had bank accounts. What had kept Homer from moving downtown to live with these Easterners, Mina knew, was his appetite, which seemed his main Greenbaum inheritance. The aromas from Mina's kitchen made him wait for one more meal before he packed up and left for the tenements. Only that autumn, he had left to study at Columbia University and live in a student residence. He turned up predictably for Sabbath supper as if he could smell the meat roasting from 110th Street.

Mina and Jacob's daughter, Mathilda, called Tillie, was the very opposite of Homer and a delight at all times. As a baby, Tillie already beamed with flirtatious green eyes and long eyelashes at everyone who looked at her. Her bronze curls seemed touched by gold, and no one had such dimples nor a more petite, precociously developing figure. She loved to dance—from waltz to ragtime—with her cousins Eddie and Sylvia. These three easy children submitted to instruction in piano, eurhythmics and painting that Homer refused. Sylvia was a talented musician and Eddie could turn fabric into a fairy's gown or clown's trousers. Tillie was their muse, the spirit of fun and lightness.

---

At five o'clock, the fragrances of browned onions and meat reached the upstairs bedroom where Mina sighed, buttoned her dark green silk dress as far as she could reach around her back, tied her apron and returned to the kitchen.

"Have you added parsley?" Mina asked Delia.

"Doing that now," Delia replied.

"Then we'll let the meat rest before we skim fat and make our gravy," Mina said. "Not to forget our secret ingredient."

"No, Ma'am," said Delia.

The secret ingredient Mina always added was a tablespoon of Cola for the caramel color and the indefinable something, the *je ne sais quoi,* to the brisket.

Mina bought generously to have leftovers for Delia to take home when she left. She never knew how many people Delia was responsible for at any particular time, nor where they fit in the Delattre family, four generations living together in a house in Harlem. Delia was half a head taller than Mina, a thin woman with smooth, yellowish-brown skin, high cheekbones, a mass of freckles from her forehead to her chin, and discerning hazel-flecked eyes. Delia was a great-grandmother but there were no grey hairs in the jet-black bundle she braided and tied in a tail at the back of her head. She claimed heritage from Seminoles mixed with escaped Africans deep inside Florida swamps. Once when Mina was particularly annoyed at Natalie, she'd told Delia that her sister-in-law's family, Sephardic Jews who had settled in Atlanta, had once owned slaves and never renounced that past. But Delia only shrugged, "Past don't mean nothing to me. My people was always free."

Mina's *matzo farfel* lay covered in cream sauce to be warmed and served after the appetizer of herring salad and pureed vegetable soup, a concession to Natalie who always tore into her piece of *challah* like a ravenous bird. And the moment Delia appeared with dessert, Natalie reached for the first and largest helpings.

"Sweets is like religion to your sister-in-law," said Delia as she sprinkled the *pflaumennkuchen* with powdered sugar. "She loves this plum cake."

"You were reading my mind, Delia. Those children would have starved in infancy if it weren't for us. Can you do this up for me please? I hope the material stretches." She turned so that Delia could complete buttoning her dress.

Delia quickly buttoned and patted Mina's shoulder. "Just fine now."

At last, Mina heard the door being opened. "Here's my husband. I wonder what has kept him so late? The entire week has been a great strain on him. If Homer comes, I hope our son will behave tonight." Mina worried when Homer didn't come that he wouldn't have eaten a good meal all week, and she worried when he rushed in that he'd upset his father's digestion and ruin the food. Tonight of all nights, Mina thought, she wanted harmony.

Mina followed Jacob upstairs to their bedroom. His mouth drooped beneath his mustaches. He looked flushed.

He unbuttoned his vest. "I won't spoil the evening by recounting our day, my dear. I know you've been at work. I smell brisket."

"I was beginning to worry. You're later than usual."

"We'd almost arrived home when Yuli surprised me with news that Eddie is leaving for Los Angeles."

"Los Angeles, so far away? I haven't heard a thing. When is he going?"

"Very soon, I believe. I don't know if he's told Tillie."

"Not a word to Tillie, Jacob. She's already on edge. Of course she's heard a lot this week. She may appear still a child but she's seventeen and understands a great deal."

"I can't bear to think of Tillie with a worry in her head. It's all my fault." Jacob's eyes began to tear.

"Of course it's not your fault, dear, and we'll not spoil our appetites with anything that we cannot resolve before tomorrow." Mina patted his cheek dry.

As Mina came down the stairs, she heard music from the salon and opened the door to see Tillie dancing by herself to "The Maple Leaf Rag" while Eddie played the piano, his wavy brown hair falling over the soft collar of his white silk shirt.

Mina beamed at her daughter, dressed in a pink silk frock with a raspberry satin ribbon at the waist. Everyone said that Mathilda was the prettiest, best-dressed girl in their crowd.

Tillie's curls bounced into Eddie's face and must have tickled his nose because he sneezed. She offered him a white handkerchief but instead of blowing into it, he turned the lacy square into a bandana that he tied over one eye. There was never too much play acting and dressing up for Eddie. His favorite artiste was Loie Fuller who he'd seen perform "The Serpentine Dance" on film at the Nickelodeon.

Out of the corner of her eye, Mina saw the ash from Natalie's black cigarette about to fall on the carpet and rushed over to catch it in a napkin. Natalie smiled indulgently as if, Mina thought, she expected her sister-in-law to clean up after her.

Yuli put down his book to kiss Mina on each cheek. *"Shabbat Shalom,* Hermina."

*"Shabbat Shalom,* Yuli and Natalie and you dearest children," Mina replied.

"I can smell the *challah.* Thank you, Auntie, for making it yourself," said Sylvia. "It wouldn't be Sabbath without your *challah.*"

Mina took Sylvia in her arms. The poor child never put on weight, Mina sighed, certain Sylvia had suffered permanent deprivation from Natalie's neglect. Of the four offspring, including her own Tillie, Sylvia had the most understanding of feelings, and was sensitive to others beyond her young years. But where would a freckled, red-headed, bone-thin, sensitive girl find a husband? Sylvia also suffered from migraines and times of melancholy. When Tillie and Eddie married, where would Sylvia fit in?

"Delia won't like it if we let anything go cold. Your father is coming down."

Tillie grabbed hold of Eddie's shirttails, pulling them from the trousers as she followed him. Mina saw he was wearing red underwear like a fireman.

When Jacob entered, he took his seat at the head of the table. Delia, starched apron over her black dress, brought water in a silver bowl for the ritual hand-washing, then passed clean linen for Jacob and Yuli to dry their fingers. Mina smiled at how Delia knew everything that should be done correctly for the Sabbath.

"*Baruch Atah Adonai Eloheynu*" chanted Jacob and Yuli together, lighting the candles, raising the silver *Kiddush* cup. Eddie walked to each glass, pouring dark Burgundy wine with the flourish of an actor portraying a waiter.

"You always make such a beautiful setting, Hermina." Yuli surveyed the dining room lit with a dozen candles in the chandelier which made the silver and crystal sparkle.

Natalie raised her lorgnette to her aquiline nose and sang *a capella*. "*Baruch Atah Heshem…*" Blessed are you Lord of the universe, Who creates the fruit of the vine." Natalie had a reedy voice with vibrato that she claimed came from Sephardic rabbis.

"We must not forget to bless our Greenbaum grandfathers," said Jacob. "They crossed the great ocean to an unknown future in America. I've told you children often that in Grandfather's time, the Kaiser was scouring the countryside to conscript young men into his army. He liked nothing better than sending Jewish men to the front lines. For that we called him the Prince of Grapeshot."

Jacob looked at Tillie and Eddie and made a small circle of his thumb and index finger. "Grapeshot, children, was ammunition used at the time, little balls bundled together and shot from a cannon. The only kind of grapes that our grandfathers wanted were those crushed into Riesling or Port, so they came to America. In difficult times," Jacob raised his glass, "may we have their fortitude. Blessed be fruit of the vine."

"Amen," they all answered.

Delia entered carrying the herring salad when the front door flew open and the candles trembled.

"Will you please remove your hat, Homer." Jacob did not look up at his son but was sure the boy was unwashed because he smelled.

Mina watched as Homer removed the workman's cap he wore to

annoy his father, and set down a satchel of the sort a traveling man carried. Her son was short and thick like his parents, but the reddish brown beard and uncut curls looked more like a rabbinical student than a young man studying pre-law at Columbia University.

"*Shabbat Shalom*," Mina said. "Please wash and sit down, Homer."

"I'm famished." Homer washed and dried his hands before he pulled a large piece off the *challah* and said with his mouth full, "In general, I wish for nothing more than a complete collapse of the bourgeoisie but I'd not like to see my own family go hungry because then I would, too."

"No such thing will happen," said Jacob. "Respect your mother, I tell you."

"Homer." Delia approached. "Good evening." She served him the herring salad. "You like good fish. You be quiet and eat."

"That I do, and thank you, Delia."

Despite his bad manners and dirty cuffs, Mina was pleased to see her son behave politely to Delia and approve of the herring. When Homer had seemed the most hopeless, Delia always had seen the boy in a positive light. The law would suit him perfectly, she told Mina. "He'll be a judge one day in the American Supreme Court." If only there were a good Jewish girl who'd ignore Homer's ranting about the earthquakes in Chile and San Francisco proving the absence of God, Mina told Delia, she'd die happy.

Delia returned with the browned, savory brisket and placed it before Mina to slice. The meat fell apart in its gravy. Jacob's plate came first, with a double thick slice, mounds of farfel, sauce, sweet and sour cabbage. Next came Yuli, then the children.

"Nothing is going to keep Knickerbocker afloat. They're doomed and you'll never get a cent out of them." Homer managed to talk with his mouth full.

"Don't be ridiculous, Homer," Mina said. "A beautiful bank made of marble!"

Jacob rapped his knuckles on the table. "Respect the Sabbath. Don't distress us."

"This brisket is delicious, Mother." Homer turned to his father,

124

"We will be distressed soon enough."

"Not now, Homer, please!" Mina's voice almost broke into tears.

"All right, Mother, I bow to your command." Homer made a mocking bow.

Yuli spoke for the first time. "Downtown at Knickerbocker, we heard the news that Pierpont Morgan was coming to the rescue."

"The Old Man won't save any of you," said Homer. "He's too smart a capitalist to throw good money after bad."

"Oh, yes, he was about to arrive." Yuli looked to Jacob for confirmation.

"The meat has touched the vegetables, Mina. You shouldn't leave preparation in the *schwartze's* hands." Natalie lowered her fork and rearranged her scarves.

Mina turned a bright pink. "Neither your soup nor the cabbage touched the brisket, Natalie. It's kosher *and* vegetarian."

"It's perfect, Mama." Tillie turned to Natalie. "Delia is part of the family, Aunt Natalie. We won't hear anything that isn't kind said about her."

"Bravo, Sis, you've developed consciousness at last." Homer clapped his hands.

"Brother, you're as rude as can be. Don't make Mama sad."

"We're fine, dear." Mina gave Tillie's little hand a squeeze. "We're perfectly fine. If everyone will have a little more brisket, I'll be perfectly content." She looked at Homer who passed his plate for a second helping. If only they remain quiet, Mina uttered a silent prayer and rang the bell.

Delia carried in the *pflaumenkuchen* alight in flaming brandy close enough to Natalie to risk singeing the feathery scarves.

"Delia, what a divine dessert! A ten-gun salute!" Eddie made a three-cornered Admiral's hat of his starched napkin and clapped his hands.

"A masterpiece!" Yuli tasted the *kuchen*. "I've never known it so drenched in brandy. Natalie, dear, do try this."

Natalie needed no urging. She lowered her head and didn't look up until she wiped up the sugared brandy off the plate with her fingers.

"Delia gets all the credit," said Mina.

"Slavery is a frame of mind as well as an institution," Homer said.

"Do you want a second helping of *kuchen* or not?" Delia pronounced the German with such emphasis that Tillie burst out in a giggle.

Jacob slammed his fist on the table. "Son, you will eat your *kuchen* and leave. I've had enough of your socialist nonsense for the evening. Go before I lose my temper."

"Jacob!" Mina glanced between them. "Homer, apologize to your father."

"I will not. I spoke the truth and have nothing to apologize for." Homer picked up a piece of the *kuchen,* and putting it into his pocket, turned to leave. "Thank you, Mother, thank you, Delia. Dinner was as good as usual. I'm tempted to call it The Last Supper."

---

As Mina set out cards for Hearts, she felt temporary peace descending at last. Could anything be so terribly wrong when a brisket turned out moist inside its crust and satisfied everyone? If only she could get out of her dress and go to bed without another mention of banks or finances, she'd be happy. Homer had eaten seconds. He was such an impetuous boy who didn't understand the importance of a solid foundation, of buying fine Persian carpets, Biedermeyer furniture, ormolu-framed mirrors. She looked with pleasure at two Louis XVII chairs that had been an extravagant purchase at the time but now seemed a solid investment that gave Mina a sense of security.

# THREE

## NOVEMBER, 1907

ALFRED HORNTHALL STOOD ON a riser facing Madison Avenue where he could see shoppers hurrying past. The November afternoon, already losing light from the shadows cast by buildings across the avenue, hadn't turned cold enough to freeze puddles into ice but on the sidewalk, pedestrians stepped gingerly around slush.

"I'm not a man who likes being right at another's expense," Alfred said to his tailor, Abraham Cogansky. "I gave my clients every possible warning. Those who listened got out of copper. But Greenbaum and his cousin Sachs adored their copper. They would not be separated from it. There's only so much a broker can do to save headstrong individuals from themselves."

"Please turn, Mr. Hornthall," Abraham requested.

From his vantage point, Alfred saw himself in the long mirror as if he were accustomed to looking down on the world. But even at this moment of standing tall, Alfred knew that when he stepped off his perch, he'd be the same slight man, scarcely five feet three inches tall, a man dependent on his tailor's skill to make his left pant leg match evenly with his right. A lift in the left shoe helped correct the difference, and Cogansky, with his clever adjustments, would do the rest.

As he looked down on the thick, brown curls that covered Cogansky's head, Alfred couldn't help taking pleasure in the knowledge that he'd raised the young tailor's fortunes with his own. Abraham Cogansky, a first-generation Russian immigrant who spoke broken

English, had talent and dedication to his craft, but without Alfred's assistance, the tailor would still be living in a tenement on Mott Street and working for a miserly boss. Now Cogansky, the father of two, had a new business and residence above the shop on Madison and 50th Street. *Mr. Abraham Cogansky, Tailor to the Discerning Gentleman* read the sign painted in gold on the glass door. Alfred liked nothing better than hearing Jewish success stories: how the Guggenheims had peddled lace, shoe polish and lye across the west, and how the scion of the fabled Seligman clan had started doing books for a coal merchant in Pennsylvania. Many enterprising men had begun with thimble and thread, and it was a pleasure, as well as an obligation, to help those less fortunate than oneself.

"Tell me about the family, Abraham. How is your wife finding the shops around here? Are things costing too much?"

"My Bella she goes downtown for shopping. Thanks by you, Mr. Hornthall, in our window comes freshlich air. Children sleep good. No more cough cough."

Alfred nodded approval at Bella's economies and the children's health. As Cogansky measured and pinned, Alfred felt as though he wouldn't be showing too much self-satisfaction if he recounted the events of the October morning that had led to great changes in their lives.

"Jacob Greenbaum, who I recommended come to you in your former place of employment because I knew he would be satisfied with your work…"

"Mr. Hornthall, you sent to me gentlemen Greenbaum and Sachs. I am thankful."

"Greenbaum and Sachs alas, the very gentlemen I could not save from themselves. In all confidence, just between us, Abraham, it's likely they won't be coming for new suits in the near future. Greenbaum chose me to handle his family's investments despite my lack of personal charm. I did my best to prevent his folly that brought them ruin."

The tailor shook his head as if to deny Alfred's absence of charm.

"I know my drawbacks. Over time, Greenbaum and Sachs did very well, that is to say, they enjoyed a considerable rise in their portfolio on which I kept a close watch. Greenbaum knew the business of undergarments but not speculative markets."

"Good dresser, Mr. Sachs. Always wanting best." Cogansky managed to speak and keep tailor pins in his mouth.

"Ulysses Sachs. There's a man who, below the neck, is a paragon of fashion, but in the head, not a grain of practical sense. He likes to play the American hero in his white tennis sweaters. Not that they'd let him in the New York Athletic Club—none of us allowed, Abraham, whether we're uptown or downtown, we're Jews to the Gentiles who don't want us in their clubs. I gather Sachs played a good game of tennis but that's all over and done with and he has only himself and Greenbaum to blame. Still, as a professional, I deeply regret their losses that I tried my best to avert."

As Cogansky worked, Alfred's thoughts returned to the value of copper shares that on Monday, October 13th, an unseasonably hot morning, began rising like a volatile gas reacting to the weather. Alfred had only reached the entrance to his office on Broad Street when he'd been accosted by a half dozen sweating men pushing each other to get close to him, noisily demanding he sell them his United Copper for which they'd pay him fifty-five dollars a share. He wouldn't know the reasons for copper's meteoric rise and fall until the full story came out several days later, but from the instant he'd been accosted by the wild-eyed crowd, he'd suspected shenanigans were afoot.

"Fifty-seven," a short man yelled. "Fifty-eight," shouted another. The buyers didn't just ask, they demanded. All around, men in shirtsleeves were grabbing United Copper shares from each other's hands, nearly coming to blows as if they were sheaves of gold rather than stock certificates. "I've no shares," Alfred protested as he slipped past them.

Alfred now changed his weight on his pedestal. "I knew there was a crooked scheme afoot," Alfred said aloud to Cogansky.

"Big *megillah*." The tailor moved Alfred around to face the street.

"*Megillah*...yes, that's the word." Alfred's mother had mumbled Yiddish to herself as she trimmed kosher meats in her delicatessen but the old language was not for Alfred, Bella said, because he was to mix with higher people.

"Once I suspected a scheme unfolding, I called Greenbaum and Sachs to come to our office. I'd bought their copper shares in the thirty dollar range and at Greenbaum's insistence, added more on margin over the summer. That morning, when they arrived, I told them if they sold at sixty dollars, they'd be truly rich men."

Alfred now remembered his feeling that the gleam in Greenbaum's eye had been akin to the madness he'd seen on the street.

"Greenbaum defended the uses of copper for conducting electricity and all else the metal was good for. Sachs had an even more other-worldly attachment. 'Copper is alchemical gold,' he said. 'And just as uncertain,' I answered. 'Value of product has nothing to do with speculation on it.' I did all I could to protect them from themselves."

"Mr. Hornthall, have no *schuld*, no guilt. Please, do not move."

"The heart of the matter, Abraham, is that men who speculate on stocks only want to hear of winners. No one likes a naysayer, the deliverer of a bitter pill. To top it off, as I was warning Greenbaum and Sachs, my partners, Singer and Lasley, barged into my office waving United Copper shares."

How fresh in Alfred's mind the next half hour remained, as if it had been only yesterday. "I bought them for sixty-five dollars!" Singer had shouted. Elman Lasley shouted that he'd also procured shares. When Greenbaum related Alfred's advice to sell, Singer and Lasley had hit their foreheads with their palms as if they'd heard the most outrageous news, as if President Coolidge himself had died.

"My god, don't listen to Hornthall! Copper will go over one hundred by tomorrow and you'll be crying tears of remorse if you sell before then," Lasley had said.

"When a stock is rising, it's like a cake. You don't stamp your feet or you bring it down." Singer did a little bit of tiptoe routine. "A boy who cries wolf doesn't get cake," echoed Lasley, a larger man, sweating heavily. "Hornthall doesn't understand success. He's good as a bear but constitutionally, you see by his constitution, he's no bull."

They had all laughed at the reference to Alfred's small stature. Singer offered Greenbaum and Sachs a cigar to celebrate their good fortune so that the office filled with smoke and Alfred began coughing.

"It takes a man to make his way among the charging bulls," Lasley grinned.

"We'll handle your account," Lasley told Greenbaum and Sachs, while moving Alfred toward the door. "Hornthall, you sound terrible. Take care of yourself. On the way home, stop and eat some oysters at Sherry's. They'll give you vigor." He heard Lasley laugh. "We'll get rid of the invalid and place our orders as soon as we can."

"We'll buy up as much copper as we can get our hands on," Singer had said.

Alfred hadn't closed the door behind him when he heard Lasley make a reference to Bob Cratchit laboring on Christmas Eve while everyone else enjoyed the goose.

"That goose," Alfred now said aloud to Cogansky, "was soon truly cooked."

"Shoulders like statue. I work on arms." The tailor stood back to view Alfred.

Why hadn't he gone back inside to say that Bob Cratchit was an honest man who supported his family and saved his son's life through his labors! But he knew that there was another meaning in the reference: Tiny Tim, Cratchit's son, was lame like himself. How they had insulted him! Alfred cheeks burned. He slumped for a moment but at Cogansky's touch, straightened up.

"What did I do then, Abraham?" Alfred gestured to a worn leather bag that looked more like it belonged to a country physician than a stockbroker. "In that satchel I had my shares of copper, that chameleon metallic element. When I reached the crowd on Broad Street, I sold every last United Copper share for sixty-eight dollars a share in cash. The men handed me wads of hundred-dollar bills and tried to kiss me in gratitude."

Alfred remembered how the pavement had seemed to move beneath him as his heart pounded in his ears. As he was fastening the clasps on the bag stuffed with cash, his eyes fell on a cigar, a fat Havana, gold band still intact, lying on the pavement. He'd wondered at the time what improvident man would leave an expensive Havana only partly smoked. A man who had just bought United Copper!

Alfred then took a cab to Pierpont Morgan's stronghold, National Bank of Commerce, where he deposited thirty thousand dollars in cash and gave an order to transfer his account from Knickerbocker Trust Company to Morgan's bank because he knew that the Heinze brothers had been using Knickerbocker to back whatever speculation was occurring.

By Wednesday, October 15, United Copper had fallen to ten dollars. By Thursday, the whole story came out in *The Wall Street Journal*. Alfred, who read the fine print to the very end of the article, learned that the Heinze brothers, formerly called Kings of Copper, had tried a "bear squeeze" to force up United Copper prices and gain majority ownership by ruining investors who'd shorted the shares and would then lose them with the rising prices. The plan had failed: for their greed, the Heinzes were caught in the unforgiving arms of their own squeeze and dragged other shareholders down with them. United Copper was now worth hardly more than the paper it was printed on.

The East Coast press had called the copper debacle the Rich Man's Panic as if it only affected New York bankers. But when the Heinze brothers' bank, Butte State Savings of Montana, declared insolvency, along with other western lending institutions, Alfred knew worse was to come. The Panic of October 1907 sent shock waves across the country; people lost life's savings. Within a month or two, without a miracle, Greenbaum and Sachs were going to lose the roofs over their heads.

Then only yesterday came a call he could not have predicted. Hermina Greenbaum, Jacob Greenbaum's wife, her voice sounding hesitant, asked for him.

"Mr. Hornthall, I hope you will be able to join us for our Friday night dinner a week from now. My daughter Tillie especially looks forward to seeing you again. She needs to see more young people these days. You do remember our Tillie?"

"Of course I remember Miss Greenbaum, who could forget her?" he replied.

Remember Tillie! The prettiest girl of all the crowd, with green eyes and a halo of golden-red curls that always made Alfred's heart seem to stand still when he saw her across a room. Tillie Greenbaum with whom he never dared to speak.

"Then you'll come? We light candles once the sun is set," Mina said.

"Thank you very much, Mrs. Greenbaum. I shall look forward to Friday."

# FOUR

THERE WAS NO WAY that Jacob could avoid the bouquet that stood in a large vase on the mantelpiece over the fireplace. The lilies assaulted him with their aggressive orange color and nearly sickening odor. Hornthall's face and the flowers made Jacob think of a funeral director rubbing his hands as he oversaw the remains of a family who'd perished together in some catastrophe. Only Hornthall didn't rub his hands together, Jacob had to admit. He was the soul of modesty—a Uriah Heap of humility.

When Homer joined them for supper, Jacob had his misery doubled—Alfred and his own son at the same table. Yuli had sent his apologies for the family, and since Eddie's departure for California, light-heartedness had gone out of their family suppers.

"I prefer a brisket, you know that, Mother," Homer said when Delia served Dover sole. "Something you can get your teeth into. I hope we're not so down and out that I can't expect roasts ever again. It's not Sabbath without the brisket I count on all week."

"Mr. Hornthall likes fish." Mina gave Alfred her attention.

"The Sole is perfectly prepared, Mrs. Greenbaum," said Alfred.

"I for one don't like variety," Homer said, pulling a bone from the fillet and laying it on the table cloth. "The bourgeoisie should remain fossilized in their habits. Habit is the best thing about you, Mother, so why turn to fish like some Irish penitent?"

"The way you eat is disgusting." Tillie made a moue with her little mouth.

"Children, please be polite. We have a guest." Mina frowned.

"Up goes the bourgeoisie flag in alarm. To the gates!" Homer brandished his fork.

After Delia took away the platter of fish, she brought in a date strudel that Jacob ate to the last crumb. Mina relaxed until she looked up and saw Tillie licking the serving spoon before her brother could grab it. Fortunately Homer ignored his sister. Everyone's table manners were suffering, Mina observed. She wondered whether being on your way down turned you slovenly, while rising improved your manners. Alfred had snow white cuffs while Homer's were tattered and grey.

"Thank you, Delia. Another beautiful Sabbath gives us strength for the week ahead." Mina closed her eyes as Jacob snuffed out candles.

Homer stood up. "Not a bad fish per se. Thank you, Mother and Delia. Pleased to make the acquaintance of a survivor, Hornthall."

"Likewise, Mr. Greenbaum." Alfred also rose to leave. "Columbia is a fine law school. I have my degree from Pennsylvania though I've never practiced the law."

"You don't say. Next week I hope we'll have brisket, Mother," said Homer.

"Alfred, I hope you have no other plans for Thanksgiving coming soon."

"I don't want to impose," Alfred answered softly.

Mina patted his arm. "We'll be disappointed if you don't come."

"Thank you, I am honored," Alfred replied.

Mina saw Alfred to the door. "I'm feeling more secure every day in my new position at Josephthal, Mrs. Greenbaum. We are allied with Loeb. The atmosphere is sober. In time, I can look forward to becoming a partner, even a seat on the Exchange."

"I'm sure you will achieve what you work for, Alfred. You understand matters we cannot possibly grasp. I knew Mr. Lasley and Mr. Singer slightly. I gather these gentlemen lacked the gravity needed for these times, a gravity that you have, Alfred."

"You over-praise me. Your husband cannot help but resent..."

"Now, now," Mina patted Alfred's arm and removed a bit of lint from the jacket. "Jacob will come to understand in time. Our son provides him constant upset."

———

Jacob sat alone in the parlor where he poured himself the last drops of brandy from the crystal decanter. How dull drinking without friends, he thought; even his wife seemed to be avoiding his company.

In the kitchen, Delia washed plates while Mina dried. When dishes and platters were put away, they sat at the kitchen table with cups of coffee as Delia smoked her small, thin cigars called cigarillos that gave off a cinnamon aroma.

"The breading on the Sole was perfect—such a light crust makes the difference." Mina breathed in a whiff of Delia's smoke that she didn't mind. "My dearest husband doesn't know coconuts about household expenses, how much we need each week. I was accustomed to buying the best without counting pennies though I never squandered, and we didn't waste. How long will credit last? Will I be able to buy a Thanksgiving goose?"

"Times hard but you're a lady. Shops be trusting you."

"I plan to sell the two Louie chairs, some jewelry that Jacob won't miss, the clocks, and pay you what I can through the end of this awful year. We'll have goose for Thanksgiving and make the dumplings from the *schmaltz,* just as we always do. Delia."

Delia exhaled a long puff and put her cigarillo out on a saucer.

"I can't bring it up directly with my husband but we both know Tillie has to marry a man who can provide." Mina began to cry quietly. "Eddie is out of the picture, and I must confess that in the circumstances of today, it's best he's in California."

Delia reached over and dabbed a tear on Mina's cheek with a clean towel.

"Now, now. Miss Tillie loves her Eddie. She surely does. She also loves her pretty clothes and won't like being poor and she knows it."

"Can you believe an ordinary metal like copper could ruin so many lives? If it had been gold, I'd understand better."

"There are mysteries. I watch people, see them tending to one way or other."

"What do you mean by that? If you're an oracle, Delia, I need to hear it."

"I don't know oracle, Missus, but I know that Miss Tillie and Mr. Eddie were only fluttering their wings with love like two butterflies. They get over it. It's Mr. Yuli I worry for. He don't look good."

"I know, I worry also about Yuli and Natalie was no help going off as she has and leaving him with Sylvia. I'm sorry they weren't with us tonight. I'll bring him strudel in the morning and insist on Thanksgiving. I won't have them by themselves. But back to my previous thoughts. After the first of the year, I don't know how I'll pay you, Delia."

"Don't need a troubled mind 'bout me. We come to that day when it comes."

"You need your money just like everyone else."

"Missus, 'bout Mr. Eddie and Miss Tillie. You never worry you leave the young ones alone, spring juices in their veins?"

"Do you mean some sort of advantage Eddie might take? Why, no, I didn't, except that he might decide to rearrange my furniture or take a scissors to the drapery."

"That all? You never catch them doing what come natural?" Delia peered into the burning ash remaining in the saucer as if consulting it for evidence.

"Eddie is such a sweet boy and a wonderful dancer. I didn't worry."

"He be a twenty-one-years-old man, Missus."

"But he's family. If I worry, it's about poor Homer's frustration— you know what I mean. It makes him contrary. Eddie is different."

"Homer will do fine once he settles."

"I only hope I live that long," Mina sighed. "What is your impression of Mr. Hornthall? He certainly appreciates our cooking."

Delia leaned closer and looked at Mina with her mysterious eyes the color of yellow smoke. "Needs fattening up. Has eyes only for Miss Tillie."

"As I said…"

"Been obvious to me for years…"

"Obvious for years? We've only just had Alfred to supper. What is so obvious to you, Delia?"

"That Mr. Eddie not be girl crazy. Mr. Alfred, he smitten with Miss Tillie. Big difference there, Miss Mina."

"Alfred won't ever replace Eddie in Tillie's affections."

Delia coughed. "That wasn't my meaning, not all of it."

"I can't guess what your meaning might be, Delia. You're too cryptic for me tonight. Who wouldn't have eyes for Tillie? Of course, someone else might turn up at one of the parties she'll be going to. Tillie doesn't appreciate Alfred as he does her, but that can change as long as she's provided for."

# FIVE

A COLD FRONT ARRIVED the third week in November, dark clouds that made the low sky as grim as the news of bankruptcies and business failures across the country. As Jacob and Yuli walked down Fifth Avenue into the Park at 86th Street, Jacob offered his cousin a hot chestnut from the warm bag in his hands. Yuli shook his head. Since the Panic, Yuli's healthy complexion had become sallow and deep circles puddled under his eyes. He'd lost at least ten pounds from his slim, athletic frame, while Jacob had gained weight because Mina's cooking was his only refuge from fear filling his chest.

J. P. Morgan, seated beside his son-in-law in the black brougham drawn by a white horse, had indeed arrived on Wall Street where he was met by crowds of hopeful, cheering men and woman calling out *We are saved! We are saved!* And though the twenty-five million dollars Morgan and other bankers raised to prevent the stock market and most banks from total collapse, the financier refused to meet with Charles Barney after the accountants' full report of Knickerbocker Trust revealed insufficient capital reserves. On November 15, Barney, whose glamour and social connections had made Knickerbocker Trust Company the most sought-after institution for investors, shot himself in his Fifth Avenue apartment.

Yuli now did something that shocked Jacob: he removed his black and gold Club scarf from his neck and hung it on a low-hanging, bare branch.

"I won't be needing this. I resigned membership in City Athletic," Yuli said.

"Why did you do that? It's a Jewish club, isn't it?"

"Oh yes, Solomon Guggenheim purchased land at 54th and built City Athletic just for us, athletic Jews."

"Why would you resign?"

"Guggenheim is adamant about collecting fees. You're out if you miss a payment. I can't pay my bill." Yuli kicked at a fallen branch. "If I have nowhere to play squash, what's the meaning of life?"

"Cousin, you have your children, and your other athletic interests."

"I've made up my mind. I'll tell members I'm moving out of town."

"Sylvia told us that Eddie will be staying in California through the holidays," said Jacob. "Is there truth in what you just said, that you'll be moving with them?"

"Not yet, though Natalie has written that she will not return before New Year's."

"Natalie will be leaving you alone through the holidays?"

"Sylvia promises to stay with me. I can't answer so many questions, Jacob."

They reached the lake and sat down on a bench to watch children float their sailboats in the stiff breeze.

Yuli looked up into the leafless trees. "I regret that I couldn't buy a Panama hat like the one Eddie purchased to go to California. He looked like a native of Hollywood. He bought enough luggage for a Rajah. It was great fun."

"Where did he get the money for all this outfitting?"

"I believe he charged at Abercrombie & Fitch. They accepted our credit."

"Won't you be humiliated when the bill comes?"

Yuli shrugged. "Eddie is clever at such things. You know, he's a magician. I think he's just right for the flickers."

"That may be, but you and I will have to think realistically, without magic."

"No magic, no sport make a dull man, cousin. Shall Sylvia and I live like mice?"

"Mice! You and Sylvia will eat every meal with us. No one is going hungry, though count yourself lucky you're not dining with us tonight. Mina has invited Alfred Hornthall for the second Sabbath

140

meal in two weeks and for Thanksgiving, imagine!"

"I warned you the small broker fancied your Tillie."

"Yes, you were right, that little clerk has designs." As he spoke, Alfred Hornthall's name pounded in Jacob's ears, giving him the same kind of headache he'd had the previous Friday when he'd found Mina in their bedroom sorting through jewelry at her dressing table.

When he'd asked her, "Why are your jewels out, my dear?" she'd replied, "I was selecting what to wear for supper tonight." She turned away so he couldn't see what they both knew was not a truth. "Our young broker says…"

"Alfred Hornthall is no longer our broker!" Jacob roared. "The brokerage house itself has failed. I see no reason to socialize with him."

"I didn't invite Mr. Hornthall for business but to share Sabbath, and I've learned that he has new employment with a good bond house, Josephthal & Company. He's told me he's fond of chicken which is good news because poultry costs less this time of year."

Jacob's face reddened. He knew that Hornthall had made a killing selling his copper as he'd advised them to do. Jacob found this a betrayal even as he knew his feelings made little sense. How had Mina come by the information that Hornthall had a new employer? Clearly, she was keeping essential news, more than the cost of poultry, to herself.

"Mr. Hornthall has sent the beautiful flowers," Mina said.

"Too gaudy for my taste. My dear, I suspect the man is taking advantage of the situation. You're far too trusting to see it."

"We have often shared the Sabbath with those who are alone."

"Hornthall is alone for a reason. He's a friendless, joyless sort of man. All brain and no social graces. No small talk. All facts and figures with him. He has enjoyed your cooking already so I do not know why you invite him again."

"He needs bringing out and Tillie is good at that. She says he has nice eyes."

"A frog's eyes, behind specs," Jacob said under his breath. "Damn it all, why did you not ask me before inviting Hornthall the first time?"

"Please, don't swear on the Sabbath, Jacob." Mina looked as if she were about to cry. "I need your help, not your doubting."

Jacob knew that his wife was unused to going against his wishes, which meant that she understood the serious nature of their situation.

"It's up to our daughter if she wants to see a young man who is in a position to advise us in difficult times. I can make economies when I have to but they will not be enough to bring us through this situation. I'm as unhappy as you are."

Jacob lowered his eyes. Never in their married lives had Mina spoken this way but he could not deny the truth of her words. Their situation was desperate. Chicken leg and Hornthall went together, Jacob thought. Man looks like a plucked bird.

Mina picked up her strand of cultured salt-water pearls, his gift for their twentieth wedding anniversary, and asked him to fasten them. Each pearl glowed with nacre and looked as large as the oysters they'd grown in. Jacob's heart swelled with remorse. He leaned forward and kissed the moist spot where Mina's chignon touched her pinkish skin. She sighed and leaned back against him. "You're a good husband, Jacob."

---

Jacob realized he hadn't heard what Yuli had been saying to him. "What was that?" he asked his cousin.

"I was saying that we have our life insurance, Jacob. We might fall on our petards to save our families." Yuli brushed a lock of his greying hair from his forehead.

"Yuli, don't be joking. You'll return to the Athletic Club if I have to speak to Guggenheim myself." He retrieved Yuli's scarf from the tree and handed it to him.

---

During supper, the three young people, Sylvia, Tillie and Alfred, chatted along so companionably that Jacob didn't need to make conversation. Alfred praised the salmon mousse and when she drew him out on the subject, Mina found him remarkably knowledgeable about fish and was glad that he appreciated the pound of rosy Norwegian salmon with dill and cream. He was smartly-dressed in a well-tailored dark suit of English or Italian wool. Feeding him for a month would improve his looks, Mina thought, and if his cheeks were less bony, his nose would appear less prominent. Behind the lenses, his eyes were a pleasant brown and he had remarkably long lashes, like a deer. She didn't know where Jacob had gotten the impression of frog's eyes.

Following roasted chicken and Delia's rice dish, Mina rose from the table to bring the dessert. She wanted to make sure that Jacob understood that his favorite strudel from upstate Rome apples, topped with marmalade and sugared cake crumbs, had been prepared specially for him.

"You made me very welcome on the Sabbath, and the meal was as delicious as one could wish for. Thank you." Alfred rose from the table before there was any awkwardness about retiring to the drawing room.

"I'll see you to the door, Mr. Hornthall," Mina said. "I was a bit concerned that my cook's exotic spices would make the hen difficult to digest, but she always insists on adding her bit of this and that. One never knows if a guest has a delicate stomach."

"Not at all, I found the meal wonderful. You've put a pound on me at least."

Then, as Mina was preparing to say goodnight, Alfred paused and seemed to wish a tete-a-tete.

"The source of my fish expertise," he said, "comes from helping my mother buy at the markets for the delicatessens we owned in Philadelphia. She never wanted me to get my hands smelly but sometimes she needed me, especially when Father was ill."

"Are they still living?" Mina suppressed her surprise that his parents were in trade.

"My father passed on ten years ago. Mother went to the shops almost until the day she died. They had three locations and did an excellent business."

"Does that mean that neither parent is alive? Are you all alone in the world?"

He nodded and touched his chest with his hand. "I especially miss my mother, blessed be her memory."

Mina reached forward and covered Alfred's hand with her own.

"Thank you once again, Mrs. Greenbaum, for the fine supper and good company. You know that when I managed your husband's account, I urged him to sell."

Mina held Alfred's hand to keep him from leaving. "I'm aware of the losses and that we must endeavor to curtail our living expenses. I shall do my best but I worry about the effect on our Tillie."

She looked down and so did Alfred, as if both regarding their shoes. Then Mina recovered and removed her hand.

"Forgive me for worrying to you out loud. I should not have done so."

"Please, I consider your trust an honor and I confess I envy Miss Greenbaum for having such a *gemutlich* family," he said.

"Thank you. To tell you frankly, I can't imagine my little girl without someone to provide for her in the manner to which she's accustomed. I'm afraid we've spoiled our Tillie—but then who wouldn't spoil such a darling? I've promised her a trip to Paris, just the two of us, for her eighteenth birthday." A silence followed. "I mean, before she is a grown woman and ready to begin her own life. Now I'll have to break my word."

"I don't think there's anything wrong in spoiling a daughter as charming as Mathilda. I'm sure I would do the same were I ever so blessed to have a child." Again, Alfred looked down, color rising to his cheeks. "Josephus avoids the type of jeopardy we recently experienced. There won't be such unpleasant surprises. I'll have security."

"It doesn't bother me at all that you come from a culinary background. We come from corsets and underwear."

---

Two days after the Sabbath, Mina and Tillie sat in the kitchen over coffee. Sunday was Delia's day off.

"Tillie, my love, we'll go shopping for new dresses for the Hanukkah parties. You never know who you'll meet among the young people who love dancing as you do."

"Why would I want to go when Eddie isn't there?" Tillie tossed her curls but the next moment, her eyelashes became moist. "He hasn't sent a word from California. I keep wondering when he'll come back but no one seems to know. I hope that he doesn't see Alfred's bouquets. Eddie despises showy flowers."

"Alfred is generous. He doesn't stint."

"He's buying out florists on Park Avenue. I'd be amazed if there were any left."

"He's a little overeager to make an impression. But Tillie, what about the new style of dress, with the wide, deep arm holes, that's just come in?" Mina buttered a scone to hand to Tillie. "You know, cut low under the arm."

"It's lower in front and drapes a little." Tillie made a half moon with her hands. "They say it's the Japanese influence. I saw a dress in a mauve color in the window at Bonwits."

"Mauve will be perfect. I can see it on you as you dance."

"Alfred is short," said Tillie. "You need a taller partner to whirl a wide skirt."

"Eddie wasn't tall."

"Eddie didn't need to be tall. He was a perfect dancer."

# Six

ONCE AGAIN, ALFRED STOOD before Abraham Cogansky's mirror to have another suit fitted because he didn't want to give Hermina Greenbaum the impression that he had only one article of good clothing for the holiday season.

*Another suit, what was wrong with the good one you had made just yesterday? What is this for extravagance?*

These words seemed to come out of the mirror he was facing though he'd not moved his lips. The voice he was hearing was his mother's, blessed be she in memory.

*Not that I want to criticize the rich man you have become, but for how long will you have money if you go on spending without putting by?*

*I didn't have the first suit made yesterday, Mother. I'm going to evening parties in some grand houses, and you'd like me well-dressed,* Alfred answered in his head.

"This suit, best Italian wool silk blend. Not over hot, not cold. Summer, man sveats much," said Abraham.

"I don't perspire even in summer. Mother always said that my glands were weaker than normal."

"Don't say so, Mr. Hornthall. God bless our healthful children."

Alfred's cheeks reddened, not only at Abraham's words but also because he'd been thinking what his mother would be saying about his feelings, his intentions, toward a girl from the Upper East Side of Manhattan, a girl who hadn't ever taken care of a home because she had maids for every need. Alfred's mother, Dora Fishbein Hornthall, would not have approved of her son's choice of Mathilda Hornthall. Dora had never moved from her small old-fashioned apartment in

146

South Philadelphia, though she could have afforded the north side when she opened the third delicatessen. It went without saying that she'd never had a cleaning woman set foot in the apartment. *What do I need they break things?* Dora guarded her savings and her hopes for her only son. She wished him to marry a sensible girl from a professional family.

Alfred had never given his mother cause to worry. He fulfilled her wish for him to enter the legal profession, but the summer he graduated from Pennsylvania University Law School, he took a summer apprenticeship on Wall Street that Dora advised against. She wished him closer to home. From the moment he had stood beneath the great windows and skylight of the New York Exchange and felt its powerful energy, Alfred wanted to be nowhere else. He had felt the heartbeat of the country pulsing through the ticker tape, pounding on the board as money flowed to the railroads crossing the country, financing the shipping lines around the globe, every hour of every day. Before the summer was out, Alfred had decided to join the business of Isaac Singer and Elman Lasley, two young men who had opened a brokerage office on Broad Street.

*This will not be for your good, Alfred.* Dora considered New York City flim flam where dishonesty and extravagance was rewarded, a city full of *luftmenschen,* souls who lived on dreams and air and would fall as hard and swiftly as they had risen.

As Alfred now looked in the lengthening mirror, he didn't know if it was love he felt for Mathilda Greenbaum or only an effect like high altitude. She dazzled him. In that dazzle, he did uncharacteristic things like having two suits made and ordering flowers every time he passed a florist because Tillie made his eyes love color. He didn't know if love was a vision of roses and copper curls, a tinkling of laughter, a whirl of little feet in satin slipper. Perhaps it was more like riding a carousel with brightly painted horses going around and around, every time circling closer to a golden ring that in reaching for, he risked falling off the rising and dipping steed.

"Abraham, you've more practical understanding of women than I have." Alfred looked around him. The shop was entirely neat, not a speck of dust, nor a dropped pin on the carpet. The mirrors were polished to a gleaming shine. The tailor's wife must be a loyal, hard-working and efficient woman who kept all this immaculate.

"I know only Bella, good wife, of women," answered Cogansky.

"I want to know what you say about a man overreaching himself."

"Over...?"

"A man who reaches for higher than he is expected to reach."

"Oi, a *fonfer*," said Cogansky. "You are speaking for Mr. Green-baum's daughter? Uptown 75th Avenue people."

Alfred's cheeks reddened. "You have guessed. How did you know?" When no answer came from the younger man, Alfred admitted the tailor had guessed. "I think of my mother. She would say I am a *fonfer*, the kind of man she had no patience with."

"Mr. Hornthall, you no *fonfer*. You do things good. " Abraham reached into his pocket from which he drew what Alfred realized was a finger of salt and threw it over his shoulder to ward off any evil eye.

"Greenbaum and Sachs townhouses will go on the block next month if their payments aren't made. I understand Mrs. Greenbaum's concern for stability."

"Move arms. Up, down, like wedding dance." Cogansky stepped back to eye the trouser lengths, pulling down the shorter cuff leg to match the longer one.

"Don't say wedding. I fear...I fear this," Alfed placed his hand over his heart, "is going too fast and high, like the day of the copper madness."

Abraham again threw a few grains of salt, this time for good fortune, and Alfred squared his shoulders and stood as evenly as he could before the tailor's mirror. He'd begun swimming at the YMCA. Though he didn't love sport or getting water up his nose, the exercise and a better brace strengthened the muscles in his foot and leg so he walked almost normally.

"Not that I expect Jacob Greenbaum ever to say, 'You were right, Hornthall, you tried to save me.' I don't expect we'll ever hear those words spoken to me."

"I say other words, Mr. Hornthall. I say *mazel tov* and *gluck*."

# SEVEN

JACOB WAS SENT OUT on errands the day that men came from the auction house. Mina stood watching the carriage recede carrying the caned-back, half-settee with green velvet upholstery, always her husband's favorite.

Mina and Delia themselves carried down two armchairs from Homer's bedroom. Then, with cash in hand, they took a cab to shop for a goose and all the trimmings. Delia would chop apples, raisins, chestnuts and prunes for the stuffing. The goose liver in dumplings that accompanied the fat bird would float amid a rich gravy. They bought brandy and would use a half-bottle for the *Linzertorte* dessert.

"Tillie always loves Thanksgiving." Mina looked out the window of the carriage and sighed as they passed the Plaza Hotel on their way home. "And right away comes Hanukkah with dancing for young people. Tillie's as light on her feet as a ballerina. I told her, 'In your new dress, you'll be the prettiest girl at the party.' Her answer, Delia? 'You want to show me off like you showed off the Louies so someone will buy me?' I never expected such words from my daughter."

---

On Thanksgiving morning, after the goose was pricked, trussed and placed in the hot oven, Mina asked Delia for brandy. "Just a half cup for the crust for our torte."

Delia returned with an empty bottle. "Nothing more than sherry be here."

"Oh, dear, Jacob must have found it and the poor man needed it more than we do. I'm remembering a Jewish saying about goose,

Delia. 'If poor people dined on rich people's goose, they'd have luck the next year.'"

"I won't mind that happening to me one year and I'm no Jew," said Delia.

---

Mina smiled encouragingly at Alfred when he accepted second help-ings. After the meal, when they got up to stretch, Mina made sure that Alfred and Tillie were alone a moment.

"Your mother makes me feel welcome in your home, Miss Greenbaum."

"Mama likes you, Mr. Hornthall. She feeds you too much, I'm afraid."

"I am a bit overstuffed, Miss Greenbaum, because your mother is such a fine cook and I appreciated every dish, perhaps a bit too much."

"You must call me Tillie, Alfred. We're friends." Tillie extended her hand until her small fingers lay warmly in his palm. Color rose from Alfred's cheeks to his ears.

"Shall I see you at the parties coming up? I'm not much of a dancer but I imagine you love the modern styles of dance," he said.

"I do. I'll enjoy meeting you next week, Alfred. I'm sorry you have to go out in this weather. Don't get wet. It's pouring out there."

"I have my umbrella. Were the flowers to your liking? I don't know which are your favorites so I leave it to the florist to make the selection."

"They are beautiful but too extravagant."

"Not at all, not at all. I'll say goodnight then."

Tillie waved goodbye to Alfred who looked back for a final moment, almost slipping off the curb as rain drops bounced from his umbrella.

"Mr. Hornthall, Alfred, be careful," Tillie called out.

Mina patted Tillie's head. "The man doesn't even feel the rain, he's so happy you're kind to him. Give him the least encouragement and you'll have him wrapped around your little finger. Meanwhile, come in before you catch cold."

---

"An admirable home," Alfred said to Tillie the first night of Hanukah when they met in the ballroom of the Warburg mansion at 92nd and Fifth Avenue. For several nights each December, the wealthiest German Jewish families opened their doors to parties for children to run about spinning a *dredel* and young people to dance as musicians played from room to room.

"How do they do it? Not to ever worry about anything?" asked Tillie.

"The Warburgs are a great banking family," said Alfred. "They have made good financial decisions when others did not. But I wouldn't exchange the *gemütlich* atmosphere in your home for a mansion such as this. Are your mother and father here?"

"Papa brought Sylvia and me but he didn't stay. Mama is home with a cold. He didn't want to leave her alone."

"Please convey my wishes for a speedy recovery. Your mother works very hard."

"It's more the mental strain from worrying about my father and Yuli who has been particularly melancholy since his wife left for California."

"I'm sorry about the distress and appreciate your confidence," replied Alfred.

"Sylvia is here but I don't know where she went, probably the library, hidden behind a book. Listen, the music is starting." Tillie pointed him to the corner of the room where a Negro was playing on a piano.

Alfred extended his hand. "Would you care to dance?"

"Yes, thank you, I'd love to."

At dancing school, where his mother had sent him to overcome his shyness, he was always afraid of stepping on a girl's foot with his heavy corrective shoe. Would he be able to remember the steps now? Forward and back, side to side.

"Here." Tillie's arm came up and she brushed his neck with her warm little wrist, sending a tingly, hot sensation from his feet to his ears. He managed to place his hand on her waist with the greatest care, but once he was ready, the music seemed to have become louder and faster.

"I'll let others ask you to dance." Alfred stepped back. "They're serving refreshments from the buffet table. Shall I bring you a glass of champagne?"

"Please."

"I'll be right back."

Tillie watched Alfred walk out the door to a landing where servants were pouring drinks. He held his shoulders straight. The poor man, she thought, he's walking on eggs.

More guests entered the room, children pulling on their mothers' arms, eager to start spinning a *dredel* on the marble floors.

Alfred handed her a flute of champagne which she drank in three swallows.

"You're very thirsty. Please, drink mine."

Tillie accepted his flute and swallowed it down.

When a young blond man wearing red suspenders asked Tillie to dance, Alfred stepped aside and watched with admiration as the two did a dance he knew was called the Turkey Trot for the way the people lifted and lowered their arms like a flapping bird's wings. Alfred heard young women compliment Tillie on her dress and smiled at the attention she received.

At the end of the song, Alfred left the room and returned with more champagne for Tillie which she drank quickly before young people pulled her into a line to dance the Bunny Hop, their arms around each others' waists.

When the piano player stood up to take a break, the dancers headed for the supper table but Tillie stood leaning against a wall.

"I'm so terribly thirsty," she said. When Alfred thought she was heading toward a fountain in the next room, he followed her.

"How cool the water is," she said, dipping her fingers in and running them across her forehead.

"Tillie, you mustn't drink that water. It's not clean."

"Don't worry." She brought her fingers to her lips and sucked. "That's better. Now come, let's explore."

Tillie took his arm and he held her up. They wandered from room to room hung with velvet draperies and filled with brocaded settees and chairs. Tillie led on toward a far end of a corridor where the music sounded Oriental, and when they looked in, they saw children dancing around in circles, faster and faster. When the little ones fell down, they laughed and got up again. Tillie laughed, too, remembering as a child how she'd spun the *dredel* to this Eastern music.

"Would you like to sit somewhere?" Alfred now felt worried that Tillie might fall if he let go of her arm.

"I'm quite all right. If you would only find Sylvia to listen to the music."

Alfred brought Tillie a chair before he left to find Sylvia.

Tillie tried standing up and would have fallen if a tall man wearing a black cap had not steadied her. "Are you all right, Miss?" he asked.

"Music and champagne," she answered.

"Please, come sit."

Tillie did not resist. The room was still spinning though the children were gone.

The dark stranger had an accent and was dressed in black like a magician. He checked again to make sure she was seated and then returned to the podium at the end of the room. Tillie, trying to make her eyes focus and not see multiple musicians, saw him step onto a podium and pick up a musical instrument, a clarinet. Another man was playing a violin, a third pulling back and forth on an accordion.

The clarinet player swayed like a snake charmer until he seemed to float up above her on the high ceilings. She listened with closed eyes, feeling only the tears that moistened her cheeks.

"Why are you crying, Miss?" The clarinetist had returned and was kneeling before her. "Come to the window and breathe fresh air. Snow is falling."

"What is your name?" she asked.

"Shimon. And yours, Miss?"

"Tillie."

Shimon walked Tillie toward the windows, drew aside heavy drapery and opened a latch. Tillie felt snow on her cheeks and leaned out until Shimon pulled her back.

"You will get cold. Where are your people?"

Before she could try to answer his question, Tillie heard him called, "Shimon we're paid to play not be with guests."

"I go to play *O Chichornia* 'Russian Dark Eyes' for you. Please stay."

"Of course I'll stay. I'll be here forever. You are the man with the dark eyes."

Shimon then returned to the musicians who played faster and faster, bobbing and swaying. Suddenly Sylvia was there, shaking her shoulders.

"Where have you been? I've been looking for you. What's wrong, Tillie?"

"Nothing's wrong. It's so wonderful. I'm so happy. Listen to the dark eyes."

"Uncle Jacob is waiting. We have to get our coats and go. Alfred is worried."

"Alfred?" Tillie said his name but saw only Shimon. "I must say goodbye."

"To Alfred?" Sylvia asked.

"No, to him, I want to say goodbye to Shimon."

"Tillie, I can't make sense of what you're saying because you're drunk. Uncle Jacob is waiting in the snow. Come, this minute. No more nonsense."

Almost out the door, Tillie turned. She could still hear the Eastern music though she was sure Shimon was calling to her to stay. She tugged on Sylvia's arm. "Wait, a moment."

"The clarinetist? He's good, isn't he? He must have been classically trained in Russia and he's put a spell on you. They were known for that," Sylvia said.

"I want music." Tillie's words slurred as they stepped out into the snow.

"You've had enough music and champagne for one night. Uncle Jacob!" she called. "Come help me with Tillie."

Together, Jacob and Sylvia lifted Tillie into the carriage.

# EIGHT

THE MORNING AFTER THE Hanukkah party, Mina tried to get her daughter to drink lemon tea sweetened with honey but Tillie said her throat was too sore to swallow. Sylvia came close and whispered, "You've only yourself to blame. In front of all those people, Uncle Jacob and I had to lift you into the cab. You must have drunk two bottles of champagne. I never saw you like that."

"Don't remember. Can't talk. Hurts." She pointed to her throat.

"And I'm sorry for that. What did you and Mr. Clarinet talk about?"

"Kiss."

"Kiss! You let that stranger from Russia kiss you? No wonder you're ill."

Tillie's eyes closed and she smiled.

By that evening, Tillie's fever rose to 103. She tossed back and forth in the sheets, murmuring words Sylvia didn't want Mina to hear.

Mina called Dr. Katz who examined Tillie and prescribed Bayer aspirin and cold compresses, but that evening, Tillie still couldn't swallow even a sip to get down the medicine. Suddenly she sat up in bed and spoke.

"All his fingers were cut off."

As Mina leaned closer to hear, Tillie threw herself back on her pillow and seemed to be struggling with something she wanted to say. It was about what happened to a family in Russia before they'd escaped to America. In her mind, she remembered Shimon's words but she couldn't get them out of her mouth because it hurt too much. The Czar's army was coming to get his brother. His father grabbed his axe and forced Shimon's older brother outside. There was a scream

155

and then weeping. Shimon's father had chopped off two fingers of Moise's right hand to keep him from being taken to fight in the Czar's army. Shimon said that his father hadn't spared Moise for a sheep or a goat, something Tillie hadn't understood until now. She sat up and said the words, "Like Abraham and Isaac." Sylvia leaned closer but Tillie had closed her eyes.

Dr. Katz returned in the afternoon, and after taking Tillie's pulse and examining the swelling on both sides of her neck, he pried open her mouth to swab her tonsils. Outside the room, he told Mina he'd seen white spots and suspected Tillie had a pneumonococcal infection for which there was no known treatment. Mina was to keep ice packs on Tillie's throat and head to bring down swelling and fever.

"We can only wait and hope the crisis will pass. She's young and strong."

At the height of her fever, Tillie saw herself bundled in rugs and walking into the snow behind Shimon. She looked up but didn't recognize Alfred's large brown eyes behind spectacles, filled with worry.

"Tillie, please drink water and swallow aspirin," he said but she shook her head away, back and forth, preventing him from pressing a cold compress on her forehead.

"Be careful, Alfred. The infection may be contagious," Mina pulled Alfred back.

"I nursed my mother when she had an infection so I'm not afraid."

"You are a brave man," Mina said.

When Dr. Katz returned, he confirmed Mina's worries about contagion. There was infection in the hospitals so Tillie could not be moved there. "I fear she's in danger," he said. Tillie's breathing was labored.

Alfred took Dr Katz by his elbow and they walked out of the room to the hall.

"I've read of a new treatment against bacteria. You must get milk, boil hard, then inject a full syringe in the lower body to draw the bacteria." He blushed. "You inject in the buttocks. Of course I would not be in the room."

Dr. Katz scratched his head. "I've not heard of this but I don't know what else we can do, the situation is serious already and if the infection closes off the breathing…"

Mina boiled milk and came back, blowing to cool it down. Dr. Katz sent everyone but Mina and Delia from the room. They turned Tillie over while the doctor drew out a large hypodermic needle, filled it with the heated milk, and while Delia held Tillie on her stomach, he injected her with the syringe.

Tillie cried out but soon she slept because the doctor gave her a sedative.

"If this doesn't work, I will operate on her throat to open it for breathing. I'll be back in two hours after she's slept."

That night, Tillie woke up with such a throbbing behind that she couldn't turn over but she realized she could breathe more easily and managed to swallow a few sips of tea with aspirin. Dr. Katz seemed amazed but he warned Mina that her daughter wasn't out of danger.

"Most unconventional but I believe Mr. Hornthall's suggestion has had the desired effect of drawing the bacteria from your daughter's neck to her lower body." The doctor pulled up sheets and showed where Tillie's small behind was red and swollen.

"We can't be sure but I believe she's in less danger and we have this resourceful gentleman to thank." The doctor bowed to Alfred who had grown a stubble of reddish brown beard and had dark circles under his eyes. He lowered his head to deflect the gratitude of all around him.

"You have saved her. My gratitude has no bounds. Of what did your poor mother die?" Mina asked.

"An infection that began with a wound we didn't realize was serious," he said. "She washed her hands many times a day because she touched food but the poison in her blood advanced and there was nothing the doctors could do. I've been learning new methods are being developed to counter bacteria. Soon there will be medicines. I intend to help further this effort, in the financial realm of course. I'm not a scientist."

"Your poor mother." Mina was holding Alfred's hands. "You good dear man."

"Mother was a brave soul and a loving woman, blessed be her name," he said.

---

In the coming days as Tillie improved, Alfred left late in the afternoon and returned every morning clean shaven to be at Mina's side when she fed her daughter rice pudding with raisins. Color was returning to Tillie's cheeks and she winked at Alfred, or at least he thought she had.

"I don't know what we'd have done without Alfred," Mina kept saying.

A day later, Tillie's first words came when she saw reddish-gold strands of hair on her pillow. "Mama, I'm losing my hair."

"It's from the fever. It will grow back of course but I think we should call Madame Marlene, the hairdresser at the Plaza, to fashion a style for you."

---

Tillie sat up and Madame Marlene placed towels over her shoulders. Then the coiffeuse, a middle-aged French woman with chestnut hair loosely gathered at the top of her head, walked around Tillie's bed, clipping as she went, picking up stray curls. "You have beautiful hair and it will all come back. For now, hold the mirror for me. I've seen pictures in *Vogue* of short hair in Paris. So adorable on a young and pretty face as yours."

Tillie sat up straighter. "So I will be ahead of fashion," she said.

"You'll be far ahead of style in New York, my dear," said Madame Marlene.

"Do mine, too," said Sylvia.

"Sylvia, you don't have to." Tillie looked from Madame Marlene to Sylvia.

"I want to. A haircut won't make me pretty but my head will feel lighter."

After the coiffeuse clipped them both, Tillie felt exhausted and lay back.

"Sylvia, don't go. Come closer," Tillie whispered. "I'll never see him again."

"Alfred? Of course you will. He's only gone to his office. The dear man comes as soon as he can leave his work."

"Not Alfred. The musician. Shimon. I'll never forget our kiss."

"That clarinet player should be banned from parties. He overstepped."

"He's a wonderful musician who has suffered."

"Tillie, we don't want to blame your illness on the Russians, but Aunt Mina and I have been speaking about the unsanitary conditions in which they live, and how easily the bacteria can grow there. They may not be sick themselves, but they can infect others. I wonder how many people came down sick after the party."

"Not all kissed him, I don't think." Tillie looked down smiling to herself.

"Tillie, you don't know how dangerously close to losing your life you were. We won't say a word to Aunt Mina. She's worn out. Alfred mustn't hear a word."

"When is Eddie coming home? Will he be here for Christmas?"

"He's working on his first picture with Misha Kaminsky who is a producer Eddie has impressed. The man thinks my brother has talent for movie settings."

"Of course he does!" Tillie exclaimed. "He can do anything with materials and furniture. Imagine a Turkish harem or Roman baths— Eddie will make them real. When I'm well, we'll go to California to see Eddie, and we'll get work, too. We'll earn money to send home because Mama needs it here. I know that Papa has lost our fortune."

Sylvia took a deep breath. "This is difficult for me to relate, Tillie. I was going to wait until your recovery was complete, but now I have to tell you. Misha Kaminsky, Eddie's producer I just told you about, is an orthodox Russian Jew."

"Does he wear long coats, funny hats and those curls?"

"No, according to Eddie, Misha dresses in three piece suits and wears a Fedora. But he was raised as Orthodox and he's superstitious. He throws salt over his shoulder ten times a day to ward off bad *mazel* he calls it."

"So does Mama, and Delia's so superstitious she wears a little bag around her neck but it's voodoo, not Russian."

"There's something I have to tell you, Tillie."

"Eddie was always inspired by picture books from Egypt and China."

In her strange state between feeling hot and cold, too weak to get up, yet peaceful lying in bed now the pain in her throat was gone, Tillie only half listened to Sylvia's long story that her cousin kept making longer before getting to the point of it.

"Misha Kaminsky made a promise at the deathbed of his mother to find a husband for his daughter, Misha's daughter, before the mother's mourning period ended in a year. If he did not marry his daughter, the mother would curse him from the grave."

Sylvia sat for a moment twisting her long fingers in her lap.

"I know it sounds very strange to us. I don't think Eddie understood it all. What he did write was that Rosa has a mustache, and that she's swarthy and perspires."

"I'm sorry she does but swarthy can be handsome, like Shimon. You can tell me everything again later but right now my head is beginning to hurt. I want to sleep."

When Sylvia left, Tillie closed her eyes but she didn't go to sleep. She saw Rosa with a mustache. She saw Shimon swaying as he played his clarinet for her. She understood the news that her cousin hadn't been able to tell her directly. Eddie was going to marry the swarthy daughter and rescue the producer from a curse. She and Eddie, their love for each other, was being sacrificed for money.

---

Mina worried that news of Eddie's engagement in California might cause her daughter to relapse. She spoke of the relationship with Delia as they sat shelling peas for Christmas Eve supper.

'You see, everyone considered the cousins betrothed but there was never a date set, nor any particulars. Tillie and Eddie were always more like brother and sister."

Delia kept her neatly braided head down as Mina continued.

"Alfred declared that he would never urge Tillie to do anything she did not wish, but in the next breath, he revealed that he'd paid our month's mortgage. I said he'd rescued us now in ways we could not possibly repay but he only answered modestly that during Tillie's crisis, he thought we might have overlooked the payment. A modest man."

Mina dabbed away tears on her cheeks. "I don't know how we'll get on without Alfred's assistance but no one can make up my daughter's mind to accept him if he summons the courage to ask for her hand. He knows he has my approval."

———————

To Sylvia, who arrived to help with the Christmas preparations, Mina felt she could talk more intimately.

"I don't know how to broach the subject to Jacob, my dear husband. Do you have any suggestions?"

"About Alfred and Tillie," Sylvia answered.

"Alfred is our only hope. I know you understand our situation, yours and ours."

"I intend to work." Sylvia walked up and down the kitchen. "At first, we may have to rely on Eddie and his Russian producer, but Natalie and I will find employment. The pictures need musicians."

"Sylvia, you don't intend to be a working girl and never marry!"

"I look forward to being a working girl. I hope that I will marry when the right man arrives, Auntie."

"I only can wonder at the ways of the world. We were all assured that Tillie and Eddie would marry once they were older. Delia once implied that they might not be right for each other, though I don't know why. Eddie so loves beauty and he adores Tillie."

"We'll never know, will we, Auntie?"

———————

"My parents probably drank champagne once or twice in their lives," Alfred said as he accepted a second glass on Christmas Eve. "I seem to be making a habit of it."

"You know *I've* tasted a bit too much." Tillie smiled at Alfred, making Mina feel that an understanding had been reached. Tillie's golden-red curls framed her face like an angel and Alfred's appearance was already much improved with his good tailoring and fuller cheeks, a sign of happiness. They would make a fine couple, she decided.

"I propose we toast to good things in the new year! And I'll just throw these few grains of salt over my shoulder to make sure I don't bring us anything unlucky by making such a wish," said Mina.

"Mama! So superstitious! Almost Russian," said Tillie.

"*Prost!*" Alfred removed his glasses to wipe them. "A good German toast. If I have anything to do with it, Tillie will never be without champagne."

"To the children," Mina lifted her glass to Jacob. "I know all will be well."

---

"He's like a son to me already," Mina said when Tillie announced her acceptance of Alfred's proposal. She didn't look at her mother as she spoke the words that would change her life and Mina did not press her.

"Alfred has fallen in love with your cooking, Mama."

"Don't be a silly girl. He fell in love with you from the first moment he saw you. I think he saved your life, Tillie, by the strength of his love."

"I'll be giving him my life now." Tillie did not meet her mother's eyes.

# Nine

"Mrs. Greenbaum suggested a honeymoon in Florida." Alfred's face flushed at the word *honeymoon*. "Before they return, I'm expected to outfit myself. Would you make inquiries, Abraham, into what a man on his wedding trip should be wearing in Florida this time of year?"

"You don't worry, I make all what you need." Cogansky's hands measured and his head nodded in response to Alfred's words.

"Thank you. You're more than my tailor, Abraham, you're my friend. On the day that makes me the happiest of men, you'll be seated on the groom's side in Temple Emmanu-El. I count on you to be there when I break the wine glass."

"My honor, Mr. Hornthall."

Alfred looked at his pocket watch, a gift from his mother. "Now I must go."

"Don't forget top coat, Sir. You get cold."

Abraham wound Alfred's scarf around his neck before he opened the door and saw him walk down the street, noting the more even step.

Abraham extinguished his outside lights. The street had become dark and there would be no more inquiries tonight. He turned the key in the double lock and pulled down the shade. Even as he extinguished them, the shop lights seemed to continue to shine in the mirrors, as if the figures of the customers he'd been fitting nearly all day remained a moment to remind him of his success. Upstairs, he could hear music coming from the Victrola he'd bought. These days, he often repeated to himself "*uff mir gesugt?*"—such good luck should happen to me? Despite the financial pinch, men came to him regularly to order suits and evening wear for which he found the best

163

quality materials at the best prices on Second Avenue. They paid their bills on time, also. He'd never give cutting or fitting to anyone else, but soon he would need help with buying. His son was still only a child and perhaps his boy would never be a tailor but a learned man, a teacher, even a doctor. How high dreams could rise! And how he loved the piano music by Mendelssohn coming from his own rooms on the Victrola. A concert every night!

---

Under a dark wintry sky, passengers on the *Mauretania* waved white handkerchiefs at the crowd below. From the First Class deck, Mina and Tillie kept their eyes on Alfred who looked very small as he pumped his umbrella in the air. "He's so proud of you," Mina hugged her daughter. Taking Tillie to Paris to buy her trousseau had long been Mina's dream, but until Alfred offered to pay all their expenses, she hadn't thought they would be able to.

"Mathilda and I will begin to save after the wedding," Alfred told Mina. "But now I want her to be happy without a care in the world."

"You are spoiling us both," Mina replied.

"That is all I wish to do."

---

At the first night's supper on board, Tillie and Mina met their table companions for the rest of the voyage. Mina's conversations with matrons from New York, Chicago and Kansas City developed as soon as the first course arrived—a delicate morsel of smoked fish in a cream sauce—leading to praise for French cuisine in general, then more intimate revelations about the digestive peculiarities of their husbands and children, and from there to family matters they mightn't have been revealed were they not at sea and feeling untethered. Tillie heard Alfred's name mentioned. She hoped her mother would not say more.

"Yoohoo, pretty copper-headed gal. Y'all come over here and talk with us."

A very tall young man wearing a shirt with pearl buttons waved an unfamiliar broad-brimmed hat in Tillie's direction. He bowed and asked Mina's permission to allow Tillie to join the young people after supper. Her mother nodded her approval, and said to Tillie, "Find out about those slender dark-haired girls. You see them over there, the two who are so stylish." Mina turned Tillie's shoulder so she could see a pair of well-dressed young women sitting by themselves.

The young man and his companions were from Texas, an area of America Tillie knew nothing about. Tillie thought the girls wore too much rouge and had too many ribbons sewed to their blouses and jackets, but they made such a fuss over her. "Look at her curls," one girl said. "Like a French poodle doggie in pictures." On their way out of the salon, the two dark-haired young women her mother pointed out stopped Tillie.

"I'm Jessie Leiter and this is my sister Rachel. Come by tomorrow morning for tea in our stateroom so we can get to know you," Jessie said.

That evening, the Texans led Tillie on a tour of the ship, showing her the marble fountains and the tapestries of hunting scenes in the salons. "Looks like the French castles we're going to see," said Harry, the boy most determined to impress Tillie.

---

In the morning between breakfast and lunch, Tillie arrived at the Leiter's stateroom where the sisters' clothes were hanging for her to see. Rachel and Jessie encouraged Tillie to touch the silk blouses, finished with elegant details like small rosettes sewn around each hand-made button hole.

"Our father is manager of Marshall Field and we take trips to Europe for the fashion shows," said Rachel. "Daddy sent us to art school. I'm not bad at it but Jessie has the surest hand. She captures a line in a minute with no one seeing."

"Which Marshall Field then copies," Jessie said. "The French are furious when we come out with their designs the same year but our people at Field's are fast."

"Of course we make changes," said Rachel. "If the French try to sue us, our lawyers make them wish they hadn't."

"The first thing you have to buy in Paris is a grey jacket of French gabardine. You will build your wardrobe around a jacket this year." Jesse walked to the closet where she found a jacket that looked long and school-marmish to Tillie on the hanger. "Don't worry, it's perfect on and gives you room to move, which is important."

The sisters had straight up-and-down figures, slim hips and almost no bosoms, physiques more like Sylvia, Tillie thought. Rachel had the prettier, regular features and extremely pale skin against black bobbed hair, while Jessie's green eyes sparkled with mischief and her wide smile was friendly and full of fun.

Jesse slipped on the jacket, turned front and back, showing how it followed her body without clinging. "Clothes will be more natural for a modern woman," Rachel said.

"Oh, I do like it," Tillie said as Rachel put the jacket on her. "But I don't have your figures. I'm more…" Tillie ran her hands from her waist to her hips.

"Curvy. You'll want the jacket fitted to show your shape. We all have different figures and we should dress for ourselves, using but not a slave to fashion," Jessie said.

"It's almost eleven, a civilized hour for sherry and biscuits, though we could have tea brought. You're not too young to drink?" Rachel opened a cabinet with bottles inside.

"Oh no, I have drunk my share of champagne this season," answered Tillie. "I guess you could say that champagne changed my life."

"You're going to tell us everything." The sisters sat on either side of Tillie.

After the first glass of sherry, Tillie found it easy to talk about the financial Panic that had bankrupted her father and caused Eddie to leave New York.

"Eddie never liked bad news. All I know now is that he's marrying a movie producer's daughter with a mustache and I'm engaged to Alfred who will save the family." Tillie sipped her sherry. "He's a hopeless dancer. He's like holding a twig. But he's loyal. He risked his health while I was very ill."

"The Panic was a close call though we were safe because Father stays away from all markets—he's seen too many go down with the price of wheat or pigs," said Rachel.

"He doesn't trust American banks, either." Jessie poured Tillie more sherry. "He keeps our money with Rothschild in England and in bonds."

"I think Alfred has gone into bonds. But what do I understand?" Tillie laughed.

The sisters exchanged a look that Tillie read as a kind of pity.

"But Tillie," Rachel filled Tillie's sherry glass, "if Eddie was inconstant, you are better without him. We've seen Mother suffer with each new secretary Father brings in."

"What do you mean?" Tillie asked.

"Father is not exactly discreet. He sends his new secretary a pearl necklace from the store and Mother finds receipts. Of course they're pretty girls, in a plump way, while mother has been dieting her entire life. We're afraid one day she will waste away being fashionable. She's a skeleton, honestly."

"Our father won't ever divorce Mother because you don't divorce a Loeb in Chicago. We've hated mistresses since we were old enough to understand the word."

"My cousin Sylvia and I used to talk about mistresses without knowing what they did," giggled Tillie. "We were nine or ten and we heard our mothers say *mistress* in a whisper on the phone. I don't think my father had one."

"Of course he did. All men do." Jessie took Tillie's hand. "Such tiny fingers and such a large diamond."

"Mama says I'll be the only girl in Alfred's life, which is probably true because he isn't tall or good looking."

"Frankly, hearing about Alfred, it sounds as if your mother traded you to him."

"Jessie!" exclaimed Rachel. "What an awful thing to say."

"It's all right, and there's truth in what Jessie says but I made the choice to accept him. I don't want Mama and Papa to lose our home and be poor. And I can't make a living." Tillie straightened her shoulders and sighed. "Eddie always had something amusing to say to make me laugh. I'll be bored listening to Alfred but I won't be poor."

"I'm sorry we didn't meet you sooner," said Jessie. "You'd be perfect working at Field. You're very pretty and you seem clever. With a little help, you'd develop your style and become a buyer. Where did you ever get your daring haircut?"

"After the fever, my hair fell out. Should I let it grow now?"

"No, it's adorable, so chic and French," said Rachel.

"You can choose less girlish clothes, because of your hair." Jessie tilted her head.

"I'm not as bad as the Texans, am I?" Tillie asked.

"Oh no!" laughed the sisters. "All those bows and that rouge are impossible."

"I still say, if Tillie doesn't want to marry Alfred, she shouldn't," said Jessie.

"Tillie did not ask for our advice." Rachel looked at her watch. "Time for lunch. Tillie's swains won't be happy if she's late. Are you always the belle of the ball?"

"I love to dance and have a good time. It's too late for me to change my mind because I gave Alfred my word and Mama is counting on me. There's nothing I can do about it and Alfred will provide for all of us."

"Have you read *Wuthering Heights*, Tillie?" Jessie asked.

Tillie shook her head.

"Kathy married the man chosen for her but she loved Heathcliff all along. They grew up together, like you and Eddie. She made a tragic mistake and broke his heart which destroyed his faith in humanity so he made everyone suffer."

"But Eddie doesn't have a broken heart over me. He hasn't even phoned once."

"Believe me, thwarted love leads to tragedy," Jessie declared.

"Jessie, stop right now. I'm surprised you're advocating a topsy-turvy life for Tillie when you like everything in order, the whole day, the entire week down in black and white on your calendar. You only like romance in books." Rachel gave her younger sister a nudge. "Let's go, and no more suggestions for our Tillie."

"Rachel thinks she's Lizzie in *Pride and Prejudice*. Always right, knows it all. She'd choose priggish Mr. Darcy over dangerous Heathcliff."

"Jessie, how many times have I told you that Mr. Darcy stirs my passion every bit as much as Heathcliff stirs yours! We have brought two copies of *Wuthering Heights* and *Pride and Prejudice* because we always find someone who should read them."

"Tillie mustn't take *another* step before reading Bronte. If she feels the depths, if her heart pounds with desire, the book will save her from a loveless marriage."

"I don't think I'm a tragic heroine." Tillie drained her sherry. "It's not my nature. I do love to read novels with dashing men. I had only one close call with romance."

"We'll hear all about it next time," said Rachel. "Let's go have lunch."

─────────

Tillie didn't have a moment alone in her cabin to read the two books the Leiters gave her. Even the dime novels from the Eagle Library she'd brought with her lay unopened. Either she was playing shuffleboard on deck, changing outfits for the next meal or dance, or sleeping through breakfast because she hadn't come to bed until three in the morning. There were handsome officers in white uniforms trimmed with gold-braid who invited her to their private parties where they popped bottles of champagne every five minutes. Before Tillie realized it, the final night of the voyage arrived.

The Captain waited until servers cleared the dinner dishes before announcing that the *Mauritania* had won the Blue Riband by sailing across the Atlantic in record time and beating the record of the Cunard Line. Everyone in the salon stood to toast before they headed for the dance floor.

The Captain asked Tillie to dance. "You're a bright penny and have given us a happy time looking at you."

"We'll see you again soon," said Jessie. "You'll come to Chicago to visit us."

"It's only overnight from New York," said Rachel. "We don't like goodbyes."

Tillie wanted to hang onto each one of her new friends and never let go the image of herself as the most popular girl on the ship, always the first to dance and the last to leave the floor.

# TEN

MINA AND TILLIE STAYED a night at the Ritz Hotel on Piccadilly and left London the next day for the sister Ritz on the Place Vendôme. Tillie spoke French with a charming lisp and little moue of her lips that had been imparted by Madame LeRieux, a young, red-headed governess to whom even Homer was courteous because she was pretty.

When she'd been to Paris as a child of ten, Tillie had loved riding the merry go round in the Bois de Boulogne. Mounted on a gold-saddled rabbit or goose, she'd leaned so far out that she almost fell before grabbing the golden ring.

Tillie was still petite enough to lift up her skirts and climb on a prancing rabbit without looking too foolish, but instead of reaching for the ring, she urged a little girl in a sailor costume to hook it with her stick.

"*Voila ma petite!* Bravo!" Tillie clapped.

"*Merci, jolie M'mselle.*" The girl grinned from ear to ear.

Later, as Tillie and Mina walked along the graveled paths of the Bois, bundled-up children rolled hoops, their tasseled caps streaming behind. Every child politely greeted them as they passed. "*Bonjour M'dame, Bonjour M'mselle.*"

"I marvel at the French children. Such good manners. I tried teaching Homer but he wouldn't learn. You were perfect, as you are now." Mina gave Tillie's arm a squeeze.

"They're having so much fun. Like we used to, Eddie and Sylvia and I, when we came to Paris together. Remember Papa and Yuli sneaking off to the Follies Bergère?"

"While I ate éclairs and Natalie read a book."

171

"Who knew what Aunt Natalie ever did with her time?" Tillie asked.

"Leaving Yuli alone through Hanukah and Christmas! Too selfish. I worry about Jacob and we'll only be gone two weeks. I hope your father keeps up Yuli's spirits."

"Papa does seem more resigned to Alfred." Tillie sighed, then Mina sighed, and they walked until they reached the Jardin d'Acclimatation where Tillie remembered that Eddie had been so mesmerized by the marionettes on the little stage that he'd wept when Pierrot fell down and got his head knocked sideways by Pierrette.

"The puppets make me think of fun I had with Eddie." Tillie looked away so her mother wouldn't see a tear she wiped away from her eyes.

"You poor dear, you stayed up too late on the crossing but you were having such a good time that I didn't mind being awakened when you came in. I'm also sorry that Eddie left us the way he did, without a word. You two were like brother and sister."

"That's not quite all we were, Mama. I won't ever be as carefree as I was with Eddie. I know we both have to do what's best for all."

"You'll always be carefree, it's your nature, as well as your good heart."

"I'll become horribly dull once I'm married."

"Oh, no, you'll be the darling of the household and popular wherever you are."

Beneath the bare trees, the grey sky seemed to weigh down on Tillie's shoulders.

"If I'm not to be happy, I'll try to be as good-tempered with Alfred as you are with Papa. I'll try in every way to live up to your example. I'll even learn to cook."

"You don't know you won't be as happy with Alfred as I've been with Jacob."

"But you were in love with Papa when you married him, weren't you?"

"Our parents wanted our match. But it's true, I fell in love very quickly—who could not love Papa? There were times that I was, well, disappointed, but I found happiness in my home and children, as you will."

"I don't know what we'll talk about. Alfred is so serious about stocks and bonds."

"Alfred will be more reliable than your father, Tillie, and that's worth a lot."

"What do you mean, Mama?"

"Jacob has his own weaknesses but there was never any need for you children to share a parent's worries."

"I don't think I'll have children."

"Why in the world not?" Mina asked.

"What if I have someone like Homer who has been such trouble?"

"He has, but you'd love him as I do and he's improving," Mina said.

"Maybe it will be impossible for me to have children after my fever."

"Not at all. You caught an infection being near someone who was contagious. It has nothing to do with children, and when you are ready and the happy day arrives, they'll do everything in the hospital to make you comfortable. You won't feel a thing," Mina patted her daughter's rosy cheek. "Let's see if we can get a carriage to the Champs d'Elysées and find that pastry shop. No one makes pastries like the French."

"Let's both have a *Napoleon.*"

"Anything you wish, my darling."

"I'll have two pastries because why should I care about my waistline any more?"

From the patisserie where they chose two *tarte aux noisettes* and chocolate covered *Napoleons* with lemon-vanilla cream inside, they strolled down shopping avenues. Tillie observed that skirts were cut shorter than in New York and hung differently, flowing with more suppleness from below bloused waists. The wide armholes and sleeves that draped from the shoulders, only just coming into New York, were worn by many women. Even overcoats had deep sleeves.

The House of Worth on the *rue de Paix* showed fashions as modern as any Tillie had yet seen. The afternoon dresses had an Oriental flair, or at least what Tillie imagined Japanese or Chinese might look like from pictures in magazines open upon tables.

"Aren't they pretty and simple? So much less fussy than New York."

"You don't think they'd look too foreign for home?" asked Mina.

"They are Parisian, that's foreign. The Leiters say they'll catch on."

"It's all up to you, darling. I have instructions from Alfred that you're to have whatever you want. But I wonder why they don't have price tags."

"Because they're so expensive," Tillie answered.

A saleswoman wearing a black jacket with a straight black skirt brought small glasses of port and chocolates shaped like rabbits wrapped in gold. She explained in a confidential whisper that Edwardian fashion was in the past, and that *Directoire* had come in, with a hint, a *soupçon*, of the East.

"*Soupçon* means just the right amount, Mama, a little flavoring, like bay leaf."

"That horrible pinching is gone, poof." The woman banished waists with a single gesture. "*Toutes les femmes, les petites demoiselles* like yourself, will not want to look like the pigeon with the chest puffed out." She made the exaggerated S-line of the corseted female body and leaned over to Tillie. "*La jeune fille* does not have to dress like her *Maman. Au naturel, comme ça,* will suit you *perfectement.*"

"I'm not enthusiastic about the reduced bust line." Mina frowned. "We women have the shape that the opposite sex expects to admire."

"Perhaps times have changed," answered Tillie.

"How is that possible!" Mina scoffed.

"For spring," said the saleswoman, "black and white will be *en vogue.* Your coiffure, Mademoiselle, is *trés advancé.*"

"*Merci.*" Tillie shook her curls.

After an hour of trying on combinations that Tillie saw through the Leiters' critical eyes, she chose a grey skirt that swung back and forth beneath a peach silk blouse with deep sleeves, and a soft grey flecked jacket that draped with a curve over the waist.

On their way back to the Ritz, they browsed the covered booksellers' stalls along the Seine for pictures of Paris to bring home. While Mina inspected the watercolors of Notre Dame and Versailles, Tillie peeked into small books with brown covers, the kind her Papa thought he'd hidden where no one would look. She'd discovered his cache when she was putting away his ties, and carried them next door to show Eddie. In his room when they were alone, they opened *French*

*Undressing*. On the first page, a man was taking off a maid's apron. Turning to the next picture, the apron was all the plump girl had on. Tillie blushed as they continued to the next images. She remembered hoping that Eddie would hold her from behind but he'd only laughed at the pictures.

Tillie saw two books with pink covers, *Claudine à l'Ecole* and *Claudine à Paris*, by a writer named Willy. The cover drawing of a little girl with long hair and a Red Riding Hood cape made her suppose they were children's books, but when she began reading a paragraph, she was shocked at the description of girls playing games with other girls, not children's games, but kissing and more. On another page, a school mistress undressed a young girl to discipline her. Tillie squirmed with warm sensations, said nothing to Mina, and bought the books by Willy.

The Ritz dining room was crowded for lunch because the chef, Auguste Escoffier, was in residence for the week.

"We'll eat everything he prepares, even snails if need be," declared Mina as they dove into creamy patés of duck and salmon that preceded the *Boeuf Bourginan*.

"Have you ever tasted the like!" Mina ate most of her dinner sighing and closing her eyes before taking another bite. "How do the French do it? Delia might know."

For dessert, Escoffier's very own *Pèche Melba*, peaches and raspberries just slightly warmed, rested on the most delicious ice cream. "Divine," Mina declared.

After the heavy lunch, Mina reclined on her bed to read her *Town Topics*. Once her mother's eyes closed, Tillie got up quietly and closed the door to the bedroom, freshened herself, stepped into her little boots with heels, new jacket, and tiptoed out.

On the street, she wandered along la *rue des Augustines*, bought a pair of green leather gloves for Sylvia and handsome foulards for her father and Alfred. She walked until she reached a stairway down to the Seine where she stood alongside the swollen grey river that was swooping up everything in its way. Papers swirled with branches until the river rushed them out of sight under a bridge. Tillie thought about the feelings she'd had looking at the Claudine books, at the passion that Jessie Leiter said she should feel. Shimon seemed more dream than memory. She knew that a passionate life would not be hers with Alfred. She held onto the rail and pressed her nails into the cold iron. Silly girl, she said to herself. Never think this way again. You are saving Mama and Papa. You'll eat lots of good food.

––––––––

The next day, they bought pastel feminine *dessous*—underclothes, little brassieres with rosettes that matched slips, panties and garter—at *La Belle Dormeuse,* the Sleeping Beauty. Lacy, tissue-thin nightgowns hung beneath peignoirs.

"I'll give Alfred apoplexy when he sees me in these," Tillie giggled.

That evening, Auguste Escoffier prepared a pheasant with truffles and the very best scalloped potatoes Mina declared she had ever eaten. "How did they make ordinary potatoes so light and crusty they melt in your mouth? The butter, I suppose, and something else German cooking lacks."

After supper, they sat sipping coffee in the lobby watching guests pass through high, revolving doors. They followed the progress of a party of over-sized men and wolf-like women in furs and hats that covered their smoky-looking eyes ringed by black kohl.

"They're Russians," someone beside Mina whispered.

"They're ever so much more elegant than our Russians," said Mina.

"Because these are the Princes and Dukes," said the stranger next to Mina.

"I don't imagine Misha Kaminsky is so handsome and Rosa has the mustache," said Tillie. "I almost feel sorry for Eddie. What a change in our lives, Mama."

"Don't blame your father too much." Mina took her hand. "He was doing the best he could to secure your future. How could he have known that copper would ruin us?"

"Alfred foresaw it. He said he tried to convince Papa to sell shares."

Mina clenched Tillie's hands. "It's too complicated for me to understand. Alfred is smart and generous. You're being the most wonderful girl, Tillie. I know you'll care for Alfred who loves you very much. You'll be a beautiful bride. Tomorrow—the dress."

———————

At Maison Jeanne Paquin, a doorman ushered them inside the narrow vestibule and up steep stairs. Dresses made of the most gorgeous colors and fabrics, greens of sea pools, lavender of Provence fields, peach and apricot of perfect fruit, as if sent by a pasha directly to Paris, hung all around them or were paraded by models with impossibly thin waists. But they'd come for a wedding dress, and Tillie saw her gown hanging alone. It had a fitted silk bodice covered by tulle and tiny pearls, and a silk organza long skirt.

"I hope the Mademoiselle will be very happy," said a seamstress called in to make alterations. "Tomorrow your dress will come to the Ritz. A pleasure to serve you."

———————

Before the wedding dress arrived at the Ritz, a telegram from Jacob was waiting. Mina had no forewarning and didn't even pause before opening it.

**Dearest loved ones terrible news stop our Yuli is no more stop Natalie returns stop**

Mina called New York and reached Jacob in the afternoon. When she finally gave the phone back to the desk clerk, she collapsed in tears. Tillie helped her to their room.

"I can't seem to get my breath. I'll relate Jacob's words if I can. It's too terrible."

"I know it is, Mama. Let's sit down."

"Sylvia had gone to the opera because Caruso was singing and Yuli urged her not miss the performance. While she was gone, Yuli swallowed enough of a concoction of opium solution and brandy so that he appeared asleep in his bed when she returned. She didn't try to wake him. The worst for Sylvia was that the physician told her that Yuli had most likely been alive when she'd left him sleeping and gone to bed."

"How awful for Sylvia! I can't imagine our Papa…"

"You don't have to. Jacob would never do such a thing."

Mina took Tillie in her arms and caressed her curls. "At least Yuli didn't throw himself out a window or disappear in the river where they'd dredge him up disfigured. When they found him without life, he was perfectly dressed." Mina stood up. "The sooner we go home the better. We must help Sylvia, and not leave Papa to brood."

"What will we do about the wedding?" Tillie asked.

"It has to be postponed at least a month."

Tillie knew that if she wanted a chance to announce a change of heart, it was now. She could plead grief. The wedding dress could be returned. They'd repay Alfred for the trip though how they'd do this she didn't know. The idea of going to Hollywood to work with Eddie and Sylvia returned, but she knew that if Alfred didn't help them, her parents would lose their home and have to live in an apartment somewhere. What effect would that have on her Papa? The image of Yuli's lifeless body on his bed came suddenly to her. She shook her head. She would marry Alfred a month later than planned.

---

The *Mauretania*'s sister ship the *Lusitania* sailed from Liverpool under grey skies as if the Atlantic winter weather was made to match Tillie and Mina's unhappiness. Mina stayed below, while Tillie walked the decks, unable to sit still. One evening after supper, as Mina played solitaire, she remembered something. "Jacob told me how Yuli had shocked him by taking out a life insurance policy. It had seemed so uncharacteristic of Yuli to plan anything ahead. And knowing that poor dear soul, he probably never did take out the insurance."

# ELEVEN

Ulysses Elias Sachs' obituary in *The New York Times* lay face up on the parlor table. Later Mina and Tillie would sit with the paper and stare at the photograph of the handsome, silver-haired gentleman, their Yuli. She read praise for the deceased, an outstanding sportsman and beloved family man taken suddenly before his time, in perfect health, at age forty-nine. The *Times* writer named the clubs that Sachs belonged to, and family connection to the well-known Smoother corset created in New Haven. Cause of death was not mentioned.

Alfred sent masses of white lilies and two dozen budding pale pink roses that even Jacob admitted were in good taste for the sad days ahead.

Sylvia told Mina that it was easier to make arrangements for the funeral while her mother was still in California. "Mama says we must wait. A Hindu spiritualist told her Yuli's spirit was circling Los Angeles. That's why she says to wait but I know Jewish law requires a speedy burial and that is what I prefer, Aunt Mina."

"You're right and I support you." Better that Natalie stayed as long as possible in Los Angeles, Mina thought. She'd heard that California was a strange place.

———

The day of the memorial, Natalie arrived, swathed in so much black veiling she looked as if she were returning from the grave. Beside her, Eddie walked in slowly wearing a long coat and hat pulled over his brow covering much of his face. Throughout the funeral service, he held tightly to his mother's arm and kept his eyes averted from Tillie who snuck glances. She wept when she saw him weep. Cantor Schlager sang *Baruch Atah Adonai Eloheynu* and the mourners proceeded to carriages to take them to Grand Central where they caught the train to New Haven. At the graveside, the sun was shining and the snow shimmered. "A perfect day for Yuli to go sculling on the Hudson," Jacob said to Mina.

---

Mina wrote personally to a hundred guests she'd invited to Tillie's January wedding. In small script at the bottom of a black-framed card announcing Yuli's death, Mina sent the family's regrets: *Jacob and Hermina Greenbaum regret that the wedding of their daughter Mathilde Helena to Alfred Frederick Hornthall will not take place as announced due to a death in the family. After a brief wedding trip, the couple will be at home on East 75th Street to welcome their dear friends.* She then struggled to limit guests for the smaller ceremony set for February. Up and down the list she moved her pen, crossing out names until she had reduced the number to twenty close family and friends.

Mina felt both disappointed and relieved that the plans were changed; a one-hundred-person wedding with a reception at the Plaza Hotel would have cost a fortune. Even though Alfred had given his blessings to her arrangements, Mina had dreaded presenting all the bills. Now, by selling a piece or two more of jewelry, Mina could cover the supper that she and Delia would prepare at home. The Parisian gown might be too elegant for the small ceremony but since Cantor Schlager was officiating, Mina thought that the dignity of the occasion merited the dress, and Tillie looked so like a princess that she must wear it this one day.

---

The morning of the wedding when Sylvia arrived to help Tillie dress, Mina met her at the door and enfolded the thin young woman in her arms.

"You know how terribly we mourn our dearest Yuli. Today we will celebrate Tillie and once they are off to Florida, I will be at your side to help pack for your move."

"If only I'd stayed home that night, if I'd not gone to hear Caruso…"

"You must not blame yourself, darling. If this is what Yuli planned, he'd have done the tragic deed another night if not that one. Please, be at peace."

Sylvia shook her head. "He seemed in better spirits, Auntie. We ate a little supper and he drank a glass of wine. He even said he looked forward to taking the train to California when the house was settled. I never thought…"

"Of course you didn't. Who could have?" Mina stopped herself from mentioning Natalie, who had left New York with Eddie immediately after Yuli's funeral, as if all the years when their children had dashed from one door and back to the other, the shared holidays, as close as families could be, meant nothing to Natalie or Eddie. Her question, *How could you leave your husband, Natalie?* remained unasked.

"I can hear my girl calling us," Mina said. "She needs fastening into her gown. I'm so pleased that Homer has agreed to be the best man. This may be the beginning of a new side to my son. He even allowed Alfred's tailor to make a good suit for him. I've never given up on Homer."

Mina and Sylvia opened the door to find Tillie sitting on her bed in her shift. "I found a white hair last week, Mama. Is that bad luck?" Tillie asked.

"Tillie, of course not!" Mina threw salt over her shoulder. "It's from your illness. Now let's get you into your beautiful dress."

"I'm supposed to do your stays to make your waist tinier but I don't think you need anything to look like a French ballerina," said Sylvia.

"Today, for sentimental reasons, I'm going to wear a Smoother," Tillie replied.

"We women must suffer to be beautiful," Sylvia, Tillie and Mina said together the remembered phrase passed down from mother to daughter.

Sylvia regarded her freckles and long nose in the mirror. "Even suffering won't make me beautiful "

"Sylvia! You must have more confidence in yourself. Once you're in California where it's as warm as Florida, and you're not worrying about the house, you'll blossom in the sunshine."

"I'll get more freckles and probably won't see the sunshine much, because Eddie…" Sylvia looked from Mina to Tillie for fear that mentioning her brother's name might break the calm, but Tillie didn't blink. "What I mean is, I've already got work playing the piano in a theater for what they call a movie serial."

"In Paris, Syl, the *Directoire* look is in," Tillie outlined a silhouette. "To wear it properly, you need a figure like yours. I'm too short. You'll be in fashion when I'm a plump little married lady with legs I'm trying to hide," said Tillie.

"Darling," Mina said to Tillie, "we haven't had a moment these past days for a real talk, mother to daughter."

"Don't worry, Mama. Eddie and I investigated that long ago."

Mina and Sylvia stared at Tillie. "You're not going to surprise me now with anything shocking, are you?" Mina asked.

"No, Mama. We consulted Papa's books from Paris, that's all."

"Tillie, say no more. No more surprises. I can't take them." Mina fanned herself with Tillie's veil. "I'm going to help Jacob with his tie and when I ring, I want you downstairs. Delia is waiting to serve coffee and wish us goodbye."

"Delia's coming, isn't she?" said Tillie.

"Of course, but she'll get dressed when we leave. We'll see her at Temple. "

---

The men arrived first at Fifth Avenue and 43rd Street where they waited beneath the high cupolas and portico of Emanu-El, sheltered from wind and gusts of snow whipping the cold air. Soon the second carriage bringing the women pulled up. Mina stepped out first, keeping Tillie's head from view, and then lifting her white skirt to keep it from getting wet.

Friday night services were ending as they entered. Alfred had been recently to Emanu-El to attend Yuli Sachs' funeral and to sign the wedding documents but tonight the temple seemed even grander than it had then. The arabesque archways illumined with dozens of candelabra branched upward like jeweled trees from the Holy Land.

When Tillie appeared in the small chapel in her lacy, bouffant wedding creation, Alfred supposed that if he traveled the world he'd never again see such a sight.

"Soon be over." Homer was standing at his side. "I've got your arm."

"I don't want it to be over," Alfred answered, his teeth almost chattering.

In the seats behind them, Greenbaum, Sheyer and Sachs relations sat together. Delia, her skin burnished and hair glistening, wore a red velvet blouse and black hat back on her head. Alfred's few cousins from Philadelphia sat alongside Abraham and Bella Cogansky on the other side.

Homer stood with Alfred to the left of Tillie, while the Greenbaums and Sylvia stood on her right, facing Cantor Simon Schlager. Homer didn't expect to feel anything special in the temple, this over-decorated palace where German Jews pretended piety while they showed off their wealth. He'd only agreed to stand up for Alfred and to be tailored by Cogansky for his mother's sake. When he'd entered the tailor's fitting room and the good-looking young man wearing an apron with many pockets asked him to mount the stand to be measured, Homer had tried to explain that he wasn't like the rest of the rich German Jews who stood on pedestals and expected to be served. "You're not my servant," he'd said to Cogansky.

"Of course not, I am tailor. Am fortunate man, thanks to Mr. Hornthall. If you please, step up for measure."

When asked, Cogansky told in detail how Alfred had helped his family.

"Two bed apartment." Cogansky pointed up to the ceiling. "Mr. Hornthall gives me business and new life. He has done good."

Homer's attention returned to Cantor Schlager instructing Tillie to take three steps forward away from her father toward Alfred, signifying her free will entering marriage. He then asked Alfred to raise her veil to look into her face. Not only was Alfred supposed to lift Tillie's veil, but the rabbi had instructed him to peer closely at his bride's face, explaining that this ritual assured the groom and his family that the woman before him was the one he intended to marry. The cantor asked Tillie if she accepted Alfred as her husband.

She responded in a whisper, "Yes."

Alfred could hardly clear his throat to reply the same. Fortunately, they had signed the marriage certificate earlier because his hands wouldn't have held a pen steadily enough to write. He gave Tillie the gold ring as instructed. The cantor nodded at Alfred for the words he'd been told to say. "Behold thou are now consecrated to me with this ring, according to the laws of Moses and Israel," to which Tillie replied, "Thou art my beloved and my beloved is mine."

Before Homer had time to become bored, the brief wedding ceremony from the Union Prayer Book was almost concluded. Alfred took the cloth-wrapped wine glass, brought his good foot down hard until everyone heard it shatter before they shouted out *mazel tov*. The shards of glass crushed beneath the white cloth signified the people of Israel broken apart and scattered in the world.

When Homer turned around to see the congregants, his eyes lingered on the pretty woman wearing a lacy shawl beside the tailor. How Homer envied men who had found their partners in life! At twenty-two, he had not yet loved nor been loved by a woman, and he was weak with longing for the understanding person who could share his ideals and his passions, warm his bed and prepare him meals. Thus far, he had only admired from a distance the dark-eyed, bold girls who took part in political discussions on rooftops and in labor halls downtown, girls who worked in garment factories all day and yet had the strength to argue for their beliefs at night. He never succeeded in speaking with them, feeling he'd be regarded as an imposter.

The cantor concluded with a mournful parting melody that seemed to reach Homer from the European villages where Jews had forever been persecuted. He found himself crying for Uncle Yuli, who wore pretentious sweaters and carried tennis racquets as if he were a Gentile, yet always had had a kind word for him.

"Mathilda Hornthall!" Alfred declared, sweeping up Tillie's skirts so they wouldn't touch the ground. "I will live for your happiness. You will never know how I love you."

# Part Three

# ONE

Tillie Hornthall, reclining on a flounced chaise, let the phone ring four times before she replaced the receiver on its frilly skirt. She sulked for a moment at Sylvia's thoughtlessness: every morning the cousins spoke between nine and ten and Sylvia should not have been away from the phone when Tillie had important news.

Tillie soon regained her good humor and patted the cushions beside her so the two silky soft King Charles Spaniels at her feet would jump up. She gave each a bite of her buttered scone, smiled at the gentle lick of their pink tongues on her fingers, and raised her eyes to her garden where the last drops of dew still sparkled on spider web tracings between glowing buds in her rose bushes. She released a contented sigh, acknowledging how she'd grown to love her California Spanish-style home that stood high at the end of a lane to catch the freshest sweet breezes, the perfumes from orange and lemon trees that flowered and ripened year-long in surrounding orchards. At night, Tillie left open her windows. Imagine that in New York! Though her spaniels, Little Nell and Sir John, were small dogs they had high penetrating barks, enough to wake Prospero, the chauffeur who occupied the garage apartment. Prospero drove Tillie and Alfred's Chrysler sedan whenever they needed to go anywhere; the dapper small man also provided Tillie with the best liquor smuggled up from Mexico so that Prohibition hardly mattered.

Twenty years earlier, Tillie had submitted to the move from Manhattan to somewhere in the wilderness of California for Alfred's delicate health. The first winter of their marriage, Alfred had caught a cold that turned into bronchitis and lasted into the summer. His asthma worsened until doctors declared his lungs presented a life-threatening situation unless he found a dry, warm climate where the air was clean. At the time, Tillie had felt she'd made a double sacrifice, first for marrying Alfred, and two years later, having no choice but to migrate to California for her husband's health.

True, there had been no Saks, Bergdorf nor Bloomingdale's, but Sylvia, almost a native of the west by then, had introduced her to Hamburger's, Robinson's and the May Company on Wilshire Boulevard in Los Angeles. Soon Tillie reported to the Leiter sisters that the west was not too far behind Chicago for fashion. The Leiters knew all about the west coast department stores and the casual styles they carried; when they came to Los Angeles on buying trips, they visited Tillie. Rachel and Jessie had remained single and as stylishly thin as ever while Tillie had indulged her appetite and put on weight, especially since the trial of childbearing. While Sylvia had also retained the 1920s boyish, athletic Gibson Girl look, Tillie knew that her sparkling green eyes that changed color in different lights, her tilted little nose and her creamy *poitrine*—the French word so much prettier than *chest*—were appreciated by gentlemen of any age, and that Alfred still saw her as his beautiful bride.

Tillie drank her cup of coffee as she studied photographs of ready-to-eat snacks in her new *McCall's*. When I finish my coffee, she said to herself, Sylvia had better answer. Finally, she rang her cousin's Escondido number and heard Sylvia's voice. "Yes?"

"What do you mean, *yes*? Who else would be calling and where were you when I rang earlier?" Tillie hoped that Sylvia would respect the drama in her voice.

"David was up all night watching the ticker tape and I didn't sleep much."

"Alfred departed at midnight from the Santa Fe station," Tillie said.

"What! He left without you? Why would he go? Didn't he take

the Limited?"

"No, the Limited was only going to leave today so we had to go to some out of the way station in Los Angeles that smelled foreign, where you felt you could be kidnapped and held in captivity with no one knowing for weeks you were missing." Tillie paused to let Sylvia appreciate her description of the event.

"Was it your imagination, thinking it was dangerous or did something happen?"

"You mean more than poor Alfred going off in the middle of the night? Just because something doesn't happen is no evidence that it couldn't have," Tillie replied with a piqued tone. "I thought you'd be more sympathetic."

"I'm shocked by Alfred's hasty departure, especially since we saw you only the night before last and he gave no hint of a plan. Why did he go?"

Tillie let a half minute elapse before she answered in a low voice as if there were eavesdroppers. "Because of the Market, Sylvia. *The Market*. You remember Alfred's concerns when we came to you for supper, and how he urged David to sell."

"I know what Alfred advised but David thinks he's all wrong and is doubling down on our investments. President Hoover himself has assured us there's nothing to worry about, though I admit, David's borrowing makes me uneasy."

"Alfred left to be in New York personally to sell all our stocks," said Tillie.

"Poor Alfred, he worries too much. It's not good for his digestion."

"I know that, Sylvia, but it's his nature to worry, and he counts pennies as I don't, but fundamentally, he is a generous man. He's traveling all the way to New York to warn Singer and Lasley, his old partners, of the dangers. They didn't treat him well but as I said, Alfred is a forgiving man and a student of history."

Tillie again paused to signal her maid Teresa to bring the morning beverage.

"Alfred waxed almost Biblical after that. 'I can't stand here on the shore and watch while the water is rising. When I reach the other side, I'll wire you.' Can you imagine, he took that old leather suitcase instead of the Samsonite I bought him! I said he could have crossed the Red Sea with the Egyptians carrying that bag since it dated from then. He looked so small, no bigger than a large child. How will he defend himself?"

"Your imagination is running away."

"He's a sparrow among hawks, Sylvia."

"I don't think I'll tell this to David. The excitement. I worry about his heart."

*You've always been a fool to trust David's heart*, Tillie thought but didn't say. Her own marriage, separate bedrooms since the twins' birth, worked better than many, especially better than Sylvia's to David Loeb, an aspiring producer who never seemed to do more than talk projects in Hollywood. An air-puffer, a *luftmenshe*, Alfred called him. Sylvia sometimes unburdened her sorrows about the girls David called in for casting.

"Before he stepped into the train, Alfred surprised me again with an embrace which is out of character. To add to all my confusion," Tillie groaned, "Margie is arriving tomorrow just as her father leaves today. A day earlier and she would have persuaded him to stay home. He listens to his daughter and vice versa. They pay me no serious attention." After another sigh signaling how much she endured, Tillie said goodbye.

---

By eleven, the sun had topped the trees and all the delicious perfumes of gardenias and roses were offering their most effusive fragrances to Tillie's senses. As she sipped her bourbon with ginger ale, Tillie remembered the moment at Sylvia and David's when Alfred had made up his mind to leave for New York to sell out of the Market.

David Loeb was a large man with thick greased black hair and large grey eyes that bulged from his face when he was excited. As he spoke, he paced back and forth on their terrace, cigar in hand. "The Market has no ceiling, Hornthall. It's only just beginning to peak. Margins are secure and broker loans are up. All you need is ten percent of purchase price to buy any company you want."

"I know about margins and broker loans, Loeb." Alfred coughed and tried to brush away the cigar smoke. "The Market has been trending down since September. That's a sign that the fundamentals are shaky."

"Hornthall, you old pessimist." David loomed over Alfred like a shaggy bad-smelling animal. "You're *losing* by *not* buying. Look into this Shenandoah Trust. Goldman Sachs is behind it so you can't miss. I'm putting everything I have into the trusts. By next year, I'll have my own production company and movies, movies, movies, just you wait and see what hits I'll have my name on."

"The trusts are based on speculation pure and simple," Alfred replied. "They own paper that owns paper. They crumbled like sand in '07 and they will crumble again."

"How can you be so dense! I've made five hundred percent in Radio Corporation alone. I wager I'll be one thousand percent to the good before it's over."

"But when will it be over? That's the question."

"Doom and gloom, Alfred. Sky's the limit." David poked the cigar between his lips and rubbed his hands together in satisfaction before he raised them above him as if worshipping the night stars. That moment, Tillie now remembered, was when Alfred had decided to read the heavens differently.

When Prospero was driving them through the darkness north toward Pasadena, Alfred had said, "Sky's the limit! Fool! When he's doing his war dance, it's time to get out."

"I wondered if your digestion wasn't affecting your thinking," Tillie said. "Sylvia's cook prepared food that was so spiced it must have given you heartburn."

"I don't understand the purpose of foreign spices in America but my digestion is not the cause of my distress. My dear, time is of the essence where the Market is concerned." Alfred had turned to his wife in the dark, thick lenses of his spectacles all she could see. "I wish to take a night train to New York without waiting until the skies that fool David thinks so highly of fall down. Will you pack my suitcase?"

Tillie chose her battles: changing Alfred's mind on taking Samsonite luggage had not been one of them. She'd also given up opposing his visits to smelly health stores where the white-coated sales clerks listened to his complaints and cared about his ailments as she did not. She was grateful that Magda, the Hungarian woman in Dr. Gregor's health shop on Wilshire Boulevard, gave Alfred gooey concoctions for his liver; when a wizened chiropractor Tillie thought looked like a *golem* came to the house and loudly cracked her husband's thin little bones, she stayed out of the way. Tillie thought her own liver and aching back got the right kind of attention from Prospero. Bourbon by preference for Manhattans, cognac before she slept, were her treatment of choice.

She'd also given up trying to pry off Alfred's green celluloid eye shade which he persisted in wearing though she'd often told him that the hideous thing made him look like a medieval Jew in a counting house. There was even a term for people who wore them—green-eye-shade men. Alfred did have an eye condition that made him extremely sensitive to light, but really, it wasn't necessary to wear it after the sun went down. Now that she thought of it, perhaps the one trait shared by her husband and Elman, their son, was the green eye shade. Elman wore one when he played cards, but then her son was charming even with that ugly thing on.

# Two

Lights twinkled in the clear autumn evening as Alfred's cab crossed west at mid-town. Tillie's reservation for him at the Plaza Hotel was an extravagance in Alfred's opinion, but once he drew the curtains closed, unpacked his pajamas and toiletries, he was grateful for the quiet suite. After a shower, he called room service for tea and a chicken sandwich and sent out his suit for pressing with a rush order. Soon after he ate, he undressed, pulled on his pajamas, and was asleep in minutes.

On Tuesday morning October 22nd, Alfred read every word he could find on the financial situation in the early morning papers. When his breakfast arrived, he opened his curtains onto a view of the southern tip of Central Park. A clear, beautiful day. Then he called his former brokerage partners. Isaac Singer answered the phone.

"Alfred Hornthall! What the dickens are you doing in the city?" Singer yelled into the phone as if Alfred were hard of hearing. "As if I didn't know, you sly fellow. The greatest Market of all time."

"I'm not confident the Market will hold up," Alfred said.

Alfred heard laughter. "Market jitters? That's the old you, weak nerves. The ticker tape is lagging behind the volume of transactions, nothing more. You used to call yourself a contrarian, as I remember. More like a man who won't dive into the water."

Did Singer suffer from selective amnesia? Alfred wanted to ask. A dive into the water! They'd drowned while he'd held the high ground in 1907.

"I don't call myself anything. I base conclusions on evidence that I've studied."

"Not another word, old man. Come on down to the new office

and join the party of the century," Singer said. "We'll all be here to welcome our *eminence grise*."

---

Traffic moved slowly downtown, stopping at red lights long enough for Alfred to read the ticker tapes over brokerage doors. The Tuesday Market was at 450 and rising. Why did he hope to achieve talking with Singer and Lasley when they'd laughed him out of their offices before the last financial disaster? Perhaps because the two had come around to his new home with an apology that had touched his heart. He wasn't a vengeful man. Now, with the Market so high, he must warn them off the cliff's edge. Alfred had a sixth sense, an internal barometer, about financial numbers: when he felt the low pressure, the storm coming in, it was time to go to higher ground.

In the elevator rising to the top floor to Lasley and Singer's brokerage office, Alfred tried to take deep breaths, as if he were climbing to the thinner air of a mountain.

At his knock, Isaac Singer opened the door and clasped him around the shoulders. "My dear Hornthall, enter our domain. Elman, here's our Alfred come all the way from California to celebrate. He doesn't have the suntan, but then, when would our Alfred ever be out in the sun?"

"Our long lost partner." Elman Lasley, fatter than ever, embraced Alfred so hard that he squeezed breath out of him.

Alfred pulled himself free of Lasley's sweaty hands and stood back to see two younger men seated in chairs around a conference table. The office furnishings were sumptuous, from Persian carpets to chandeliers.

The two men, who looked like twins in their snug-fitting suits, stood to introduce themselves as the Kahn brothers. "We've heard a lot about you, Mr. Hornthall. A real *eminence grise*."

"Exactly what I was calling him," said Singer.

"A drink will put color in his cheeks!" Elman Lasley rose and pressed a button on the wall. A bar swiveled out. Alfred looked at the array of bottles and thought of Prospero and Tillie's smuggled bourbon.

"A glass of water will be fine. No ice."

"No bubbly? Just look at this morning's numbers!" Singer extracted a bottle of Mumm's from a small refrigerator, showed the label as if he were reading stock quotes.

"Water, that's all." Alfred drank down the glass. He had a little dry tickle in his throat, probably a reaction to the colognes and hair cream the young men had perfumed themselves with. He'd try not to cough.

"The Market is too high." Alfred struggled to suppress the tickle. "Today, tomorrow, Thursday at the latest, it will fall. You must sell."

A fit of coughing, deeper down in his chest, overcame him.

"Have you brought disease with you?" Isaac Singer moved back his chair.

"I think he's come east to warn us," said one of the Kahn brothers. "I'm listening. Your reputation merits it."

"You must call in your margins while you can," Alfred said.

The second Kahn brother shook his head. "You may have been a genius, a wizard, in your time, but we're in new territory. President Hoover is a businessman himself."

"Boys, listen," Elman Lasley addressed their younger partners. "Lo those many years, Hornhall was right and we were wrong but the mistake he's making is equating past history with the present."

"You can imagine that Jewish Cassandras aren't appreciated at times like this, Hornthall. Paul Warburg is already a pariah for doubting the Market," Singer said.

"Warburg is right. Sell," Alfred wheezed.

"Who have you been talking to in California? Bolsheviks? We're not dealing in sales right now. Department of sales, closed." Singer made a pantomime of slamming shut a door. "Our investors want to buy, buy, buy, no matter how high."

Lasley placed his hand on Alfred's knee. "Old friend to old friend, Alfred, the professors, the wise men, all say there's no ceiling."

Alfred closed his eyes. This ceiling as well as its floors seemed to be moving.

"Nothing to worry about. We hold Goldmann Sachs trusts. We're in Shenandoah. Better than gold in the bank," Singer said.

"Shenandoah's not even listed, it's selling from the Curb," Alfred protested.

"So much the better. The Exchange is too small for it," said Harry Kahn.

"Shenandoah! Sheenandoah! Blue Ridge! Shenandoah!" The men chanted the trust names, words that danced in air Alfred was trying to breathe.

"The moment confidence erodes…" Alfred could manage only a whisper before one of the young Kahns snapped a finger in his face.

"Boo!" he said. "You're an old scaredy cat. Time to retire to the attic."

"You've had a long journey and need rest and to take care of that cough. Come back tomorrow, all will be well, old friend," said Singer.

The four men ushered Alfred through the door. Before they closed it, Elman Lasley said, "There's always a seat at the banquet when you've come to your senses."

Laughter rang in his ears all the way down the hallway, no end in sight.

Alfred staggered and limped as he had down school corridors with boys' taunts following him until finally he opened a door to the stairway and closed it behind him. Though his chest felt every descending step pounding like a hammer on an anvil, he walked from the top floor to ground level and out the service entrance.

On Broad Street, a strange cold darkness surrounded him. The sun had been shining when he'd entered the building but now he had the impression that night had fallen, or another season advanced. He consulted his watch. Noon, he read, as he peered into near-darkness. Noon. Tuesday 22, October 1929.

———————

The rest of the morning, Alfred sat in his hotel room hunched over newspapers, reliving the denials from his old partners as they once again sent him to the woodshed. He had Magda's drops with him. He squeezed them into water and drank. In California, without the winter cold and the smoke-filled air, Alfred's asthma was so improved he could walk without wheezing. He did spend most of the daylight hours holed up in his study, but when he took his familiar route down their hillside street and back again, even his limp was diminished.

After a nap sitting up in an armchair, Alfred's coughing had subsided but he was too anxious to stay put in his room. It was three o'clock when he decided to go out.

As he went along the edge of Central Park, a fine mist clung to the air and made the bright leaves of the park look almost black. When he turned downtown onto Broadway, the sky was even darker. Was there an eclipse, he wondered? Or was something happening that an ancient seer would have taken for a portent of disaster?

Alfred walked until he saw a brokerage office on Times Square. The ticker tape was wildly flashing numbers as if calling men to sin rather than to buy more shares on margin. Alfred entered an establishment that could have been taking bets for the races but had paper spitting out stock quotes. He gave his account numbers and told the man behind the desk to sell half his RCA through the Boston Exchange. The agent mumbled disapproval under his breath as if he would refuse an order as disgraceful as a sell in this Market. Alfred hated to go against Radio Corporation, but once he'd given up his favorite company, the rest came easier despite the agent's increasing growls of disgust. He moved on to another small office where he put both sell and short orders for half his General Electric and Westinghouse, feeling as if he were being watched by agents on the look-out for traitors to American free enterprise and all the country stood for. Alfred was patriotic and it hurt him to be betting against the great corporations that had brought such prosperity to the United States.

By the time he returned to the Plaza, having sold three quarters of his portfolio, he felt like a fugitive arrived at a border that once crossed was closed to him forever.

# THREE

TWO MORNINGS AFTER ALFRED'S departure, Tillie woke up early and pulled on a navy and white striped blouson top with red piping at the neckline. Almost patriotic, she thought as she looked at herself in the oval mirror and primped her silver hair. She'd found a grey strand the day of her wedding when her bobbed red curls were still growing back after her fever. By the time she turned twenty-five, the copper waves were almost all silver. She could have tinted but she didn't because her fine skin and green-flecked hazel eyes made a dramatic contrast with her premature grey. As the years went on, no one believed she had a twenty-two-year-old daughter and son, twins who couldn't have been less alike if they'd come from entirely different parents.

At the moment, her daughter Margie was asleep in her childhood room after three days en route from New York to California. Margie lived alone in Manhattan and worked in advertising. She had earned straight A's at Stanford, while her twin brother, Elman, had been kicked out of the University for playing cards in a sidecar of a motorcycle that had crashed. Though Elman had inherited his father's gift for numbers and Tillie was sure he could have been a great mathematician, he chose a life playing professional cards with wealthy partners. Alfred's cavils that his son never did an honest day's work fell on deaf ears as far as Tillie was concerned: she felt Elman, who didn't have his sister's athletic nor studious ambitions, was her more compatible child.

Much as her own father had disparaged her brother, Homer, Alfred disapproved of everything his son did. How strange that these family patterns repeated themselves, Tillie thought. In fact, children, like husbands, were a mystery to her. She had disliked the marital relations that had engendered her twins, followed by gestation and births she had barely survived. Before she realized the years had passed, they were grown and gone.

Tillie walked down the corridor into a room where the windows were curtained with brown damask. Contemporary, lighter furnishings filled the rest of her home, while she kept dark what she called the library. Here her parents' prized Biedermeier buffet and matching armchairs upholstered in the original maroon velvet were protected from the California sun. Bookcases lined the walls and Dresden figurines, lighted by ringed Tiffany lamps, had survived Jacob and Mina Greenbaum's move west. Tillie kept the room as if her parents might surprise her sitting in their chairs with highballs in hand, appreciative that their precious belongings were as they'd left them. Even the paintings, a horse race at Deauville from the Barbizon school, and two paired Corot-school landscapes, hung in the dim light.

After the financial Panic and Tillie's marriage, Mina and Jacob Greenbaum had continued to live in their Upper East Side brownstone thanks to Alfred's support. In 1921, they joined their daughter in California, but Tillie's dream of family reunion under the same roof had lasted only a year. A pain in her mother's hip that made Mina wince when she walked was diagnosed as bone cancer, and the disease moved rapidly toward its end. After Mina died, Jacob, always a man with a large appetite, began to pick at his food no matter what favorites Tillie had her cook prepare. Nothing in her life was as painful as watching her robust father wither to a stick. He didn't seem to want to fight a cold that turned into pneumonia. His final days, Alfred sat holding one hand as Tillie held the other, the men reconciled in these final hours. When her father had breathed his last, Tillie felt as alone and vulnerable as she had at eighteen leaving with Alfred on the train for their Florida honeymoon.

Tillie now moved silently around the room, dusting a bronze Italian sylph that had been dear to her mother. Above it hung photographic portraits of scarcely-remembered relatives, their cheeks painted pink on the sepia tint, young roses in faded beige foliage, she always thought. Perhaps no one told them to smile for the camera or maybe the women couldn't because they'd been so tightly encased in their Smoothers. Tillie regretted knowing little about her family history, only as far back as her great grandfather who had arrived in New Haven around the time of the American Civil War to join a community of Bavarian Jews in the corsetry trade. There, one of Jacob's grandfathers had created the combination corset and girdle they called the Smoother that made their fortune. Tillie could still remember that her dear mother never went out without being fastened in, compressed and distributed into the S-curves of the day. She wished she'd kept at least one pink satin Smoother to remind her of Mina. "You must suffer to be beautiful," Mina would say, repeating in French, "*Faut souffrir d'être belle*"

In a formal portrait with their parents, Tillie and her older brother Homer, dressed in a sailor suit, glared out at the camera. Poor impossible Homer! He'd so hated everything their parents wished him to be while she'd loved dressing up in pretty clothes and enjoying the praise of all who gazed down on her. "A joy to all eyes," her father used to say as he bounced her on his lap.

Not long after her parents moved to Pasadena, Tillie had engaged a photographer named Edward Weston, recommended for his talent and because, after a romantic scandal, the man had needed patrons. In his photograph of Tillie's mother, Mina was a serene study, swirls of greying hair drawn loosely back in waves, her dark brows arched wide over her pale eyes. Mina's aquiline nose turned slightly downward, shadowing thin, curving lips, and her shoulders took on light as if bathed in air. At the gauzy shadow of bosom and overlapping folds of her dress, a diamond brooch glistened.

Tillie supposed the picture of Mina was valuable now because Mr. Weston had gained a following, but she wouldn't have parted with it for any amount of money. He'd brought out something in her mother's luminous skin, something fragile and fleeting, almost haunting, as if he'd seen his subject would be leaving them soon. Mina was just fifty-seven when she died. Tillie was now forty-one and relished her creature comforts, the taste of good food, the pop of a champagne bottle, the sharper smoky *parfum* of bourbon and whiskey. She was, as her mother had predicted, happy in her life, romantic dreams past and nearly forgotten, but how she missed her beloved parents! She wiped her eyes with a kerchief and closed the library door.

In the chaise under her umbrella, *McCall's* lay open to the article on food for card parties, mostly plates of cheese on crackers that looked appetizing as she waited for Margie to join her for lunch. She'd remember to ask Margie if advertising photographs made food appear better than it really tasted.

Just then her daughter came onto the verandah in shapeless blue pajamas. That young woman had never known how to dress for her figure, Tillie thought: there were ways to draw the eye from short and sturdy legs, ways to create the illusion of height.. Admittedly, her daughter excelled at sports, jumping a horse over high hurdles, playing tennis with experts, and those accomplishments seemed to matter more than style.

"Good morning, Mother." Margie said.

"It's almost noon, time for a drink, but I'll wait for you to dress."

"Coffee for me, then I'll change. I've got a tennis game planned."

Tillie rang the bell for Teresa. "Have you heard any news from New York?"

"I've been sleeping."

"What I mean, Margie, is whether you think that there's that anything to worry about in New York. I know it's a beautiful day here but it might not be there and Alfred may have caught cold in the miserable train. I am sorry he missed you. You're his favorite. What do you think of his unexpected departure over the Market?"

Margie yawned. "*The New York Times* issued warnings all summer that stocks would fall but they kept climbing so people I talk to are staying in, nervously staying in. Tommy says that like Prohibition, the Market can't go on. I trust Papa's instincts."

A young woman with a dark round face above a starched white apron appeared.

"Teresa, you haven't met my daughter, Margie. I'm sorry she's not dressed yet but she'd like coffee, please. I'll have my usual. We'll be having lunch later."

"Thank you, and welcome Senorita." Teresa smiled and left.

"Thank you for introducing us. When did Teresa come?' Margie asked.

"Not long ago and she's ever so much cheerier than the last one. You're right, dear, that no one understands the ticker tape like your father, but speaking as you did of the awful Eighteenth Amendment, I want you to know that I never want for provisions thanks to my Prospero. He recently found a cache of blended Seagram's on a beach in Mexico. The bottles just turn up for him."

"Blended is smooth but I doubt the case on the beach was by chance."

"You mean you think he deals with gangsters?"

"Seagram's doesn't wash up on California beaches anymore than it does on the shores of Lake Erie. In case you didn't know, Seagram's is Samuel Bronfman's proprietary blend. Tommy says Lake Erie is called the Jewish Lake because Bronfman and Meyer Lansky get their booze across it in boats, guarded by men armed to the teeth."

"You are a fount of knowledge, dear. I'm glad it's not all gruel and work."

"No, Mama, work is interesting and I like the people in the new agency that I joined. It's called Benton & Bowles. They're just starting up and have all sorts of talent to create modern advertising campaigns. I've been wondering whether we should go to New York to be of help to Papa?"

"You just got here! Let Alfred be our knight in shining armor. We'll shop."

"Mama, I don't need to shop. What surprises me is that Papa didn't give any warning. He knew I was coming in. It's so unlike him to act hastily."

"He was waiting eagerly for you to come, but he was distracted by Sylvia's David and off he went on a derelict train in the middle of the night. I'm afraid he might have been taken for a tramp with the old suitcase he was carrying when I had the new Samsonite waiting for him. At least I made him take his own pillow because he never knows about dust and his asthma."

"Papa alone is vulnerable. We should go to New York."

"Your father will perform his miracles and return within a week, so no more talk about leaving me."

"I'm not leaving you. We'll take the train together. We'll have company."

"It's so perfect here!" Tillie kicked off her sandals and walked barefoot across the tile, leaving small moist footprints as she stepped inside to see if Teresa was making her cocktail. "How will racing after Alfred affect anything? Aren't there rules and regulations to prevent 1907 from happening again? And you have your tennis game."

"I can fit that in this morning. I haven't unpacked. If we catch tomorrow's Limited, we'll be in New York on Thursday," said Margie.

"But I'm happy here. Let's not rush."

"Tomorrow morning isn't rushing. You said you want time with me alone."

"All right, Margie. As long as we take First Class Pullman. I won't undergo the hardships that Alfred submits to for economies."

# FOUR

A Negro wearing a white jacket led Tillie and Margie down the carpeted aisle of the Pullman sleeping car. He plumped up cushions on the couch and asked, "May I provide you with anything, Ma'am?"

"Very kind. We're provided for at the moment, though we may need something later." Tillie gave him twenty dollars. "We're in good hands with you, George."

"Thank you, Ma'am, anything at all, I provide. Just pull this cord."

After the porter closed their door, Tillie kicked off her high heels.

"That's a lot of money to start out with," said Margie.

"I like George and I'm sure he carries a regular supply of liquor, though not the quality Prospero gets. Your father, who is frugal as you know, always tips at the start."

"Really? You think the porter supplies booze?"

"Didn't you see him wink when he asked twice if he could *provide* us?"

"I guess you're right. How do you know his name is George?"

"I don't, but he didn't say it wasn't."

"Mother, that's condescending. The man has his own name."

"Of course he does, dear, and we'll ask him in time." Tillie lifted a starched doily from the table beside her seat and saw there was no dust under it.

Tillie brought out a pinch bottle.

"Tommy says Prohibition is the single least popular legislation ever passed," Margie said.

"It appears that Tommy knows many things."

"Seagram's Blended has a royal crown which makes it taste even better, don't you think?" She held up her mother's kidney-shaped bottle with brown liquor swishing inside. "Royal, the drink of kings. It does give comfort to know you're drinking what the royal house drinks. I wouldn't be surprised if Samuel Bronfman, who is a short squat Jewish man and far removed from royalty, designed the bottle and label himself."

"You're spoiling my illusions, dear. A bucket of ice will bring them back."

The porter appeared almost before Tillie lifted her finger from the buzzer. A few minutes later he returned with a bucket, ice and ginger ale.

"You wonderful man. What is your name?"

"Marvin," he answered.

"Thank you, Marvin, we have two days on our hands until Chicago and I know you'll make them pass easily."

"Yes, we will," he answered, then turned. "You will see how the time flies."

"Isn't this smooth!" Tillie said. "Let's toast Prospero, my miracle man."

"I like his Shakespearean name. Here's to Papa!" Margie lifted her glass.

"Your father isn't as fond of Prospero as I am. Alfred scarcely touches a drop."

"What will Prospero do when they repeal?" Margie sipped.

"Prospero is a man of many parts. He's invested in the Market. I wonder if Alfred communicated his views to him. In appearance, Prospero is not as you may imagine."

"What do I imagine?" Margie squinted as if the image would come. "I can't help seeing this Shakespearan bootlegger as rather swarthy and tough, with a beard perhaps."

"Wrong, and that's the beauty of the man. He's bald as a banker, has a baby's complexion and sweet dimples. He can fit in anywhere socially."

"Prospero sounds like a chameleon."

"That's it. You always find the word. Prospero gets into Hollywood shindigs attended by my former fiancé, Eddie Sachs, Sylvia's brother, the movie producer."

"Your voice always goes up a dramatic notch when you speak of

Eddie Sachs, as if you were auditioning for radio. The Market is all we need in drama."

"Oh dear, let's not think too far ahead. For the present, I wonder if we'll meet any decent card players on board. Bridge is where Elman is my natural child. Never forgets a card. Isn't that a form of higher intelligence? Alfred insists our son is incapable of making an honest living but Elman is still so young."

"We're the same age, Mama. That's what twins are."

"Of course, but you always rushed ahead and did things more quickly. Getting born first, you were there earlier. Elman hasn't been as efficient with his time as you."

"Where is my so-called younger sibling?"

"He's keeping company with very rich people cruising in the Mediterranean. They employ him to be their Bridge partners because he's brilliant. They treat him swell, all expenses paid. Elman will be a Grand Master before he's thirty. Don't frown with disapproval if you don't know what that means. Bridge is all-American."

"Tommy told me that Meyer Lansky started out playing cards, or maybe it was craps on street corners, before he got into more lucrative gambling, booze and murder."

"Elman's on a yacht where beautiful women in gowns and gloves come and go."

"Mama, you let your imagination run away with you when it's about Elman."

"And you don't give him a chance," answered Tillie. "He's apologized to me for the problems he caused while you were both at Stanford."

"He's never apologized to me," said Margie. "He just called me a prude."

"You were a stickler for rules. I suppose Elman was just having fun," said Tillie.

---

Sunset turned the granite face of the San Gabriel range rich mauve and rose. Tillie gazed out the window and Margie had just opened *Dodsworth,* her new Sinclair Lewis novel, when her mother looked over at the title.

"I've never heard of the author, Margie. Must you read it?"

"It's got wonderful reviews. You'd like the main character, a successful Midwesterner who decides to follow his wife to Europe. Tommy recommended it."

"Why would I want to read about that part of the country? Would you stop for a moment and answer my burning curiosity about this Tommy fellow who comes up again and again in the conversation."

"If Tommy's free, he'll squire us around. You'll like him."

"I reserve judgment until I know more about a man for whom you have a special affection, if I'm not mistaking that blush of color in your cheeks."

Margie closed her book.

"Is he attractive?" Tillie asked.

Margie sighed. "Much too attractive, that's the problem. Tommy is the best looking guy I've ever known. He dates girls all over town. We're pals, that's all."

"There's nothing wrong with the way you look. We might dress you differently—less utilitarian. I had plans in Los Angeles that we can pursue in New York."

"Mama, I'm fortunate not to have a noticeable disability but I'm not a beautiful New Yorker with show-girl legs like the ones Tommy knows. He's six years older than I am and a foot taller. He sees me as a little sister, even calls me Sis." Margie looked out the window. "When I wire Papa to tell him when we're coming, I'll send one to Tommy. He'll meet us at the station unless he's on a deadline or hung over after a big night."

"What about *your* feelings for Tommy? Are you content with being Sis?"

"You're the sleuth, what do you think?"

"Darling, I'd say that you can't hold a poker hand when it comes to handsome Tommy. You care very much about this young man."

"I'm crazy about him but it's not reciprocated, believe me. He writes about Broadway for the *News* and dates the chorus girls."

"As we were saying earlier, or perhaps I was talking with Sylvia, Flapper skirts are on the way are out, thank heaven. Even during their dreadful reign, I successfully managed by sleight of hand to conceal what I wished to conceal and show off my best features. We'll dress you so you could have showgirl legs if you chose to reveal them."

Margie looked at her plump little mother with her short legs and couldn't help smiling. It was wonderful, she thought, to have so much confidence and self-approval.

Tillie stretched and patted her stomach. "You feeling hungry?"

"I'm always hungry though it wouldn't hurt me to miss a meal."

"I wouldn't think of missing a meal on the Limited. It's a blessing to have an appetite, Margie. You wouldn't want to be like Alfred or Elman, pecking at this and that because of their delicate stomachs. And their fragile bones, always susceptible to injuries the way yours and mine aren't. You can jump around on horses and dash after tennis balls but the minute Elman looks the other way, he breaks something. Elman has a tendency to have bad luck in everything but cards. You should be more sympathetic toward your brother. You had the advantages."

"Advantages? He did sums in his head I couldn't count. He's got twice my IQ."

"Whenever I tell your father that Elman inherited his brains, Alfred says, 'Why doesn't he use them?' He never criticizes you. If I gave you some necessary corrections, it was for your own good. To this day, you're prompt and Elman is usually late which explains to me why he takes shortcuts. You see, my side of the family, unlike your father's, was given to fleeting pleasures. Greenbaums didn't rise to the very pinnacle of our crowd. Not enough *pflicht* and *arbeit*—that means duty and hard work in German. Alfred is more typically German. I feel much more French or Italian." Tillie scrutinized her daughter. "I'd say you've got Hornthall determination mitigated by Greenbaum love of sport. Uncle Yuli was an excellent athlete, rest his soul. Fortunately you're not too high-minded to be fun, at least sometimes."

"Thank you, Mother, I'll take that as a compliment. Sylvia has told me lots about her father. Did you say you were hungry? Let's see if they've begun serving."

Tillie raised her hand in front of her face and drew a shape like a cloud. "I'm caught up in memory, Margie. Just look at that water reflecting where the moon is rising. Isn't that beautiful. Is it Great Salt Lake already?"

"Hardly. We'll be in the Mojave desert all night. It's a mirage."

"As is life, I believe the Hindustanis say. You never met Sylvia and Eddie's mother, Natalie, who became a Hindustani and visited the Indian continent from where she has never returned, as far as anyone knows. Such a blow to a child, losing both parents to unnatural causes."

Tillie stood up and regarded the scrub and sand that stretched to the horizon in the last light of the day. "The desert makes me thirsty." She poured another finger of bourbon into her glass. "Is the compartment smaller than it should be? I thought we'd have more space in here but we're surrounded by luggage."

"Your luggage, Mama."

"You rushed me so I took everything I might need. I haven't been to New York in three, no four years, and you never know about the weather. Let's go have supper."

––––––

"I'm relieved that they still use good table ware," Tillie said after they finished their roast chicken and wild rice. When apple crisp and ice cream arrived for dessert, Tillie lifted the pinch bottle from her bag. "Saving the best for last."

"I wish we could get in touch with Papa," said Margie.

"What could possibly happen to Alfred? He won't leave the hotel room. Speaking of seeing the town, we'll have to rely on Tommy to take us to speakeasies."

"He'll be happy to oblige."

"Where's our good-looking Tommy from?"

"He's a native westerner, born in Colorado, but he and his mother moved around after his father died. He's lived in New York, Chicago and San Francisco."

"Like a native Indian," said Tillie.

"Why do you say that?"

"All those migrations. Is he mixed-blood?"

"His grandparents were German Jews like us but instead of staying in the east, they went west." Margie sipped her bourbon-laced coffee.

"Did they strike it rich like the Guggenheims?"

"No, they didn't get rich. Tommy's mother was widowed young and raised him alone. She taught school but now she's a dean of a high school in San Francisco. Tommy feels guilty that he hasn't made life easier for her."

"I thought all the Jews made fortunes in mining. The original Guggenheims started out in stove polish, or so people said. Solomon's wife Irene and my mother were good friends, and you adored the oldest girl, Eleanor, who moved to England."

"I still love Eleanor and we stay in touch," said Margie.

"She was always bossy. I'm surprised she landed a count. The middle girl is a dwarf, such a pity."

"Her name is Gertrude and she's swell," said Margie. "She loves animals."

"But a dwarf. I'm on the shorter side, what is generally called petite, but I can't imagine what I'd have done if I'd been a dwarf."

"You weren't, Mother."

"Let me tell you something you don't know about your mother that will make you appreciate the way I brought you up. German Jews of my generation were over-trained and over-supervised as children. Everything we did came under scrutiny, including our morning performance, what they called our duty, if you know what I mean."

"What!" Margie coughed as the coffee and bourbon went down.

"It's true. Early morning, I'd dash next door to perform for Sylvia before her governess arrived. Sylvia had a nervous constitution."

"You're not serious. You never told me this."

"It's not exactly dinner-table conversation but we've finished eating. Digestion and elimination had to be regular, which was one reason Homer hated governesses. He used to chase them around the dining table with a carving knife."

"Homer with a knife! I don't believe that either! He's a judge. He obeys the law."

"You didn't know him then. After our kind of upbringing, many children in our set had breakdowns or developed bizarre habits for the rest of their lives. Any number of Guggenheims and Seligs would be under lock and key if not for who they are."

"Tommy's mother June's maiden name is Selig," said Margie.

"A Selig!" Tillie raised her eyebrow appreciatively. "Comes from good people."

"Not the same branch as the ones with all the bank money."

"Still, a Selig. They were the brightest stars in the crowd, along with being among the craziest. Shall we try the Bar Car without the bar for old times' sake?"

They stood up and took their purses.

"One reason I love California is that you don't have to *perform*—whether it's hygiene commandments or the way you dress or what you cook. In California, I can drink mimosas for breakfast and smell roses all day long and who cares? All the awful things they called our duty, thankfully I'm well past those, as well as never cooking a brisket."

"And I got to attend public school where I had a normal life and regular teachers and played sports," said Margie. "Like Homer, I would have hated governesses."

Tillie's answer was lost in the noise of the wheels and rush of air between cars as they opened and closed doors.

The Bar Car looked as pitiful as Tillie feared, a few older people sitting in a dimly-lit carriage as if their lives had been suspended. The wide bar was shuttered.

"This is tragic," Tillie said, taking Margie's arm. "They might as well be knitting socks. If your Papa delivers us from danger once again—though I don't believe there's any need to worry—I'll get my hair done and wear Mother's foxes for a brief visit with my brother in a neutral place like the Plaza, though he'll have to wear a tie."

"Homer certainly wears ties. He's a professor, Mama, at Columbia Law and he's one of the youngest judges. He writes opinion pieces for the *Times* on labor issues."

"He was always too much of a radical for Alfred," Tillie sniffed. "Your father hates the Bolsheviks."

"Homer isn't a Bolshevik. He's a Socialist Progressive. He's wonderful to me."

"You two have probably discussed all my faults."

"No, Mama, we never do. We talk about politics and economics."

"How dull. Homer was not exactly dull when he was young but he disapproved of family and childhood, both which I loved. Homer called us parasites. He reproached us for not having Russian souls, whatever that meant. We used to bring our old clothes to the Lower East Side where people came from all the Russias. The girls were ever so grateful for my pretty dresses but you wouldn't want to invite them home. Margie, don't look at me that way. I'm being honest. The German Jews didn't like the eastern Hebrews flooding New York. They gave us a bad name when we were fitting in. There was one Russian exception in my girlhood and he almost sent me to an early grave."

"What are you talking about? Did he have a knife, like Homer?"

Tillie waited until they'd reached their cabin, opened the door and stepped in. Once there, she found a clean glass and poured in Seagram's.

"I had my brush with Russian romance, Margie. What you don't know about your mother! Enough about me. What, dear, do you do in advertising?"

"Coincidentally, I'm working on a radio show right now with a wonderful writer and actress named Gertrude Berg who is creating a program about immigrant lives, mostly Russians, in greater New York. It will be the first national Jewish-themed show."

"Like Amos and Andy?" Tillie asked. Before Margie answered, Tillie continued, "Why would anyone want a radio program about Russian Jews? Of course they're talented and entertaining. Eddie's first wife was a Russian, with a mustache. Her father got Eddie into pictures, the reason why he married her and not me. They divorced."

"Mrs. Berg grew up performing in the Catskills at her father's hotel," said Margie.

"Well, I could have guessed." Tillie gazed out the window and yawned. "We've gotten through one full day and it wasn't bad at all. Let's have our beds made up and enjoy our nightcap in our little home away from home."

Tillie changed into a white silk nightdress with lace ruffles at the sleeves and neck. The moment she lay down, her eyes closed and she began lightly snoring. Margie savored the calm to think about the radio show, *The Rise of the Goldbergs.*

Before she'd met the writer and star of the show, Gertrude Berg, Margie had stepped into the elevator going up to a top floor of the Empire State building to the NBC executive offices. Before the doors closed, a short and rather stout woman wearing furs and a hat with a feather came in. At the door to the NBC suite, Mrs. Berg introduced herself to Margie who still didn't know who she was.

Once in the executive offices, Mrs. Berg began reading her script in the words of her character, Molly Goldberg. She spoke her lines as naturally to the men in suits and ties as if she were talking to a friend by telephone. She managed to make the men laugh with Molly's malapropisms without making fun of her character. David Sarnoff, the most important man in radio, laughed out loud.

"It's *Mamala!*" he clapped his hands.

Margie then read the commercial she'd written for Sunshine Soap, a possible sponsor for Mrs. Berg's show. She was nervous and her hands trembled with the script. The next moment, Mrs. Berg had the mic and began reading the ad copy, bringing Margie's words to life as if she truly loved washing the glassware in Sunshine.

On the way down in the elevator, Mrs. Berg patted Margie's arm. "Your words made those soap bubbles come to life. I just added the hot water."

# FIVE

AT BREAKFAST BEFORE REACHING Chicago, their white-jacketed waiter leaned over the table. "I have understood, Madam, that you are close to those in the know. I have placed my life savings in the shares. Do you believe the Market will prevail?"

"You and your family will be safe," said Tillie. "My husband is doing his best." When they were alone again, she turned to Margie. "Is there cause to worry?"

"Everyone's got jitters," Margie said, "but Tommy always says the right words to do when he sees people worried, 'Let's have another drink.'"

"Music to my ears. I'm going to fall for your handsome Tommy."

"You'll also agree with his claim that Prohibition makes people drink more. 'You never know when you might get the next one,' I quote him. When he has a hangover, I give him a Bicarb of Soda and an aspirin." Margie looked out over spent fields of corn. "There's a product you can praise without needing to exaggerate. Bicarb of Soda washes dirt from windows and settles the stomach. I doubt anything will ever replace it."

"You see Tommy at bedtime?" Tillie leaned forward. "That you didn't mention."

"He sleeps on my sofa with a blanket when he can't get to his upstairs, a studio which is one room the size of a large closet. My apartment is bigger, you'll see."

"You put him to bed like a baby but nothing more? For a modern girl, you're an innocent child, Margie." Tillie sighed. "I hope this fast-talking, hat-over-one-eye-newsman isn't a rogue like Sylvia's David who has led my poor cousin a merry chase."

"I'm so sorry about that. Aunt Sylvia is so independent and smart. Tommy is sincere and never tries to fool anyone but he's too likable for his own good."

"I'm not sure I understand you."

Margie sighed. "He can't say no to a drink or a pretty face."

"I didn't mean to compare your Tommy to David who lacks charm and only talks about himself." Tillie patted Margie's hand. "Let's concentrate on the challenge ahead."

"What is that?"

"Tommy, of course. When you appear in the French hat we'll buy at Bendel's you'll be irresistible to Ronald Colman himself. Hats, in your mother's opinion, transform a woman. Forget about cooking your way to his heart. It's the chapeau."

"I thought you were warning against a man who chases women. Not that Tommy actually does the chasing. They fall in his path. He does resemble Colman, you'll see."

Margie pointed to buildings in the distance. "We're almost into Chicago. The time passed so quickly, aren't you glad we came?"

"It's not been so bad at all," Tillie replied.

"You're all packed, nothing left behind because we'll need to get right off to make the connection with the Century to New York."

"I have an idea, Margie. Let's not rush. We can stop in Chicago overnight. I haven't seen the Leiter sisters recently. They're in charge of fashion buying for all of Marshall Field. They'll help create your new look."

"Mama, we can't lose a day in Chicago. We need to see Papa as soon as we can."

"What day of the week is it? I've lost track."

"It's Wednesday, October 23rd."

"Wednesday! Nothing ever happens this late in the week. We'll stop in Chicago."

"No, we're catching the Century and going straight on through." Margie stood up and waited for Tillie who was looking for the waiter. When he arrived, she gave him a twenty-dollar tip, and patted his sleeve. "Don't you worry, the Market will be fine."

On the 20th Century Limited, Tillie had her hair done in the beauty salon while Margie stayed in their cabin to read the newspapers. Tillie returned, her cheeks flushed from the hair dryer and her silver waves perfectly marcelled.

"Daisy or Sally, whatever her name, was the smartest little girl who knew just what I needed." Tillie held up a bottle with brown liquid sloshing in the bottle.

Tillie took Margie's arm as they walked through several cars to the dining lounge with low lighting and candles on every table. "I should have gotten more dressed," she said.

"You look very smart, Mama. The girl was good with your hair."

"Thank you, dear. I'm a woman who needs to be admired. I know that much about myself. Best of all, we're provided."

Tillie poured bourbon into their water glasses and asked for ice.

"You see how civilized life can be," Tillie whispered. "A speakeasy on wheels."

Dinner began with Russian caviar, followed by Maine lobster, a filet mignon, potatoes gratin, watercress salad. Tillie finished with apple pie a la mode.

After supper, they went to the Lounge Car where fumes of good whiskey rose in the air with cigar smoke, and Tillie declared, "I feel at home. Do you know, I've actually been missing Alfred but I've enjoyed your company, Margie. I don't know if I ever had the character to be the independent woman you are but now we'll never know, will we?"

A waiter brought two glasses with ice and asked if they wanted soda or ginger ale. Tillie asked for the ginger ale, poured herself and Margie bourbon over crackling ice, and topped off their glasses. She took a sip. "I did choose my creature comforts over wild romance, not that I would have had that with Eddie. It's only that I never had it at all." She looked down at the diamonds on her finger and smiled at the her brright red nails that sparkled with gloss.

"I know I'm silly and superficial and care for trifles. Don't contradict. It's what I've got instead of...well what you feel about Tommy."

"If only it were that easy, Mama," Margie replied.

215

# Six

THURSDAY, OCTOBER 24TH, ALFRED woke early with ringing in his ears. His throat was sore and his head hurt. The whine in his head wouldn't stop. From the windows to the back recesses of the room, the *fleur de lis* tridents in the wallpaper seemed to march up the walls and over the ceiling as if these little three prongs were weapons to chase him out of their sight. On the table before him lay the morning papers with their conflicting banner headlines. WALL STREET PANIC AS STOCKS FALL! A second seemed less dire. BROKERS BELIEVE WORST OVER.

His daughter's telegram sent the night before from Chicago announced their morning arrival at Grand Central Station. Alfred calculated that if the 20th Century came in on time and they had their baggage unloaded efficiently, and their cab didn't get stuck in cross town traffic to the Plaza, he had forty-five minutes before Tillie and Margie arrived.

He folded his clothing and sat down to compose a letter. But he couldn't make his hand move across the stationery because he didn't know what he was thinking of writing that would make sense to his beloved daughter and wife. He himself didn't understand the cause of his malaise, the suffocating anguish he felt, feeling the walls and the carpet so oppressive. To get air in the room, he pulled apart the red curtains and opened up the view to 59th and Central Park. Light streamed in as if it had been dammed-up. The cool, rain-washed air smelled as spotless as the sky. Overnight, light showers had cleared the atmosphere so the morning sun glowed and shimmered on the autumn russets and golds of the trees along pathways in the Park.

He stepped out on a narrow balcony that extended from his window, less than a foot wide between the building and an iron railing

His knees trembled. As he steadied himself against the railing, he realized it would take so little to end the whirring in his head, a roaring of oceans between his ears. He felt choked up with anger at his former partners, regret at letting himself be driven away, a dismissal that hurt all the more because it was so unjust.

A horse whinnied and a high-hatted coachman helped two stout women into his carriage where blinkered horses, their heads buried in nose bags, were eating their oats or mash. In October 1907, despite the laughter his partners had packed him off with, he'd gone his own way, rid himself of copper and triumphed. Mina Greenbaum had recognized his wisdom. She never forgot to let him know that he'd saved their family. Abraham Cogansky, whose wife Bella conveyed the family's good wishes with a packet of her delicious sweets every Rosh Hashanah, owed his prosperity to Alfred's cool head in a time of turmoil. Alfred had intended to visit *Cogansky, Father & Son, Tailors to the Discerning Gentleman,* on Madison Avenue, but now the words that Singer and Lasley had assailed him with made him doubt why he was alive. Was he that much of a fool to be mocked and insulted yet once again?

He gripped the window drapes behind him like an understudy waiting in the wings for his moment on the stage, torn between stepping forward into the unknown or back into the room where his corrective shoes stood waiting for him.

---

As the 20th Century came up the Hudson River toward Manhattan, Margie's eyes went from the rolling grey of the river to the headlines on Thursday morning's papers the porter delivered with coffee, eggs and croissants. Some reports indicated serious trouble with the Market while other issued words of assurance.

Tillie primped her hair and chose a pewter grey silk blouse with ruffles and a grey gabardine skirt.

"Help me with my zipper, dear," she said.

Margie zipped the skirt but the waist band button wouldn't reach the button hole.

"It's too tight, Mother. Put on something else."

"No, I want to wear this!" Tillie stood with her little legs firm and stamped one foot. "I'll hold my breath. Just being on Fifth Avenue makes me look slimmer."

"It makes me feel fatter because other women are so slim."

"It's all in your mind," said Tillie.

"We have different minds," answered Margie.

"Don't be stubborn. When we arrive, first thing we do is liberate my little furs. They belonged to Mama so they don't mind spending most of their time stored in the east, close to where they grew up on Long Island, but now I'll bring them out."

Margie stifled her laugh about dead foxes and their feelings. She had no answers to most of Tillie's illogical remarks. She watched as her mother sucked in her breath until the button finally went into the hole. "Sorry," Margie said, pinching a little pinkish flesh.

"Suffer to be beautiful," said Tillie. "Now sit with me on my suitcase to close it."

The train slowed until it was barely moving alongside the platform.

As soon as Tillie caught sight of a tall man in a fedora waving a bouquet of yellow daisies tied with a red ribbon, she mouthed *Tommy?* Margie blushed and nodded.

"Aren't you going to wait for the red carpet to be rolled out, Mama?"

"I can forego the red carpet for this handsome young man," said Tillie.

In a moment, Tommy bounded into their stateroom. "Sis!" he said, and "Ma'm," he bowed.

"No such formalities. I'm not that stuffy, young man. And daisies, my favorites, how did you know!" smiled Tillie.

"Tom Grensky, Mama. My mother, Mathilda Hornthall," Margie said.

"Honored." He bowed and handed Tillie his bouquet.

"How is it out there?" Margie asked.

"A perfect fall day," Tommy answered.

"I mean, what's the ticker tape doing?"

"The bear is growling up and down Wall Street but the bull seems to be showing his horns also. Total uncertainty that could turn into chaos at any moment."

Tillie clapped her hands. "Drama! Either way, my husband will save the day."

"I wonder where Papa is? I sent him a wire. I thought he'd meet us," said Margie.

Tommy took Tillie's hat box and picked up the largest suitcase.

"I've heard much about you, young man." Tillie patted Tommy's arm.

"Oh, dear." Tommy lifted his fedora, revealing thick, wavy black hair.

"I feel familiar enough already to tell you that you don't need a hat, Tommy. It's a shame to hide such an outstanding head of hair."

"Thanks. The 20th Century is some swell train, isn't it, Mrs. Horn-thall?" Tommy gave Tillie one arm and Margie the other. "Mind you don't trip on the red carpet."

"Please, call me Tillie. I understand your mother is a true woman of the west, like you and Margie, while I'm merely a transplant. I hope she's well."

"Mother's fine, thank you for asking. Margie was a peach with her. Took some of the heat off me when she visited the last time."

"You didn't tell me about that, Margie. I've never been to a mining town. It must be exciting when they take the gold out of the ground."

"In Leadville, gold came first, then silver in lead ore. Rich while it lasted. By the time we left, after my father died, the riches of Leadville were gone. I've never returned."

"I am sorry that your mother lost your father so young. Although Alfred doesn't have a strong constitution, he takes care of himself. You can't imagine the smelly drinks he consumes in the name of his health."

"Mother, Tommy doesn't care what Alfred drinks." Margie looked pleadingly.

"And on that subject, Tommy, Margie assures me you're the man who knows how to provide remedies that are healthful in a special way." Tillie stopped in the middle of the passageway opening into glimmering lights of Grand Central "Isn't it beautiful?"

"How would you describe the symptoms before I prescribe?"

"Dry throat, very dry throat." Tillie coughed. "Can you help?"

She adjusted her hat so the feather waved in Tommy's direction. "As dry as if we'd crossed the Mojave sands on foot—which at times this trip felt as if we had."

"Sounds serious but I have just the remedy for a desert crossed and a dry throat right with me." Tommy produced a silver flask that he handed to Tillie.

"How can anything be wrong in New York City with this brilliant fellow anticipating our every desire?" Tillie tipped her head back to swallow and gasped.

"Mama! Can't we wait until we're out of the station?" Margie asked.

"This does taste medicinal. My bootlegger, by the happy name of Prospero, wouldn't touch it. He gets me Seagrams blended."

Tommy whistled. "That's good stuff. Costs a lot."

"What exactly do you call this drink?"

"Gin, with a hint of vodka. I'll get you better. I have a pal who owns a Prince Alfred custom-made jacket with zinc-lined breast pockets. He uses one pocket for ice and the other for the essentials. He says the suit was originally made for a loony who chewed charcoal and ice together with whiskey and considered himself nourished."

"As long as I haven't gone blind yet, I'll have one more sip. A chilled glass and an olive—you'd hardly notice the taste. You'll take us to a speakeasy, won't you? Alfred refuses. He says driving around at night looking for a peep hole would be too dangerous."

"Like going into a blind pig, Mrs. H.," said Tommy.

"And what is that, young man?"

"It's a low-level joint. We'll only go to the best with you and young Miss H."

"I'm not averse to a little slumming. Look at those pumps on that young woman, Margie. Aren't the heels an unusual shape!"

"Wedges, Mama. They're new."

"I haven't seen them in Los Angeles. We'll stop off at Bergdorf and try on a pair. I knew it was a good idea to come and shake off the country dust of California."

"I want to see Papa first. I sent two telegrams."

"Don't worry about your father. He has nine lives. First we'll get my foxes from storage, only a few blocks east and uptown. Not every woman can wear the chunky heels but if they're in fashion, we should try to make a good show of being up to date while we're here. Look at that cute cape lined with fur."

"If you need warmth, I'll lend you a cardigan sweater," said Margie.

"I'm not Jane Eyre, dear. My little foxes don't want to stay in that horrid place when I'm here. When I wear them, I feel as though Mama and I are communing. The darlings grew up in New York and cavorted in the nearby forests."

"You already told me about their upbringing, Mama."

"Why don't we take one cab and you drop me off at Mendel's on Third, give Papa a kiss and tell him I'll be right along. Look at that headline. **Black Thursday Crash**."

"I'm afraid the hit song of the season is going to die a quick death," Tommy said.

"What is the song?" Tillie asked.

"It's called 'I'm in the Market for You.' to Porter's 'I'm in the Mood for You.'"

Tommy stopped a cab, helped Tillie and Margie into the back seat. "Driver, uptown first, take Lex. Then we'll go back to Fifth, the Plaza. Traffic looks light."

Tillie leaned over to whisper in Margie's ear. "He's so wonderfully *American*! Such perfect Continental English. Much more *western* than most Californians."

Tillie caught sight of two women who seemed to be holding each other up.

"Oh dear, is that woman wearing black bunting? Did someone die? Did we declare war? Bunting gives me a chill. Where's my hat box?"

When Mendel's Fur Storage appeared, Tillie rapped on the cab partition. "Here we are, dears. Later, I'll expect a proper dry one, young man. Someone in the hotel is bound to come up with real gin."

"Come on, Mama, you get your furs. I have a feeling we shouldn't waste time going to Papa."

# SEVEN

"Papa!"

Alfred heard Margie's voice, and before he could react, a pair of strong arms were holding him around the waist.

"Mr. Hornthall, Sir! Forgive me, but you're close to a large open window and there's a breeze out."

Alfred's white bony feet had somehow lost their black socks as well as their shoes. Margie kneeled beside him and hunted for the stockings, but seeing her father's small bare feet made her gasp. Even in the summer, her father padded around in slippers or shoes with socks, never sandals, never barefoot. She didn't realize how his flesh around his twisted ankle was shrunken, as if he'd been in shackles. He must be in constant pain, she thought as she knelt closer to touch the cool bone with her cheek, stroking the veins and tendons before slipping his foot back into the sock.

"Papa, were you sleep-walking?" Alfred coughed and shook his head. "Do you have a temperature?" Margie touched her father's forehead which felt warm and moist. "Come and sit beside me." She held both his hands to warm them in her own.

"I was letting in the air. Where is your mother?" Alfred took deep breaths.

"Mama's on her way. Tommy, give Father a drink."

"I don't know your name, young man."

"Excuse me, Mr. Hornthall. I'm Thomas Grensky, a friend of your daughter's."

"Tommy has already met Mother. She'll be here in a few minutes."

Tommy handed a glass to Alfred who coughed as soon as he tried to swallow.

"I've never liked strong stuff and this tastes like denatured alcohol."

"It isn't highly refined but it won't blind you," said Tommy.

"What's the word out there? I haven't seen papers in the last hour," Alfred said.

"The news keeps changing—worse, better, worse. The tickers can't keep up. They're calling it Black Thursday." Tommy held the flask up.

Alfred shook his head. "Black Thursday, not very original. You should have seen what copper did on Black Thursday in '07. Went up to seventy in the morning, down to ten before you could blink, so fast you'd have thought it was a gas, not a solid. The sums lost were immeasurable."

"I know a little of 1907 and what was lost when copper fell, Mr. Hornthall," said Tommy.

"But you can't have been more than a child in 1907," said Alfred.

"I was six. My father lost his life's savings in copper, had a heart attack and died a week later. He'd been ill but my mother said the shock of his losses caused his death."

"I'm sorry to hear that. Copper never was a reliable investment," said Alfred.

"Best not to look back." Tommy raised his glass. "To a brighter day! Cheers!"

"This stuff could light the room on fire." Alfred tried to sip again.

"You haven't lost your sense of humor, Papa." Margie still held her father's hand.

"It was easier to be objective from California when the Market was all numbers and not complicated by people who try to sway you from your certainty."

"What do you mean, Papa?" Margie asked, but her father didn't seem to hear her question and went on, as if thinking aloud.

"Low interest rates, people and businesses with too much money to speculate. I'm not a soothsayer but I read the signs."

"You can get superstitious about Octobers," Tommy said.

"You certainly can but it's really a matter of fundamentals not magic."

"Papa's always been ahead of his time," Margie said.

"This summer, while Mathilda was shopping downtown in Los

Angeles, I visited the La Brea tar pits where I saw a creature rise from the black bubbling goo. You might say I was hallucinating, but I saw a flare and felt heat as if a mammoth was returning to warn me. Perhaps it was a warning from myself—what that Viennese doctor calls the unconscious. On the strictly rational level, I knew the trusts were too large."

"Papa, I've never heard you so philosophical." Margie squeezed his hand.

"Anything you got rid of is to the good, Mr. Hornthall. I've never saved a dime to play the Market but I've watched ordinary Joes in the press pawn the wife's wedding ring to buy a few more shares of Shenandoah. Don't want to run into them today."

"The trusts were pure shenanigans, then and now." Alfred shook his head. "The truth is, I've never been a well-liked man. I lack the common touch. I'm not saying this because I'm a Jew. There are charming Jews. Elman Lasley is one. Mathilda disarms everyone. Margie, you inherited Mathilda's touch."

"Don't berate yourself, Papa. You've given Mama and me every-thing and we love you. Even when you were in the middle of some calculations, you'd stop working to answer my questions or help me with my homework or answer my questions."

Alfred stood up and limped across the room. Tommy rose to follow but Alfred stopped him. "Don't worry, Thomas, I'm just pacing. I did sell a good amount and shorted other positions—a dirty word in a bull market—so we are safe. But Mathilda expects heroics of me and I backed down on my certainty that the Market would crack."

"You may still be right, Sir," said Tommy.

"I don't want to be right about this," said Alfred. "I hate being a Cassandra."

"Mama will be here any minute so let's order champagne, Papa."

"How shall we do that, my dear? It's prohibited."

"I've learned a lot about the loopholes, Papa. Tommy will call room service and before we know it, champagne will appear. Let's get club sandwiches, too. I'm famished and I think we could all use something to settle the nerves and stomach."

Tommy picked up the phone. "Of course I'll pay cash," he said into the receiver.

"Fetch your suitcase, Papa. That old one Mama always wants you to throw out."

Alfred didn't seem to hear her. He was talking to himself. "If tomorrow is as bad as today, I could buy back in. Or perhaps I won't buy at all and let time tell how far the Market will fall." He turned to Margie. "Your mother may have to give up the races at Del Mar but we won't lose our home, as her father would have done in '07."

"If my father hadn't stepped in, my grandparents would have been without a roof over their heads," Margie said.

"If you have any cash from your transactions, you can buy up Broadway for a song." Tommy whistled a tune. "It's a new show tune from *No, No Nanette*. Can't get it out my head. 'Tea for two and you for me.' I hope it won't close before you go to see it."

"No theater for me, young man. I don't understand the point of make-believe but my wife loves the shows, the sillier the better."

"The suitcase, Papa." Margie stood beside the battered brown case.

Alfred unfastened a hidden compartment and pulled out one-hundred-dollar bills.

Tommy whistled. "That's quite a bundle. Weren't you afraid of being robbed?"

"If I followed Mathilda's advice and dressed like a rich man who carried Samsonite luggage, I probably would have been relieved of it."

"*Samsonite, strong enough to stand on*, that's a great ad line!" said Margie.

They all heard a knock on the door and then Tillie's voice, "Anyone home?" Tillie's fur foxes seemed to precede her, pointed glittering eyes staring from her shoulder.

"Alfred, you look pale."

"We were just discussing the situation, Mathilda."

"And I'm looking at Tommy who's even more handsome without his hat. No more fedoras for you. They'll wear down the scalp and suppress your natural waves."

Margie cleared her throat. "Mama, would you like something to drink?"

"Of course I would. What a ruckus out on the street. I survived the young man's medicine and I can still see daylight, but I don't want to push my luck."

"Your husband anticipated. Champagne on the way." Tommy bowed to Alfred.

"He's always clairvoyant. My own genius." Tillie kissed Alfred on the cheek, which caused a blush to rise on his pale cheeks. When he coughed, Tillie moved away and walked to the window to pull the drapes completely open.

"I'm pleased you let in the fresh air, Alfred. Usually you keep everything closed up as if you were a mole. Did I hear a worrisome cough?"

Before Alfred could deny a hint of illness, Tillie continued, "I have an idea. Let's all go for a carriage ride in the Park. What memories the view brings back. We were naughty children, Sylvia and Eddie and I. When the parents dined here in the restaurant, they left us with a maid in an upstairs room. We'd stand on a sill and pour water from windows onto people's heads as they walked by on 59th ."

Alfred seemed to shrink back at the mention of a window. Margie patted his arm and brought him to the sofa to sit down.

"Mrs. H, you were a rascal," said Tommy.

"We liked having fun. Otherwise, life was so boring. Is someone at the door?"

Margie opened for a white-coated waiter rolling in a tray with four champagne flutes, ice bucket and two bottles wrapped in brown paper.

"Oh, Alfred, you magical man. You don't even need to make a call and champagne materializes." Tillie kissed him again.

Tommy lifted the Mumm's, green and sweating with cold, and held it aloft.

"To your liking, Sir?" the waiter addressed Tommy.

"Allow me." Alfred pulled a bill from his pocket. "Keep the change, lad."

"I love it when Alfred is munificent. To our good fortune! I should send you off alone more often, my dear. You become as chivalrous as when we met and I drank far too much champagne."

"Mr. Hornthall, to your wisdom." Tommy clinked glasses with Alfred. "Never let the bubble out of the bottle that's destined for the glass. Let me fill you up."

"I knew Tommy would make Alfred merry." Tillie found the nearest mirror and primped her hair. "I was only a *little* concerned, Alfred, when I saw the headlines, *black* this and *black* that, but you take away my cares. I only need to freshen up a moment before taking our daughter for a new wardrobe."

When her mother left the room, Alfred said, "I wish Mathilda would not go on so. No one likes a survivor when others have gone down, especially Jewish survivors. If she'd go shopping and stay busy, I'd do some calculating here." He reached for his green eye shade on the table.

"I won't drive you into bankruptcy," Tillie called out to Alfred as she snuggled the foxes around her neck and fastened her hat with a pearl pin. "Margie, we'll have a bite of lunch and onward to Saks and Bergdorf where we'll find you everything that spells style. I saw more of those darling wedge heels on the street."

"Try for the bargains, my dear." Alfred handed her three hundred dollars in bills and kissed her on the cheek. Tillie kissed him back and tweaked his ear.

"Keeping us in clover. I'm the one person in the world who knows you're a genius, Alfred. When girls come around wanting your attention, I'll say, 'This brilliant man is my husband, he's married to me, so keep your eyes to yourself.'"

"You're quite sure you'll be fine alone, Papa?" Margie looked first to her father and then to Tommy who waited for Alfred to speak.

"I'm perfectly well, my dears. You go off and have a good time."

Tillie kissed him on his cheek and held him so close that her perfume almost made him sneeze, but as soon as the door closed behind all of them, he let out several coughs and sat down because he felt faint.

# EIGHT

MARGIE LEFT TILLIE AT Pegasus, a speakeasy on 50th and Third while she dashed downtown to the new Benton & Bowles offices in the Chanin Building on 42nd and Lexington. She told Dick De Vere, the head copywriter, that she'd take work with her and return after lunch.

"My mother and father are in town. I hope you don't mind," she said.

"Stay as long as you like. It's crazy out there," De Vere answered. "No one's working, they're all watching the ticker or going downtown to the killing yards, unless they're drowning their sorrows. I'm not invested. I hate risks."

"Good for you." Margie grabbed a folder.

"Say, weren't you in California on vacation for two weeks with your folks?"

"I went and then I turned around because my parents decided to come to town. I only hope Mrs. Berg will have a chance to go on air with all the confusion everywhere."

"It's up to the gods now." De Vere lifted his ink-stained hands.

Margie caught a cab back to meet her mother at Pegasus, knocked three times below a winged horse and gave the new password, Tea for Two, from the hit song. The door opened and she entered darkness.

"Mind your step." A hand took her elbow. "Hello, dear, where's the gentleman?"

"Tommy says hello. I'm meeting my mother."

"I see the resemblance, Miss. She's there, in a booth. Doesn't waste time."

"You don't have to force drink on her. She takes to it naturally, like a camel crossing the desert to an oasis."

"What will you have?" Tillie waved and beckoned Margie. "The martini is perfectly dry and it's real gin. I don't mean to malign your Tommy's firewater."

"It's early for me. I need coffee. It's been quite a day so far."

"Hasn't it, and we haven't begun shopping. Now don't disappoint the waiter, darling. Order alcohol—that's what we're here for. If necessary, I'll drink it."

"A short beer for me." Margie said to the waiter.

"Beer? Who drinks beer when there's gin?"

"I do, this early in the day, and I have copy to write," said Margie.

"Never go by the sun for drinking time, which is why darkness at noon is just right." Tillie lowered her nose and sipped. "You know, Tommy is a man with perfect pitch. The way he mixes with people! Alfred's not sociable by nature but he was taken with your beau. Tommy could go to Hollywood and be in pictures."

"Tommy isn't my beau, we've talked about that."

"Did it not go well at work, dear?"

"Dick De Vere, a man usually not known for his friendliness, seemed happy that the big spenders were suffering. Our owners come from money—Mr. Bowles and Mr. Benton—and De Vere resents it."

"Why in the world would anyone resent money of all things?" asked Tillie.

"If you don't know, Mother, I can't tell you. Right now, I'm hoping that RCA stock doesn't crash and take NBC and Mrs. Berg's show with it."

"You must marry Tommy, Margie. He's already like a son to me. I'm sure Alfred would trade in Elman if he could. I wouldn't, of course. I want them both as sons."

"Mama, don't talk that way. It's ridiculous."

"Not at all. We are buying you a cocktail dress for dinner tonight that will begin a new chapter with Tommy. Bendel's first. The girls will be happy to see me back."

At Bendel's, Tillie snagged a young salesgirl and told her they wanted her personal help. "Bring an array of dresses, my daughter's size, into the fitting room. Current fashion for evening, smart, and well-made. She's on a tight schedule."

The salesgirl returned with an armful of dresses.

"Here, what about this?" Tillie asked of a frilly number. Margie shook her head.

"I don't need to look like a meringue."

Finally, the woman brought Margie a black faille with an interesting neckline.

"It's smart and hints at a special *someone* in the wings," Tillie said.

Margie held up the black ruched top with a bias-cut skirt that fell below the knee. She looked at the price tag. "My god, Mother, it's so expensive. More than three month's of my salary. We can't afford it."

Tillie examined the label. "Yes, they know how to charge, because it's French, look here. Imagine we're in Paris."

"It's too expensive."

"My daughter works for pennies," Tillie told the girl, "so sometimes her mother has to step in and take charge. We'll buy it, and black pumps to go with."

As Margie was trying on heels, Tillie returned holding a close-fitting black hat with a sequin chevron and a feather. "We wouldn't want to miss this chapeau. Now we need shoes, the kind with wedges or maybe more a heel for evening and height."

Margie slipped into black heels with a rosette as if they'd been made for her.

"O.K., now I'm Cinderella complete, and thank you, Mother, for a beautiful dress that I'd never buy myself. Are you going back to Papa right now or having this sent?"

"Sent, with hat and shoes," Tillie said as she pulled her large bills from her bag. "There's enough left for me to shop and keep out of Alfred's way while he works more miracles."

———————

Once Alfred felt sure that his wife wouldn't come back for something she'd forgotten, he called down for the newspapers. The *Daily News'* headlines were big enough for a Balkan revolution. WILD-EYED BROKERS RUN FOR COVER.

He wanted to see the damage for himself, but downtown he risked being recognized, and if Lasley or Singer learned he'd sold and had cash, they'd strangle him with their own hands. He had no taste for confrontation. He needed to go undercover.

He took Tillie's black raincoat from the closet. In the pocket he found a scarf, large black sunglasses and a rain hat. He put them all on, and on his way out, picked up his wife's long black cigarette holder and refitted one of her cigarettes. In the mirror, he saw some sort of small bohemian or an Italian who reminded him of Prospero.

The ticker tapes Alfred glanced at through windows on Broadway showed a slight upswing. He didn't care if US Steel was doubling its worth: his mind was made up, he was staying out. He kept on the dark glasses and hat and entered a broker's office where he issued a sell on the rest of his Steel and RCA despite their falling price.

Before he took the first downtown train to Battery, he lowered the hat over his ears until it reached the top of the dark glasses. What struck him most when he emerged at the tip of Manhattan and walked toward Broad and Wall was the ominous change in the weather. Uptown, the sky had been blue and the sun shining. Here, the air was smoky, as if there were a fire. Perhaps it was just the crowds, police and vehicles all trying to make their way through masses of men on the streets.

Alfred found a spot on steps at the end of Broad and Exchange Place from where he had a view of the Street. As he read the words "Integrity Protecting Works of Man" written in great marble letters above the columns of the Stock Exchange, he reflected that once again Integrity had not done her job as promised.

He tied the scarf higher around his neck until it reached his chin. His cloak of invisibility made him feel removed from the furor, a Babel of sounds that suddenly was followed by the strangest kind of sighing that ran down Wall Street as if a collective being were letting out its breath.

---

Tillie hoped to run into an acquaintance, a familiar face, but everyone on Fifth Avenue seemed to have their eyes on their newspapers or at their feet. On the upper floor of Saks, a dark blue outfit caught her eye. On closer inspection, it wasn't a dress but pants with wide legs and a top that had a criss-cross bodice. When she tried it on, she liked the way the pants flattered her legs, and the clingy fabric fit over her bosom. Another French design, she saw, and so expensive she'd have to go back to Alfred for more cash.

She told the salesgirl she'd like to have the pants hemmed before five o'clock. "Three inches up on the pants. Be sure not to let this go to anyone else. Here's fifty dollars just to make sure you hold it. I'll be back before you close with the rest in cash."

"Madam, take your time, it's yours. It's like a funeral parlor in here today."

At the Plaza, Tillie asked the front desk clerk whether the Guggenheims were in their suite on the 14th floor. "I'm not at liberty to say, Madam," the boy replied.

"They're old friends. You're too young to know me, but they do."

"Sorry, Madam. If you will be so kind to wait, I'll ask my manager."

"Don't bother, I'll call, and I'll remember that you were not helpful." Tillie flipped her fox heads so the eyes stared at the clerk. She felt slighted that the young man didn't believe she knew the Guggenheims well enough to drop in. Did he imagine she might want to rob the master suite? But what would be the point, she thought as the elevator rose, of striking up the old acquaintanceship with Irene Guggenheim? Irene had become an important philanthropist whose good works appeared in the *Times* social pages and Tillie felt that she had nothing worthy to match that.

When Alfred didn't answer her knock, she let herself in. A maid had tidied up. She slumped onto the couch where Alfred had left some papers with numbers on them that she didn't bother to read.

The noise of horns and cars and the bustle of New York around the Plaza hurt her ears. Perhaps she was just tired after the busy day, she said to herself. New York made her feel older. It was four p.m. When would Alfred be back and where was Margie? Tillie didn't like being alone without a drink or anyone to talk to. She didn't often get the blues but she felt the low pressure coming on just when she heard a bustle at the door and leaped up, checked lipstick in the mirror and turned on her smile for handsome Tommy whose deep voice she could hear.

# NINE

"YOU'RE NOT TELLING ME that Delmonico's is no more! That's the most devastating news I've heard all day." Tillie didn't look devastated as she sat with a drink in her hand, little stocking feet dangling over the couch.

"I guess it will have to be Sherry's," she said. "I can still remember Mr. Sherry's Egyptian quail and his Sweetbreads Terrapin. Divine!"

"I'm sorry to say, they closed two years ago when Mr. Sherry died," Tommy said.

"No, not Sherry's gone, too! What is left in New York!" Tillie pouted with the indignation she'd been feeling all day. "Everything's changed and gone. I feel abandoned by New York."

"There are plenty of good places to eat," said Margie.

The discussion was interrupted by Alfred's arrival in his wife's hat and scarf.

"It's Groucho in *Cocoanuts*!" Tillie howled. "Are you taking up a career on stage now? What did I tell you two about the way Alfred changes like a chameleon from moment to moment. This time you've outdone yourself, my dear."

Alfred removed the sunglasses and returned them to Tillie. He hung her scarf, coat and hat in the closet. "There, all in order," he said.

"Oh Alfred, things don't have to be in order. You should kick up your heels more often. Where *did* you go in that unusual outfit? To an audition to replace Houdini?"

"To the shortest street of sorrows on earth at this moment," Alfred said.

"You went downtown to Wall Street, Mr Hornthall? I tried to get down there but with so many shows closing, I had my plate full

234

consoling pals. I heard the street was pandemonium, a Roman circus. Men were flying out windows."

"It was more like a funeral. At one point a man appeared on a roof to the side of the Exchange. We were all looking up and I swear everyone held their breath. Fortunately, he then disappeared inside and a huge sigh of relief went up and down the street, as if the entire crowd was connected by an invisible wire."

"Alfred, I hate to miss a poetic word but I need to pick up a small purchase I made, anticipating your success. I must bring a little of your cleverly gained wealth."

"Mathilda, we're not out of the woods."

"I don't want to hear about any woods or street of sighs." She held out her hand.

"The man on Wall Street was only working on the roof," Alfred said as he gave Tillie bills.

"I'm glad for that," Margie said.

"Wait until you see how well Margie and I did amid the gloom. We'll brighten your spirits." Tillie pulled on her coat. "I'll be back before you know it. Hold the drinks."

"Good luck, Mrs. H."

When Tillie was out the door, Tommy scanned the papers. "Bad to worse."

"Not the worst yet," said Alfred. "Everyone in America will feel the effects."

---

As soon as Tillie returned with her dress box, Tommy handed her a drink.

"Have you conferred? I won't eat here in the hotel where the widows dine."

"I came up with 21 Club," said Tommy. "It's on 52nd, right around the corner, newly relocated from downtown where Jack and Charlie started their first place. Word is they have a direct line across Lake Erie to Mr. Bronfman."

"I told you, Margie, you'll become a worldly woman with Tommy."

"I certainly have learned to drink more like a New Yorker," said Margie.

"I like your girl as she is, Mrs. H. She's the most honest and brainiest person, for her young age, of course. She can write circles around me but she doesn't show me up. Don't get a big head, Sis. I need you to correct my grammar."

Margie blushed to her ears.

"Since my daughter made nothing but straight A's when she could have been having fun, it's excellent her education is of use. Tell me more about this 21 Club."

"At 21, their motto is *Spirits keep the Spirits up*," said Tommy.

"I'd like that over my bar at home," Tillie laughed.

"When they get raided—and everyone does—you never see a bottle. If you ask Charlie, he might show you the padded exit chutes where the bottles go for safe keeping."

"Have you been there, Margie? How dressy is it?"

"Not too dressy," Margie answered.

"We will dress it up then."

"Rummy news hounds call it home but women give it class," said Tommy.

"Margie, the new outfits, all the trimmings."

"Like a turkey!" Margie said.

Tillie shooed Margie into the adjoining room where she laid out their new clothes.

"What do you think? The girl at Saks gave me a discount when I paid her the balance in cash. She must have thought I wasn't coming back. My first pair of pants, if you don't count sleeping pajamas." Tillie held up the bottoms for Margie to touch.

"Quite an outfit but won't you be cold? It's October and that's summer silk."

"My foxes will protect me. Tommy said it was just around the corner."

As Margie struggled to hide her white brassiere under the low-necked black dress, Tillie said, "How stupid of me to forget black lingerie. Yours is institutional!"

Margie looked down at her décolletage. "I'm afraid I might fall out."

"Don't move too much. Now for hats." Tillie placed Margie's with the feather at an angle. "Just so, at a naughty angle like a delivery boy. Ready! Hold your breath."

Margie followed her mother into the sitting room. Tommy stood up.

"Sis! Will you look at my best gal. She's magnificent." Tommy toasted.

"My little black swan." Tillie patted Margie's arm. "Alfred, did you see Winston Churchill on Wall Street? I heard he was there."

"I didn't go inside the Exchange, Mathilda. To my mind, Mr. Churchill has very foolish economic ideas. Politicians and doctors should stick to their professions. Margie, your mother is right, you look stunning."

"Thank you, Papa. You just bought this French dress for me."

"We're on our way to 21. Alfred, what will you be wearing? Will you let me dress you up again?" Tillie asked.

"No, my dears, go without me. I'll order up a club sandwich and chamomile tea."

Tillie sighed. "All right, my genius, but we'll drink our first toast to you."

---

A heavy-set man in a tux opened the 21 Club and lighted their way down stairs.

"The usual?" the maitre d' in a tux asked Tommy.

"I like being with a man who has a usual. What is it?" Tillie laughed.

"A Long Island Tea." Tommy sat with Tillie and Margie facing him.

"I spent happy summers on Long Island. Of what does the tea consist?"

"Different establishments mix them differently. There's vodka or tequila or rum or gin or all three. Triple Sec and Ginger Ale may be added. No tea has been detected."

"One for me!" Tillie grinned.

"What will you drink, Margie?" Tommy asked.

"A Manhattan with the blended bourbon that Mama likes. Two cherries."

"Good choice, Sis. Blended not only tastes better but it's safer."

"Safer? How so?" asked Tillie.

"Something about the esters in blended is easier on the stomach than straights."

"I'll tell Prospero about the health benefits. He's our bootlegger, you see." Tillie paused. "Why do you think such a moronic and unpopular law punishing us for having a good time has lasted this long?"

"I've heard it's because of Russia, Mrs. H.," said Tommy.

"Russia?" asked Tillie.

"Bolshevism lives on vodka, or so we believe. Russia means godlessness, revolution and vodka, so ban booze, the masses won't revolt. That's just a theory."

"Say Russian Revolution and you say Jews." Tillie lowered her voice. "Trotskys, Einsteins, Guggenheims. Like your Tommy said, Russians."

"Only Trotsky is Russian, Mother. And the rest aren't revolutionaries."

Tillie shrugged. "You're so literal, dear. Information isn't everything."

Tommy stood up. "I'll put in our orders, two Teas and a blended Manhattan."

The band started playing, "Oh! How I Hate to Get Up in the Morning," and Tillie tapped her feet. "You know, Margie, I don't find these trousers unfeminine at all. I may buy several pair before we leave. Tommy is so democratic, so *American*."

"You said that earlier but do you mean as opposed to revolutionary, Mama?"

"Don't argue details. I heard him say you're his best gal."

"I'm his *Alka-Seltzer and Bayer Aspirin* grammar-correcting gal."

"Margie, I know from life observation that couples who vie for attention usually clash. Only one of a pair can be the peacock."

"Am I the pea hen? So much poultry this evening."

"Of course not. You're a remarkable young woman, and believe me when I say that a man like Tommy can't live on his looks and charm forever. He needs you."

"A pea hen?"

Tillie tapped a cigarette into her holder and held it out for a passing waiter to light. "Like Alfred, though differently. My intuition seldom fails me. I predict Tommy really wants a woman with a good head, not a dandelion on her shoulders. And darling, no brown hen ever wore a feather in her cap that looked so adorable as it does on you."

Margie blew the feather out of her eyes and tried to feel glamorous when all she truly wanted to take off her new shoes, unfasten the dress, and lose the damned feather.

When Tommy returned, the waiter took their dinner orders and Tillie sang off-key to "A Pretty Girl is like a Melody" and "Blue Skies."

"I could get used to this." Tommy forked in a medium rare steak smothered in mushrooms and onions. "I usually go for the Mulligan Stew. How about another round? If there's a raid, you'll see Charlie leading his staff into action."

"I wouldn't mind being arrested with this cocktail in my hand. Of course it would shock Alfred if they put it in the papers." Tillie took a sip.

"We don't have to be arrested." Tommy signaled to the house cameraman. Tillie raised her glass while Margie felt such tingles down her arm where Tommy's hand rested on her bare shoulder that she could barely hold still until the flash bulb went off.

"You'll come to visit us at home, Tommy. I'll make sure you're not thirsty."

"I've always wanted to see La Jolla. It's where my parents had their honeymoon. Mother said they were perfectly happy there but Father had to return to the salt mines."

"How dreadful. Did they mine salt? I thought it was silver."

"Not literally, but my father slaved for his uncles. My mother always told me the uncles wouldn't let him go, or pay what they owed, though the altitude was killing him."

"Sea level is always best. Was it truly the Wild West there?"

"My grandfather Max told me that in Leadville, if a stranger asked for the time, you pulled out your gun and not your watch and said, 'Time for you to get out of town.' Otherwise you'd get your timepiece stolen and a knock on the head. Grandpa's wife, my grandmother, was hit over her head with an ax by a rogue from Jesse James' gang."

Tillie patted Tommy's arm. "That's a frightening story. An ax, how dreadful. I'm sorry you lost your mother, and in what a way."

Tommy's eyes went misty. "Actually, it was my grandmother. Mother is well."

"I knew that, silly me. It was hearing about that ax that confused me."

"After all Mother went through bringing me up, I've pulled pranks and got myself expelled from schools. And this," he lifted his glass, "she considers near poison."

"Well, poison me again." Tillie patted his arm. "Margie didn't give me enough to worry about but her brother made up for it."

When the band started into "Tea for Two," Tommy held out his hand and Tillie took it, sashaying behind him to the floor.

Margie watched her short, vivacious mother, head tilted back, gazing up.

After Tommy steered Tillie in one more tipsy twirl, he came back to take Margie onto the floor. She didn't know if she could stop her legs from trembling long enough to move her feet.

"The feather tickles." He settled his chin on her head.

"It's a foolish hat." Our first dance, she thought. May it never end.

"In a good way." He pressed her more tightly to him as the tenor sang, "Just tea for two, and two for tea, me for you and you for me…alone."

Margie closed her eyes. The solid warmth of his chest, the sweetness of snuggling in the spot where his arm and shoulder touched her cheek, made her wish the song would have a third and fourth encore.

Tillie had paid the bill before they returned to the table.

"Thank you, Mrs. H. They overcharge on drinks, but they serve good stuff."

"I've had the best time! When Alfred worries we won't have enough money tomorrow, I'll say, don't worry, I spent it last night while we had it."

Tommy laughed. "No quibbles with that philosophy."

"Alfred and I like Herbert Hoover and we trust his instincts. My daughter went to Stanford with Mr. Hoover's daughter, the shyest possible girl, wasn't she, dear? And didn't you sleep in Abraham Lincoln's room when you visited the White House?"

"Next door, and the bed was hard."

"You never told me that," Tommy said. "You keep the best parts quiet."

"Not really. You know pretty much all. There's no mystery about me."

"Margie, of course there's mystery to you. Aren't you my daughter?"

On the street, there was a strong cool wind as they walked.

"What do you see up there?" Tommy pointed to the uptown corner.

"Are you testing *my* sobriety? I see two fire hydrants on either side of Fifth and another across 53rd," Tillie answered.

"The same number but they're not hydrants, they're Olympic hurdles. Margie?"

"In this dress and shoes?" She looked down at her skirt and her pumps, trying to ignore her breasts half out of the bodice.

"I'm giving you a head start because of the outfit," he said.

"Those are fighting words!" Margie removed her heels and took off toward the first fire hydrant, leap-frogged, and headed across 53rd toward the next.

"What are doing, young woman! You're not a horse. The dress!" Tillie cried.

Margie dashed across 53rd and hopped the second hydrant to 54th before Tommy caught up and pulled her to a stop as she pushed one breast back into her dress.

At that moment, a police car pulled up to the curb with tires screeching.

"You see, they've come to arrest the both of you." Tillie caught up. The policemen ignored them and headed toward the 21 Club.

"A raid!" Tillie clapped her hands. "Did we miss all the fun?"

"Do you want to go back inside to see?" Tommy asked.

"I'm too distressed by my daughter. Whatever possessed you, Margie? I was brought up in New York and I've never seen such behavior."

"Mother, you poured water on people's heads and the dress is fine."

---

Friday the bankers and financiers who had promised their organized support bought into the plunging Market. Share prices went up again but Alfred had made up his mind. He was out and would stay out. Tillie went shopping without much enthusiasm while Margie worked. "Incantations" was all Alfred said as prices slipped and rose all day Saturday. In the afternoon, Tommy appeared with tickets for *Naughty Marietta.*

"I hope it's the kind of show where there's nothing serious to think about and everyone leaves the theater with a song in their heads," said Tillie.

---

Sunday, Tillie kept humming lines from the lead song in *Naughty Marietta*, "Ah, sweet mystery of Life." Then she said, "Alfred, I'm ready to go home if you are."

"You've only been in New York five days."

"You delivered us from harm and I can do nothing more to help my daughter relieve Tommy of bachelorhood. The weather's turned cold and I miss home."

"What are you referring to when you say relieving Mr. Grensky? Of what?"

"Alfred, if you don't understand without being told, then you never will."

"He's a nice enough young man though I wonder if he'll have stable employment. This advertising business seems all hot air. I don't see that household maintenance is improved by new products. My mother cleaned with baking soda and vinegar."

"I wouldn't worry about Tommy. He'll land on his feet. I only hope that Margie has more savvy than you do, Alfred, and learns how to hook her fish."

# TEN

"WE WERE LUCKY TO have seen *Naughty Marietta*, Mama, because the show closed in a week," Margie, back at her desk, told her mother over the phone in California.

"How wrong that is! People need to forget their troubles," Tillie tilted the receiver to her chin so she could sip her bourbon.

"Broadway's nearly dark. Right now, people seem to be walking around not knowing what hit them. So many actors are out of work. Tommy's looking for a job because there isn't much call for Broadway newshounds."

"If he's out of work, marry him and bring him home. He can work on his play. Alfred will provide." Tillie coughed. "Dry throat, just a moment." She sipped her drink.

"Are you OK, Mother? What play are you talking about?"

"The one your Tommy wants to write, about the wilderness out west, his miserly aunts who wore black that scared him, and something about a dreary boarding house where he and his mother had to live, where he almost died of the influenza in 1918."

"He did live with his mother in a boarding house in San Francisco but I didn't know about the Spanish flu part or the play."

"When you're married, he'll tell you everything."

Margie took a deep breath, knowing it wouldn't make any difference if she protested that as far as she knew, Tommy had never thought of marriage with her or anyone else, least of all with her.

"People are losing jobs. I'm fortunate to be working, and Tommy's crowd is out looking for work," Margie said.

"Given his charm and looks and gift of gab, Tommy will have no problems."

243

"It's not that simple but I'm working on getting him into my agency."

"That's the first sensible thing I've heard you say. Dedicate yourself to making that young man successful."

"Are you giving me confidence or taking it away, Mother? I've got a job that's interesting. I'm using my history degree."

"About kings and queens?" Tillie asked.

"No, Mother. I studied America history. When I meet consumers to survey them about our products, I let them know I understand we've been through hard times before."

"That's all well and good, but make Tommy successful and he'll propose to you because a man needs to feel he's prospering. If you fall off a horse, let him pick you up."

"I don't fall off horses, Mother. You and Papa gave me riding lessons so I could keep my seat. You sent me to Stanford so I could take care of myself no matter what happened. I may be a pea hen in the looks department but I've got an educated brain. I'm out of arguments and I've got to run."

"Bring me home a son-in-law just like you brought home straight A's and blue ribbons before I get too old to dance again with Tommy."

When they hung up, Margie pushed back from her desk and exhaled. Since her parents left New York, there had been Black Monday, Black Tuesday, black nearly every day of the week until the end of October, banks closing, jobs lost, farmers turning under their crops because they couldn't sell them. She and Tommy had returned to the big brother, little sister footing. The moment of magic in his arms, the "Tea for Two" moment, hadn't been repeated and probably never would be. Fortunately, she was so busy she hadn't much time to think about it. Mr. Benton kept his dictating machine spitting out memos in triplicate keeping her in the office, time only to grab a split pea soup or turkey pot pie at the Automat on her way home and fall into bed until her alarm went off in the morning.

There had been some bright moments: despite company losses, NBC had debuted *The Rise of the Goldbergs* live November 15th, barely three weeks after Black Thursday. Margie thought the operetta-style opening music, "Toselli's Serenade," was a perfect antidote to despair, both upbeat and wistful. Gertrude Berg herself had come up with the opening message, "From our family to your family." In troubled times, she said, people needed to feel like a family all over the country, needed to talk to neighbors across a hallway or in their neighborhood, to invite them into a cozy kitchen where it was safe and warm, where something fragrant and familiar was cooking on the stove. When Gertrude's character Molly kneaded dough on air, Margie could feel fingers pressed together. When Molly peeled spuds on the show, Mrs. Berg would use real potatoes and drop them into real water. She fried up real eggs so the pan sizzled.

---

The last days before the Christmas holidays, gusts of frigid December air whipped Margie's cheeks red and made her eyes smart as she passed window displays with baubles on trees, tumbling bears, sleighs carrying gifts resting on cotton snow piles. She supposed there must be shoppers wanting to believe the bounce in the Market meant a better new year, or at least allow them to give their children a moment of joy.

Christmas Eve, Margie was buttoning up her coat to leave when Tommy called her work phone. "You busy? Meet me at Yang's. Chop Suey on me."

She walked down to 14th Street where Yang's Chinese was bustling and Tommy, wearing a fedora, was waiting for her at a table in the back.

"Merry Christmas, Sis. I already ordered the Chop Suey and Chow Mein. I write Mr. Wang's ad copy and he's throws extra shrimp and chicken into the Special."

"It's better than anything I've eaten for weeks," Margie said after the first bite into spicy noodles and pork. "I didn't realize you did this side work. Is this how you're paying your rent?"

"A little here and there. Wang's sister runs the laundry so I'm kept in shirts. Got the bathtub gin operation running pretty well. Don't worry, I've improved the recipe since your mother's critique. How are they? Mrs. T. is swell and so is your father."

"Papa has been busy watching everyone else collapse but he doesn't gloat."

"No, he wouldn't. He'll stay away from windows, I think."

"That was a crazy moment. Mother said you were working on a play."

"She asked me what I most wanted to do, so I told her about the idea I've had. Guess I got it from *The Bridge at San Luis Rey*, you know, the Wilder novel. Mine would have the people in a boarding house in 1918 when the Spanish Flu hit. Who gets it, who doesn't, something on that order, but your dear mother is getting cart or play ahead of horse. It's only in my head at the moment."

"It's a good idea. A play set in a boarding house…a cross section of America."

"Thanks. I did really get sick and Mother never left me, not for a moment because young people died the fastest. Maybe the play is not a good idea." Tommy picked up his tea cup and poured in gin.

"I think it is a terrific idea. Family, strangers, thrown together, real drama."

"Thanks, Margie. You're like Mrs. T. You encourage. Got you something."

"Tommy, what's this? I didn't get you a present. And my hands are sticky."

"You got me a foot in the door with B & B. I've several irons in the fire but I'll get serious after Christmas when I have my interview with Mr. Bowles."

"He's a good man and I think he'll like you. He has a soft spot for panache, which you do have."

"Flattery. But please, open the box."

The gift nestled in tissue was a small bottle of *L'Heure Bleue*. Tommy turned the blue glass stopper to release the fragrance, carnations with a touch of cinnamon competing with the rest of chow mein and noodles. Margie sneezed.

"Hope that won't happen when you use it. Sugar and spice, like my gal."

"Thank you, I didn't expect a gift."

"You're good to me, Margie Your mother and father were good to me."

"My mother can be so silly! She's smarter than she lets on."

"Smart as a whip. Knows how to read people. Show me a smile, Margie. I've got to go. Merry Christmas, Sis."

Tommy came around to help Margie with her coat and kissed her cheek.

Margie walked a block east in the frigid air before bursting into tears. *My gal?* What did that mean? He liked her, and maybe felt a little something more, but not the way she loved him, hopelessly, one-sided, every-waking-moment love and confusion, hopelessly. She suspected that wherever he was going, whoever he'd be with over the holidays, he'd not think of her.

———

Margie could have gone home to California for the week between Christmas and New Years, but it meant half the holiday on the train. Instead, she accepted her mother's cousin's invitation to Long Island for the 31st.

The Sheyers' dozen guests were determined to banish bad times by throwing sheets over their party clothes like Halloween ghosts, marching through the drawing room carrying out the bones of their goose along with all the empty bottles of French wine into a clear, starry night. "1929 begone, begone," they chanted.

"Elijah will come next year and markets will go up!" Isaac Sheyer closed a door.

"You're mixing up the holidays," said his wife Helene, who wore a magnificent long strand of pearls on her large, warm bosom.

"Hoover will rescue us!" Isaac poured champagne. "He's just biding his time."

"Hoover, Hoover!" chanted the guests as 1929 ended and 1930 began.

"Do you have a sweetheart?" Helene asked Margie.

Margie shook here head. "No, I don't."

"How about a ride tomorrow with a nice Warburg boy who's rather shy but sits a horse beautifully? My boots will fit and you can belt my breeches at the waist."

———

Tillie called New Year's day. "How did Tommy like Helene and Long Island?"

"Tommy didn't come."

"Oh, I thought he was going with you."

"He didn't. The weather was terrible but I went riding anyway."

"Alfred carried me off to the Hotel Coronado for New Year's! I wore my pajama pants from New York—you remember them, very silky, deep blue."

"Must have been a lot warmer than here. I wore my beautiful French dress and almost froze when we went outdoors."

"You didn't go to Mendel's to pick up my furs? They love going out in winter."

"I'm fine. Tell me about the Hotel Coronado."

"We ate little lobsters from Mexico, not as sweet as the big ones from Maine but tasty. I haven't slept in the same room with Alfred for years. It wasn't at all as inconvenient as I imagined."

Margie didn't know if Tillie was being intentionally vague about a romantic moment, or simply reporting a fact.

"Alfred was right, of course," Tillie said. "Sylvia's David lost everything."

"Oh, that's terrible. What will Sylvia do?"

"Poor Sylvia, married for love, didn't get much of that, and now no security."

"I'm sure Papa didn't like being right about David," said Margie.

"Don't be so sure. Your father has never been more cheerful. He spent all last year worrying that the Market would crash and now that it has and he saved us where nearly everyone else lost their shirts, he's magnanimous." Tillie paused. "To top off the week, Sylvia told me that Eddie is divorcing again. You remember Eddie, our cousin?"

"Volume of your voice going up, Mama. Speak more softly so Papa can't hear."

"Well, Eddie is single again. His *second* divorce." Tillie's stage whisper was still loud. "His wives get plenty of money. He'll help Sylvia. You do know that movies are making more money than ever because people go into the dark to forget their troubles. Eddie can turn Tommy's play into a movie if there are happy songs in that boarding house. Happy New Year, darling. May this be the lucky one! You know what I mean!"

# Part Four

# ONE

## PASADENA, CALIFORNIA
## AUGUST, 1937

WHENEVER JUNE GRENSKY CAUGHT sight of her son during the pre-wedding dinner, Tommy had a highball glass in his hand. She thought she should speak to him about his drinking but as voices rose and fell on the terrace of the Hornthall's home, and in the background music played softly on the Victrola, her son was nowhere to be seen.

"I think I spied him headed toward the garden," Dr. Morris Selig said to his sister.

Their older brother, Dr. Max, shook his head. "He's never taken on the responsibility he should have."

"I believe that young woman can handle anyone," replied Morris.

"I shall find him and bring him back to the table where he belongs," said June.

Margie watched her future mother-in-law fold her napkin, push back her chair and get up. June began down the path toward twin Japanese ponds at the bottom of the garden. Lanterns lit the way but the decline was steep so Margie stood up and followed. She stayed close to June whose white collar shone in the moonlight. Her own outfit— black and white geometric silk with wide shoulders—must have also seemed to shimmer as well. Two nighttime butterflies, Margie thought.

They both stopped, June ahead and Margie five feet behind, to avoid a body lying on a bed of flowers. Margie heard June cry. "Son! Thomas!"

Tommy turned his head, a smile on his lips. "Evening, Ma."

"He's just been sleeping a little." Margie took June's arm to pull her away.

Though she was shaking, June didn't budge. "He gave me such a scare."

"I'm sorry about that, June. I really didn't think anything serious had happened."

"Dear Marjorie, I'll understand if you call off the marriage. He's no credit to our family. You see, he grew up without a father, and though I did my best, it seems that wasn't enough to establish his moral grounding."

"Oh, June, please don't be unhappy on this lovely night when I'm so happy. Your son is a good man. He's just been independent a long time and this is his last night as a bachelor. I understand your worry but please don't let it spoil your evening."

June sighed. "How can he behave in such a way? I did try to hold up the standards of his dear father before him, but I couldn't make up for the lack, and Tommy just didn't take discipline seriously when it came from me."

"Let's leave him to have an hour's sleep and rejoin our families."

"Words cannot express my disappointment in him. You are a brave woman."

"I'm not being brave, dear June. I love him through and through. I know he drinks too much. I believe he'll slow down when we begin our lives together."

June still refused to take her eyes from Tommy who was now lightly snoring.

"His father had a weak heart. You know Tommy barely survived the Spanish Influenza? It was touch and go for weeks. And I must confess, my own father drinks."

"I'm sorry Grandfather Max couldn't come." Margie was holding June by the elbow, still trying to get her to leave Tommy and return to the company on the terrace. "We're going up north to visit your father in San Francisco on our way east because Tommy feels so close to him. I believe Tommy wants to do his best, June, but since Repeal, there's such availability of liquor."

Someone had put Cole Porter on the Victrola and "I've Got You under My Skin" sounded so lovely that Margie wanted to twirl June in the moonlight.

At that moment, Uncles Max Jr. and Morris met them on the path. The men had serious faces.

"Is our nephew unwell?" Morris asked.

Margie pointed to Tommy snoring upon the flower bed. "He's actually sleeping peacefully. You needn't worry."

"I've told you, our nephew needs professional attention," Max took his sister's arm. "Everything *we* tried to teach him just rolled off his back."

"Max, with due respect, it's not your choice. It's Marjorie's, if it's anyone's." Dr. Morris, whose Hollywood practice included numerous alcoholics and addicts, continued, "In my experience, no one can make a man give up his drink except himself."

"Thank you, Uncle Morris. I'm not worried, really. The wedding isn't until four tomorrow afternoon and Tommy makes an amazing recovery," Margie said.

Dr. Max took his brother aside. "The bride appears as non-plussed as her peculiar mother. I suppose it's the New Yorker in them."

"Let's look on the brighter side," Morris answered. "You won't find a more lovely estate, which says something for Nephew's choice of family. The Pasadena crowd is generally more respectable than Hollywood. Frankly, I was worried he'd get some silly flapper pregnant and we'd have that on our hands."

"I'd say he's damned lucky. He's thirty-five. You can't call advertising a real profession. All those ads do is sell horse lineament to gullible patients. The boy has always relied too much on his charm and good looks," Max said.

"In this town," Morris replied, "you can't fault good looks. As for myself, I'd like another glass of excellent French champagne. Brother, I predict Tommy's marriage will be happier in some respects than our own. His admirable wife is made to have children."

"You're surprisingly insensitive to my feelings, and to Susie," said Max.

"Yes, yes, I know. We would both like it otherwise. My Fanny is a perfect angel but she's been ill for many years, and neither you nor I have offspring to take our name. My poor darling can no longer swim in the pool I built for her to exercise."

"I'm sorry, Morris, truly I am. There seems no diagnosis for her disease of the muscles. Let's return to the table and give our sisters our support."

"May seems to be getting on very well with this crowd," Morris said. "She must have experience with the bohemians in San Francisco."

"The less I hear of May's alliances in San Francisco, the better," Max grimaced.

———————

"You're not taking May away? She's too much fun! We're just getting acquainted." Tillie, hanging on to May's arm, signaled the server for more champagne.

"Thank you, Mathilda, for the excellent supper but we must all go together back to Morris' for the night. The weather looks promising for tomorrow," Dr. Max said.

"It's always near-perfect weather in southern California, which is why we call it our paradise, isn't that true, doctor?" Tillie addressed Morris. "If I hadn't insisted we leave the horrible winters, Alfred's asthma would have killed him in New York."

June forced down a lump in her throat. Perhaps she was just feeling the loss of Tommy to a woman who appeared to understand him better than she did. She thought Margie a sensible person and should have been happier, but how different it would be if Nathan had lived to guide his son through difficult years. She stifled a groan that rose from deep within her throat. She missed Nathan so much tonight it was as if she hadn't gone through decades of mourning him.

Mathilda Hornthall saw June's eyes fill with tears and pulled a hankie from between her décolletage. "There, there. I'll weep plenty tomorrow, June, but life doesn't stop for anyone. One big carrousel we can't get off."

June clenched her lips in disapproval. How dare this over-dressed plump little woman philosophize at her expense? She pulled away when Tillie seemed ready to plant a liquory-kiss on her cheek.

When the Seligs were leaving, Tillie held on to May and whispered, "I like you, May, much better than your sister who seems a terrible prude. Does she ever smile?"

"My sister will never be truly happy again. She lost the man she loved."

"So I've heard. But what a fellow your nephew is. I've had my heart set on him from the moment we met and you can't imagine how much time and effort I've put into getting him here. My daughter was hardly any help at all. Tomorrow, you and I will be as happy and tight as clams."

"May, it's time we go!" Dr. Max called out, then to his brother, "The daughter seems a notch above her vulgar mother, fortunately."

---

After the Seligs left, Alfred excused himself to go up to bed. Margie, Tillie and Sylvia remained on the terrace drinking a brandy in the moonlight.

"I'll go have a look at my groom." Margie stood up. "June was not amused."

"She's a stiff woman who doesn't approve of me." Tillie stretched. "My back is telling me that one more brandy will be good for comfort's sake and then to bed."

"I think Tillie should see Alfred's chiropractor," Sylvia said to Margie.

"Sylvia, you know that health is Alfred's domain. I'm never ill, only overworked. A lovely dinner tonight but I'm holding back the masterpiece for the wedding supper."

"I'll come up with you, Tillie. It's time for me to get some sleep. Unless you'd like me to go help you," Sylvia paused, "with your sleeping beauty out there."

Margie laughed. "Thanks, Aunt Syl, you go with Mother who has outdone herself. If there's a duck or lobsters left alive in the Los Angeles area, I'll be surprised."

"Now that the Depression has ended, we're not counting pennies," said Tillie.

"The Depression hasn't really ended, Mother."

"For me, it's like Prohibition, gone to the Lord. Prospero is invited tomorrow and I hope he comes. And that tailor your father liked so much, whose shop he financed, I believe he's coming from Florida. Bye the bye, Margie, you don't have wedding night worries, do you dear?"

"No, Mother."

---

The night was balmy and the lunar light fell on Tommy's cheeks like pale silver water. A slight breeze spread sweet fragrances of citrus and gardenia. By the peaceful, upturned curve of his lips, Margie supposed he was taking in the scents and the breezes in his sleep. It was best that he hadn't registered his mother's disapproval. He often berated himself, telling Margie how he'd let down his mother, how he wished he'd been a better son. Few people knew how sensitive Tommy was to criticism. He looked so confident and jaunty, the broad shoulders, the dimple in the firm chin, the head of thick black hair that other men envied and women wanted to run their fingers through. How many times he'd been told he could be a Hollywood leading man. And yet he doubted himself and, she thought, drank to dull the harsh words that his boss De Vere seemed to enjoy leveling at him, or the letters June sent never quite giving him approval.

Margie pulled a garden chair near and reflected on the uneven course of their romance; if she'd been a gambler, she wouldn't have given herself odds that eight years after the Crash, and thirty years after the Panic that had changed their mothers' lives, she and Thomas Grensky would be getting married the next afternoon in Pasadena, California.

# **T**wo

ONE WEEKEND IN THE middle of a sweltering August in 1932 when everyone else at their advertising agency seemed to have fled to the beaches, Margie suggested to Tommy that they drive to Connecticut. *The Goldbergs*—the show's name had been shortened from *Rise of the Goldbergs*—was a hit, and NBC had raised Mrs. Berg from her starting salary of seventy-five dollars a week for a fifteen minute program to three hundred dollars and a half hour on air. Margie, who was writing commercials for the show's sponsor, Proctor & Gamble, also got a raise. With her extra twenty-five dollars a week, she saved and bought a used green Chevy coupe that Tommy named The Frog Prince.

As she drove, they gossiped and talked shop. She'd gotten Tommy on at Benton & Bowles and he'd proved good pulling in talent from his Broadway reporting days. In a speakeasy in New Bedford, two whiskies gave Margie the courage to say, "I've never been away over night with a man." She concentrated on looking at the floor strewn with peanut shells. Eyes still averted, she said, "You're the only one I want to lose, my uh, what they call my reputation, uh with."

"Sis!" Tommy raised his hat, fanned himself, and replaced it on his head.

When she looked up, she saw he was blushing. "Are you sure?" he asked.

"I'm sure. If you want me, no strings attached."

Tommy still looked surprised and seemed not to have an answer but he leaned forward and took her hand. "I'll show rather than tell."

When they located a hotel on the water, Margie kept silent as

Tommy registered them as husband and wife. She followed him up a flight of stairs to a white room with a window where the salty breeze again seemed to cool the heat she was feeling. He isn't a stranger, after all, she told herself as she looked at the double bed with its maritime blue coverlet. After work, they often left together for drinks with colleagues but usually she got tired of cigarette smoke and was ready to leave long before the rest of them. "Night, Sis, sleep tight!" he'd wave a farewell, echoed by friends and strangers. Tommy would be the last to leave the bar or party, wherever drinks were being poured. Some late nights, when he couldn't make it up another two flights to his closet-sized studio above hers, he used his key to let himself in to fall asleep on her couch. In the morning, Margie made him coffee, eggs and toast, then got him up and out to work.

"You planned this, Sis?" Tommy asked when she scurried from the bathroom to the bed in a nightgown that Tillie would have approved of—black and lacy—and so embarrassing to buy that Margie had told the shop girl she was giving a gift to a cousin, an actress.

"I hoped it might happen, but I didn't know how until I asked." She pulled up sheets to her nose and began to giggle. He was soon laughing and then they were in each other's arms.

---

Over the following days along the shore, between lobsters on wharves and whiskey in brown bottles, Tommy, to his own surprise, felt eager to take Margie back to their hotel bed. "There's so much you have to learn. I wouldn't have guessed you were ticklish," Tommy said as he tickled.

"I'm not the only one." She tickled him back, slowing her fingers, fascinated by the curls of hair that covered much of his broad shoulders and down his back.

There was no tub. They took showers together. She was a foot shorter so the first lesson in standing-up making love was trying not to lose her balance or laugh. There was always teasing and laughter, even in passion.

"I hold you accountable for making me as happy as a clam." Margie collapsed on top of him and he turned them side by side for deep kisses.

———————

From his studio two floors above hers, Tommy sent messages down the side of the building attached to a potato on a clothing line. "Hungry" or "Starved" or "Tonight Sweets?" Margie pulled on the cord and sent the potato back up with her reply, "Meat loaf" or "Mac 'n cheese." She didn't extract any vows of fidelity but it was hard to sleep the nights when Tommy hadn't climbed into her bed. She didn't want to think of who might be sidling up to him wherever he went, who he'd gone home with. The easy-come, easy-go relationships among actors and writers, newshounds and ad agency people, that had been fueled by drinking away the years of Prohibition hadn't stopped with Repeal earlier in the year: now there was a celebration every night with the booze poured legally from rows of bottles that stood proudly behind a bar.

One cold morning in January 1935, after a week in the Midwest where she'd conducted consumer surveys for Pepsodent and Oxydol, Margie decided that instead of another night in a hotel in Chicago, she'd catch the overnight sleeper to Grand Central. She'd left her apartment to her cousin Lucy Benjamin from Atlanta who'd come north to Manhattan to try out for shows. At the station, Margie drank coffee and bought doughnuts for their breakfast.

Before turning the key to her apartment, Margie heard two voices inside, a female giggle, a male laugh. Lucy was a pretty redhead with a high little voice and chorus-girl legs, the cousin she'd had in mind when she'd bought the lacy black seduction nightgown. Margie supposed her cousin had brought one of the theater people back for the night, so she knocked and called, "I'm back."

Margie knocked and opened the door wide enough to see Tommy in the bath robe that he kept in her closet. Lucy, in nothing but a nightshirt, opened her Betty Boop lips, but before she would say word, Margie put up her hands for silence. She didn't look at Tommy, who couldn't hide a guilty expression and turned his face away.

She walked past them to the bathroom where she stood staring at herself in the mirror as she splashed water on her face and washed her hands. Her short hair was stuck to her head. She wished she didn't look as if she'd been dragged up from somewhere.

"It's all my fault," she heard Lucy through the door. "Oh Margie, honey, I feel terrible, I swear you've been so swell to me and I'm an ungrateful silly girl who just drank too much with this good-looking New York beau of yours."

Margie came out and, without looking at Lucy, gave Tommy her angriest glare.

"You should get dressed now. Leave the robe. It doesn't belong to you."

"But it was a Christmas gift, Sis. You had it monogrammed with my initials." He pointed to the slanting black cursive above the pocket. "See, TMG. No one else fits the description and it's just my size."

"All the more reason I don't want to see you or it anymore."

Margie cursed tears she couldn't keep from sliding down her cheeks.

———————

Margie's own small office had a door she could close because actors on *The Goldbergs* and the variety program, *Showboat,* sometimes shouted or sang the commercials she wrote for their shows. That morning, she was grateful for the door that kept her from seeing Tommy. After work, she walked west to the Fifth Avenue Schrafft's where she ordered a banana split, double hot fudge and marshmallows. The first warm chocolate spoonful almost came back up in her throat. She took another spoonful, swallowed, and then another. She thought of Tommy's affectionate nickname for her, *my little sweet potato bottom.* She might as well spoon in the last sticky spoonful and get broad as an Idaho spud for all he cared. *I'm twenty-seven going on twenty-eight,* she thought. *I've always wanted marriage and children. What are the chances Tommy is going to change his life and make this possible?* It was years past time to tell Tommy that she wanted him and no one else, and if she didn't hear the same words from him, to tell him that she couldn't go on. If he didn't want her enough to forego the appeal of any girl close and drunk enough to fall into bed with him, she had to break her own heart and give him up.

She hurried out into the cold where air dried her tears as soon as they fell. *You will not cry again*, she instructed herself, though once she opened her own door and saw Lucy, dressed in a smart travel suit, nothing could turn off both their tears.

They sat down on the couch and sniffled. "Oh honey, I tell you the man loves you. How you've been crying, you poor dear. I am so sorry, believe me."

Margie handed her cousin a tissue and Lucy handed her one.

"He's just God's gift to women, honey. He loves you, not me. We drank a godawful lot. He's upstairs. He's been letting down that potato every hour."

Margie looked toward the kitchen window where a knobby spud was moving slightly up and down like a fish on its line.

"Where are you going? It's almost dark." Margie pointed to Lucy's suitcases by the door. "I thought you had an audition tomorrow."

Lucy shook her curls. "They're so damn many talented people up here in New York City. I'm taking the night train home to Momma before I become a full-fledged lush and get in some real trouble. I'll choose one of the nice boys in our crowd who's been after me. I had my dream of being up there on the big stage, dancing in a beautiful spangled gown with men in coattails behind me and Astaire waiting in the wings. It's not going to happen, I know. You're a brick, Margie, just like your Mother. Aunt Tillie is counting on you snagging Tommy. You mustn't ever tell her any of this or I'd never hear the end of it."

"Of course I won't, Lucy. It's not just you that's happened to fall for Tommy."

"You just pull in that potato, honey, 'cause he wants to make amends. He talks about you as the best and smartest girl in the world. What happened was that his mean boss made him feel bad and he didn't have you around to boost him up like you do."

"De Vere is a jealous man. He doesn't give Tommy a chance," said Margie. "One day Mr. Bowles will take Tommy's ideas and use them, no matter what de Vere says."

"He's just a beautiful baby boy. I'll be coming to your wedding, darlin'."

---

Tied to an especially wrinkled and pitiful potato that descended on the laundry cord outside her kitchen window, Margie read, "Forgive. In repentance." After taking minutes to push a stool to the sink so she could stand and open the window, she pulled in the potato, detached the note. "Talk," she wrote and tugged on the cord.

---

"We were having such a swell time. If I hadn't been a horse's ass... won't happen again, I promise." They were sitting on her sofa with two feet between them. He was looking dramatically repentant, Margie thought, and she wasn't going to be swayed by his furrowed brow. She took a long sip of bourbon he'd brought.

"Tommy, we've been sharing the same bed most nights for going on four years. If anything, I love you more than I ever did but I want to have a home and a family. Nothing you've ever said leads me to believe being a husband fits that description of you in the future." She paused and took another long sip to clear her throat.

"I never dared say these words for fear of scaring you away, but now I have to. I want to be married and have children, and that means being able to count on a husband."

"Lucy is a sweet girl but she didn't mean anything to me."

"Lucy has almost nothing to do with what I'm saying though I feel grateful she's made me see more clearly what I do and don't want for the rest of my life."

"I'm a horse's ass. Should I get down on my knees and beg forgiveness so you won't be mad at me any more, please?"

"I am mad at you because she's my cousin and I trusted you both but Lucy is not the reason I'm telling you what I'm feeling, so don't make me repeat myself."

Margie pushed her seat back and started to get up. Tommy held her wrist. "I'm the black sheep in the family, I know it."

"Tommy, that's no answer. I'm not going to feel sorry for you and

I wish you'd quit feeling sorry for yourself as if you don't have any choice. I know you're a good man and you care about your family, your friends, and I hope about me. So let's kick the black sheep in his tail. Make up your mind about what I said because I won't go back on it."

Margie didn't let his touch on her shoulder stop him from leaving. When he was gone, she drank another shot of bourbon and got into bed.

The phone woke her at two in the morning.

"Margie, I'll go through with it. I'd be a fool if I lost you."

"Oh Tommy," she cried into the receiver. "Come on down right now. I'll make us scrambled eggs and bacon because you just made what most girls wouldn't call a romantic proposal and I accept, I do, I say *yes*."

———————

Margie had told her mother she wanted a small wedding, only families, a few close friends. Tillie pretended to agree but immediately started making a guest list and began looking for her daughter's wedding dress. In the end, Margie accepted the big party as well as a gown sent from Bullock's Wiltshire, a creamy, skinny white lace sheath that was too tight.

Before leaving for California, Tommy invited friends to celebrate their engagement at the Algonquin Bar where he wondered aloud about the whiskey gentlemen in Scotland and England, wine and champagne makers in France. What were they doing to enter the American market since Repeal of Prohibition?

"Anyone remember single malt whiskies? Nothing tasted quite as pure," he said.

"And French champagne, that's a fond memory," said a man down the bar.

"We're still only receiving a trickle," the bartender added. "If I had a supply of the good foreign stuff, I'd display those fancy bottles like chorus girls behind the bar."

"All the Brits and Scots and Frenchies need is our advertising expertise. Olde England where they drink like kings and queens has a ring." Tommy lifted his glass.

"Hear, hear!" their friends shouted with raised glasses.

"Let's make it our honeymoon project, Tommy," said Margie. "We'll go to Europe and you can send stories back with local color and interviews from those grand old masters of the art. You'll get contacts at *Advertising Age* to begin with and I bet you can sell stories on both sides of the Atlantic. Your drinking will be a revelation."

"We'll be at the source of an historical revolution!" Tommy clasped her hand. "You are a very smart sweet potato bride-to-be."

# THREE

THE WEDDING MORNING, TILLIE was up with the first rays of sun. Her two elderly King Charles Spaniels reluctantly rose at the early hour from their beds and followed her into the kitchen with feathery tails wagging. Tillie gave each waiting dog a slice of cheese, then heated water for Alfred's chamomile tea and her own coffee.

She sat with her cup on the terrace. The sky, perfectly clear, had faint streaks of white clouds in the pink and blue distance. In his bedroom, Alfred's calculating machine was clacking away; Tillie hoped her husband wasn't already adding up the wedding bills. Alfred might grumble but she knew he'd do nothing to keep the wedding from being his wife's triumph. The Leiter sisters had already arrived in Los Angeles. Her brother Homer was coming alone without his wife and family. As for Elman, he'd promised his mother he'd arrive to see his twin sister married. Alfred's tailor, Abraham Cogansky, was arriving from Florida. Cogansky's sons ran branches of his gentlemen's tailoring business in New York and Miami. Tillie would introduce him around Los Angeles after the wedding festivities to help establish him in the west.

One guest alone caused Tillie anxiety. Eddie Sachs. Tillie felt her heart flutter at the thought of seeing her once-intended, for decades a successful Hollywood pictures producer. Tillie had seen his musicals but in all the years that had passed, they'd never met each other. "It's your fault, you've kept us apart," Tillie reproached her cousin Sylvia. "I insist that you invite your brother to my daughter's wedding."

"Do you think that twenty Peking ducks will be enough for our *canards à l'orange*?" Tillie asked Margie and Sylvia as soon as they joined her on the terrace. Both assured her that twenty ducks with all the rest on the menu would be more than enough for their guests, but Tillie shook her head.

"I'll have Teresa call to bring five more, just to be safe. Lobster to start, then duck, then filet mignon. Trimmings to match. Charles and Simone should be arriving at ten with their assistants and I want everything to be ready for them to plunge into work."

Margie noticed that her mother's face and neck looked a bit scrawny and that she braced her back with her hand. She must be dieting, Margie thought. Tillie always was competitive and perhaps wanted to be thinner than her daughter who'd been on an excruciating regime to fit into the wedding dress her mother had picked out for her.

"How old is June? You can't tell by the way she dresses," said Tillie.

"She's only a few years older than you are—I think she's in her early fifties."

"She's eons older than I am!" Tillie exclaimed.

"June has a very good position as the dean of a girls' school in Oakland," Margie said. "After her husband died and Tommy was growing up, several men proposed marriage to June. She always asked Tommy if he wanted this or that man for a father, and he said no, so she turned them down. Tommy feels guilty that he spoiled her chances, though he thinks she wouldn't have loved anyone except his father."

"What child would want a new man to come in and discipline him? Alfred criticized his son's every move. My father couldn't abide Homer. That's the way fathers are toward their sons more often than not. I do hope your brother's ship arrives in time for the ceremony." As soon as she sat down, Tillie's Spaniels jumped on her lap. "I like June's sister. May's the rebel in the family. She promised to tell me about her love life."

"I like May also. She was always softer, more affectionate than June, Tommy has told me. Her love life should entertain you. It's entirely unconventional though she tries to be discreet, according to Tommy."

Tillie clapped her hands. "There's so much to look forward to with May but I'll have to get through the day pretending with June."

"You don't have to, Mother, and June will probably see right through you. She may not be as easy going as her sister but according to May, June was a different person when she was with Tommy's father. She loved him passionately. His death so young devastated her."

"Hard to believe the passion," said Tillie.

"It's true. She melted like a candle to his flame, those are May's words."

"What a romantic turn of phrase," Tillie said.

"May writes romantic poetry for greeting cards." Margie smiled thinking of May with her untinted wispy hair pulled up into a bun, her pen poised above paper and the heated words of passion she penned while her own lover waited in the next room. "Is Elman really coming?"

"He wired three weeks ago from Marseille that his ship would be passing through the Panama Canal and up to Los Angeles, but I haven't heard a word since."

"The Panama Canal! Wouldn't that be fun to see! Elman's been everywhere but if he's docked in New York, he's never called me."

"He hasn't forgotten you stiffed his friends at Stanford."

"Mother! The friends were gamblers who dunned me for *his* gambling debts."

"Hasn't Elman been in Africa this time?" Sylvia asked.

"Yes and he's coming for his sister's wedding because he has true family feeling." Tillie paused to be sure Margie heard. "Syl, I was wondering, what if Eddie asked Tommy to stand in for Ronald Colman in a picture? Tommy looks like Colman."

"Tommy doesn't do stunts, Mother." Margie was beginning to feel annoyed, then decided that her mother's mind and words would go where they will. "It's all beautiful today and everything is perfect. Our guests will never want to leave Pasadena."

"The roses and gardenias are my special friends. Every petal is releasing its perfume." Tillie took a deep breath. "I've employed Teresa's entire family, including the gardeners, for the last two months. Our president, whose name I dare not say in Alfred's presence, wants everyone to work and I'm doing my part. Alfred blames the president for everything though Franklin comes from a good family. If only his wife wore better undergarments. We'd all feel safer if Eleanor wore a Smoother. The country likes to feel that everything is controlled, not being left to flop around."

"Oh Mother, that's ridiculous. The country doesn't care if Eleanor Roosevelt's bosom is corseted or not. If Smoothers are still in existence, they're in the Smithsonian."

"I also admire Mrs. Roosevelt, drooping bust-line and all," Sylvia said.

"You two have no sense of style. By the way, Margie, our Smoothers were updated by the Russians who bought the business from Papa. They call them Vanity somethings now and they're not as uncomfortable and lots prettier than they used to be. Sylvia wouldn't know because she never prodded or stuffed herself into a corset, but I remember squeezing myself purple in those things. I always envied you your stylish figure, Syl."

"You never envied anyone, Tillie. You've always admired yourself."

Tillie patted each dog's head. "Is that so?"

"I only mean you believe in your personal right to happiness," said Sylvia.

Margie felt surprised by the bold choice of words though she knew that over the years, Sylvia had learned to confront Tillie rather than sidestep confrontation. "It's her narcissism," Sylvia had recently told Margie. "Dr. Berg, my analyst, says Tillie's self-regard protects her from understanding her own limitations."

"That is so true of mother," Margie had answered.

Now, while Tillie stepped into the kitchen for another check on the ducks, Sylvia confided to Margie she was taking a big step away from mourning her dead husband, David, who had taken his life a year after the Crash. "After the wedding, I'm going to Palestine to assist refugees arriving from Europe. Ever since I heard that brilliant man Chaim Weitzmann speak about persecution and the danger to Jews living in Germany, I've wanted to go. I won't tell your mother yet, it would upset her."

"This is such a surprise, so adventurous, Aunt Sylvia. I'm proud of you."

"I feel the calling and it isn't as if I'm leaving a husband or children the way my own mother did when she went to India."

"Mother will miss you."

"I'm just a comfortable old shoe to her. I'll be back, don't worry." Sylvia hugged Margie. "This is your day, darling, and I'm so happy for you."

At that moment, the Spaniels ran barking from the kitchen around the house.

"The caterers can't be this early and flowers aren't supposed to arrive until eleven. Perhaps it's Teresa rounding up more ducks." Tillie followed her dogs.

In the driveway, a long black Lincoln was being parked by a chauffeur who then stepped out and opened the back seat. Before anyone emerged, the driver unfolded a wooden chair with high wheels.

Tillie ran across the gravel drive with her hands over her mouth. "What has happened to you, my son! You're not paralyzed, are you?"

"No, Mother, I'm not paralyzed. I had an accident on safari. I may be left with a limp but I'll walk. I'll be like Father." Elman Hornthall placed a bush helmet on his balding head as he accepted the chauffeur's help into the wheelchair.

"That's not kind to say but I'm so relieved to know that you're not paralyzed." Tillie leaned over and kissed Elman. "I can't imagine a paralyzed child."

"I'll tell you the story in detail as soon as the surprise member of my party emerges. Carmela, love, do come out. The little dogs won't bite you."

The driver opened the other side to help out an extremely tall woman with long legs in Spectator pumps, wearing sun glasses the size of saucers. With one hand, she held a large bag made from an animal, and in the other, a gigantic conch shell she pressed to the side of her head. Her hair was egg-yolk yellow, her skin dark and wrinkled.

Margie and Sylvia stepped closer, staring at the shell and then at Elman.

"Well, hello, Margie and Aunt Sylvia. You ladies look very fine. May I present my wife, Carmela Estevez de Ruiz de Leon."

"Your wife?" Tillie and Margie asked together.

"Two years, isn't it, darling?"

The woman with the shell did not answer.

"Elman, I didn't know you were even engaged." Tillie said.

"We've been traveling almost constantly. Everyone, say hello to Carmela though she may not hear you over the sound of the waves."

"Waves?" Tillie asked.

"Carmela is from Cuba, an island, surrounded by water, so she must have the sound of the ocean at all times. She can never be without the waves. Carmela, my darling, my mother Matilda, my sister Marjorie, and Sylvia. We've always called you Aunt but I know that's not exactly our relationship."

Sylvia nodded, then all three women obediently greeted Carmela who seemed to register their presence from behind the dark glasses but did not speak.

"Carmela and Elman, come in and rest. You'll be the center of attention today, after Margie, of course. You never did anything ordinary, Elman."

With the chauffeur pushing his wheelchair and Tillie beside him, Elman said, "We met at the Sans Souci in Havana where Carmela was performing. She's a piano bar singer, much admired by the cognoscenti. If you ask, she might oblige tonight."

"Were you nearly eaten by lions and tigers in Africa? Did a ravaging beast cause your injury?" Tillie asked once they were seated with drinks.

"I never saw wild beasts devouring each other on the veldt. It's bad enough to hear their mortal cries at night. The rogue that caused my accident wasn't a carnivore nor aiming at me particularly. We were sitting in the back of our bush truck holding our cards. I'd made a bid of six no trump, with a combination of thirty four points between myself and Lord B. As we were laying down cards, I felt a terrible stab in my leg. The impact almost turned us over and the hullabaloo that went on! Shots fired! My last thought before I fainted from the pain was that one of our bearers had gotten me with his spear. Only later in the hospital, I learned that a rhino had impaled me with his horn through the canvas side of the truck, right in the middle of my move. They have terrible eyesight, it turns out. Lord B's bearers shot the animal and sawed off the horn as a souvenir. Carmela has a bag from his hide. Unfortunately, I couldn't bring the horn because a Chinaman offered me a fortune to grind it to powder, for sexual vigor, he said."

"Elman, you never stop surprising me. I can't believe you're now a married man speaking in a foreign language. Isn't that amazing, Margie?"

"I'm still speaking to you in English, Mother."

"Yes, I guess so but it's so exotic that it seems like another language."

"It must have hurt terribly." Margie remembered feeling a twinge in her own leg about two months ago and wondered if twins were really sensitive to each other's pain.

"Lord B saw to everything and paid for first class care in Nairobi. The doctor said I'd walk with a cane and should be grateful I hadn't lost the limb."

"What a dull life the rest of us lead in comparison. I heard that Havana was wild during Prohibition." Tillie poured herself a trickle more bourbon in the glass she was holding.

"It still is. Men always think of new ways to sin and an island is a good place for it, but Carmela and I lead a quiet life. We go on cruises. Carmela plays piano and I partner gents so they can win at Bridge. Nothing terribly exciting except for the occasional rhino."

"Was it really Lord Beaverbrook?" Margie asked.

"I'm not at liberty to reveal my patrons' names. By the way, Margie, you look very smart. You used to be a square, muscular little girl."

Margie kissed her brother's cool forehead. They were as different in character as they were in physique, she thought. As a child, Elman's purpose had always been to take the shortest way possible to satisfaction while she'd been the responsible do-all-the-homework girl. She practiced piano while lacking all talent, while Elman could sit down and pick out a melody by ear. What they shared was Tillie's adaptability, Margie thought, and that wasn't a small thing.

---

Margie peeked in on Tommy who still gave no sign of waking. She nudged him and said it was time to dress. She would put on her gown in the next room. "Don't peek."

She supposed that the creamy lace gown that fitted over a jade green silk slip, emerald green glass buttons all the way down the front, would never fit again because she didn't intend to starve herself on her honeymoon or thereafter. She fastened her strand of fine pearls and her earrings. In the next room, she could hear Tommy getting up just as cars began arriving.

---

June complimented Margie on her dress but seemed to be searching among the guests standing behind her.

"Tommy will be down any minute," she said.

"It's his wedding day. He should be here with you, Margie," June said.

"He will be. He's just finishing his own toilette."

"I don't know how she takes everything in stride," June said to her brothers.

Carmela, wearing a large black sun hat and a black form-fitting dress wheeled Elman to greet his sister and her in-laws. He'd changed to a white tuxedo jacket on the top, while on the bottom, one leg was in black pants, the other covered by a cast, which included the signature of Winston Churchill that everyone wanted to look at. "Underrated Bridge player, very sensible," he replied when asked what the man was like.

Homer Greenbaum appeared to be hot and uncomfortable in his tuxedo. With his bald head, Margie thought he looked like a Jewish Herbert Hoover. She kissed him. "I'm so glad you're here, Uncle Homer."

"Thank you my dear, I've rented the suit for a day though I hope no one sees me as a tux is against my principles."

A distinguished looking older man in a light weight silk suit introduced himself. "I am Abraham Cogansky, friend of Mr. Hornthall. I have been to his wedding also."

"Mr. Cogansky, it's my pleasure." Margie extended her hand.

"My wife wishes to say *mazel tov*. Such a fine home she would have liked to visit but daughter is expecting any moment and she said she must stay with."

"*Mazel tov*, Abraham. I'm grateful that you are here," said Margie.

"Are all these tall people your husband's family?" Homer asked.

"They're from the west," Margie answered. "Tommy's father was tall, too."

"Under the right circumstances, a Jew becomes taller in every generation, isn't that right, Abraham? I imagine that your son towers over you." Homer wiped his brow.

Cogansky nodded. "He had good food and fresh air, thanks to Mr. Hornthall."

"Where's the lucky man, dear? I believe the rabbi is lurking nearby," said Homer.

On her way to find Tommy, Margie caught up with her Atlanta cousin, Lucy, dressed in such a pretty floral blouson top and skirt that she felt a moment's twinge of irritation toward her before they embraced in the sunshine.

"I told you I'd be here for your wedding, didn't I, Margie?"

"It was more than I knew." Margie hugged her. "And I see a sparkler."

Lucy held up her diamond ring to catch the light. "There's decent local theater in Atlanta where Louis is an up-and-coming district attorney. One day I may be a governor's wife, but how I would have loved a little room in New York and a role on Broadway. Still, it's good this way and you got a dreamboat, Margie."

Margie was sure she recognized the guest who approached her: Eddie Sachs, inches shorter than his sister, Sylvia, plump as she was thin, wearing a reddish toupee.

"That toupee looks as if he's stolen it from an orangutan outfit on a studio movie lot," Lucy whispered to Margie.

"Shh, it must be from *his* studio lot. He's a producer."

"Oh, heavens. I might still change my mind and stay in Hollywood," Lucy said.

"I know we're cousins but we've never met." Margie extended her hand to Eddie.

"We are, and not as far removed as it might seem. My sister told me your groom was handsome but she didn't prepare me for the gorgeous man I just met. *Mazel tov*."

"Thank you, Cousin Eddie. I've always heard so much about you." Margie saw he wasn't the least interested in her, only in looking at Tommy standing with a drink talking to her father. Margie felt a rush of love and protectiveness for her small, loyal father who waited in a white dinner jacket to give her away.

Alfred took Margie's arm and quietly asked, "You're sure of this, my dear?"

She nodded her head up and down. "As sure as I can be of anything, Papa."

"You're happy, I see that. I was the happiest man when I married your mother."

"That's very sweet," Margie kissed him.

"And I still believe I'm a lucky man," he said.

The guests parted to let Margie and Alfred enter the circle where Tommy's uncles stood beneath the shade of a *chuppah*. Tillie darted in like a dragonfly in a green silk jacket and pajamas with a cape that reflected sunlight bouncing off its wings.

Tommy walked forward wearing a navy jacket, white wool pants and a polka dot Sulka tie gifted by Tillie. All he needs, Margie thought, is a captain's cap and he'll be ready to sail our ship across the Atlantic.

The wedding ceremony was as brief as Tillie had instructed the Hollywood rabbi to make it. Margie and Tommy responded to the posing of questions and a brief instruction on marriage quoted from Maimonides before they exchanged rings. The rabbi's final admonition was to be devoted to each other. "Love is a sacred trust," he declared as he joined their hands.

Tommy broke the wedding glass under his shoe to a burst of applause and more *mazel tovs* from the guests. Margie squeezed his hand and he kissed her so passionately that she squeaked, "I can't breathe but don't let me go."

"I won't, dear wife. I do love you and I'm very happy."

"I love you, too." Margie leaned up to him for another kiss. "We will be happy,"

When Margie looked around, she saw June who had a far-away

look on her face.

"Mother always told me that when she and my father were pronounced man and wife, he kissed her with such a smack everyone giggled a little," Tommy said.

"Like father like son." Margie turned to hug her mother-in-law.

"I hope you will be happy, my dears." June wiped away tears.

---

Tillie's seating plan placed people she thought compatible at the same table. Eddie sat with Sylvia and their Atlanta cousins. Prospero, looking as young as ever, chatted with the Leiter sisters who were smart in dark suits with new larger collars and longer skirts, reminding Tillie of Mrs. Walllis Simpson herself. In order, the caterers served Lobster Thermidor drenched in cream, ducks bathed in Cointreau, filet mignon with truffles, and wine with each course. The wedding cake would make its appearance after a pause to stand and move about.

As soon as she could, Tillie left her spot at the head table with Alfred and the Seligs to join the Leiters and have a closer look at Eddie.

"We're staying in Los Angeles for a few days," said Jessie Leiter when Tillie sat herself at their table. "We'll have chances for good talks."

"I took your advice to heart. I read Miss Austen and have become Mrs. Bennett, marrying my daughter to Mr. Darcy," said Tillie.

"Oh, Tillie! A Jewish Mrs. Bennett is so funny! How amusing you are and what a shame we don't see each other more!" Rachel Leiter laughed.

"One day you may move to Pasadena which is the perfect place to live on earth."

"I doubt we'll leave Chicago. We do go to Florida in the winter," Rachel said.

"You two are wonderfully stylish as always. I hope you'll meet a few interesting people here while I play hostess. Let me introduce you to Prospero, on whom my happiness and well-being depended before Repeal, if you know what I mean."

"My dear Tillie, Mrs. Hornthall," the bald man raised his glass, "I am sorry you didn't need me to provide for this beautiful wedding. I toast your good health and happiness. Since we last met, I've taken up other endeavors. I am invested in real estate."

"Real estate will never go dry. Oh, I made a joke." Tillie clapped her hands.

Tillie returned to the head table where she had May as a buffer between herself and June who was speaking to Homer about the education of young women. Tillie whispered to May what she'd wanted to confess all afternoon. "As soon as they've brought the cake, I'll introduce you to my intended, before fate separated us."

"There's nothing I write more feelingly about in verse than thwarted love and lost opportunities for happiness," answered May. "If I'd met you earlier, I'd have composed ditties for the tables, as I did for my sister's wedding to the man I loved."

"You loved Tommy's father?"

"Oh yes I did, but my sister stole him from me."

"Did she steal him off your arm? You must tell all, May."

"Of course it's all in the past and I've had a sweetheart in San Francisco for many years. His name's Jerry Murphy, as Irish as he sounds. We've been living in sin for ages and I'm as proud of it as my sister is scandalized. Her disapproval adds a certain fillip."

"Is that like spice or sauce?"

"Yes, mixed with a little revenge. But Jerry and I really don't need more than we have in our little love nest."

"You mean you live together as lovers? Oh, May!" Tillie took a deep breath.

"I followed him to San Francisco. He's been jailed ever so many times."

"Jailed? Is he a jewel thief?"

"Of course he isn't. He's been jailed for the working class. Jerry's away often organizing strikes."

"Is he a Bolshevik as well as an Irishman? Now you're frightening me, May."

"Jerry is IWW. He believes workers should have rights and be paid honestly."

"Alfred's a staunch Republican and won't hear about strikes or unions but you will find a friend in my brother Homer. Don't abandon me because I have no interest in politics. It was never fun gossiping with my cousin Sylvia but I have to thank her for bringing Eddie, my first love. He's the man wearing a strange pelt on his head."

Tillie pointed out Eddie who must have just told a funny story to his table because they were all laughing.

"I wish I could have sat myself beside him but that wouldn't do," Tillie said.

"You never thought of taking him as a lover?" May asked.

Tillie looked thoughtfully toward her roses and inhaled the fragrances. "I believe I've become under-sexed married to Alfred. If I'd married Eddie way back then it might have been different, as I certainly had stronger feelings in my youth, but who knows, our love may have all been in my mind and this is the first time I've seen him in over twenty years. He was once very slim and graceful." She paused. "But then, so was I. Just before I married, I read a French book I bought in Paris. It was very naughty and made me feel all sorts of things. I admit that if I'd married a handsome fellow like your nephew or someone I once met ever so briefly when I'd had too much champagne, but that didn't happen and I have Alfred."

"I adore Tommy but Margie will have her hands full. Women fall all over him. As they would have over his father had not June entranced him. It was mutual, I have to admit. There was no one else for either of them. They must have lit quite a conflagration on their wedding night after waiting so long."

"I'm not sure of your references, my dear, but I'm jealous all the same of passion requited or not. As for Margie, she has resources of strength." Tillie squeezed May's hand as Carmela, who'd gone to the piano, began to sing "Summertime."

The music almost drowned out Homer saying something Alfred took exception to.

"You're simply all wrong there, Homer," Tillie heard Alfred say.

"Homer! Alfred! Don't make me separate you so I can listen to our diva. Talk about Gershwin or athletics, please. Didn't someone famous just hit another home run?"

"Di Maggio hit for the cycle," Homer said to Tillie. "Is Delia still alive?"

"Oh yes, and she would have been here if she weren't so far away. The clever woman returned to her island, whichever one it was. She bought a home for her multitudinous family. I have her address. She's living a life of ease which she deserves."

"I admired and loved Delia," said Homer.

"She always thought the best of you when no one else but a mother could."

Homer blew Tillie a kiss that felt like a moment of understanding.

"Mark my words, Homer, our president is going over to the Russians. We should have boycotted the Olympic Games. Leave Europeans to fight themselves," Alfred said.

"Look how Owens showed up Hitler. That was magnificent. On the subject of Europe, do you think it's wise for Margie to travel there with the mad Bavarian and his storm troopers on the move?" Homer asked.

"I'm also worried about their travels, though what can be called safe at home? Roosevelt is in bed with the unions and squeezing credit. He's sending us right back to the worst days of '29." Alfred held out his champagne glass for more.

"Alfred, Homer, no more politics. Drink champagne. Look at your happy child! And listen to your daughter-in-law."

"Daughter-in-law?" Alfred looked bewildered. "I know I have a son-in-law."

"Over there, playing the piano. I told you that Elman married a chanteuse."

Alfred shook his head and drank another sip of champagne while Tillie clapped her hands at the end of Carmela's song. Everyone had grown quiet until several voices called out, "More! More."

Carmela played "Lady Be Good" as if George Gershwin had written it for her. She segued into "Rhapsody in Blue" and "The Man I Love." When she began, "Love is Here to Stay," Tillie walked over to give Alfred a kiss on his cheek.

"It brings back our youth, doesn't it? Everything's a great success," Tillie said.

"If you'd like to dance, my dear, I'll try not to step on your feet."

Alfred stood and Tillie followed him in a two-step hardly less plodding than the first time they had danced at the Hanukah party three decades earlier.

––––––––––

After all but a few guests had left, Alfred showed no signs of wanting to come up to bed.

"Homer, you're a wicked influence on him," Tillie said.

"Alfred is secretly a Keynesian who may in time become a socialist," Homer said.

"Not a chance, Homer. But I do see the larger picture. We need money to finance a recovery that isn't complete and still appears fragile."

"I give up!" Tillie raised her hands in the air. "I'll bring Alfred's cardigan."

"You had the foresight in '07 and again in '29 to get off the bandwagon, Alfred. I admire you for it even though I do wish the magnates and corporations would go to hell." Homer paused. "I saw my father humbled. On top of being ruined, the poor man had to put up with a son who bit the hand that fed him. I speak of myself, not you."

"Mr. Greenbaum behaved decently without ever liking me," Alfred said. "I worry over Tommy's earning possibilities and his tendency to drink."

"I also share your concerns that Tommy is not settled but your daughter can take care of herself. Fill me in on your son married to that talented piano player."

"As far as I know, Elman has not done an honest day's work in his life. Imagine having an accident on a safari while playing cards, if he's to be believed. I'd prefer not to speak of my son. Even now he gives me a stomach ache."

"Runs in Jewish families," said Homer.

"What do you mean?"

"Mothers indulge, fathers disapprove, both to excess. My wife and I had our children later, so perhaps age is on our side. They're both fine kids and good students."

"My boy is with me in the business, thanks to God," said Abraham

Cogansky who had been silent during the conversation.

"Let's drink one last glass to our children while sharing a deep pessimism about the world." Homer lifted his champagne flute. "We agree that Hitler must be stopped."

Alfred lifted his glass. "I don't understand Chamberlain encouraging the villain."

"Jewish people must leave all Europe lands if they can," Cogansky said.

"Just so Margie comes home safely." Alfred couldn't help noticing that Tommy was draped over the piano listening to Carmela and hoped he'd not wander off again to sleep somewhere on a flower bed.

---

Upstairs, Margie shimmied out of her dress and girdle and into a dark blue tunic and trousers for the night train to San Francisco.

"You bought that without me?" Tillie sat up from where she'd been reclining on the bed. "It's not bad at all. Show yourself to the Leiter sisters if they're still here and make apologies for me. I'm too tired to get up. Do you mind if I don't see you out?"

"Mama, you rest, after all you've done from morning to night."

"I admit I'm feeling a bit peaked though I look a decade younger than June. Dr. Delicio has refilled my prescription so I'll rebound tomorrow. Eddie is still great fun at small talk but wasn't that a terrible toupee he was wearing?"

"Like Baby Faced somebody or other in the gangster pictures."

Tillie laughed. "Sylvia said his daughters look like their mother, poor things, with the mustaches. You and Tommy will make children with beautiful heads of hair."

Margie blushed. "Everyone but you worries about me and Tommy."

"Worry! I'm ecstatic and I can't wait until you settle in California. Give me one more kiss, my beautiful bride." Tillie lifted her head from the bed. "Didn't we already discuss the facts of life? If not, it's rather late and I'm sure you'll manage. Between you and me, I believe Eddie has more of a fancy for gents than ladies."

"I thought the same when he looked at Tommy, gazing as if he'd never stop." Margie kissed her mother on both cheeks. "We'll call from San Francisco, just to make sure you have gotten some rest. I'll say to goodbye to Papa."

# FOUR

<u>FOUR</u>

SEPTEMBER, 1937

MARGIE AND TOMMY GRENSKY waved their goodbyes to friends on the Hudson River pier and were heading to the lower deck of the *SS Champlain* when they saw Hal Bloom, a newsman who'd also landed in advertising after the Crash.

"You two lovebirds running off together?" Bloom greeted them with handshakes.

"Legal. Got hitched in California. Taking a few things to the other side of the big pond." Tommy pointed to Margie's heap of luggage waiting on the deck.

"Congratulations. Where's your cabin, kids?"

"Somewhere in the deeps." Tommy wiped his brow. "Hope it's cool down there."

"Not a chance. A real steam bath below. Stay above the water line."

"What do you mean, Hal? Swim?" Margie knew that Hal Bloom had been hired by Young & Rubicon and was wondering what big shot he'd been seeing off.

"We have the French Line account and a cabin has been reserved for the boss but he can't make it. You two ready to move to First?"

"With the Vanderbilts? Saw one of them being brought on in a wheelchair. We can't afford those kinds of heights." Tommy placed his arm on Margie's shoulder.

"Cost you nothing. If you don't take the suite, it goes empty. Flowers delivered and champagne already on ice. Want you to have it, kiddos."

284

"Gee," said Margie. "Think we should?"

"We'll take it for the price, thanks, if you let me offer you a drink."

"You can pop champagne in the cabin but I've got to run."

"All this and we didn't bring real evening clothes," Margie said.

"You've got style, you two. Won't matter what you wear, you'll be a breath of youth among the generation that can afford First. I'll settle it with the purser and scram before we're a threesome on your honeymoon."

---

Overnight, Tommy became the most popular man in First Class, bowing in gracious defeat as he lost at shuffleboard to elegantly dressed white-haired ladies whose strings of pearls dangled down their décolletage, and drinking late into the night with their husbands, who kept pouring whiskey into his glass and offering stock tips and introductions to their daughters. He engaged three pretty French girls who worked on the *Champlain*—Antoinette, Delphine, and Cécile—to have drinks with an older gentlemen.

Each night around ten, Margie said goodnight to Tommy and his drinking companions and went to their cabin. Shoes off, she took up a book and stretched on the sofa where a moon reflected in the sea. Their luxury suite had the largest windows she'd ever seen. Two Agatha Christies that she and Tommy liked reading aloud, each with their own Inspector Poirot accent, lay on the night table for them to share. As she waited for him to join her in bed, she thought about Elman's safari adventures, how he'd surprised everyone with Carmela and her conch shell. She'd never understand her brother.

Margie woke up when Tommy came in and snuggled next to her, his warm body a source of constant pleasure. By the third night, though, she wanted Tommy to leave the smoky saloon and come to bed earlier. When she signaled with a yawn the next night, he mouthed "five minutes." Again she lay awake for a half hour before she fell asleep, Agatha Christie unopened on the bed table.

The final night of the voyage, he vowed to be up for the first sight of the English coast as they came into British waters. At dawn, when he didn't wake up at her nudging, she pulled off the covers and poured cold water down the neck of his pajamas.

"You devil!" he shrieked.

"Your fault." She shoved him in the shower that was larger than her entire New York bathroom. She still didn't want to reproach him but five nights drinking was testing her patience. Out of the shower, she slapped him with a towel on the bottom.

"Meet me on deck. England is off the starboard side."

---

In London, they found a small hotel near Charring Cross Station but within two hours after Tommy left to meet a newspaper friend, he returned with a grin on his face. "Pack up, dumpling. I just had a glass of stout with Bob Halliday," he said.

"Doesn't Halliday write for the *Herald Tribune*?" Margie asked.

"Yes. He's been covering Germany for the *Trib*. Going to be over there for three final weeks and then he's leaving at the end of the month for home. He's offering us his furnished flat near Drury Lane until he gets back. He didn't want anything for using it but I insisted. We'll stand him drinks whenever he's back in town."

"I'm glad I didn't unpack. We can use more room. I got used to all that space on the ship, especially when I was on my own." Margie didn't look at Tommy; she didn't want to complain that evenings in the honeymoon suite had not been what she'd hoped.

"Halliday also introduced me to a *Trib* ad account guy who's leaving. I'll take that over for now."

"Tommy, you're either too good or too lucky. I'm so pleased, it's wonderful."

"Just wait. That isn't all. No time wasted. Made my first contacts with whiskey representatives. Swell guys in starched collars. What about you, young spouse? Lazy?"

"Almost lazy. Relaxed, I guess. It's been years since I wasn't on a deadline. I did some shopping. You won't believe the prices. I'm outfitting you in tweeds."

Margie held up a heather-grey tweed jacket that she'd picked out on Bond Street. "You can take it back for tailoring but I had someone try it on and it looked about right."

The perfectly-fitting jacket brought out the hazel in the green of Tommy's eyes.

"Spouse, it is wonderful."

"You have important business in London and I'm discovering an inherited talent for shopping, as long as I have you to buy for. Take a look at these trousers."

Tommy held up a pair of dark grey wool slacks. "They look perfect. You treasure. You encourage me as you always have. Come sit down, my feet hurt."

They sat on the small hard couch. Tommy took Margie's hand with her wedding ring. "I think the British are secretly in love with advertising but won't admit it because they don't like spending or appearing too forward. We were so very polite and they gifted me with something for my bride, payment on the installment plan."

He crossed the room and drew out of his satchel a beautifully sculpted round bottle with liquid amber jiggling inside. "Aged single malt, my sweet. I can get you blended, barley, wheat, rye, Scottish, Irish for writing promotional ads. I'm hoping I'll be paid in pound sterling, but this liquid reimbursement won't hurt in the meanwhile."

"I've never tasted anything so smoky." Margie sipped. "Delicious. Dense."

"Keep the adjectives coming." Tommy scribbled in his pocket notepad. "We're all about product which shouldn't be difficult as the British Isles make the best whiskies in the world. Americans have been painfully deprived. Now a Yank disembarks to tell them that Prohibition is gone, and that America has awakened with the thirst of a million Paul Bunyans. They're listening."

"Happy awakening!" she toasted.

"Look how grey it is. A shame to go out. I'm not hungry, are you?" He winked.

She shook her head though she'd felt starved before he'd arrived.

———

They emerged holding each other close. Rain was falling and the

Soho streets were slick. "Italians, we have spaghetti! Chinese, chow mein. What is your preference my darling?" Tommy kissed her damp head.

"Candlelight and red wine and pasta, hands down."

They pulled open the door to Ribbolini's and were instantly embraced by its aromas of tomatoes, meat, garlic, and the warm handshake of a woman with strands of black hair out of its bun and a white apron. "Call me Julietta, luvs, and come with me."

Julietta beckoned them to a checker-cloth covered table with a carafe of wine, bread and candles already set up.

After a heaping plate of decent Bolognese and rough red wine, Tommy said, "Wouldn't be here without you, sweet potato pie."

"I'm happy to be off the boat and all the swells you spent long hours with."

"They wouldn't let me go, Margie."

"Sometimes you have to disappoint people, say goodnight and come home."

"Don't be a task driver, all right?"

"I missed you at night, that's all. I prefer spaghetti and you to be here."

"We're here and if I have another mouthful of spaghetti, I'll burst," he said.

Tommy said that Halliday had recommended a pub called The Cheese on a side street a few blocks from the flat. Theater girls laughed loudly, still bright-cheeked with rouge from their shows, while men with notepads dripped cigarette ash on the bar. They could have been the actors, publicists and reviewers off Broadway, except, Margie said, their teeth revealed British or Irish lack of dentistry.

Tommy ordered two gins from a rumpled-looking bartender drying glasses.

"Yank, don't miss Ruth Gordon in *The Country Wife* at the Vic. She's a scene stealer. Does the very naughty very well." The bartender was named Ian.

"Let's go to lots of plays, Tommy. The British are the best actors."

"Half of them seem to be here." Tommy looked around

A man in tattered clothes with an aristocratic face raised his glass to deliver King Edward VII's farewell speech as if he were the resigning monarch himself.

"I have found it impossible to carry the heavy burden of responsibility and discharge my duties as King as I would wish to do without the help and support of the woman I love…I lay down my burden… God Save the King." He deposited his glass.

Someone called out "Prince, Farewell, another drink." Tommy raised his glass to the loyal Brits mourning Edward's dismissal because the prince would not give up Mrs. Simpson. By closing time, Tommy was arm in arm with men who leaned on each others' shoulders while Margie waited for the last call from the bartender to take him home.

———————

Later in the week, Tommy stepped into The Cheese for a quick pint before going home. A reviewer with the penname Mr. Duck said, "Yank Thomas, take a look."

A pretty, slender woman in a trench coat and hat had stepped into the pub and was shaking off dampness. She removed her hat and a mass of chestnut curls tumbled out.

"Another countryman of yours, "said Duck. "She's in *Pride and Prejudice* at the St. James. Not bad at all."

"That's a show we want to see," said Tommy.

When the actress asked for a whiskey, half the men stepped up to buy.

"Raise your hand, lad, stand up for the U.S.A.," said Duck.

"Here's a gallant countryman, Miss." The bartender pointed to Tommy.

"Thanks." The pretty girl tossed down a shot glass and kept her eyes on him.

"Have another," Tommy said.

"Thanks again, I will. Come see the matinee soon. Say you're my brother Hank and there's always a ticket. What's your name anyway?"

"Thomas, called Tommy. And yours?"

"Adrienne Lynne is what I go by."

"Adrienne, that's a top-drawer name. Thanks for making me hero of the hour." Tommy was about to say, "My wife and I haven't yet seen a play," but he did not.

―――――――

At their flat, he opened the door and smelled a beef stew.

"Wifey, you're such a peach. So smart and you can cook. How did I ever convince you to marry me? Why did I wait so long?"

"You kept begging until I accepted. Tell me what triumphs you had today."

"*Advertising Age* wants pieces on the revived cross Atlantic whiskey trade I said was about to happen. They want production numbers, plus details from the source, human interest, interviews with master blenders, sniff, inhale, drink. Guess we can do that."

"All this on your second day out! Let's drink to blended and single malts!"

"Never refuse to drink when requested. Once the distillers see their names and stories in print, they'll take out ads, I'd bet on it."

"You're a natural. I did tell you that already?"

"You make me feel darned good. I'll hammer out some copy after mystery stew."

"Don't leave out the funny men in starched collars you told me about."

Tommy sat down to his Remington where he typed with two fingers.

"I can help, I use all ten of mine," Margie offered but he shook his head.

She cleaned up and started writing post cards. After family mail was taken care of, she wrote to Mr. Bowles. He'd promised to keep her job, but what if the unexpected happened? They always took precautions because Tommy expressed negative feelings about the responsibilities of children. "I was a burden to Mother," he said often, to which she replied, "But she loved you," and the conversation ended.

"The British have offices that are like a living room, so cordial, so different from ours." Tommy looked up at her. "They appreciate restraint. They're more cautious than Americans, slow to change. The older men seem to have more power than the younger ones—different from home. Loyalty to brands and your firm."

"At home, you almost have to be young to have the nerve for advertising."

"Tradition matters here. Along with smoothness."

"That's a good line, Tommy. I was also thinking of another. *Bootleggers were man's best friend a little while back, but now you can order directly from the source where tradition matters.* Something on those lines."

Tommy typed. "How about a lead, *Refined old world taste makes a return?* Too bad premiums won't work but you can't expect a drinker to save a bottle top or steam off a label for a prize."

"How do you know that?" Margie asked.

"Drinkers aren't savers like housewives. They're almost the opposite. A housewife plans ahead. She knows she'll be doing the wash a hundred times so she buys more than she needs and appreciates a gift or a discount. Drinkers' minds, and I speak from experience, are in the moment. Tomorrow, feeding the kids doesn't enter their heads until it's too late and they come staggering home without the paycheck for the missus."

Margie's stomach sank a moment. No kids. He seemed to be mind-reading her.

Tommy took a sip of his whiskey and returned to typing his copy with his index fingers.

# FIVE

Tommy picked up the phone in Bob Halliday's office. "*Herald Tribune.*"

"Adrienne, the girl you stood to whiskies last night at The Cheese," a husky voice said.

"Hello Adrienne, what can I do for you?"

"The actress I'm understudying for Jane has a sore throat and I'm on with Hugh Williams. Short notice, but come to the matinee this afternoon. I want to have you there."

Tommy hesitated. He and Margie had planned on seeing *Pride and Prejudice* together but Margie might not be in and there was only one ticket before the curtain time in only an hour. He did want to see Hugh Williams as Mr. Darcy.

"You'll have to hurry up and get over here."

"That's swell, thanks, I'll be there," Tommy answered.

Adrienne's ticket was third row center, close enough to see she was as much a knock-out as he remembered. He clapped vigorously when the cast took their bows, and as Adrienne looked down from the stage, she saw him and mouthed, *Come see me.*

As he walked around to the stage door, he calculated that he'd have enough time to congratulate Adrienne on her performance and be back for supper with Margie.

Adrienne's dressing room door was ajar. "Come in, tell me what you think."

He stepped in. "You were wonderful." He took off his hat to Adrienne.

"You should never cover that head of hair."

Though the actress was much younger and slimmer than Tillie, her comment on his hair in her ironic New York accent reminded him of Margie's mother. Like Tillie, Adrienne knew how to take control from the moment she met a man.

The fragrance of bouquets and Adrienne's face creams made the heated room cloyingly sweet. Tommy felt relief from the excessive sweetness when the actress unscrewed the cap from a bottle of whiskey, releasing smoky fumes. "Here's to a new friend." She poured amber into his glass. "You seemed to have good taste in the stuff."

"Tell me, where you from, Adrienne?"

"When I'm not putting on the British Ritz?" Adrienne swiveled to face him. "I'm a dressmaker's daughter from Queens. Mother sewed me into my first costumes when she was making party clothes for rich girls. Gypsy Rose Lee has nothing on us 'cept Gypsy's in movies now and I'm understudying the second lead so maybe I should have stripped."

She shimmied and her breasts bobbed in her flowered dressing gown.

Tommy looked down so she wouldn't see the blood that rushed to his face.

"Your family from New York? I come from Colorado."

"I had a western grandpa who called himself Ely Sands. Sold fancy clothes to the miners and got into trouble. Mama said the name was Sandovsky but he made it shorter."

"This might sound crazy," Tommy said, "but I remember my aunt telling me that Baby Doe—a dance hall girl who married a Colorado senator—had arrived in Leadville on the arms of a Mr. Sands who sold fancy dresses. Maybe that's your grandpa."

"Wow, that would be a co-incidence. I'll ask Ma when I talk to her. Maybe we have more geography in common. A refill? Whiskey's cheap here." She tilted the bottle.

This was his moment to come clean and tell the pretty actress he was in London with his wife on their honeymoon where they were researching whiskies. Margie's name should have come up by now, but every minute he bantered with Adrienne and their eyes sparked something, the harder it was to introduce his new wife into the conversation.

"You like the theater?" she asked.

"My passion. Used to do reviewing. Like all us hacks, I had a dream of writing a play, a Noel Coward kind of droll comedy though what I've had in mind is more drama."

Adrienne, still sitting at her dressing table, got up and sat beside him on the sagging couch covered by a silky spread. "Duck said you have a soft spot for poor King Ed. I'll never forget the day about a year ago. I was on the Strand where every living soul was weeping their eyes out. The good King's speech still makes me cry."

"The abdication was like a death." Tommy was now coming closer to violet brown eyes ringed with dark shadows, his senses whirling while somehow he managed to speak. "Upper classes did everything but tar and feather one of their own."

"They're the most terrible snobs here." Adrienne said. She was almost in his lap now, too close not to come closer, the attraction of two warm bodies and lips governed by a law of physics and chemistry that wouldn't be denied. If Margie hovered somewhere in his mind, Adrienne's voluminous, soft reddish curls tumbling from ribbons put anything but fragrance and skin far away. Adrienne's little nose with its dab of cold cream blurred in Tommy's vision, and then they were deeply in each other's arms.

"Miss Lynne!" called a voice from outside followed by a rap on the door.

She pulled back to answer, "Yes, Mr. Durbin."

"Miss Hyson is recovered for the evening. Just letting you know, luv," he said.

"Thank you." Adrienne raised her hand to stop Tommy from standing up but he took one step back, then another, and somehow managed to find his hat and coat.

"Handsome, where are you going?"

"Got to fly. You were smashing. How'd you reach me, by the way?"

"I know Bob Halliday's office phone. We used to see each other here and there."

"You know Bob Halliday?"

"Swell guy who hates Hitler. He's met a girl to rescue in Berlin."

"That's him. Good old Halliday. I have to go, really, must finish a story."

"You newsmen! You'll come again?"

Tommy slammed his hat down on his brow and staggered out. He felt ridiculous almost running down the narrow hall behind the stage, pushing open the door to the cold air and nearly falling out onto the pavement as if he'd been bounced rather than voluntarily made his exit.

———————

Margie thought Tommy looked a little flushed when he came in.

"I hope you're not catching a cold. Maybe pop in the bath while I heat soup."

"Soup and bath, just what I need," he said, escaping behind the bathroom door and running the tap for a bath.

"The evening has a nasty chill," he heard Margie say. Then she came to the door.

"I called an old friend, Tommy. Eleanor and her husband Arthur live near a village called Nutley, in Sussex. With your love of British history, you'll find it fascinating to visit. She's the eldest of three Guggenheim girls and the one I was closest to when I was growing up. El married a minor count so she's now Countess Castle Stewart. Her middle sister, Gertrude, lives on a neighboring farm. Gertrude is a dwarf. She always loved animals. To an animal, she wasn't different from anyone else. Tommy, are you coming out? The soup is ready."

"Heard every word, dear, about the ruminants and some dwarves."

"One dwarf. A witty and kind one, if you please. Dry off and come eat."

As they ate, Margie continued talking about her childhood adventures with the Guggenheim girls, how Eleanor's mother Irene and Tillie had been friends, and how Solomon always had two mistresses, one chosen for brains and one for beauty.

"According to Eleanor, he's lost his head over a German baroness who has ideas about helping him collect modern art like their cousin Peggy."

"You're talking about Solomon Guggenheim, *the* millionaire Guggenheim?"

She scooped out more potatoes from the soup for Tommy. "Eleanor is as down to earth as anyone you'll ever meet."

"What I remember is the whole Guggenheim clan picked Leadville clean. Why don't you go visit without me? I won't fit in with Guggenheims."

"Tommy, Old Lodge was a hunting stop for royalty. There will be all sorts of historical things to see, and I want you to meet Eleanor. She's very strong-willed with a great sense of humor. As a girl, I was one of her devoted slaves who did whatever she wanted. You know, there's a certain age when younger girls idolize older ones. I once spent most of a night in a tree where El had posted me as a look-out while she and her older girl friends smoked and drank inside a barn. Summers, we sometimes traveled with them to their ranch in Idaho on their railroad car."

"Private railroad cars definitely sound outside my price range."

"You can talk to Arthur about whiskies. Quote a real Count of the Realm. Do you want to stay all alone in London without me?"

Tommy had to look at his plate. "I'll go with you," he answered.

Margie jumped up and hugged him. "You'll have a wonderful time, I promise."

# Six

The little train from Victoria Station stopped at gritty, grey London suburbs before chugging into the green Sussex countryside. At a small brick station, Margie saw the sign for Nutley, grabbed Tommy's arm and ran to the end of the carriage where she saw a thin woman wearing a tweed suit and hat with a feather waving an umbrella.

"She's got the head of a Roman senator dressed like Peter Pan," Tommy said.

"All three Guggenheim girls look like their father. Their mother was a Venetian creamy beauty but they didn't inherit her looks." Margie stepped off the train.

"So this is Thomas. I've heard so much about. Very glad to meet you." Eleanor gave Tommy a firm handshake. "And my adored Margie. I can see you're a happy woman."

"I am happy," said Margie. "Thomas Grensky is a main reason."

"Thank you for having us, Countess. Please call me Tommy." He made a small bow.

"None of the countess stuff between Americans, Tommy. Just Eleanor, please."

Eleanor drove her sleek black Jaguar at break-neck speed between hedge rows on either side of narrow, winding roads. From time to time, a farmer in a cart appeared and she swerved around the slow-moving vehicle while leaning out to wave and honk. Tommy watched everything with an amazed look on his face, then a broad smile.

"I suspect they had more than tea to drink at the village fair. We were there earlier, cutting some ribbons." Eleanor drove uphill beneath

297

a leafy green tunnel that opened onto an imposing, turreted stone edifice with three floors of windows.

"It's grand," said Tommy and Margie together as Eleanor slammed to a stop.

"Cold and uncomfortable but we keep it up because the villagers expect us to be here. It gives them security to know we're looking after them."

Tommy raised his eyebrows at Margie as if to say, *These are your people?*

The Count, a tall, lean man in country tweeds, shook Tommy's hand. "The ladies look forward to a jaunt on horseback if it's possible. Do you enjoy riding, Mr. Grensky?"

"It's not my chosen sport except when they race around tracks," Tommy said.

"You're right, young man. I never liked riding to hounds which my wife, though American, thinks un-British of me. Shall we give the ladies a chance to talk while we have something restorative before dinner?"

"Nothing would suit me better than a restorative."

"I understand that you Yanks might be on the way back to prohibiting drink."

"Oh no, Count, we're not going back to Prohibition." Tommy raised his hands in protest. "I'm in England to sell advertisements to the biggest whiskey makers in the British Isles because our American market has opened up and it won't close again."

"Advertising? I've heard of it, of course, but you'll tell me more."

Arthur took Tommy's arm. Gardeners doffed their caps. *Good afternoon, Sirs.*

They entered a dark hall through a massive door, walked on stone paving to a book-lined, carpeted study with a fire burning.

"What a grand fire." Tommy came close to the grate and rubbed his hands.

"And you'll be even warmer when I get you the whiskey I promised," Arthur said. "You'll tell me what you think of it."

Eleanor took Margie in the direction away from the house toward the stables where horses greeted them with neighs.

"Here, you give sugar." Eleanor pressed a handful of cubes into

Margie's palm. "We loved our horses and our dogs, didn't we? Now I've got boys, four of them, but I don't neglect the ponies, either." Eleanor put two fingers between her lips and whistled. Dogs bounded in first response, rangy brown liver and white hounds with wide grins and wagging tails, followed by two slim boys in short pants with high-colored fair skin and gold-red hair carrying what looked like flat hockey sticks.

"Afternoon, Mum." Both made small bows.

"Afternoon boys. I'd like you to meet Margie Hornthall…sorry, what it's now?"

"Grensky but just call me Margie. I'm an old friend of your mother's."

"Pleased to meet you, Ma'am." The boys stood politely waiting until Eleanor said, "All right, off with you," and they dashed back around the stables and Margie kept stroking the tender muzzle of a grey mare.

"They're on a holiday from school. Practicing their batting. It's cricket. Don't ask me to explain. My two eldest don't come home so often."

"El, four boys! They're so lively and polite. I'm truly envious."

"Two years apart and I consider myself fortunate to be done with breeding though it still surprises me that I've had four of them, all robust, all adored."

"I'd like three, with a girl. Tommy doesn't know about it yet."

"With your hips, you'll have no trouble birthing, Margie. Personally, I'd have done fine with the vet in attendance but that wasn't possible. Let me show you around."

As they walked on, Margie said she hoped they didn't talk too much about Edward and the Mrs. Simpson business. "Tommy's obsessed with Edward."

"Then I won't say that I'm glad we're quit of him," said Eleanor. "He's a damned anti-Semite who'd have fed us to Hitler. Albert—now King George as you know—is less flashy but made of finer stuff."

"Tommy's attachment is intense. I'm not sure why. British history and kings."

"It's so much twaddle compared to what's going on over on the

Continent." Eleanor planted her walking stick into the gravel lane. "Just imagine an exhibit the Nazis put on in Munich they called 'Degenerate Art'—that's all the modern painters Father collects these days. Unless an artist has milkmaids and blond youth, the paintings go into the fire. We've forbidden Father to go to Germany though he's dying to buy as much 'degenerate art' as he can for the new museum he's building in New York."

"How is Aunt Irene? I haven't been to see her in several years but I've read about her good works in the press."

"Mother is fine. They'll be here later for supper."

"Oh, I'm so glad to have a chance to see her again."

"Have you heard the news that our crazy Cousin Peggy is also collecting modern pictures and opening a gallery in London? She can't do anything that doesn't shock. She embarrasses Arthur and me. Tell me about you, dear. It's been so long."

"I've been working since I graduated from college. Mother objected but now she thinks it's clever of me. I love working and meeting people for our ad campaigns."

"Ad means advertising I gather. What is that precisely?"

"I write radio commercials for products. One is a variety program for singing stars and another is for the first Jewish woman on national radio. It's called *The Goldbergs.*"

"I've never heard of it, but isn't a bit risky to be so openly Jewish?"

"If you mean, does it draw too much attention to Jews, the fact is that the show is so outspokenly Jewish that it's an antidote to anti-Semitisim. It was a gamble for NBC but Gertrude Berg, our star, has made Jewish families seem like any immigrant family, Italian or Polish, with the problems anyone new with a funny accent and eating different food has in assimilating. President Roosevelt is supposed to have said that he didn't get the country out of the Depression—the Goldbergs did. I think Jews owe her a lot."

"How different it is over here. The British lower their voices when they say Jew. It's becoming fatal on the Continent." Eleanor paused. "My dear, because you've got a good head on your shoulders, I'd like you to take some papers to France. You are going?"

"Yes, when Tommy's finished business here with the whiskey it's on to France for champagne."

"Good. It's nothing to get you in trouble but I don't dare risk the mail for residence permits and our promise of support to Jews to escape Hitler's grasp."

"I never realized it was so bad, or so close," said Margie.

"You have the Atlantic between yourselves and the Reich. To make matters worse, we have that horrible Chamberlain congratulating the little German on his restraint. I believe you've met Siegmund Warburg in New York? He's recently left his home in Berlin and brought his wife and children here. He's coming to supper tonight."

"I haven't met him but my aunt, Sylvia Loeb—she's actually a cousin but I always called her Aunt—Sylvia believes the Warburgs are doing a world of good for refugees, setting up bank accounts to help them emigrate and much more I don't know about. She's on a committee for Palestine where she's planning to go herself."

"The Warburgs are buying time for Jews to get out. Jews can't stay in Germany. The sooner we realize it, the better." She sighed. "Enough. Shall we dress for dinner?"

"I have this suit and riding pants, and Tommy's got the clothes he's wearing."

"Arthur's second man will find Tommy a jacket and I'll give you a good string of pearls that will go with anything you're wearing. You're both so attractive that it really doesn't matter what you wear."

"Tommy certainly is. He can wear anything."

"So can you, my dear. You're *most* attractive, Margie, and you have character."

————————

Arthur's second man found a dinner jacket and trousers for Tommy so that he appeared for cocktails looking the country squire. Margie noticed he was drinking like one, accepting a butler's large pourings of whiskey before supper.

Gertrude Guggenheim arrived in a rattling green truck wearing a brown wool coat to her ankles and straw clinging to her rustic cap with a feather. She was about three and a half feet tall, and if she'd had a cape, would have looked like a diminutive rustic from *Midsummer's Night Dream*, Margie thought. Two dogs followed her, a waddling male Basset Hound and a yellowish female, something between Corgi and Shepherd. The castle's hounds followed to the drawing room table where one began to pass gas.

Gertrude giggled, "That's my boy Toby. We call it passing Tobes." She gave a pat on the head of the Basset who squirmed with pleasure and let out another stink.

"I'd call them Limberger and Gorgonzola," said Tommy. Gertrude roared. Tommy grinned and kissed Margie's neck where Eleanor's large pearls were glowing. "It's not half bad here."

"I thought you'd like Arthur. No pretensions. And I love seeing El again."

"What *did* you feed the dogs, Gertie?" Eleanor asked.

"The odd innards. They love kidneys."

"Oh. Lord!" Eleanor shook her head and looked at her watch. "Mother and Father are always late. Siegmund is upstairs. He arrived while we were dressing and said he needed a nap. Cook hates it when we let the soup go cold so we better go in."

Eleanor rang her dinner bell and led them into a wood-paneled, coffin-ceilinged dining hall with crests and banners on the walls. The two boys appeared, scrubbed and combed. Gertrude's dogs waddled after, installing themselves under the table at her feet, while Eleanor's hounds lay against walls.

"The dogs look like ones you see in medieval tapestries," Tommy said.

A young maid began passing a tureen of potato-leek soup. As Margie spooned the first mouthful, Gertrude's dogs bounded from the table to join Eleanor's pack of hounds rushing toward the door. Arthur stood and Tommy followed.

The two people Tommy saw emerge from a silver Rolls Royce couldn't possibly be Solomon Guggenheim and his wife Irene. All Guggenheims were giants of legend—whatever they touched turned to gold—not these two old, small people.

"Such a rush of cars that Hanson had to contend with. We're

famished." Irene Guggenheim, engulfed in furs up to her chin, shook hands with Tommy when Eleanor introduced them. "I don't suppose there's any food for us. Hanson will eat downstairs."

"Do sit before the soup is entirely cold, Mother."

"Is that really you, Marjorie? I hope you're still an excellent horse-woman. Dear, this is Mathilda Hornthall's daughter. She used to ride at Madison Square Gardens, in the steeple chase, is that correct, my dear?"

Margie nodded. "Other people's horses."

"I received an invitation to your wedding but we were heading east and not west. This must be the lucky man. So good looking!"

There was still charm in Irene Guggenheim's kind smile, especially in her eyes and her thick brows. She'd been a true redhead, Margie remembered, but now had silver curls, like Tillie. "She's a social reformer," Margie said to Tommy. "Child welfare."

"I can't think of them as anything but Guggenheims." He swallowed wine.

As they talked, two servants passed a large fowl. Overdone roast beef and boiled potatoes followed. Tommy kept his nose in his excellent French Burgundy bottle.

They'd finished eating by the time Siegmund Warburg appeared wearing a black suit and an impeccable white shirt. Tommy said to Margie, "Lord, he's expensive."

"I don't know if he'll talk about Germany. I hope he will," she answered.

They waited until Warburg was served and had eaten before Eleanor asked him about his family. "When I'm in Berlin, Aryan friends invite me home to dine which still gives me hope that the German people will realize they've been misled by Hitler and come to their senses, but for the moment, I've moved my wife and children here."

"You won't convince me about Germans. They'd snuff me out," said Gertrude.

"Gertie, thank goodness none of us are there." Eleanor patted her sister's hand.

Solomon Guggenheim spoke to Tommy. "I understand we share a locale, young man. Leadville! Remember it well! You in mineral sciences?"

"I left Leadville when I was young and I've never been back."

"1887—I was never allowed to forget that date." Guggenheim went on to yell in Tommy's ear how his father had started out as a peddler with a cart selling lace, stove and shoe polish all over the west before coming to Leadville. "Father took his first mines for debts in 1887. He didn't have any use for mines but silver paid off, as I'm sure you know, young man. Name Grensky sounds familiar. In trade?"

"Yes, they were. Beverages." Tommy drank. "I come by it naturally."

Guggenheim seemed satisfied with Tommy's answer. "Father understood you had to be in production for the real money. Smelting was what we grew up with. Dark, dirty and smelly it was."

Tommy grumbled into his wine glass and drank.

When nine chimed on the clock, Gertrude announced her departure. The elder Guggenheims and Warburg went off to bed. "Goodnight, you charmer." Solomon kissed Margie on the cheek.

"Remember me to your mother," Irene Guggenheim said and Margie replied that she'd write to Tillie tomorrow.

Once Margie got Tommy upstairs he flopped on their small bed.

"You can't sleep in Arthur's jacket. Let me help you out of it."

"Should have told Guggenheim a thing about kings of silver and barons of copper. Did my father in."

"Tommy, you can't blame Solomon."

"You don't understand." Tommy resisted having his shoe laces untied and Margie backed away. "My father died leaving nothing and Mother worked to bring me up."

"I know she did. June is an admirable woman."

"Never supported her. Been a bad son." Tommy began to weep.

"Tommy, go to sleep. Your mother is fine now."

"Leadville, no place I'll go back to. Guggenheim a bore and a bully."

---

In the middle of the night, Margie woke up to hear him snuffling.

"Sorry. Feel terrible. Head splitting."

"I'll get the remedy." She got up, fumbled for aspirin, Alka-Seltzer and water.

---

In the morning, Tommy slept while Margie and Eleanor went for a ride. At lunch, Tommy entertained the boys with stories of his own delinquent school days.

Eleanor drove them back to the station. "We'll see each other in London. I'll bring you the packet I spoke of." Eleanor shook hands with Tommy and kissed Margie on both cheeks. "Come again, any time, and stay longer. Tommy, I'm sorry you had to listen to Father." Eleanor shook his hand.

"I'm sure he didn't mind." Margie embraced Eleanor. "Thank you, I loved it."

———

The trip back to Victoria seemed to take twice as long as it had going out to the country. Tommy glared at the green fields from under furrowed brows. Margie asked if he still had a headache and wanted another aspirin. He grumbled a few words and she didn't ask again. At Victoria Station, she had to run alongside to keep up with him. Her eyes smarted as she carried her heavy bag toward Drury Lane, increasingly angry.

"Tell me, before we bring bad feelings upstairs, what's gotten into you?"

Tommy put his suitcase down and shook his head. "I did mind Guggenheim, just so you know. I don't understand why you mixed me with your royals, your nobs. In New York, I felt out of place in their country houses when you brought me along like a pet."

"I never did that. A pet! That's ridiculous. I wanted everyone to meet you."

"I'd appreciate not being pulled along again."

"Tommy! Eleanor and Gertie are truly old friends, and Arthur isn't a snob. I wanted them to know the man I married because I'm so proud of you."

Margie was standing with her hands on her hips as people and cars passed. Tommy had faced her anger only a few times; fortunately her most furious moments not directed at him but at the unwise man or woman who had mistreated an animal. Margie had once held

Tillie's horse trainer at the edge of a pitch fork for beating a retired race horse for failing at stud. "You're a bully and you're going to be fired," Margie had told him before letting the man escape the tines of the pitch fork.

Tommy also knew from past experience that Margie's anger died out as quickly as it flared, leaving no trace. She never kept a slow burn that lasted the way his mother did. His mother nursed resentments in silence for weeks: every time she visited the awful Grensky aunts who were still alive and living in a San Francisco hotel suite, she said she felt sick remembering the way they'd dismissed her, cutting her off without a penny, but she persisted making annual visits to them. Margie, he knew, would have let the aunts know her feelings and never looked back.

"Let's have a drink. I need it. Hair of the dog," Tommy said.

They backtracked to The Cheese. Tommy carried Margie's case. He hoped and prayed that Adrienne Lynne would not be there.

When they were seated with two mugs of ale, he said, "You've never wanted for anything, Margie. You don't see the privilege you've had." Before she could react and answer, he emptied his glass and ordered another. "You're no snob, not in the least. You're a swell democratic gal with a huge heart and I haven't a leg to stand on when I criticize. I'm an ass. But I've got my pride and I don't find it easy being married to a woman who knows one of the richest men in the world and calls him Uncle. Good Old Uncle Sol Guggenheim." Tommy snorted. "Robber baron Guggenheim to me."

Margie stifled several responses off the top of her head because she knew that Tommy needed to talk. She never thought visiting Eleanor and Arthur would trigger old hurts. She liked Tommy's friends, all sorts of friends, and was liked back for herself. She had the innate confidence not to worry what others thought of her, nor second-guess herself, but, she realized, they still had deep differences, misunderstandings that might not be so easily fixed.

# SEVEN

ADRIENNE LYNNE CALLED SEVERAL times and sent letters to Halliday's office while Tommy and Margie were in Scotland and Wales tasting whiskies from the island of Oban to St David's Head, ending their tour in the distilleries of Edinburgh. Halliday's office secretary Alice was curt with Adrienne on the phone and placed the perfumed letters separately from other mail as if to quarantine their aroma. When Tommy checked in, Alice never mentioned the calls and handed him the letters with a look of disapproval.

"Mr. Halliday used to wonder whether the lady swam in these scents," she said.

Tommy knew he was an avoider who hated confrontation with a woman, so he made excuses to Margie about why they weren't going to The Cheese or to see *Pride and Prejudice* before they left for France.

Tommy's second day back at the office, Alice brought in a wire. "Boss postponing return to London. Getting married tomorrow. Grensky stay," Alice read.

The phone rang and Tommy answered to hear Adrienne's breathy voice. "Celia's giving me the matinee. In just four hours, I'll be Elizabeth Bennett, not mousy Jane but fabulous Elizabeth, the brains of the play. You gotta come, Tommy, so I'll be spectacular." Adrienne pouted her words as if he could see her mouth.

"Congratulations, Adrienne. Thanks, but I got a Macbeathan cold in Scotland."

"So that's where you were. I thought I was being snubbed and now I won't accept excuses, not even the murder play. You come. I won't take no. You got my letters?"

"I'll probably cough and ruin your lines."

"You won't ruin anything unless you don't show. Missed you, Tom. Come."

As Tommy's cab pulled up before the theater, he remembered how Uncle Morris had taken him aside at the wedding and said, "You married a fine woman. Cherish her. You're a grown man now, Thomas. I've seen hanky panky in this town, and without exception, it leads to bad ends."

Adrienne got all Elizabeth Bennett's lines right but she didn't seem to believe herself in the part until Mr. Darcy, Tommy's idol Hugh Williams, insulted her and she rose to the challenge. From then on, intelligent lines carried her through to the end. At the curtain, Tommy stood to applaud and saw Adrienne give him her signal to visit her dressing room.

"I'm free this evening, Tommy." Adrienne swiveled away from the mirror toward him. "Will you do the honors?" He poured two glasses of Scotch and drank his in a gulp.

"I'm afraid that I'm not free. I shouldn't even be out." He coughed.

Looking at him with her kohl-rimmed eyes, she asked, "Has it to do with the short woman you were with one night at The Cheese? I heard about her from friends."

Tommy cleared his throat. "My wife."

"No ring that I can see." She looked at his hands and he looked away.

"I don't wear one but she does. We're newlyweds in town on our honeymoon. Should have said so before, very sorry."

There was no air anywhere to breathe that wasn't perfumed by the girl or the whiskey. He should have defended Margie from Adrienne's 'short' remark. What drew him to Adrienne, he thought, wasn't her height or good legs, but a certain frailty beneath her bravado, her need to earn his approval. She was a very pretty girl and an adequate actress but he guessed she didn't have the confidence, the singular personality that made a star stand out and thrill. He'd known plenty of self-absorbed stunning girls and fallen for a few but Margie was different. Margie was fun. She made him happy. If it went further with Adrienne, he'd be ruining everything and hate himself for it.

"She looked more like a friend," Adrienne said in a Joan Crawford tone of dismissal, eyebrows raised. "Rather unspectacular for the likes of you, Tommy."

"She is a friend and a swell wife. I'm better off with than I was without her."

"Real life Nick and Nora Charles, huh? All you need is the dog." She swiveled away, took a cigarette from a case and placed it in a long holder. Turning back, he saw that her eyes glistened with tears and smoke.

"You're a swell actress and a beautiful girl. I wish you all the success."

"You're the perfect man, but *of course* you're married. *Good men always are.*" She put on her British accent. He smiled a little sadly and left.

---

That night, Tommy came down with the full Scottish chest cold and slept on the couch. Margie brought him hot drinks and massaged vapor rub on his chest.

"I don't like that sound deep in your chest. I'll call El and ask the name of their doctor. I know they have someone on Harley Setreet." She stroked his damp dark hair.

"I don't want you to ask for some fancy doc she knows."

"Oh stop!" Margie stepped back, hands on her hips. "There's not enough room here for you to be sick and feel sorry for yourself. No more complaints about El."

"I don't know what you see in me, Margie." Tommy looked up from bleary eyes.

"Tommy, I see a man with a cold who will soon get better."

After he'd blown his nose, Tommy said, "What I make isn't anywhere near enough to help Mother pay off a debt that causes her sleepless nights, while *your* mother—and I love Tillie, don't get me wrong—doesn't know what she has in the bank."

"Tommy, I admire June. She's earned every penny through hard work. You're absolutely right, Mother never made a cent except on a hand of cards, which is why I wanted to support myself and not be dependent." She sat down with her knees curled up beside him. "I didn't know June had a debt that worried her."

"Mother put her savings into a real estate investment that the recent slump may cause her to lose. She's only paid half she owed on it. She expected land prices to rise."

"Prices will rise again, but in the meantime, we'll send June the rest of my parents' wedding gift to pay off her debt so she doesn't lose this property."

Tommy reached for his mug of toddy, drank and cleared his throat. "It's not chump change and I'm the one who needs to help her. I need to hold up my end."

"Eat your eggs and tinned peas on toast. It's all getting cold and will taste even worse than when it's hot. You need strength. We'll talk later."

"More canned peas? English food here is as dull as the weather. What time is it?"

Margie looked at her watch. "Just past two p.m."

"Too early for a drink?" he coughed.

"I can improve the tea and lemon…maybe that will give the peas more appeal."

"Improve, please."

Margie poured whiskey into Tommy's tea and handed him the cup. He sipped.

"Much improved." He looked into his cup. "I always wanted to write plays. I don't know if I have the talent and I've never saved a dime to go off to Provincetown or somewhere to try. I never wanted to live off a wife's money even if she had it."

"You never lived off me. We shared expenses."

"You must have gotten my job back for me three times," he said.

"You didn't deserve to be ignored. You always had the best ideas and the best way with words of anyone at the agency, otherwise you wouldn't have had a job. It was your ability, not my influence. Beside, I loved you for years before you knew I existed. Didn't want you out of my sight."

"I knew you existed, Margie."

"Tommy, write a play or great copy. I want you to do good work whatever that is, that's what I want."

"Once I'm no longer down with this cold, I'll see things less darkly."

"I know you will."

"Why don't we pack up and leave dreary England and go to France? I'll finish the pieces from Scotland and Wales. Half a dozen distillers said they'd buy ads."

"I loved the brew makers there. I loved everything about being with you there."

"Then onwards to Paree where you speak the lingo."

---

Margie called Eleanor to tell her they were leaving London.

"You wanted me to bring some papers to France?" she asked.

"I do. How about the Dorchester tomorrow at noon," Eleanor said. "I'll get the train and there will be time to catch the last one home."

---

Margie saw Eleanor's green hat among a crowd of men at the bar.

"I'm drinking gin and bitters," Eleanor said. "We'll get a table and have lunch."

"I need whatever you're drinking. I won't get too close because Tommy caught a cold in Scotland and has been coughing. I'm feeling fine but I don't want to give you anything. Paris will be a good change."

"Beastly weather here," Eleanor replied.

"Oh, El," Margie began. In a rush, she described Tommy's discomfort in Sussex and their argument on the way back. "We never disagreed before over something so small. I know he drinks a lot. It's a habit from years of never turning down a forbidden drink when offered, during our Prohibition, and then it carried over to the Repeal. Then there's the question of my money and his lack of."

"You might learn the English way of avoiding talking money. For instance, Arthur never mentions that I'm gossiped about. Hebrew heiresses is what we're called. We bring the money, the husband doesn't see bills and keeps the estate and title. Be that as it may, England suits me and it's good for Gertrude. Here they don't stare at her. The real problem is that our two older boys are already talking about joining the RAF and I'm worried sick. Hitler will come after us, no matter how many countries we appease him with. My boys will in the air fighting against Reich pilots. God, what a dreadful man."

Eleanor dabbed her eyes and then handed Margie a packet. "I only have some of the signed documents. Can I send on the rest to you in France?"

"American Express in Paris should be safe. I'm just happy to have seen you and Arthur, and your two lovely young sons. I hope there won't be war."

"Until we meet again." Eleanor embraced her. "You and Tommy will be fine."

---

After several good nights of sleep, Tommy returned to his office to finish up his articles. He worked better on a deadline, and with Paris to look forward to, churned out three pieces on malts, two more on single and double whiskies of Scotland. Too bad they never got as far as Ireland, he thought. When the phone rang, he hesitated, then was relieved to hear Halliday on the line. "Back in town for overnight. Meet at The Cheese in two hours? I'll bring Betty."

"Thanks so much for the desk, Bob. It's been great to have it. The bride and I are headed to France in a few days. And thanks for the swell apartment. We can get our stuff out in a day."

"I've booked us in a hotel. Will be leaving day after tomorrow, Grensky, so don't bother clearing out for us. I heard you were front row center at *Pride and Prejudice* a few Wednesdays ago. Newsmen are worse gossips than hairdressers," said Halliday.

"Haven't told Margie about the play so maybe you wouldn't mention it and if you have another watering hole, I'd rather not go to The Cheese."

"Course not. Let's make it six. The Plough, around the corner and two streets over from The Cheese, won't see anybody we know."

---

Margie sat beside Bettina Halliday whose small head was set off by an angular black boyish haircut.

"Bettina was a fine actress until the Nuremberg Laws against Jews forced her director to replace her in his film. We met the day she got fired." Halliday took his wife's small hand.

"I fell into his arms," Bettina said. "Bobby says I can work again in America. But he's going back to Berlin. I fear it's not safe." Bettina looked at her husband.

"Let's have another round." Tommy signaled to the bartender. "Sorry to hear you're going back, Bob. I know it's dangerous."

"Betty is going ahead of me back to New York and I'll follow shortly, maybe with her mother. If you want to read the writer who takes real risks, read Bill Shirer's latest. He's walking down Friedrichstrasse in broad daylight when he hears screaming, looks up to see Jews hanging out the window of some sort of detention center. This is in the center of town. Shirer got himself noticed and powers-that-be are kicking him out. He doesn't want to go but he's a marked man. Braver than me."

Bettina seized Halliday's hand and gave him a frightened look.

"No, *liebchen,* don't worry, I'm going to be in Berlin only as long as it takes to convince your mother to leave, and we'll sail to New York together before you know it."

"*Mutte* must agree to go," said Bettina.

Only when Bettina got up to go to the Ladies, Halliday leaned over and told Tommy and Margie how Hermann Goering, one of Hitler's intimates, had just declared new anti-Jewish laws, including one declaring that no Jewish chimney sweeps or housekeepers could work in Aryan homes.

"Chimney sweeps and housekeepers!" Halliday mopped his brow. "It's like the Moscow trials. The Nazis are like the Communists—they enjoy executing people. You two, don't linger over there. Isn't safe."

# EIGHT

Early morning crossing the English Channel, Tommy settled Margie with tea and their luggage in the saloon. "I'll take a turn around the deck." He kissed her cheek.

"Don't get cold. The wind's howling. Why go out when you're still coughing?"

"Stomach's a little queasy. Be right back after a breath of air."

The wind howled and the sea frothed in the wake behind the Channel ferry. Tommy tightened his scarf and walked determinedly to a spot far from the windows where he removed a packet from his inside coat pocket.

Perfume from the half-dozen envelopes, pink and lavender and robin's egg blue, seemed to hang in the air before they floated out and down into the Channel where the dark water swallowed them up.

———

The concierge of the Hotel de Bourgogne et Montana handed them their key. Margie pointed to the stairs. "We're on *le premier étage*. What we call the second floor. We'll need to haul up luggage."

Their tiny room had a double bed, armoire, wash basin and so little space to move that Tommy declared, "Either us or the luggage, not both."

"It is small but we have a view." Margie pulled Tommy around the bed to the window where they looked out on grey slate mansard rooftops and a grey sky.

"I think I see the Eiffel Tower out there," Tommy said.

"That's a bit far to see from here but we'll go visit it and everything," she said.

"Let's stay a year." Tommy leaned out and proclaimed to the court-yard: "I love Paris. This room costs two dollars forty cents a night, with daily maid service. I can support us here."

"You can support and hold me close anywhere." Margie led him to the bed.

———

Their first stroll down the cobbled streets of the Latin Quarter, Tommy felt he was in a film and that the couple strolling by, hats low over their eyes, cigarettes at their lips, were Charles Boyer and Danielle Darrieux. "Everyone looks so French! I thought being French was what you saw at the movies but it's really true, and I'm here with my swell bride!" Tommy gave an admiring look at Margie in her fitted black coat, her hair tucked beneath a little maroon toque.

That evening, Tommy declared the Boeuf Bourguignon he ordered at their first dinner was the best meal he'd ever eaten. Liter bottles of red wine kept being refilled and crusty bread warm from the oven brought to the table. "What isn't the best in Paris? If there's anything, I can't name it." He dipped his baguette into the thick, dark wine sauce.

Early the next morning, Tommy offered to pick up mail at American Express and bring back croissants from the corner boulangerie. He found one large packet from Castle Stewart for Margie, and two slim envelopes from Pasadena and San Francisco addressed to them. To his relief, there were no perfumed pastel envelopes.

The mail girl with whom he flirted only a little offered him a dozen back issues of American magazines, including *Look* with Greta Garbo's wax incarnation at Madame Tussaud's on the cover. In high spirits, he entered the boulangerie and bought croissants by pointing at them in the case. He left feeling as though he'd spoken French.

He gave Margie her letters. "You've got the mystery one from Stewart's Castle."

"Eleanor wants me to transmit these to someone I don't know."

"What's going on, or can't you tell me her secret?"

"No secret. The recipients of these papers are French people helping Jews leaving Germany. Eleanor said she would be offering a place and employment at Old Lodge."

"That's good of her. I think about Halliday, Bettina, and the mother in Berlin."

"I do, too. I hope the mother decides to leave. Do you think Bettina will find work again? She's so stunning."

"I don't know. There are many German directors in exile in California and they may want her in their movies."

Margie pushed herself back against the bedstead to read her letter from Pasadena. After a few lines, she lifted her head. "A little worrisome news. Mother says her low back pain hasn't gotten better so she's agreed to see your uncle Morris."

"He'll serve her martinis after his consultation. Mother got the check from us." Tommy looked up from June's letter. "She thanks us and I thank you for letting it come from me. I'll pay you back." Tommy came to sit on the end of the bed. "Margie, I'm glad you didn't put up with a sulker. I'm sorry about being so touchy."

He rubbed her nose with a bit of flaky pastry on his fingers and scooted close to lick it off. She could do nothing but try to reach it with her tongue and met his.

Afterwards, they lay on their small bed glancing through the *Look* magazines.

"Tommy, what would you think, after France and maybe Italy, of going home via the west coast through the Panama Canal? It will take longer, but work will pretty much stop from before Christmas until after the New Year, so we'll hardly be missed."

"I won't be missed but they'll fall apart without you. You're the glue that holds the copywriters and creative together, and Mr. Bowles secretly carries a torch for you."

"Mr. B. is happily married. We just get along."

"I'd love to travel more but what about the French Line tickets we already have for New York? Not that we'll be in First but it would cost to buy new ones."

"I can try to exchange them. A smaller ship like a freighter would be more fun than a big passenger liner, wouldn't it, and landing on the west coast, we can see our families? My brother Elman just went through the Canal and I think it would be fun, don't you?" Tommy nodded. "I've also been thinking about my work. I can't do it just a little. You know how I am."

"You have an admirable quality to focus. You don't let stuff interfere."

"I'm just dogged, not creative as you are. What I mean is, let's take time getting home and see what happens with your new accounts. Maybe there's a better job around Los Angeles and I could help you with your work. I've loved advertising but I don't have big ambitions. B & B can find someone else to write dish and laundry commercials."

"I'm all for adventure."

"In the past, being far away from Mother suited me. Now I'm independent enough to enjoy her company. Father never complains, but I know he misses me."

"My mother sees all my bad points that you somehow miss." Tommy placed his chin on Margie's shoulder. "I'm not saying she's wrong, but you know what she used to tell me? 'Your father was ever seeking to improve himself,' which I heard as, 'You're not improving yourself.' Father's picture was always looking at me from the mantle."

"So handsome. I've seen that picture."

"I can still hear his terrible cough. I never understood why she didn't make him leave Leadville."

"I'm sure she tried. How about we start planning visits to the champagne makers, and after that we can think about our trip home."

Margie wrote letters to *les grandes domaines de Champagne* in the northeast region around Épernay, asking if they might visit their establishments. *Vous êtes bienvenues* came the answers. On a chill morning, Margie and Tommy caught a train at the Gare de l'Est and soon were travelling east through gently rolling hillsides where vineyards still had their autumn golds, reds and cinnamon.

———

The champagne makers toured them through dark, cool *caves* filled with barrels and dark bottles, explaining to Margie the elaborate process of double fermentations, ageing and riddling that were the secrets of *méthode champenoise.*

"This is astonishing. To think we just pop the corks!" Tommy said when Margie translated.

"They're intrigued by us, Tommy. They wonder if their competitors will try advertising and if they should commit to it first. I've told them we'll stress the uniqueness of vintages in a landscape where the grapes have been grown and harvested for centuries. The French word is *terroir*, meaning locale, the air and the soil, everything that goes into their grapes. We'll describe why it's unique and important. The process itself isn't well known and will make good copy."

"I'm amazed how you're never daunted by these Gallic flirts. And the way you purse your lips, oh la la."

"The men are *gallant*, the women all potentially amours, no matter our age."

"I think I'd have *beaucoup* competition if we stayed here."

On the train traveling back to Paris, vineyards gave way to brown rectangles of farm land plowed under, alongside dark green forests and meadows shorn of their wheat.

"You'll write about how popping a gold-wrapped French cork on New Year's Eve is something special," Margie said. "How anyone can feel on top of the world."

Tommy looked at his notes. "The names themselves, Piper Heidsieck, Moet et Chandon, Caves Mercier, are a selling point, and we've been there."

"*Les patrons* all told me the same thing, Tommy. They're afraid what's looming over the border, the Germans, *les Boches*. They're all worried about Germany."

---

Paris in early November held back the cold with a final burst of sunshine, blue skies and warmth. They ate good cheap meals in bistros and kissed in the middle of every bridge they crossed over as French couples did. In the hotel room, Margie listened as Tommy read out the copy he hammered on the Remington and added her touches.

He asked Margie to whisper a few sexy words to him in French in their room as they made love. "Which words?' she asked.

"Any words," he kissed her. "They do something to me."

"*Ail*," she extended her breath.

"And what does that mean?"

"Garlic."

"You can do *much* better than that if I squeeze a little."

———————

Everywhere they walked, announcements for the International Exposition at the Trocadero Palace were affixed to walls.

"Let's go to the Exposition." Margie stood before a kiosk while Tommy sat on a bench reading newspapers. "Mother was here with Sylvia and her family for the Fair in 1900. She told me the Eiffel was lit up like a big candle you could see all over Paris."

"That's looking at the bright side." Tommy looked up from reading William Shirer's last report from Germany. "Listen to Hitler's physician speaking. 'The Reich Chancellor is a border line case between genius and insanity…potentially the craziest criminal the world ever saw.'"

"If Hitler's that crazy, won't someone get rid of him?"

"We can hope they'll be better at it than they've been so far. What happened to the letters from Old Lodge? You don't have them anymore?"

"While you were buying us croissants yesterday morning, a nervous young man asked for me at the desk. He asked me if I had recently married and visited Sussex. I ran back upstairs and got the packets. That was it."

"Good luck to them," said Tommy.

"And I got a lead on a ship. The *Pacific* is a Swedish freighter that sails from Antwerp via the Canal to California. Less splendid than the French Line but the companies seem to have a mutual agreement. Maybe I can exchange our tickets."

"I'd love to stay in Paris, but it doesn't feel right enjoying it as much as I am with everything going on next door, being lucky in an unlucky time."

"Let's go see the Exposition, Tommy. We might not get another chance."

———————

"*Dedicated to all Nations, to Harmony, Art and Commerce.*" Margie read the plaque at the base of the giant Peace Column before the Trocadero Palace.

"They're whistling in the dark," said Tommy. "Just look across the river."

On the opposite side of the Seine, two monumental white stone-clad structures seemed to glare at each other in the grey light. The pavilion of the German Reich was adorned with a gigantic bronze swastika and the imperial Reich eagle. Facing it, the Soviet Union's pavilion had massive statues of workers unfurling banners and brandishing the hammer and sickle.

"If stone and marble could move, they'd be at each others' throats right now. Spain's been their dress rehearsal."

"Don't you want to see any exhibits?" Margie asked.

"Not without something strong to drink. I want Paris to be little hotels with geraniums in the window, vineyards and old wine cellars, you pronouncing garlic so it sounds delicious in the afternoon."

"We're close to Spain's exhibit. Let's go see."

Tommy removed his fedora and ran his fingers through his hair. "I'm thinking of all the malt whiskies and champagnes the good people are making. All anyone wants is a little happiness, a little bubbly, a shot of single malt."

"Let's go to visit Spain." She took his arm. They hadn't heard of Pablo Picasso nor the village called Guernica but standing before the long mural, the silent screams of horses and women under the bombardment made the pavilion a hall of dumb terror. Many visitors wore black armbands and had tears streaming from their eyes.

Tommy crushed his hat against his chest. "If I could pray, I would. This is enough for me of the World War Fair of 1937. Let's get out of here."

———

The Paris agent for the Swedish Johnson Line let Margie exchange their French Line tickets for passage on a freighter with a fifty-dollar charge.

"Where will we be stopping?" Tommy asked.

"The *Pacific* doesn't list ports of call. Freighters sail for cargo, not passengers. We may stop in Lisbon, Havana, Port au Prince, depending on what they need to on or off load. The only sure thing is we'll go through the Panama Canal and arrive in Los Angeles or San Francisco."

"Oui, Madame," Tommy answered, "Heads we win, tails we win. If it's Los Angeles, we'll see your papa and mama first. San Francisco, my mother, grandfather and Aunt May. Have you heard more about Tillie?"

Margie shook her head. "I'm ready to go home, too."

———————

Tommy chose Versailles for their last day in France. "The foppish powdered kings will be a relief from daily news of Spain and Hitler's advancing," he said.

At the metro, Margie picked up a French paper. "My god, Tommy. Look at this photograph. Edward, Duke of York and Mrs. Simpson are visiting Hitler! They have a picture of the Duke giving the Nazi salute."

"I don't want to see it," Tommy said. "Let me see."

He looked at the picture of Edward and Mrs. Simpson in a raised arm salute. Tommy held onto the Metro railing. "I don't understand it."

"Eleanor told me the Duke was soft on Hitler but I thought she was exaggerating. It's sure to let down people who've stayed loyal. It's almost treasonous, I'd say."

"It's a damn shameful way to get back at his country that gave him a military cross in 1916. Common soldiers loved him. Darling, enough heroes with clay feet. Let's go visit King Louis and Marie Antoinette who lost their heads long ago."

At Versailles, they paid to follow a small man in a beret who seemed to delight in telling racy stories about the boudoirs of kings and queens, going from English to French to Italian. When the tour ended, Tommy invited the guide for a drink.

Lieberman introduced himself and said he was from South Africa. "I'm a socialist, not welcome in my country."

Lieberman's life, like his lined face, was a walking map of Europe. He'd been everywhere, but Paris—he tapped his large nose—was his favorite city, the center of his world. "The smell of Paris, even *les poubelles*, better here than anywhere else. And the *femmes*!" He sent

321

kisses to passing girls in pretty hats with little furs over their shoulders. "I don't believe the Germans can take Europe with their pig feet and potatoes. They'll never conquer *les Francaises.*"

Before they parted, Lieberman whispered to Tommy. "I'm not ever moving again. I'm tired, young fellow. They can come and get me, but you two, you're young and you're Jewish, aren't you?"

"We are. Families came from Germany. Probably some relatives are still there."

Lieberman gave them a lop-sided smile, tipped his beret and said, "If they don't get out soon, god help them. And you two, go. Soon it won't be good here for any Jew."

# NINE

THE TRAIN CAME TO a halt outside the girded metal arch of the Antwerp station. Tommy walked into the corridor to see what had happened and saw other passengers stepping down to peer ahead. There was no movement for fifteen minutes, then half an hour. Several delays along the line had already made the train late and Tommy remembered Margie telling him that the Johnson Line didn't wait because cargo was more important to a freighter than passengers. It was now eleven. The *Pacific* was scheduled to sail at noon.

"I'm nervous," Tommy said while pacing. "Something doesn't feel right."

"You're thinking about Lieberman." Margie walked behind him along the track. "Don't worry, the only problem is with the train, I'm sure."

"The sooner we get out of here and on the ocean the better."

"We're not going to miss the boat. The Swedes know we're coming," she said.

Finally freight cars were shunted onto another track, whistles blew, and their train moved toward the glass-covered station. Before they came to a complete halt, Tommy jumped out to start unloading luggage while Margie looked for transportation to the port.

She spoke French to the Belgian driver who maneuvered his cab by warehouses to the Johnson Line office where seagulls looked in no hurry to leave their perch on its roof. Inside, a dozen passengers sat around the waiting room.

"You made it in plenty of time," the representative told Margie. "Your vessel is loading. You'll get used to being second place to cargo. Do you have passports ready?"

"Yes. Are we going to Havana?" Tommy asked over Margie's shoulder.

The man laughed. "If there's a stop in Havana, buy lots of smokes."

Margie took care of the tickets and picked up mail waiting for them care of the Swedish Line office in Antwerp. The envelope she grabbed first was light, almost weightless, addressed in her father's perfectly spaced script. She hurried to a corner of the waiting room to read. Her father usually appended a greeting at the end of one of Tillie's long, chatty letters, but this was different. Though his small print stayed in the center of the onionskin, Margie felt his nervousness.

*Your mother's heart and liver are not in danger. Attention was given to female portions but our new relation, Dr. Morris Selig of Cedars of Lebanon, believes there's nothing dangerous that a two-week rest in his clinic won't improve. Dr. Selig confided in me that your mother's former physician is hardly more than a charlatan and has provided her with the means to damage her own health. In other words, that the consumption of pills he has prescribed for her back pains have created a dependency on them. Dr. Selig has seen many desperate drug cases in Hollywood and assures me that your mother's full recovery is certain. I have recommended the naturalist way to health but this has never been your mother's choice. A letter assuring us of your well-being and plans to leave the Continent will make us happy. Your loving father, Alfred Hornthall.*

I suppose it's a relief, Margie thought, that Tillie was addicted rather than something worse. Drinks weren't mentioned but alcohol had to be contributing. The thought came to her that Tommy might help, then her second thought was: how in the world would one drinker advise another to lay off?

Margie wrote out a wire to her father. *ArriveCalifornia4weeksloveStop.*

Tommy stood frowning alongside their luggage, staring out to the grey river where ships anchored in choppy waters. She heard the call for all passengers on the *Pacific* to proceed to board their vessel. Everyone in the waiting room stood. Four unmistakably British women wearing cardigans and grey skirts crossed the tarmac to the boarding site first. Missionaries, Margie thought. Won't have much fun with them. A muscular young couple holding hands crossed the hall—Scandinavian or Dutch, not German, Margie guessed. Two more Brits, a couple, both heavy, needed help with the step and heaved groans.

"They'll be big eaters on our little Noah's ark," Margie whispered to Tommy who didn't seem to hear her. "I don't see promising company so far."

Just then, four people, Germans, Margie realized after hearing a few words, rushed across the waiting room. The two men were dressed in dark suits, wore Homburgs, and carried their valises and bags. The slim woman with them wore a heavy coat and a cloche so low on her forehead that it covered most of her pale, finely-featured face. She clutched her bags as if they might be ripped away. Her black pumps looked good but had gotten splashed with mud. A child came last, a slight blond boy in short pants. Margie could see the goose bumps on his white calves. He might be seven or eight, and the metal case he gripped seemed too heavy though he didn't let go of it for a moment.

"How did two people get so much stuff?" Margie looked at their suitcases and trunks being boarded onto the tender waiting to take them to the *Pacific* moored further out in the harbor. "We're only tourists. Some of these people are taking important journeys with half of what we've got. Where do you think the Germans are going?"

On board the tender, Tommy didn't follow her gesture toward the four people who appeared to be shivering in their heavy coats. "Did you notice the little boy with the case? A family running for its life—it's what we've been hearing."

"Wasn't looking." Tommy wiped his own eyes with his sleeve and turned away from the passengers to stare into the dark, oily-looking water before them.

"Anything wrong with your family, darling? What was in your letter?"

Tommy's eyes filled with tears. "Grandfather Max died in his sleep two weeks ago. Mother said she didn't know where to send a wire. They had the service and buried him in San Francisco. Mother didn't want to go back to Leadville. I loved Grandpa Max."

Margie took Tommy's hand. "I know you did and I'm very sorry. We did get a chance to see him before we left. Such a twinkle in his eye. I think he approved of us."

Tommy pulled out a handkerchief to wipe his eyes. "I'll never see that twinkle."

"How old was he, Tommy?"

"In his late eighties, I think. Don't know the year he was born. I vowed I'd prove myself to him, though he never asked for proof. He loved me no matter what stunts I pulled or the stupid trouble I got into. He had faith in me."

"Of course he did. He told me you were the best grandson. 'Tommy's got the warmest heart,' he said. He wanted me to know how dearly he loved you."

Margie's words prompted a flood of tears. She stroked his cheeks.

"In a winter sleigh, he looked like Santa Claus and he loved giving kids candy. I'd find pieces of taffy behind my ears. Never knew how he got them there. He was good at cards, and taught me a trick or two. I think Grandpa was born in the 1840s. Maybe he was ninety."

"That's a fine age, Tommy."

"I wanted to see him again." Tommy wiped his eyes.

"I'm sorry you didn't. You couldn't have known. Well, here's my news. Tillie is in a clinic where Uncle Morris sent her to get off pills. I could see how she'd have lots of energy and then be exhausted, but I didn't think of pills. I'm relieved it's not worse."

"Morris will take care of her. You know, I remember when I was seven, a year after my father died, what I wanted most in the world was to whistle, but no matter how hard I tried, only squeaks came out. One day when Mother and Aunt May went to Denver, Grandpa said we'd clean the stove. We ended up covered with soot. I remember he was whistling as he scrubbed me down in the tub. 'My boy, have a sip and try that whistle,' he said. The whiskey burned and when I pursed my lips, a real whistle came out. 'You see, God rewarded you for your good deed. The whiskey didn't hurt either.'"

Ahead of their little boat bobbing in the current, the *Pacific* loomed long and narrow on both ends. From the deck far above them, standing in front of tarps and ropes that covered up the center of the ship, a bearded, round-faced man with gold on his shoulder bars called down.

"Mind your step, ladies and gents. Wait until we're attached and come across."

The cargo hold opened and a gang plank was lowered, then fitted to the tender.

"Like Noah's Ark." Margie squeezed Tommy's hand. "What creatures are we?"

"Honeymooners *homosapianis*," he answered.

They crossed over and into the dark hold where a crewman held a lantern and directed them up steep stairs. They emerged into a grey light on the deck. The Antwerp docks and cranes, warehouses and train station, all of Europe seemed shrouded in mist.

Margie wanted to tell the little boy who looked so cold and sad holding his suitcase that soon the sun would shine and the sea would turn blue and green, and that whatever he'd seen, life would be better for his family now.

"We've learned more about the danger Jews are in these few months than we'd ever have known without making the trip," Margie said to Tommy. "I won't forget once we're home. I'll find out more from Aunt Sylvia what I can do to help. Oh, I forgot, she's probably in Palestine by now but I'll find a way to do something useful."

The bearded. round-faced man with gold strips now shook each person's hand.

"Hello and greetings to you passengers. I am your Captain Anderson. I come from Stockholm. Welcome to the *Pacific*."

Tommy whispered to Margie. "He looks like Grandpa Max. A good sign."

"He looks like my Grandfather Jacob."

The Captain stood before them. "You may think the *Pacific* don't look like much, but when we see German flag, we go skidoo to other direction fast, like this." He made a darting motion more likely for a speedboat than a laden freighter. "And we leave German behind quick quick."

Margie stood on tiptoe to see the Captain over the heads of other passengers. "I didn't know we might meet up with Germans on the open sea," she said to Tommy.

"We like German people," the Captain continued, "not so Nazis.

Second Mate Bang shows you your cabins. Dinner is early today. Again, please, welcome aboard."

Their cabin, located in the rear of the freighter, was a narrow room with two small portholes, no bath but a shower in a compact little box with a toilet. Tommy declared it a fine home away from home.

"I just happen to have one bottle on hand. Mercier. Vintage '28, my darling. We should pop it before the ocean upsets its balance and ours," Tommy said.

"Let's toast the long and full life of your Grandfather Max."

"He never got over his wife's murder by an outlaw." Tommy took the elegant, gold-tinseled bottle from Margie, turned the neck under a towel and eased out the cork. "We don't want the British ladies to think there's a domestic dispute going on."

"You identified them, too." Margie sat on the bed and removed her shoes.

"Missionaries, I'd put money on it."

Tommy poured a pale stream of Mercier into water glasses. Margie joined him on the bed for a toast of bubbles. Wiping away tears, he said, "Grandpa loved his champagne but he never got to see France, he only imagined it. Here's to Lieberman, too, and the little boy with his metal case."

They drank until the bottle was empty and the gentle rocking motion of the ship at anchor gave them a rhythm for particularly tender lovemaking.

———

The four British women and the four Germans were already sitting at the larger tables, while the two couples each had a smaller table to themselves.

"We're being summoned. The Captain wants us at his table." Tommy steered Margie toward the officers' table.

As they passed the Germans, Margie greeted them with *guten Abend* and the two men answered, "*guten Abend*" in reply. The woman, who still wore her hat and hadn't changed her travel suit, didn't look up. There didn't seem much resemblance between the blond boy and the three dark-haired adults, Margie thought. If he's not their son, who does he belong to?

"What's your name, son?" Tommy kneeled beside the boy.

"Markus Gabriel Rosen."

"You speak English?"

"A little."

"We're pleased to meet you, Markus. Are you going all the way to California?"

The boy shook his head. "No, I am going to *Kooba.*"

The German woman placed cheese and bread on his plate. "*Muss essen,*" she said.

"Cuba is an exciting island to go to, Markus. We'll have plenty of time to talk about cigars." Tommy mimicked a big inhale and tapped the boy's shoulder. Markus broke into a half smile, then looked at the adults for approval.

"That was sweet, Tommy. Will you make candy come out of ears?"

"I might have left some in yours, pumpkin. Look at this spread. A thousand times around the deck or we'll end up like the British hippos. Oh oh, introductions."

"This is First Mate, Mr. Tarzan Bang." The Captain and the First Mate gave small bows from their seats.

"Pleased to meet you." Tommy bowed back. "Did I hear that right? Tarzan?"

"Everyone at ease, please, no more formality," said the Captain.

"Mother was reading Edgar Rice Burroughs when I was born and Father was at sea. To your health, Thomas and Mrs." Mate Tarzan handed Tommy a foaming, dark stein.

"This looks promising. Tarzan meet Tom and Jane, I mean Margie," Tommy said.

Captain Anderson raised a glass. "We have a light Scandinavian supper, please enjoy. You may like our beers or French wine."

"Either and both," answered Tommy. "I'm not particular."

Margie saw the bottles lined up, beer, whisky, rum, wine all within Tommy's reach. She sighed, knowing this might be a long night.

The salads and cold cuts, followed by plates of sardines in tomato sauce, herring with gleaming black skin over creamed potatoes, and peach-colored salmon mousse, seemed more than a light supper. The young waiter kept bringing more. After the fish dishes, he brought platters with thin slices of cold beef, tongue and ham for sandwiches. Cheeses, pickles and relishes followed.

"Friends, a moment to pause." Captain Anderson held up his hand.

The cook in his white apron and muffin hat came out holding a pitcher of thick yellowish, bubbling liquid.

"This is hot Swedish punch you will not find outside my country but on the *Pacific*, like Swedish land. We call it *glug*. Can you say it, friends?"

"Gloog came the reply from around the tables.

Mate Tarzan Bang raised his *glug* glass the level of Tommy's eyes. *"Skål!* Mr. Tom, I think you will like our Swedish punch." He drank the cup in a swallow.

"To your health likewise!' Tommy drank it down. "Whew! Medieval brew."

"My American friend dares another?" Tarzan gave Tommy a wild look.

Tommy held his cup for a refill. "To the King and Queen of Norway and our Democratic President of America!"

"Maybe that's enough, Tommy." Margie nudged his arm at the same time Mate Bang slapped Tommy on the back. "Good man, Tom, don't let me down."

Bang and Tommy raised newly filled cups. The Mate had a fox-like face, pointed nose and blue eyes under sun-bleached brows. Complicated wrinkles traveled from his eyes to his receding hairline. Maybe in his forties, Margie guessed, browned like a nut from sun and sea air. Capable of drinking Tommy under the table. The Captain leaned toward Margie. "Mr. Bang is Norwegian. He has seen the world. I make him honorary Swede every Sunday and then I lock up the *glug*."

"Good idea," said Margie. "Lock it away from my husband, too."

Just then, Tommy's head began to go forward until it reached the table where it stayed. "Damn right!" he managed to say to no one in particular before his eyes closed.

"Don't worry, Missus," said Captain Anderson. "No one keeps up with Bang."

"But he'll try every Sunday," Margie replied.

"I know very good stories, gentlemen." Captain Anderson cleared his throat and Margie understood the old-fashioned invitation for the ladies to retire. She stood up, folded her napkin and led the way toward the door. The air on deck was cold and damp. The British women took one turn and disappeared. The large British pair and the Swedish honeymooners were soon gone. The Germans, to whom she would have liked speaking, never came up on deck. She leaned on the rail for a long time looking out into deep fog. The captain must be leaving Tommy for her to retrieve. I'll give him time to sleep a little, she thought.

When she felt the cold under her coat and dampness seeping down her neck, she returned to the dining salon where lights were dimmed and the tables cleared. Tommy wasn't sleeping, head on table. He wasn't in their cabin. Her heart pounded. The state he was in, and with the dense fog, he could have fallen overboard without anyone knowing.

She found him outside in a deck chair wrapped under a blanket fast asleep.

"You've got to get up. You'll catch cold." She tried to pull him up.

"Tarzan one goddamn drinker." Tommy burrowed his head under an arm.

"Come to bed. You'll catch cold lying here, Tommy."

"Sleep," he mumbled, burrowing deeper.

"No sleep."

Margie layered two more blankets over Tommy's body and stood over him. She leaned her head on a cold railing. Her tears felt warm against the cold night air. She didn't want a drunk for a husband, even a sweet and loveable drunk. What would happen after the honeymoon when they settled down? She tried not to make Tommy feel she was badgering him because she didn't want to be his mother. Ironically, she thought, I could be June's serious daughter, while Tommy would have fitted right in as Tillie's fun-loving, charming son.

Margie again shook Tommy and this time he stumbled to his feet. "Damn cold here," he said. She led him to their cabin where he banged around getting out of his clothes. In bed, his warm nearness made her want to bring his furry body closer to hers but she stayed on her side, awake a long time feeling lonely with him so near and yet so far away. She thought again how a wedding ring did not make a husband.

# TEN

Margie sat alone for breakfast at the captain's table. The young waiter poured her coffee and hot milk, returned from the kitchen with a fragrant basket of fresh breads and savory rolls and a plate of butter and jams. "Eggs prepared as you wish," the boy announced.

The British women, already seated, gave their order. Margie said, "Two fried eggs, please," and heard the British ask for boiled, "four minutes." Margie picked up her coffee cup and scooted her chair to the table next to hers.

She and Tommy had guessed right that they were missionaries, and now she found out that the reason for their travel from Europe was connected to a longer journey and close encounters with war.

"We are forced to return from Dacca, India, because our Canadian Mission believes the Japanese offensive in Burma endangers us," one of the women said.

"I am ignorant about your part of the world. I haven't the slightest idea what it's like or where you were in India but you must experience many hardships," said Margie.

"Do not think it's only a hardship," said a woman who introduced herself as Miss Callenbach. "That would be a mistake. The land is beautiful as are the people."

"Terribly hot and prone to flooding but we have no cause to complain," said a second woman who spoke with a Scottish brogue.

"We are teachers at the Episcopal Mission School in Dacca in eastern India, where the Ganges and Brahmaputra rivers flow into the Bay of Bengal. A rice-growing region," said Miss Callenbach.

Dressed in dark long skirts, white blouses buttoned up high, with large silver crosses over their cardigans, at least two of the women had grey in their hair. There were two younger missionaries, the Scottish girl with red curls and a pallid blond with her hair pulled into a bun under a cap.

"We cared for so many orphans we could hardly manage toward the end. Refugees from Burma, and points east, you see. What will become of the children if the Japanese reach them? We've heard horrible stories." Miss Callenbach lowered her eyes.

"You're very brave. My husband will want to know just where you were living in India. I'm sure the captain has maps. After breakfast, I'll tell him how adventurous you are." Margie pushed back her chair to return to her table where her eggs were waiting.

"Oh no," called Miss Callenbach, "we are not brave. God is on our side."

An hour later, Tommy met her on the way out of the dining salon. He wore a blue cashmere sweater Margie had bought him in Scotland and looked as robust and nautical as if he'd been up early doing exercises. He seemed never to suffer ill effects, nor have much memory of his drinking the night before. "I'm hungry as a bear," he said. "What happened to breakfast?"

"You slept through it. I met the missionaries from India and they're interesting. They'll be with us to California and then travel by land to Calgary where there's a Mission house. They'd like to go back home to the British Isles but they're being sent to Canada. What a life they lead, never choosing for themselves, always being obedient."

"Darling wife, you are a born reporter." He nibbled at her ear.

"Tommy, stop. I want to talk to you."

"Bang drank me under the table last night. Won't happen again." At that moment Tommy's stomach growled as if issuing an order for food.

"I grabbed you a roll so you won't starve. Let's go on deck."

Margie led the way to the back of the ship, sat down on a deck chair, wrapping herself with a blanket against the cold. Tommy sat beside her chewing his roll.

"Bang had me at a disadvantage on an empty stomach, and he's a Viking."

"Bang is not my concern. You drink too much and on top of passing out in the middle of supper, it's no fun for me."

"End of supper."

"End of supper, any time, I'm tired of being left alone all night. I worried you'd fallen overboard."

They both stared down at lines of misty wake the ship was churning up.

"We had such a swell time in Paris. I loved every minute. Why be cranky now? It's not as if I squirrel away bottles in my socks. I don't drink alone. I'm a social drinker."

"Cranky!" She stood up and walked to stand at the railing, then turned back to Tommy. He saw the anger in her eyes. "I truly was worried. I couldn't find you. And I don't buy your social-drinker palaver."

"Margie, I wasn't going to fall overboard. I know I'm a sucker for a drink but that's something you knew about me over many, many years."

"I hoped you'd realize I wasn't happy quite a few times. The last thing I want this marriage to be is some sort of hide and seek, with me trying to pull you away from bars or find out who sent the perfumed envelopes with no return address."

Margie no longer was looking him in the eye and he swallowed before he replied. "I never answered those letters."

"So it was a one-sided correspondence with the perfume-envelope lady?"

He shook his head. "I'm not proud of myself. I swear, nothing happened."

"I'm not going to spend my life on some kind of patrol for women and booze. I'm truly not. I hope you understand there will be a point that I can't continue."

Now Margie's look was shrouded, calm on the surface, roiled beneath.

"Want me to stop drinking completely, go cold turkey? I could try."

"No, it's not all or nothing, just not getting so soused that you pass out and don't know where you are and I'm left alone thinking of pastel letters, about which I won't ask further. I will not become a nag. It's not in my nature." She looked out at the sea and her eyes seemed to have turned a shade lighter. "I keep telling myself you made up your mind to marry me, and except for the time at Eleanor's, you've seemed happy."

"I have been very happy." Tommy rose from his chair and stood beside her. "I love you, Margie. No more smelly letters, that's a promise. I'll drink less if you wish."

"I do wish you would drink less. And I do know you're a very good-looking man and a sweet man and that women of all ages are drawn to you. Way back when Mother first met you she said I would be the brown hen to your peacock."

"Margie, it never occurred to me that you weren't the prettiest girl…"

"I'm not fishing for compliments. I wanted to get married and you agreed."

"Because I knew deep down you're the mainstay in my life and I need you. That's the truth. I don't want to hurt you. I'll watch the drinking, I sincerely will." He took her hand and she didn't pull it away. "Lunch?"

"Two hours."

———

A day later, as northern mists vanished and the southerly sun began to shine, passengers came on deck like hibernators emerging from sleep, strolling toward each other, stopping to exchange weather reports. Margie and Tommy speculated on professions, never guessing that the heavy-set English couple were glass blowers.

"That's why we wheeze. Going to visit the son in Hawaii for holiday. The boy's done well in shipping. Don't know what we've got to look forward to back home with the jerrys arming up. Lived through the first one." The husband wiped his brow.

"We're going to lie out in the sun and forget it all, George," his wife added.

"Like Hawaiian royalty, weighed and paid for by the pound." He patted his girth.

The Germans in their dark clothes passed by, lifting their hats.

"Poor sods. And where are they going?" the man asked.

"We'll find out," Tommy said.

The lunch gong rang. Everyone had renewed appetites and hurried to eat.

By suppertime, Tommy had discovered enough about the Jewish Germans to tell Margie that the men were brothers, Leopold and Frederick Asher from Hamburg, formerly employees at the M. M. Warburg bank. The woman was Frederick's wife, Lisel. Lisel's brother owned a mine in Colombia, where the three were going because even their banking patron Max Warburg, with all his connections, could no longer protect his employees. As Margie surmised, young Markus Gabriel Rosen didn't belong to them.

"They found him at the Hamburg train station alone with his case and shoulder pack. A stroke of luck along with all the hardships because it turned out the boy had tickets for the *Pacific*, so the Ashers took him under their wing. The last sight of land wasn't easy for any of them but having the lonely child helped take their minds off their own losses. Leo speaks English with verbs at the end of the sentence. His brother is less fluent. 'Imagine,' Leo said to me, 'a child that age alone sending off.' Markus told him that his mother, who lives alone in Vienna, took him as far as Hamburg. She's separated from the father who lives in Cuba, where the boy is going. He's studied English but doesn't know Spanish. He's from a good milieu, Leo said."

"We don't know for sure that we'll stop in Havana." Margie looked out at the horizon. "The only port we know for sure is in Colombia."

"Leo may not know this. Markus isn't their responsibility, at least not by birth. The Ashers gave up everything they had to get out of Germany. If they'd left a year earlier, they could have sold their property and had money, but they waited. Now the Reich allows Jews only forty marks, of all they possess in the world—houses, accounts, furniture—forty inflated marks worth nothing. Added to this, border guards stripped Lisel and took her jewelry. She didn't speak for days. There's one hopeful spot besides getting out. The Warburgs have established foreign accounts for their employees, not much but something."

"Does Leo have children?"

"No, he's divorced without any children. Neither does Frederick. Lisel had a miscarriage before they left Hamburg. It was the strain, Leo told me."

"I can't imagine what they've been through." Margie squeezed Tommy's hand.

"Everyone we meet seems to bring this war closer. Certainly puts a perspective on my small worries. Drink less, as promised."

"Of course you will. And if you want to stay home to write a play, I'll work."

"What would I do without my cheerleader?"

"Tommy, you'll do it on your own. You made Markus smile. He needs that. Wonder what his father does in Cuba?"

"Manufacturing, I think. Leo says the Nazis will try to get rid of all the Jews. Even the Warburgs will have to flee."

"I doubt that Siegmund Warburg will be going back," Margie said.

---

Over the next days, the Ashers and Markus appeared to fill out as if the three large Swedish meals served daily were being infused directly into their cheeks and waistlines. "They're like plants given water and light," Margie told Tommy. Markus' eyes seemed less huge and moth-like and his nostrils fleshed out so there weren't such adult hollows between his nose and cheek. Leo still wore his black suit jacket with wing collar and thick glasses, but the Homburg had come off so his face was getting tanned. Margie thought he looked taller; perhaps he simply wasn't as bent over. The brothers, Margie learned, were younger than they appeared to be, close to Tommy's age, late thirties, but looked much older. Lisel Asher changed the least, never losing the haunted look in her grey eyes as she trudged around the deck in her winter shoes, taking her constitutional.

---

By the time the *Pacific* was a day away from its first announced port of call at Lisbon, Tommy passed more of Leo's confidences to Margie. "He told me he wished for a wife like you."

"We've hardly spoken," she said. "You're the one walking the deck for hours."

"It's your way of making a person feel at ease. His former wife was a high-born Hamburg Jew, demanding, snobbish."

"It's not too late for Leo to meet someone else," Margie kissed Tommy's cheek.

"You know what's amazing, Leo knew of the Selig and Grensky families when he was growing up, before he went to Hamburg! The Rhineland Jewish world was a small place. He said now that it has almost ceased to exist. Leo thinks the Nazis count on pacifist feelings in England and France to give them time to get rid of the Jews and arm for war. Remember Shirer's pieces about the Wehrmacht war games, how the Germans displayed defensive weapons while it was clear to everyone who saw the troops marching that they had tanks and planes hidden."

"Eleanor is terrified her sons will join the air force because they love flying. How can you blame Europeans for doing anything to avoid war?"

"Everyone wants peace if you just read the words on that pillar at the Exposition, before you see how the Soviet and German pavilions were a call to blood."

"And the Spanish pavilion. Sorry I brought you there," Margie said.

"Paris was such a pleasure and an eye-opener, Margie. Leo thinks the Nazis *want* to spill blood and move east. Germans today are projecting pagan and blood rites onto Jews, accusing us of using Gentile blood for Passover." Tommy wiped his brow. "The poor Jews in Europe, cursed by superstitions. America is such a haven."

"You're learning a lot. Neither of us will be the same."

"Leo and I have talked more about our heritage than I ever did at home. I remember Mother being shocked that my pals weren't Jewish but I just thought she was old fashioned. I didn't see myself as a Jewish newspaperman, just a news hound. Girls I met weren't Jewish, until one who cooked the best Mulligatawny stews."

"With bacon," Margie smiled. "My family wasn't at all religious and yet I remember playing tennis at a country club that never asked me to join, and at Stanford, where sororities didn't pledge Jewish girls, friends I was close with didn't invite me in. I felt they could have stuck with me rather than have joined."

"We're in this together." Tommy held her tightly around the shoulder and she could feel his hand was steady. He'd been drinking beer and wine at supper but staying up only to play cards with the Ashers and Markus before they all went to bed.

# ELEVEN

THE *PACIFIC* MADE A sharp turn east and began sailing close enough to a rocky coast to see red-roofed towns nestled against hillsides, bright umbrellas along beaches, a medieval fortress.

"The Estoril Casino," First Mate Bang pointed out to Tommy. "Very good place to gamble but we don't have time for you to lose your money."

Soon they entered the green mouth of the Tagus River and caught the first sight of a city that appeared entirely white, as if it might rise and float airborne in the morning sun. On the highest spot, Tommy saw ruins of what appeared to be a castle with flying buttresses. The white outlines made him think of something he couldn't quite remember.

"That is the ruined cathedral," said Bang before he joined the officers to sail the *Pacific* under a slender bridge. "Here comes our ride," he pointed a tugboat approaching.

The tugboat navigator guided the *Pacific* past fishing boats toward a quay. As the crew uncoiled thick ropes and lowered anchor, Captain Anderson called all passengers on deck. "We get mail. Three, four hours in Lisbon. Please remain on board."

"Oh no, Portuguese shoes are so inexpensive," moaned Miss Callenbach.

"Are they really so good?" Margie asked.

"Like nothing in the world, and the colors! Sinfully attractive, my dear!" Miss Callenbach sighed. "I was planning to ship several pair to my sister in Brighton."

Margie approached the captain. "If we promise to be gone only as long as you need to load cargo, you'll make the women happy,

Captain. Personally, I'd like to buy Lisel Asher summer shoes for the tropics. She needs to tan her pretty legs."

"If you put it that way, Mrs. Tommy, how can a man refuse to make a woman's legs pretty? Be back by 15:00 hours, not one minute later."

"You darling man." Margie hugged the Captain. "What can I get you?"

"I'm partial to their Cointreau made with bitter oranges. It is not costly here. Make sure you return in three hours. Otherwise, you must swim." He winked.

The British ladies ran below to get purses and hats. Margie tried to ask Lisel for her shoe size in German but couldn't think of the words. She removed her own shoe, held it up and gestured from toe to heel.

"How big is the shoe?" Margie searched for words. "*Wie Shuhe grosse?*"

"*Habe ich kein Geld*," said Lisel.

"OK, *kein problem*." Margie got onto her knees and placed her shoe beside Lisel's whose foot was narrower and longer by at least two sizes, she guessed.

Mate Bang met the land representative who brought mail to the dining saloon.

"We can't look now, thank you." Margie said. "We've got a date with shoes."

---

Once on land the four missionaries, Margie and the Swedish bride piled into two taxis while Tommy went off on foot. The taxis headed up the Avenida de Liberadade until the drivers let them off at the entrance to a narrow alley. The moment they got out, Margie thought the lane should have been called *Shoe Street* because every window had displays of exceptionally beautiful footwear, from dressy high heels to boots to tailored walking flats, all in suede or polished leathers of deep red, burnt orange, moss green, earthy sienna. The canvas espadrilles came in brilliant colors like tropical parrots.

They wandered up and down and selected the shop with the largest window display. Margie bought six pairs of town shoes, four bags and a half dozen espadrilles in sizes and colors that would suit everyone at home. For Lisel Asher, she selected red with black ribbons and black with white ties. Her total came to a hundred dollars in American Express Cheques and Margie covered what the missionaries didn't have in cash.

By the time they left the store two hours later, the salespeople were still asking them to drink coffee and Porto which they regretfully refused. "Bateau," Margie pointed toward the harbor. They barely had time to catch two cabs with a stop at a *Licores* shop where Margie bought the captain three bottles of Cointreau for a dollar each.

———

Tommy crossed the vast Praça de Commercio into smaller Rossio Square, always keeping his eyes on the white buttresses he'd seen from the ship as if a ribbed cloud hovered above the city. He climbed cobble-stone alleys, passed open windows spilling out red and pink flowers, kitchens where fish was being fried in garlic. Higher up, he breathed in citrus from lemons and oranges that reminded him of Tillie's gardens in Pasadena. Finally, as he reached what appeared to be the summit, an oddly-shaped glass box clanged behind him and slid into a berth. A funicular, he realized, that came up from the port and would bring him back down.

All that remained of the cathedral in the sky were arches and the soaring points of buttresses. Suddenly Tommy knew where the memory of a castle had come from: on their mantel, beside the portrait of his father, there had been a picture of the Leadville Ice Palace of 1896. There his mother and father had danced together for the first time. "Our first dance was the Viennese Waltz," June told him in the sad years after his father's death. "No one could have been so happy as we were."

Below the hill lay tiers of tile roofs and streets, then the river, blue-green under the midday sun, while overhead, swallows circled like white cut-outs against blue sky.

Tommy realized a man in blue work overalls was trying to get his attention.

"*Teramoto*," the workman said, his hands shaking up and down to show more and more movement, all the while his last inch of a cigarette burned in his fingers.

343

"San Francisco," Tommy replied with the same motions of earth moving.

Tommy wished he could have accepted the man's invitation to share red wine from his bottle, sitting on warm stones bathed in sun, but when the funicular returned, clanging in its berth, he called goodbye and ran to catch it.

He clung to a bar that held him upright as the car shuddered down the steep grade. More gardens in windows on twisty streets as colors and fragrances filled his eyes and nose. At the bottom, he caught a cab to the dock under the eyes of Mate Bang.

"Thought I'd lost my drinking companion," said Bang. The *Pacific's* deep horn blew and the engines churned water beneath them. "You see things you like?"

"I liked everything. To live with my wife in a city as beautiful and white as Lisbon would be a dream come true." When Margie came up beside him, he hugged her shoulders. "Let's return soon. Maybe the Germans don't know about Lisbon."

"I hope so. For now I bought everyone at home beautiful things." Margie pulled out the espadrilles and then remembered there were letters to read.

One from Tillie mentioned nothing about a clinic or health. Her mother's main subject was Sylvia's desertion. "She's left for Palestine. Imagine! As bad as her mother running off to the spiritualists in Hindustan. Natalie won't smell washed again."

Margie paused and tapped Tommy's shoulder. "Listen to this. Remember my mother's old flame, Eddie Sachs, from the wedding? Sylvia's brother, a movie producer."

"The bad toupee? Hard to imagine him marrying so many women when he…"

"You've got it. A photographer caught Eddie in a compromising situation with a young actor. Mother writes her own conclusions. 'We loved as children do. Why did Sylvia keep the secret from me all these years? Now that I know, I will get in touch. We will become great friends again.'"

Tommy laughed at the thought of Tillie and the toupee, and felt a deeper warmth thinking of his mother and father dancing the night away in that Norman castle of ice before it melted back into the cold hard earth of the Rocky Mountains.

# TWELVE

THE DEEP BLUE ATLANTIC rocked them into a daily routine of meals and time on the deck with books or just staring at the sea. Margie and Tommy bronzed first, followed by Leo Asher and Markus, who day by day colored from light brown to a deeper coffee color. The vast girths of the British glass blowers pinked around the edges of their bathing costumes as they turned over, with grunts and sighs, for an even roasting.

Neither Lisel Asher nor the missionaries worshipped the sun, still it gave their cheeks color, while the Scandinavian newlyweds, always polite but never part of the socializing, kept to their cabin between meals.

Four mornings out of Lisbon, Tommy heard a heave of gentle puffing, a sound of steam rising, surrounding them. First Mate Bang called out, "Whales! To starboard."

Everyone on deck rushed to the right side and pressed against the railing to see the pod of humpbacks breaching only yards away. Three or four giants mounted swells and sank, then spouting, rose again. They seemed to be looking with one great eye at her, Margie thought, leaning toward them until something grabbed her sleeve.

"Mrs. Grensky, take care, don't fall over." Miss Callenbach still wore her long skirt and cardigan but the yellow espadrilles gave her an almost jaunty look.

"Thank you, Miss Callenbach," said Margie.

As suddenly as they'd arrived, the whales were gone. Later in the day, flying fish darted like silver arrows from the water before falling back and disappearing into the ship's wake. Some landed on the deck where Markus ran around to scoop them up and toss them back before their shine faded.

Tender air and gentle seas continued as they passed the Azores to warmer waters. Only the Captain's wireless reminded Margie that the seas beneath might be hiding German subs. Every afternoon, she listened in his quarters to catch international news, then typed a summary with three carbon copies to inform other passengers of events.

They all gathered in the saloon to hear President Franklin Roosevelt speaking from Chicago. Tommy and Margie sat closest to the radio, with Leo Asher and Markus helping translate for the Germans.

"The epidemic of world lawlessness is spreading," President Roosevelt's voice only seemed a room away. Tommy repeated, "He's calling for quarantine on Germany."

"He said we'll quarantine the Nazi contagion," said Margie to Leo.

"The Americans must for Jews do something," Leo said.

"You can count on Roosevelt." Tommy took Leo's hand and squeezed.

Roosevelt ended his address by declaring that nations of the world were dependent on each other. America would not allow "innocent people slaughtered and the foundation of civilization threatened." Margie wrote fast in her notebook to get down the words that would go into her daily bulletin for the ship.

Captain Anderson poured drinks to toast America's stand against the Nazis.

"It is not possible to make peace with Hitler. If America says so, then it will be a very big war. It will be a terrible war."

Frederick asked Tommy if Roosevelt were Jewish.

"No, though he's been accused of it. America has many anti-Semites and the President has to be cautious, but he'll open immigration from Europe."

"Weimer made promises and now look at us, refugees with nothing to the world. You know *Lebensraum* in German?" asked Leo.

Captain Anderson replied that he heard the word all the time in the Nazi speeches. "It means the Germans want their living room in all the backyards of Europe, but the American president will be stronger than they are and stop them," he said.

"I'll be in America one day." Markus made a windmill with his arms. "Charlie Chaplin in the clock."

"Of course you will but first you must learn to swim. Every American girl and boy must swim. Tomorrow we'll begin lessons."

---

Overnight, the blue ocean turned into a Caribbean aqua and the crew set up a five-by-five metal pool on the deck, filled it with sea water, and lined up chairs.

Lisel fashioned a pair of trunks for Markus that must have been her husband's long underwear cut off at the knees and tied with a cord around the middle.

"Like Charlie Chaplin." Markus turned around and bowed to Tommy.

Tommy took Markus to the edge of the pool. "We'll start with this little sea. By the time we reach Cuba, you'll be able to swim like a fish in the big one. My mother is a strong swimmer. I didn't have a father to bring me up, Markus. My mother did everything and in the end it will be all right for you as it was for me."

---

Captain Anderson's face was such a deep red against his white uniform that Margie thought he looked like a tomato on a plate.

"What are you picking up on the radio, Mrs. Tommy?" he asked Margie who was seated at the typewriter with the radio nearby.

"Nothing but bad news from Spain. Cities being bombed by German planes helping out Franco and Falangists." Margie stood up and stretched. "Markus is being met in Havana. Will we stop in Cuba?"

"We have fine times in Havana, that's for sure. Beautiful tall Negro girls dance with coconuts on their heads, and here." His hands circled round breasts over his own vast chest. "But we stop only if they say we have cargo."

"What about the other German passengers? They believe that we'll be taking them to Colombia."

"We have scheduled stop in Ciénaga, in Colombia. We stay two, three days. Ciénaga means swamp in Spanish, and it is a miserable place but with a good sheltered harbor. We have much cargo to unload there. You'll have time to visit Barranquilla."

"What will Markus do if we don't stop in Cuba?"

"There are boats to go from Barranquilla to Havana."

———————

Tommy and Margie stayed on deck with Mate Bang as the *Pacific* passed the island of Martinique on the eastern side, sailing close enough to see twinkling lights of Fort-de-France. Bang pointed out the volcano emerging from white clouds.

"When Mt. Pelée erupted, many people died. There is Dominica. We must watch carefully here to avoid shoals. I go back to the bridge."

"You know what this means," Margie said.

"I do. I've looked at the map. We're not stopping in Cuba. We've gone hundreds of miles from it." Tommy paced away and back.

"I had a feeling this would happen. What will Markus do?"

"I don't know. I'll speak with Leo tomorrow. We'll figure out something."

———————

The next day, Leo added another piece to the puzzle of Markus' history.

"A few days out of Antwerp, Markus apologized to Leo for smelling badly," Tommy told Margie. "He was washing his one pair of underwear in his sink."

"How can that be? He carried a heavy case."

They were standing on deck in the shade after lunch. Even Tommy, who seemed to brown without burning, now kept out of the white-hot sun.

"When Markus' mother packed him off, she made him promise not to open his suitcase until he was on the ship."

"When I first saw him getting on board, he was glued to the case," she said.

"When he opened it for clean underwear and clothes on board, you won't believe what he found." Tommy wiped his brow. "Bricks wrapped in newspapers. No clothes, nothing else, only bricks. He was so ashamed that he told only Leo days later."

"Why would anyone pack bricks? His mother must be crazy."

"Leo thinks the same, or perhaps she's trying to get back at her husband through Markus. When the boy arrives in Cuba, if that's where his father really is, he'll find a son with no clothes except what he's wearing, like a beggar."

"Using a child to carry your message is unforgiveable. We'll get him outfitted in Colombia with whatever they have to sell." Margie squinted into the sunlight. "You've been spending such a good amount of time with Leo and Markus, helping them keep up their spirits. You've become a real friend." She squeezed his hand.

"I don't want to let them down. I'm a slow learner and I can't promise I'll be perfect, but I'm feeling a lot better about myself." He looked down at her. "About us."

"Tommy, I don't care about perfect. I was afraid of losing you."

"You won't." He gave her a kiss behind her ears.

———————

They headed south and east along the Caribbean coast of South America beneath ice cream clouds. Markus worked at swimming, arm over arm, from one side of the little pool to the other, back and forth until finally he let himself duck his head underwater to stroke the crawl, as Uncle Tommy told him to do.

As they rested on their stomachs after swimming, Markus told Tommy how he'd cried the day he was dismissed from the Boy's Choir in Vienna.

"It was not fair, Mr. Tommy. I went never off the note. All Jewish boys were expelled from Choir. *Mutti* cried all the time and said bad things about Papa leaving us."

After Markus left, Tommy stayed on deck gazing at the light-colored sea that had grown restless, almost sullen, under a sheen of tropical sun. He thought of holding Markus' thin body in the water while the boy learned the back stroke, the light bones balanced on his hand with complete trust. He was already thinking of Markus developing muscles to play baseball.

———————

At supper, Captain Anderson announced they'd soon be at the 10°

latitude and could expect to dock at the port of Ciénaga in Colombia the next day.

After the meal, the captain asked Leo and Tommy into his cabin for a drink.

"We land in Colombia with the boy tomorrow." The captain paced and smoked his cigar. "It's not difficult to find a ship from Cartagena or Barranquilla to Havana. But Cuba often turns away refugees and the boy would be alone then. Perhaps it is best he goes with you for a time, Mr. Asher. He's an easy child and seems suited to your family. You can write to the father to come to Colombia for his son. It will make less trouble."

"My wife and I will be happy to take Markus with us to California." Tommy stood up. "We're ready to provide him a home until his father comes for him."

"Tommy, that is good but American immigration won't allow the boy to enter your country without proper papers. He will be taken from you and sent somewhere, perhaps back to Europe. If you give the Colombian customs man ten dollars, you can bring in a dozen boys. Mr. Asher will include him in his family, no questions."

"It's such a burden for you, Leo, and it would be easy for us."

"It will be good for Lisel. She's fond of Markus, and so am I," said Leo. "We'll make contact as soon as possible with the father in Havana. Then we shall see."

# THIRTEEN

A HAZY OUTLINE APPEARED, and then, like a negative coming into focus in a developing medium, the coast of Colombia emerged, ragged peaks rising above green forests. Up still closer, Tommy saw murky, muddy foam-tinged whitecaps off the shore.

Mate Bang, always a source of information, told Tommy that mining tailings washed down from the mountains in the Magdalena River made the water brown.

"The Sierra Marta range you see, there they mine coal, gold, copper, emeralds. The *trapiche* emeralds are not like any other on our earth. They form in a star pattern from how crystals grow. Men lose their minds and kill for *trapiche*."

"I'm sorry the Ashers are going there. It sounds dangerous. I wish they could have stayed in Portugal and been safe in Lisbon," said Tommy.

———

At breakfast the next morning, Captain Anderson informed the Ashers that he'd received a cable ordering all Colombian-bound passengers to disembark in Ciénaga.

"I apologize, it's a hell hole," Captain Anderson said. "Customs laws, my friends." He promised the Ashers that First Mate Bang would arrange land transportation to Barranquilla, from where they'd catch their boat up the Magdalena River. All other passengers could re-embark after passing through customs.

That morning, the sun obscured by dark clouds, Tommy walked back and forth on deck, staring at the mountain peaks. How would the Ashers and Markus, city people from a northern climate, survive in the

Colombian uplands? Like his own father, forced to leave London, the Ashers had no choice. His father had suffered the altitude nearly eleven years for love of his mother. Tommy realized how desolate he'd feel when Leo left the ship. Leo was his age but seemed like a wise father, and in a strange way, Markus was like his son. He might never see them again.

———————

Captain Anderson called the passengers on deck after lunch.

"I must give you news. I learn by radio that Ciénaga has one berth for tonight. German warship also making for port." Anderson pointed to the horizon where a speck appeared in the murky light.

"Germans!" the missionaries looked at the Ashers and went to stand by them.

"Bad weather coming. We must skidoo ahead of German ship or there will be no parking," Captain Anderson said.

"We won't let anything happen to you." Miss Callenbach touched Lisel's arm. "I know how to stand up to bullies. If only they'd let us stay to defend our little ones."

All at once the unappealing Colombian port looked hospitable compared to the ship on the horizon which was moving up on them.

"I know this German *Zerstërer* class destroyer," said Captain Anderson. "Built recently and capable of 36 knots. You know my *Pacific* speed?" No one answered. "We make twelve knots at speediest. They'll be catching us soon. We must go close by coast or be caught and Germans board us."

"That must never happen, Captain!" Miss Callenbach raised her chin.

"No, friends, this will not happen. I alert you to dangers. We must be close to rocks for we do not wish to meet representatives of Reich Navy." The captain balled his fist on the railing. "No Germans on this ship."

"You must win the race for our refugee passengers," Miss Callenbach said.

"You do not tell Captain his orders. The passage is dangerous, Madam," Mate Bang said quietly.

"Of course not. As we say, all for one and one for all. Sisters, we must pray." All four missionaries retreated to a corner of the deck and bowed their heads while the Swedes, English and Tommy with Margie beside him waited for more news.

"So now we go top speed." The captain read out latitude and longitude. "You will be surprised what this good ship can do."

Tommy thought that Captain Anderson looked like a Viking as he stood beside Tarzan beneath the Swedish flag of blue and gold.

By mid-afternoon, the spot on the horizon had drawn closer; an hour later, the destroyer was near enough to see its long grey outline, bulkhead and the German flag, red and black with a swastika in the center. By the time the sun was turning the sea salmon and orange, they could make out uniformed men on the decks. Over all, an ominous, black sky hovered as if a curtain would fall to obscure everything in darkness.

Tommy heard Anderson shout, "One more knot from engines or they catch us."

Bang gave Tommy binoculars to see ahead into the twisting, turning rocky passage the *Pacific* had to enter as the Germans, now one hundred yards behind, drew close enough for Tommy to read the destroyer's name, *Max Schultz*. A harmless sounding name, though the guns facing them didn't look harmless.

Under Anderson's direction, the *Pacific* zig-zagged at almost right angles with ominous shifting of cargo beneath ropes. The maneuvering kept the destroyer from passing but below them in the churning water, rocks poked up like teeth on either side. Tommy held Margie's shoulder as the *Pacific* turned like a slippery eel, passed a last great black rock and shot into a gap almost too narrow for it.

"We are good! The berth is ours!" shouted the captain from the bridge.

Their ship's horn sounded above the waves, once, twice, three times, a defiant hoot from the small vessel before rocks blotted out the surrounding land and water whipping the hull. The captain raised his cap to the German officer on the deck of the destroyer. The German lifted his then disappeared.

The machinists emerged on deck covered in sweat and oil, letting out shouts and raised fists at the Germans.

"Holy Mackerel!" Captain Anderson threw his cap in the air. "Only snowball's chance in hell's fires we make it. Germans are stuck on open sea with storm and will leave us alone. Swedish punch, cook. All passengers to saloon. We celebrate, friends."

Captain Anderson leaned close to Tommy. "You don't say this to anyone, but if I were a praying man, I should have requested the British ladies give us all they can. Tonight we sleep safely, thank heavens. Shall I tell you what cargo we carry?"

"Isn't it mostly mining equipment?"

"Yes, dynamite, for the mining. Only Mate Bang and I know this. As I say, we ran a snowball's chance in hell. I've got such a thirst for punch! Ladies and gentlemen, please dress for supper quickly. I like to see ladies well-dressed."

---

In the half-hour between dressing and coming to the saloon, the *Pacific* secured its place in Ciénaga at a single dock so poor and deserted that Tommy, who'd stayed on deck while Margie typed below on the Remington, thought it hardly a port at all.

After Swedish punch, the ship's stores of meats, cheeses and fish were laid out. Captain Anderson grew expansive about the brave passengers and the triumph of the ship. "Especially to friends who have escaped the German iron hand." He raised his glass to the Ashers. "You will be safe here."

Margie whispered to Tommy, "I composed a few lines for our Captain, if you think he'd like to hear doggerel in his honor."

"Of course he would!" Tommy turned toward Anderson with glass in hand. "My poetess wife has committed to paper verses in honor of today. Your title, Margie?"

"Modestly, I'll call it 'The Epic of the *Pacific.*'"

"Hear, hear!" Captain Anderson raised his glass. "All be silent. Mrs. Tommy, stand here before us!"

Margie took a long drink of the punch and cleared her throat.

> *Twas dark October thirty seven, the ship was the Pacific*
> *The sea was not precisely calm, nor was it yet horrific.*

"Wonderful!" shouted Anderson, motioning crew to come closer to hear.

*At noon our Captain's brow was dark, to wireless he'd been harking.*
*We must 'skidoo' like the fleet shark or tonight there'll be no parking.*

"Read again, Mrs. Tommy. From beginning for all to hear."

The cooks and engineers raised glasses, called *huzzah huzzah* as Margie repeated the first two stanzas and then began the final lines.

*Her prow into the channel nosed, her stern it followed suit*
*To Germans just yards behind, she blew a derisive toot…*
*'The berth is ours'—the Captain chimed—'We beat them to the harbor!!'*
*Oh, what a day—oh, it was fine, and did we cheer the Johnson Line*
*And 'specially, our Captain!*

"I rushed on the ending. Not nearly heroic enough." Margie reached for her glass.

"Not to change one word. This poem hangs here in saloon." The captain's eyes were streaming tears. He planted a large wet kiss on Margie's finger tips. Then he and Bang lifted Margie in her chair and tossed her three times, bouncing her up as she came down, shouting *huzzah huzzah*. For a final gesture of Scandinavian cheer, the engine men put pats of butter on the captain's and mate's chairs and made the two sit on them.

———

When they were alone in the cabin, Tommy hugged Margie. "You have all the brains this family needs to become poets and astronomers. I hope our children…"

"Oh Tommy, what did you say? Children…!"

"Identical to you!" He kissed her.

"You'll get good work done, too. I know you will."

"Thanks, sweetheart, you're my biggest inspiration."

Their cabin was dark as they found their way into each other's arms.

"We can accompany the Ashers to Barranquilla and be back here in time to catch our ship. Isn't that what you were thinking?" She snuggled close.

"We'll see them to the last. My dear little sweet potato pie, I do love you."

Later that night, Margie lay awake as outside a heavy downpour fell, thick slanted lines of rain that dashed against their cabin window. She heard thunder and saw lightning that must be high in the mountains where the Ashers were going. She and Tommy would find a way to help them. She moved closer to Tommy. With each breath he took, she sighed. *Oh Tommy, how I do love you.* She felt that right now the hearts of Greenbaums and Seligs and Grenskys beat somewhere within her, already beginning a new life.

# ACKNOWLEDGMENTS

To my family, Strouses and Kahns now deceased, who lived much of this story, I hope I'm forgiven for what I didn't know and had to imagine. I owe Stephen Birmingham gratitude for making me see the possibilities of my family story in his two histories, *Our Crowd* and *The Rest of Us*, which I read not long after the 2008 financial meltdown. I've especially drawn on Birmingham's depiction of the Guggenheim and Selig families although some of the details of these two clans came to me from my mother's stories. Ron Chernow's *The Warburgs* also gave me information that corroborated my mother's recollection of that great banking family. Robert F Bruner and Sean D. Carr's *The Panic of 1907* educated me, as did John K Galbraith's *The Great Crash*, about the financial crashes of the 20th century. Numerous books and pamphlets published about Leadville and the Ice Palace were of help. Gertrude Berg's memoir, *Molly and Me* filled in gaps. I'm indebted to articles of war reporting, especially William Shirer's dispatches, from online newspaper archives. I found the ditty celebrating the *Pacific's* dangerous race to port written by my mother, Carolyn Strouse, in a trunk of old letters, a treasured ending to the story.

I had many helpful readers, thank you to all: my writing group in Sonoma County, Robin Beeman, Marylu Downing, Susan Swartz, Liza Pruneske and Mary Gaffney; my childhood friend Glenna Matthews; playwright/director/actor John Schak; my cousins Katherine Meyering, chanteuse extraordinaire, and Susan Silk; an early reader and friend, Judith Moorman, helped me keep writing. In Leadville, William Korn gave so many good leads to follow for Jewish life at the end of the 20th century. I thank, as always, my son Michael Antony Levitin, for his impeccable editing, and my husband Michael Morey, an historian, for his sleuthing skills. You kept me going.

Made in the USA
Monee, IL
04 February 2020

21273982R10213